The *Highw*

ROUTE
666

HIGHWAY
TO HELL

J.D. Toepfer

ISBN: 9781737360308

Edited by Emily Marquart

Cover Design by Fatima Khan

Book Formatting by Victor Rook

With Sincere Thanks...

After writing my autobiography at age six, it seemed inevitable that I would become an author one day. So, you might say that the publication of Route 666 fulfills my destiny as much as achieving a lifelong dream. Regardless, making your dreams come true often requires the contributions of others, and I am no exception. I want to extend my heartfelt gratitude to the following persons who helped make the publication of this novel possible:

My beloved wife, Christina, is more than my wife and best friend; you are my soulmate. Your love and support make everything possible for me, and I thank you for believing in me, even when I don't believe in myself. I love you more than I can say!

My brother George. As identical twins, we've been *"wombmates"* from the very beginning. Your contributions to Route 666 are immeasurable. Thank you for your words of encouragement and creative input. I could not have done this without you!

My sisters, Tracy and Susan, and my sister-in-law Joanne. Thank you for reading the original manuscript and providing honest comments that helped improve my story. A special thank you to you, Susan, for your help with my author's website and social media accounts!

My editor, Emily Marquart, working with you was an absolute pleasure! Regardless of how many books I sell, I do not doubt in my mind that your efforts made Route 666 a far better story, and I look forward to working with you again on the next installment of the Highway to Hell series!

"I fear not the dark itself but what may lurk within it." Anonymous

Prologue

September 1728
Woods outside present-day Culpeper, Virginia
Sunset

Alsoomse was running as fast as she could through the dense woods. Drenched in sweat and with blood dripping down her face from cuts caused by razor-like thorns that engulfed the trail, she had managed to stay on the one recognizable path in the forest, but now the sun was setting. Soon, the night would fall, and it would be too challenging to stay on the trail.

Alsoomse knew she would then become hopelessly lost, just like when she had arrived in the Manahoac village about thirteen moons ago to support a group sent to negotiate a pact for peace between the Manahoac and her tribe. As a result, she had little knowledge of the local region. The only way she knew could lead her out was the same way she had come in, and Alsoomse was still very unsure how far away from the main access road she was.

She felt like her chest was about to explode, so she stopped, leaned against a tree, and tried to catch her breath. She could hear those vicious Hell Hounds in the distance and knew that her disappearance was no longer a secret. Along with the howling *Mya Aoemwa* she heard crashing through the woods, that hideous Evil Shaman Matchitehew would be leading his Red-Eye Warriors after her. She shuddered, thinking of the consequences if they caught up to her, but she knew she would not survive the forced labor much longer.

She also sensed that with the digging approaching its conclusion, it was unlikely she and the remaining Manahoac would continue to serve any useful purpose. Her death, along with the remaining Manahoac, was inevitable. She had been planning her escape for weeks, and there would be no going back. She started running down the trail once more.

***

September 1728
Manahoac labor camp

Lying on the dirt floor of his wigwam after another back-breaking day of hard labor, Eluwilussit heard the howling of the *Mya Aoemwa*. Too exhausted to even eat, he barely could lift his head from the ground. The dampness in the air combined with his sweat-soaked clothing caused him to shiver. He knew his physical condition was deteriorating, and he soon would be dead. The food rations were barely enough to keep the remaining Manahoac alive, and with the burial mound excavation nearly complete, he knew that Matchitehew would kill them all. Eluwilussit had been the Medicine Man for the tribe before Matchitehew had arrived several years ago. He knew that the remnants of the tribe now regretted replacing him with Matchitehew, but he was a forgiving man and held no animosity toward his friends. His only regret was his inability to convince the tribe that Matchitehew would lead them into ruin. Unfortunately for the tribe, Eluwilussit's horrible visions had become a reality.

The years before Matchitehew's arrival had proven to be difficult ones for the Manahoac people. They were continually being pushed westward by the white man, and the small size of their tribe made them an easy target for larger groups. These larger tribes would steal their food and their women. He did his best to protect his people, but his spells were no substitute for a shortage of warriors, and his pleas to The Great Spirit appeared to go unheard. Then one day, Matchithew suddenly appeared, and everything changed.

He claimed to be a member of the Manahoac tribe, but no one recognized him. Eluwilussit recalled that he called himself Lucius, which was not a name that the tribe had ever heard before. Later

Eluwilussit would rename him Matchitehew because of the evil that he would inflict on the people. While Eluwilussit was initially suspicious, he knew it was common for Medicine Men to leave the tribe and live many years on their own to forge ties with the spirit world and master spells and incantations. After all, he had done this very thing himself, many moons ago. This lifestyle was a challenging one and could result in spiritual changes and physical ones. Matchitehew indicated that his family members had been kidnapped from the Manahoac generations ago when he was a child, and he could only find his way back to the tribe with the help of The Great Spirit.

Matchitehew promised that he brought *"good medicine"* and that the tribe would prosper with his leadership. The seed corn he provided led to a crop like nothing the tribe had ever seen before. He also recruited great warriors who successfully defended the Manahoac against the tribes that had previously preyed upon them. These new warriors were, in fact, such fierce fighters that the neighboring tribes sent emissaries to the Manahoac to negotiate a peace agreement. For the first time that any Manahoac could remember, they were at peace and were prosperous. The prestige of the tribe amongst its neighbors was so high that tribute gifts poured in from these other groups. Matchitehew had delivered on his promises, and Eluwilussit had no choice but to step aside and abide by Matchitehew's leadership.

Staring through a gaping hole in his tattered shelter, Eluwilussit looked to the sky and noted that the moons of change, known as Ptanyetu, had begun, which meant the cold season was coming. This change mirrored the fortunes of the Manahoac. Just as the season of plenty always follows a time of scarcity, the prosperity that Matchitehew brought with him soon gave way to hardship and eventually calamity. The following season's harvest was meager, which led to a shortage of food. The visits and tributes from other tribes began to become less frequent and eventually stopped altogether. Rumors circulated that the road through Manahoac territory and the forests surrounding the tribe were *mya-li,* and the woods were now frequently avoided. The isolation and inability to trade for what they needed only increased the misery of the tribe.

Matchitehew said that the Manahoac had not been thankful enough for the previous year's bountiful harvest, which angered the Great Spirit. He told them that they needed to construct a wiki ni for the Great Spirit and fill it with repentance offerings to appease the entity. Initially, the tribe welcomed the guidance and began to dig a deep hole. At Matchitehew's insistence, they piled the excavated earth on top of the hole they were digging in a manner like how they would construct one of their burial mounds.

Eluwilussit began to doubt the project when Matchitehew insisted they dig day and night and had them ignore their typical activities such as storing food for the cold months. They also came across bountiful amounts of copper and gold, which were highly valuable to the white man and that the Manahoac could trade for food and other essential supplies. Matchitehew showed no interest in either of these prized minerals or stockpiling resources. Finally, Matchitehew also insisted that they call the Great Spirit by a new name, Lucifer.

When he had raised concerns about this with Matchitehew, the warriors turned on him and the people. The Manahoac became slaves, and Matchitehew worked them until they began to get sick. As the hole became cavernous, the mound grew higher, and the Manahoac started to die. Once dead, they were buried in the growing pile of dirt. There were escape attempts, but those who left never returned, nor did any help ever arrive. In a last-ditch effort to save the remaining members of the tribe, Eluwilussit began to counsel Alsoomse on how she might escape.

Unfortunately, the sounds of the *Mya Aoemwa* confirmed that Matchitehew was aware that she was gone. As he closed his eyes, he hoped that she would succeed where others had failed. Otherwise, he knew the Manahoac would be no more.

***

Alsoomse had thus far managed to avoid the *Mya Aoemwa,* but she knew they had closed the gap between them. It was getting more difficult to move down the path, not only because it was dark but because the wilderness had begun to reclaim the trail. The vines and brambles grabbed her ankles and had caused her to fall more than once. The forest was eerily silent, with the only sounds being her muscling through the brush and the beasts in hot pursuit.

Eluwilussit had told her that she would be near the main road that led through Manahoac territory and connected with other tribes when she crossed over the third stream that cut across the path. Once she got to that main road, he told her to head east toward the white man's settlements and find help. He believed that only the white man would have weapons that might work against Matchitehew and his warriors. She had just crossed over the last stream and felt a surge of energy. She knew she had to be close to the main road.

Just then, Alsoomse heard a noise to the right that caused her to stop and look around. She began running again and was startled by noises to her left. Alsoomse looked all around and saw nothing but darkness. A sensation of being watched made the hair on the back of her neck stand up. Starting down the path once more, Alsoomse eventually came upon a road. She had made it! She tried to orient herself and figure out which way was east. She looked down, and it was evident that no one had traveled this way for some time. There were no footprints or hoof prints on the muddy edges of the road.

Many people had disappeared while taking this road. Alsoomse hoped to change that. She turned left in a direction that she believed to be east. She had taken just a few steps when red eyes peering through the darkness surrounded her. Then, she heard growling and a menacing voice emanating from the night.

"Alsoomse, my dear. You should not be out here after dark. You never know what terrible things could happen."

Screams echoed through the forest. Then, there was nothing but silence. No one was there to see Alsoomse's body being dragged from the road back into the deep, dark woods.

Chapter 1

Jack Aitken sat staring at the plate of bacon and eggs on the table in front of him. The Cosmic Café had a reputation for serving the most delicious breakfast in Lawrence, and typically Jack would have eaten a meal like this with gusto, but this morning he had no appetite. Nervously sipping his coffee, Jack waited for Father Mark Desmond to join him. He had not seen Mark Desmond since they were teenagers, and were it not for his clerical collar, he would likely have difficulty recognizing him.

Jack's thoughts turned back to his family, and his anxiety began to build. A bead of sweat dripped down his back, and he tapped his fingers on the table incessantly. He knew they were safe for the moment, but how was he going to rescue them? How could he fight a force that he still could not comprehend? It was an ancient evil so horrific that he found it impossible to articulate the magnitude of its destructive power. Jack fought to maintain his composure, but his fear and unceasing worry were overwhelming him, and while he struggled not to hyperventilate, he felt tears slowly roll down his cheeks. He hoped that he could find the right words to explain all of this to Mark and, even more importantly, convince Mark to help him. *What do I do if Mark doesn't believe me?* He struggled to push the negative thought from his brain, but Jack knew he was running out of time. Failure was not an option.

The waitress poured another cup of coffee, and Jack checked his watch. It was just about 9:00 a.m., and he looked out the window, scanning the parking lot for Mark. At the same time, he was on the lookout for the police. Jack was sure that the authorities in Virginia now knew he was on the run, and it would not be long before they put out a nationwide APB for him. The cloaking spell that he hoped temporarily shielded him from the view of his adversary would not provide the same protection against law enforcement.

The door to the café opened, and a bell signaled the entrance of a new patron. The waitress greeted Father Desmond by name. Jack slid out from the booth and waved to get Father Desmond's attention. Father Desmond saw Jack and made his way over to the booth. They shook hands, greeted one another warmly, and sat down in the booth across from one another.

The waitress approached and asked Father Desmond if he would like coffee.

Father Desmond smiled. "Yes, thank you, Mary. I will have my usual as well, please."

"Coffee coming up," Mary said. "And I'll put an order of pancakes and sausage in right away."

Mary turned over the coffee cup in front of Father Desmond and poured the coffee. She left, and the two men sat looking at one another, with neither of them knowing just what to say.

Jack was the first to speak. "It's been a long time, hasn't it, Father?"

Father Desmond quickly interjected, "Jack, please call me Mark. My friends still call me Mark, despite my chosen vocation."

Jack took a breath and said, "Okay, Mark. It is good to see you, my old friend."

"It is good to see you too," the Father said. "I must say that it was quite a surprise to hear from you after all of these years. I am looking forward to catching up, but tell me, what brings you to Lawrence?"

Jack hesitated. "I have some business that I need to attend to here. But before I get to that, seeing you reminded me of something. Do you remember our St. Aidan's soccer team?"

"Oh, yes." Father Desmond smiled. "Ever since I received your e-mail, I have been thinking about CYO soccer. I was trying to recall the names of our teammates. Tommy Rogers played left-wing, didn't he?"

Jack nodded. "That's right. Paul Bradford played right-wing, and you were the striker."

Father Desmond continued, "You were the right halfback, and your brother George was the goalie. Your twin brother, right?"

"Your memory is excellent, Mark. George lives in South Carolina and is married with three kids. He teaches history and coaches soccer. His son is an up-and-coming goalie himself. Guess it's in their genes. Do you remember Camp Marydale?" he asked.

"That is where we played our games, wasn't it?" Father Desmond laughed. "I think it was in Farmingdale on Long Island."

"I wonder if they still play soccer games there," Jack added. "Do you remember the championship game against Holy Spirit?"

Father Desmond quickly answered with a slight tone of disappointment in his voice. "Yes. How could I forget it? That was the game we lost two to one in overtime."

Jack sighed. "I think George still has nightmares about that game. Every so often, he will bring it up, and it makes me think he's still processing why he couldn't stop that penalty shot."

"There are some things I guess you never get over."

Mary returned with Father Desmond's breakfast. She turned to Jack and asked, "Was there anything wrong with your meal, hon? It looks like you have not touched it."

"Oh, no, ma'am. I guess I'm just not very hungry this morning. I'd love some more coffee, though."

Father Desmond poured syrup on his pancakes, and as he began to eat, Jack mindlessly stirred the coffee in his cup. He enjoyed their trip down amnesia lane but felt pangs of guilt for enjoying himself while God only knew what was happening to his family. Putting down his spoon, he said solemnly, "Mark, may I ask you a personal question?"

Mark put down his fork, matching Jack's change in demeanor. "Sure, Jack, what would you like to know?"

"What made you decide to become a priest? How does one go about it?"

Father Desmond looked surprised and joked in a blatant attempt to lighten the mood a little. "Are you interested in becoming one, Jack?"

"I guess that would be difficult since I'm not Catholic. I'm just curious, I guess."

Father Desmond continued to eat his breakfast. "I know that becoming a priest is not something that you hear a lot about today. It was not necessarily something that I set out to do. When I was younger, I was an altar boy. I served many masses with Father Richard Malloy, and he was an inspiration to me. He would allow me to go with him to minister to the sick in the parish, and as I approached my high school graduation, I felt a calling to serve God. After graduating from Chaminade high school, I studied theology and philosophy at Notre Dame. I got involved with the campus ministry while I was there."

Jack shifted in his seat. "What did you do after college?"

"I returned home to Williston Park and enrolled at the Seminary of the Immaculate Conception in Huntington. After completing seminary, I served as a Deacon at St. Aidan's and then was ordained as a priest about two years later. I eventually found my way back to Chaminade as a priest, hearing confessions and being a spiritual advisor to the young men who went there. I was transferred to the Saint Lawrence Catholic Campus here in Lawrence about ten years ago." He studied him. "Now it's your turn, Jack. What have you been doing all these years since the end of your illustrious soccer career?"

Jack hesitated. Should he tell Mark the real reason he was here in Lawrence? He decided he wasn't quite ready to do so. "Well, I graduated from Herricks High School in 1984 and went to Stony Brook University. I wasn't sure what I wanted to study when I was there, so I ended up taking a wide variety of courses, ranging from astronomy to the history of Judaism. I graduated in 1988 with a degree in Political Science and History."

"Stony Brook has an excellent academic reputation," Father Mark said. "What did you do after college?"

Jack felt his lips tug into a smile. "I got married to my high school sweetheart Amanda, and we have two wonderful sons. I'm not sure that my degree had anything to do with my career as I've been working in insurance for almost thirty years. I can't say I love it, but who truly loves their job, right?"

Mark chuckled. "I guess that is true. I love what I do, but there are aspects of being a priest that can be, shall we say, challenging."

Jack was about to continue when his phone began to vibrate. He had purchased a burner phone to avoid being tracked by the authorities, but there was nowhere he could run to escape this caller. Jack checked the screen, a knot building in his stomach at the all too familiar number. He felt the blood draining from his head and thought he might faint, but he knew he had to collect himself and answer the call.

Excusing himself, he got up from the booth and pressed the answer button. Jack heard a voice that struck fear right to his very core.

The genteel English accent on the other side of the line could not mask the cold, calculating tone of the voice. "Good morning, Jack. Are you still in Lawrence?"

"Yes. I am here."

"How are you progressing in regard to fulfilling the terms of our bargain?"

Jack took a deep breath. "I'm working on it. Are my wife and children okay?"

"Of course, Jack. They are okay, for now."

Jack was growing agitated. He struggled to keep his cool. "I want to speak with them now," he demanded.

The icy voice replied, "Mr. Aitken. You are not in a position to make demands. I would suggest that you act with greater restraint if you wish to see your family again, alive."

Jack regained his composure. "May I speak to my family, please?"

"That is better."

Relief flooded him as Amanda's voice came on the line. "Jack, are you there?" she asked. Her voice was quivering.

"Yes, Amanda, I am here. Are you and the boys okay?"

"We are, for now. Where are you?"

Jack tried to sound reassuring. "I am in Lawrence, Kansas. I'm going to find what he is demanding, and I will see you all soon."

"Jack, please hurry." Amanda did not sound convinced. "I'm worried about what all of this is doing to Louis and David."

While she was speaking, Jack heard his sons sobbing in the background. He closed his eyes and tried to picture Amanda and the boys. He wanted to remember them with smiles and laughter, but the only vision that came to his mind was the three of them clutching one another inside a ring of fire. The fear on their faces seared in his memory forever.

Jack tried to sound composed and confident, but there were tears in his eyes. "Amanda, I know this is hard on all of you. I promise I will make this right."

The voice that he dreaded returned. "Jack. You have heard for yourself that your family is unharmed. I would suggest that you make haste. Remember, midnight November first, Mr. Aitken."

Before he could say another word, the line went dead.

***

After Jack excused himself, Father Desmond continued to sip his coffee. He enjoyed talking about their glory days, but he could not help but wonder why Jack was here in Lawrence. He said he was here for business reasons, but as a priest, Father Desmond had become pretty adept at sizing people up and knowing when they were hiding something. There was something Jack wasn't sharing with him. But what was it?

Jack returned to the booth, his face ashen. The mood, which was blissful with nostalgia only a few minutes ago, was now somber and subdued. One clear thing was Jack's call had not gone well. "Jack, are you alright?"

He sat down and rubbed his eyes. Father Desmond didn't miss that they shone with tears. "I am okay, Mark," Jack stated unconvincingly.

Father Desmond grew more concerned. "You do not look okay, Jack. Did you receive bad news?"

"It's… complicated, Mark. I will be alright. Do you want some more coffee?"

Father Desmond could tell Jack was not ready to talk just yet. "Sure, Jack, let us have one more cup." He motioned to Mary, who brought a fresh pot of coffee.

Jack added cream and sugar to his cup and stirred it with a spoon for what seemed like an eternity. Finally, he looked up at Mark. "I'm sorry for that interruption and for being so distracted. Where were we?"

"I do not have to be a priest to see that you are troubled, Jack. Sometimes it is beneficial to have another person help to bear a burden. I am not trying to pressure you or pry into something personal, but perhaps I can help."

Jack took a deep breath. "I know this is probably the last thing you would think I'd be asking you, but… what can you tell me about good vs. evil? What I mean is, what did they teach you in seminary about it?"

Father Desmond tried not to appear shocked. Were it not for Jack's grave appearance, he might have grinned or possibly attempted to change the subject. It was clear, however, that Jack was waiting for an answer.

"Well," he began slowly. "The Catholic Church teaches that there are three kinds of evil. Physical evil encompasses all those things that can cause harm to us. These include injury, illness, and even death itself. All of these are things that prevent human beings from fulfilling the normal progression of their lives. The second kind of evil is what we refer to as moral evil. Sin is the manifestation of this. It is where a person does what they know; eventually, it causes a guilty conscience." He paused. "The final type of evil is called metaphysical. This form of evil prevents natural objects from attaining their ideal potential or what we might call perfection."

Jack nodded as if he understood, and Father Desmond continued, "I believe more people abandon their faith in God because of the influence of evil. This temptation to stop believing leads a person to feel resentment toward God and causes them to rebel. Some people refer to evil as a thing, but I see it as the wrong choices we make and their consequences. Evil is the freedom to choose sin and selfishness. God is the ultimate example of joy and love, and rebellion on our part causes us to lose these things."

Jack's shoulders slumped, and he stared at the table. It seemed his words had hit close to home. "Mark, why do bad things seemingly always happen to good people?"

Father Desmond collected his thoughts before responding. "Jack, this is a question we all ask ourselves. It is hard not to, at times, feel persecution despite trying to do what we believe to be the right thing. However, there are three thoughts that I would like you to consider. First, who says all people are good? Isn't the opposite true? Don't good things happen to people who do not seem to deserve them? I find that sinners often think they are saints, but a real saint would know they are a sinner. Indeed great people are the ones that are most reluctant to say that they are.

"Second, is all suffering terrible? Isn't true wisdom derived from suffering? Even Eastern religions like Buddhism refer to true knowledge only coming from pain. Ask yourself, what does a person who has not suffered truly know about life?

"Finally, are we destined to know the rationale behind God's actions? The man the Bible calls Job may represent the ultimate exploration of the concept of evil. Even at the end of that book, we do not know what God is actually up to."

Jack removed his glasses and rubbed the bridge of his nose. "I have to admit that I never really thought about the challenges in my life from this perspective," he said. "Perhaps it's the consequence of being a lapsed Methodist. I know that part of a priest's job is to hear the confessions of their congregation. I guess mine is that I have not set foot in a church in more than twenty years. Thank you for indulging me. I do, however, have another question that I would like to ask you. Mark, what is the position of the church on the existence of Hell?"

Father Desmond fought every instinct that told him to ask Jack where this was all leading. Something in Jack's face, however, said to him that this was not that time. "If you are looking for proof of its reality, I have none to give you. Taking things on faith is part of my job description. The church affirms its existence and that Hell is the chief punishment for being separated from God. You see, to be united with God means to love him freely. Suppose we sin against God, our fellow man, or ourselves, then we are not loving God, are we? Dying without repentance and refusing to accept His mercy means we are separated from Him forever. Ultimately, this is what the concept of Hell truly represents. Perhaps it is a state of being as much as a place. Hell is a consequence of our free will. In some respect, we choose Hell for ourselves. For some, Hell seems unreal, and its existence impossible. However, when we acknowledge the inhumanity of Auschwitz or what happened to Christ at Golgotha, then the existence of Hell seems all too real."

Jack took this all in. "It's easy to forget in all of the discussion about heaven that there even is a Hell," he said. "The concept of free will sometimes is lost when we are making excuses for our behavior. Being a victim of circumstance is a lot easier to accept than taking responsibility for our actions. I have to admit that I am guilty of doing just that."

"If you are searching for absolution, you are talking to the right person."

Jack gave him a rueful smile. "Be careful, Mark. Some souls are beyond redemption. After all, the devil does not live in Hell all by himself." Before Father Desmond could respond, Jack continued, "Mark, I have one final question."

Father Desmond looked at Jack. "Okay, Jack. I'm listening."

Jack hesitated and then asked, "You have given me your explanation of what the Church says about evil and Hell, but I would like to hear what your personal view is on the subject. What do you believe about the reality of these things? Do you believe in the supernatural?"

Father Desmond looked up sharply.

Jack persisted. "Mark, I need to know." His agony was apparent.

Father Desmond had not discussed the topic of the existence of supernatural forces with anyone in many years. He had somehow managed to bury his experiences, but they came flooding back in a torrent of fear. He had promised himself that he would never open this door again, but Jack's anxiety was palpable, and he knew that his friend needed significant assistance.

Father Desmond said a silent prayer and began to speak, "Jack, I have not spoken about this in many years and promised myself that I would never do so again. However, I can tell you are carrying a great weight on your shoulders. If it helps you, I will tell you what I believe."

***

Father Desmond's demeanor had changed as soon as Jack asked his question. His fingers were tightly laced together and held under his chin. He stared downward at the tabletop as if he were about to pray. Jack sensed he'd struck a nerve, but there was no turning back now. He listened intently as Mark spoke.

"The church walks a fine line when it comes to the supernatural and paranormal. Faith requires us to believe in the extraordinary, but ghosts and spirits can just as easily be deceptive instruments of Satan as they are souls of the departed. I have had several experiences with the paranormal and what some would call the supernatural. When I was in third grade, I woke up in the middle of the night and saw a vision of what I believed to be my grandfather in my room. It was perplexing since my grandfather lived in Florida. I asked the vision what it was doing, and it disappeared. The next day I found out that my grandfather had passed away. I was not scared and tried to tell my parents about what I saw, but they dismissed it as the imagination of a sleepy nine-year-old. I can't tell you why he appeared to me. Perhaps it was to say goodbye. But as we sit here today, I know what I saw, and it was real to me."

Father Desmond took a sip of water and continued. "As a teenager, I went on a camping trip with some of my friends. One of them had packed a Ouija board, and we thought it would be cool to play with it. That night we gathered around the campfire and sat in a circle holding the board. We started asking questions about girls and other things teenage boys discuss. Then one of my friends asked if there was anyone there with us. The planchette began to move and hovered over 'yes.' We then requested whatever this was to identify itself. The planchette started moving independently, spelling out D-E-M-O-N. The board then flew out of our laps into the campfire. We were startled and began accusing one another of trying to pull a prank. We narrowly avoided a fistfight over the whole incident. Although none of us would admit it, we were scared. We talked about what had happened for hours, and eventually, we all agreed we should go to sleep."

Jack swallowed hard.

"I was jarred awake by what sounded like something was scratching at our tent. I glanced down at my watch, and the time read 3:00 a.m. As I sat up in my sleeping bag, I saw something so hideous that I cannot even describe it to you. Its claws were holding open the flaps of the tent as if it were beginning to pull itself inside. Its red eyes met mine, and it growled. None of my friends moved a muscle. It was almost as if this entity was coming for me. I instinctively reached for my crucifix, which I always wore around my neck. I held it in front of me, and the entity reared back as if the vision of the crucifix was causing it pain, and it disappeared.

"My heart was pounding out of my chest, and I was fighting to catch my breath. Eventually, I slid back down into my sleeping bag, but truthfully there was no getting any sleep after that. The following day we found footprints in front of the tent. They looked like claws, and everyone else figured that some animals had visited us. I knew better but kept silent as I thought no one would believe me. I only found out years later paranormal investigators consider 3:00 a.m. to be the so-called witching or devil's hour and that demons appear at that time as an affront to God and the holy trinity. The next day was when I decided to become a priest."

Jack was speechless. Before he could utter a word, Father Desmond began to speak once more. "As a priest, I have witnessed and participated in exorcisms. I have seen things that have no earthly explanation. Modern psychiatry and science cannot account for them. I believe that evil is present in forms that we cannot and do not want to comprehend. Satan and his legions are real, and they have a voracious appetite for souls. The battle between good and evil has raged since Satan fell and continues to this day. I am haunted by what I have seen and experienced. You asked me what I believe. What I have told you is what I feel entirely and unequivocally."

Jack sat dumbfounded. He had come to Lawrence for a specific purpose and hoped that Mark could give him some insight into the adversary he faced. Somehow this seemed to become even more surreal than could be imagined. How could it be possible that reaching out to a friend who he had not seen for nearly forty years would provide him with the hope that he might still find a way out of what appeared to be a no-win situation? That he even might yet save his family and himself from eternal damnation.

It couldn't be just a coincidence. Jack did not believe in predestination, but was a higher power guiding his steps?

Although Father Desmond asked Jack to call him Mark, it no longer seemed respectful. Father Desmond had shared so much of himself with Jack and had done so despite his fear and dread. The only way he could think to repay Father Desmond was to tell him the truth. He owed him that.

Regaining his composure, Jack leaned in closely and whispered, "Let's go for a walk."

Father Desmond insisted on paying the bill, and Jack acquiesced. They stepped out into the bright sunshine.

***

The air was crisp but invigorating. The reds and yellows of the changing leaves made it clear fall was in full swing. It was late October, and Halloween decorations were everywhere. Father

Desmond led the way to Lawrence Nature Park, several blocks from The Cosmic Café. They made small talk, continuing to catch up on what had transpired in their lives over the years. They arrived at the park and walked an unpaved trail surrounded by oak trees, hickory, and redbuds. Jack almost felt like he was back home, walking a path along Bull Run Creek in the Manassas battlefield.

He searched for the courage to tell Father Desmond the real reason he was in Lawrence.

"Father, I greatly appreciate the time we have spent together today and everything that you have shared with me. Now, I need to share some things with you. There is no easy way for me to say this, so I will just say it. I am on the run. The police in Virginia are likely looking for me right now, and it probably won't be long before they figure out that I've left town. Several weeks ago, my family went missing." Their conversation stood in stark contrast to the tranquil park surroundings. "They were victims of a kidnapping, but the authorities think I am responsible for their disappearance."

Father Desmond didn't appear to be surprised. "I see, Jack. I sensed something terrible had happened, and I was waiting for you to tell me what was going on. Please continue."

Reassured, Jack continued. "The ransom for the return of my family is not monetary. If I don't meet the demands of the kidnapper, then my family will lose their eternal souls."

Father Desmond's eyes widened. "Jack, did I hear you correctly? Did you say, lose their souls?

"Father, I'm sorry for dragging you into this. If I hadn't lived with this knowledge for several weeks, I wouldn't believe it myself." He shook his head. "I had nowhere else to turn, and when I found your name while searching for a priest to converse with here in Lawrence, I was relieved."

"You did the right thing," Father Desmond reassured him. "As Christians, we are here to help bear each other's burdens. Please go on."

Jack blurted out, "Father, I am here to retrieve an object from Stull Cemetery."

Father Desmond stopped dead in his tracks. Jack couldn't blame him. Stull Cemetery, located twenty miles west of Lawrence, had a well-deserved reputation for being one of the world's evilest places. In truth, many believed it to be the gate to Hell itself.

He looked Jack directly in the eyes and asked sternly, "Jack, what could you possibly want from Stull Cemetery?"

"Father, are you able to hear the confession of a non-Catholic?"

"Yes, if the danger of death is present."

Jack put his hand on Father Desmond's shoulder. "Father, perhaps it would be best if I start at the beginning…"

Chapter 2

Jack sat down on a bench, joined by Father Desmond. They sat with neither of them, speaking a word for what felt like an eternity.

"Don't stop believing!" Jack's cell phone suddenly went off, causing him to leap off the bench.

As Jack frantically checked the caller's number, Father Desmond asked, "Jack, what is it?"

Jack let out a deep breath and fell back onto the bench with his hand on his chest. "It's an Amber Alert about a missing child in the area," Jack said, still gasping for air. "I was worried it was him calling again."

"Are you alright?" Father Desmond asked with concern. "You look like you could have a heart attack."

"He calls me constantly. Sometimes it's for a report on my progress in fulfilling our so-called bargain, but most of the time, it's to taunt me and remind me that my family's souls depend upon my successful completion of this mission."

"Jack, let me take you to the campus infirmary. We can get you a valium or something else to help you calm down. I'm worried about you."

Jack shook his head and waved Father Desmond away. "I just need a minute or two; I'll be fine. Really. I'm okay."

A few minutes passed, and Jack picked up his phone to read the alert. It hit way too close to home. He could not help but think about this own family and the search that must have been going on at that moment to find them.

"It's a fifteen-year-old boy that is missing," Jack said somberly. "Donnie Gilbert, about five feet tall and one hundred pounds."

Father Desmond closed his eyes and said a silent prayer for the family and the child's safe return.

"Sadly, there have been several similar abductions lately. Jack, why don't we get back to your confession."

He nodded. "I believe the dire circumstances I find myself in have their origins deep in my past. In 2001, I was diagnosed with Major Depressive Disorder, but looking back, I'm certain that I suffered from depression most of my life. I remember periods of melancholy going back to my childhood. Earlier that month, I'd seriously contemplated committing suicide. I sought help from a psychiatrist who put me on medication that, along with the love and support of my wife, stopped me from acting on those dark feelings."

Jack suddenly stopped talking.

"Something wrong, Jack?" Father Desmond asked.

"Two people are coming down the trail."

Jack instantly recognized them as police officers. His fight or flight instincts took over, and he began to search the area for a potential escape route. He was sure they were coming for him, and his arrest would all but seal his family's fate.

Sensing his apprehension, Father Desmond grabbed his arm. "Wait. Don't do anything suspicious." He smiled at the officers, and both men stood up as they approached. "Good day, officers. A fine day to spend in the park, is it not?"

"It is, Father," said one of the policemen. "I'm Officer Marshall," he said, pointing at his partner, "and this is Officer Pulaski. Unfortunately, we're not here just for the exercise."

"Oh," said Father Desmond, sounding concerned. "Is something wrong?"

"I'm sure you are aware that there have been several child abductions in the past few months. Now, a fifteen-year-old boy has gone missing, and we're searching the park for him," Officer Pulaski stated.

Jack stood silently by Father Desmond's side. At the moment, it was all he could think to do.

"We have not seen a child, have we?" Father Desmond glanced over at Jack.

"No, we haven't," Jack agreed.

"Do you have a description of what he looks like?" Father Desmond asked.

"Roughly five feet tall and weighs about one hundred pounds," Officer Marshall replied. "His mother dropped him at school, but the principal said he never made it to his class."

"His name is Donnie Gilbert. He's wearing blue jeans, a white shirt, and a light tan jacket," Officer Pulaski added.

"Do you have a way we can contact you if we see him?" Father Desmond asked.

Officer Marshall handed him a card. "Call this number if you see him. By the way, Donnie has Autism."

Almost immediately, Jack's fears for himself faded. Hearing that the little boy was autistic touched his heart deeply. He knew all too well the worry and panic that Donnie's family was feeling at that very moment. Ignoring the risks, Jack stepped toward the police officers.

"My sons are both autistic," he said. "I've worked with law enforcement officials to educate the police on autism. What has happened to Donnie is an all too frequent occurrence. Nearly fifty percent of families with autistic children will experience an event like this in their lifetime. My youngest son, David, wandered away from us once. I never want to feel that feeling again."

"Neither of us has any training on how to handle someone with Autism," Officer Marshall said. "Do you have any tips you can give us?"

"Water," Jack said. "Check lakes and ponds first. Drowning is the primary means by which an autistic child who has wandered away will perish. Do you know if Donnie has verbal skills?" Jack asked.

"We really don't know," Officer Pulaski answered.

"Okay. Donnie is likely to be disoriented and may not be able to speak to you even if he is verbal. The situation will require a lot of patience on your part. Don't make any sudden movements, and avoid using the siren in the patrol car. Many people with autism don't like to be touched, so you'll want to warn Donnie several times before you try to touch him."

Officer Marshall had pulled out a notebook and was taking notes feverishly.

"It's likely that Donnie will be practicing some form of repetitive behavior to try to calm himself down. For example, he could be hitting himself, saying the same sentences over and over again, or rocking his body back and forth. I can tell you from personal experience that it is hard to watch your child hit himself in the head, but it's better to ignore that behavior and praise him and encourage him when he stops doing it. In other words, ignore the behavior you don't want and praise what you do."

A message came over Officer Pulaski's body radio. "10-101, what's your status?"

"10-101 here. We've finished our sweep." Officer Pulaski paused. "We're going to head toward the lake."

"10-4, roger that," said the dispatcher.

"We truly appreciate your help, Mister…I don't think I caught your name," Officer Marshall asserted.

"Jackson," Jack quickly responded with his hand outstretched. "Jackson Grieve."

"Thanks again."

The officers departed. Jack let out a sigh of relief and looked at Father Desmond. "That took a few years off of my life for sure."

***

Father Desmond reached into his jacket pocket to make sure he still had his house keys. A compulsive habit he developed as a child and had never conquered. While feeling for his keys, he felt another more rectangular object.

"Yikes! I forgot to put this bill in the mail," he said. "Would you mind if we walked over to the post office so I can make sure it goes out today? It's across town, which gives me more time to hear your confession."

18

"I guess so, Father," Jack said, anxiously checking his watch.

As they headed to the park exit, Father Desmond said, "What you did back there for those police officers was very risky. It might not have been the best thing to do under the circumstances. You must take care not to bring unnecessary attention to yourself. Do you understand, Jack?"

"What you're saying makes all the sense in the world," Jack responded. "But I couldn't stand by knowing the anguish that Donnie's mother must be feeling right now." He cast his gaze to the ground. "It's what my wife Amanda would have done. It's what she would expect me to do."

"It was admirable, Jack. It says something about the kind of man you are. Putting the needs of others ahead of your own is the Christian thing to do. It must be very challenging having two children with autism. I am aware of the epidemic of newly diagnosed cases in our country but confess I don't know as much about it as perhaps I should."

As they made their way down Massachusetts Street, Jack periodically looked over his shoulder.

"What's worrying you, Jack? I've noticed you looking behind us every so often."

"I don't know, Father." He rubbed the back of his neck. "I just have a feeling. Like we're being watched or followed. I guess it's just my nerves. Sorry, where were we?"

"Tell me about when you found out your oldest son was autistic," Father Desmond suggested.

"When we found out that Amanda was pregnant, as you might expect, we were elated. We were looking forward to all the milestones that new parents wait for with great anticipation—the first smile, first tooth, first steps, first birthday, and so on. The first year was an adjustment, but we experienced all of these wonderful events pretty much on schedule, with one exception. Louis turned two, and he was still not speaking."

"Is it uncommon for a child to not start speaking by age two?" Father Desmond asked.

"Not necessarily, but Louis didn't even babble. Our pediatrician gave us information about services that we could access for Louis, including seeing a speech therapist. As the year went on, the caseworker started to hint that Louis needed to see another specialist, a neurologist. It was clear she could not share her suspicions, but the persistence with which she urged us to have him seen told us we needed to follow up on her suggestion. As the holidays approached, we booked an appointment with a neurologist, but the earliest appointment we could get was around Louis's third birthday, which was in February. We headed back to Long Island to celebrate Christmas with both of our families."

Father Desmond sighed. "Unfortunately, Christmastime has become as much a season of stress as a season of joy. Something evidently happened that Christmas."

Jack continued, his voice choking with emotion. "We'd barely put Louis down for a nap and sat down for Christmas dinner at my sister's home when we heard him screaming. We dashed upstairs and found him sitting up in bed, crying hysterically. We attempted to comfort him, but it was almost as if he did not recognize us. The more we attempted to comfort him, the more upset he got. Amanda and I looked at each other, and we started packing up our things and left without eating dinner. As soon as we got in the car and pulled away from my sister's house, Louis calmed down. I turned to Amanda, and before I could say anything, she said, 'I'll call when we get home and see if they have had any cancellations. We were able to get a slightly earlier appointment. Thursday, January 13th, 2000, is a day I will never forget, although I wish I could. The neurologist spent some time with Louis and did some testing. Afterward, he said, 'Louis has Autism.'" Jack lowered his head and stared down at the concrete sidewalk.

"Looking back, I believe we both had our suspicions, but neither of us wanted to admit it to the other. We left the doctor's office in silence. No matter how prepared you think you are to hear something like this, the truth is you aren't. On the way home, as is usual, we got caught in traffic on Route 66. We held hands, and both broke into tears.

"I called my parents that night to break the news to them. All I remember is my father saying, '*Oh God no,*' and I heard my father begin to cry for the only time in my life. I thought about how I was going to tell my twin brother about this. He and his wife were pregnant with their first child, and even though there was no family history of autism, I was concerned that maybe this was genetic."

The twenty-year gap between his son's diagnosis and the present day had done little to ease his pain. Teardrop after teardrop fell to the ground.

Father Desmond stopped at the intersection, but a bleary-eyed Jack continued into the crosswalk. Distantly, he registered the screaming siren from the ambulance racing in their direction. Father Desmond reached for Jack's shirt collar and yanked him back to the curb before it was too late.

Jack gasped. Jolted back to reality, he realized how close he had come to being another dead pedestrian.

"Jesus, Father," Jack said. "I'm sorry. I'm glad you were paying attention. You saved my life."

Panting, Father Desmond replied, "I think we both need to sit down for a minute." He pointed toward the bus stop to their left. "There's a bench over there."

Despite the cool fall temperatures, both men were sweating profusely.

"I'm sure glad you still have your cat-like reflexes," Jack joked in an attempt to bring some levity to the moment.

Father Desmond laughed. "If you think you can make it across the street in one piece, the post office is around the corner."

Jack stepped to the curb and exaggerated the act of looking both ways before he entered the crosswalk. Father Desmond grinned at Jack's antics, and even Jack himself cracked a smile.

Leaving Jack outside, Father Desmond entered the post office.

***

Across the street, Jack saw a sign that read, *9ᵗʰ Annual Zombie Walk*. It reminded him that Halloween was only three days away, and he was on the clock.

"Three days," Jack muttered to himself. "I need to find this object and get back in three days."

His phone vibrated, and he quickly pulled it from his pocket. "Damn!" Jack said.

Father Desmond exited the post office. "What is it, Jack?" he asked.

"My cell battery. It only has twenty percent life left in it, and if it runs out…"

"Give me your phone, Jack."

Jack handed his phone to Father Desmond.

"If you go into settings, there should be a… ah, here it is." Father Desmond swiped and put the phone in a power-saving mode.

Handing the phone back to Jack, he said, "I also turned off the vibration. You can still hear if a call comes in, but the vibration mode uses more battery. This hack should help for a little while anyway."

"Thanks," Jack said with a mixture of surprise and appreciation. "Where did you learn so much about cell phones?"

"Oh, I've always had an interest in electronics," he said with a shrug. "Let's head back to the rectory," he suggested. "We can talk more privately there."

***

As they made their way across town, Father Desmond reflected on what Jack had shared with him thus far. While he had no children, he felt empathy for Jack and understood how such a diagnosis might impact a family.

He turned to Jack and said, "Having counseled many couples over the years, I know that news like this can put a strain on a marriage. Tell me, how did you and Amanda cope with it?"

A smile crept onto Jack's face. "Father, I'm sure I don't have to tell you about the state of the institution of marriage today. The divorce rate is pretty high, and it's even higher among couples with an autistic child. Some estimates are that nine out of ten such marriages end up in a divorce. Fortunately for us, Louis's diagnosis brought us even closer together. We feel fortunate that we were on the same page from the beginning regarding the priorities for his treatment. Amanda is strong, like a rock, and has just the right temperament to deal with the chaos in our lives. There's a serenity that allows her to live in the present. She should be a role model for me, but while she seems to find a way to cope with it all, I seem to fall apart."

Father Desmond put his hand on Jack's shoulder. "Jack, you have been through a challenging time. I know it is easy for me to say this, but you might try letting up on yourself a little bit." He offered a sympathetic smile. "Not advice but a suggestion."

"Father, I know I've taken up quite a bit of your time already, but there is more."

"Somehow, I thought there might be. I'm listening."

"The year after Louis's diagnosis was filled with a lot of ups and downs. While the Internet is a valuable tool, it has a dark side. We started educating ourselves on autism and how to treat it. Most of the information we found wasn't helpful, and at times it was frightening. It did nothing more than reinforce and worsen our fears. While searching for answers, we still had additional testing for Louis that the neurologist had requested. I had to pin Louis to the table for blood tests, and the sheer terror in his eyes is something that I will never forget. We then took Louis for an EEG. He needed to be sedated, which involved forcibly feeding him the tranquilizer."

"Jack, I'm sorry that you had to go through that. No parent should have to do this to their child."

Jack accepted Father Desmond's compassion with a sad smile and continued. "We sat in the waiting room for the sedative to take effect. A father came in with his son. The father sat down, and the child flung himself to the floor. He started running his fingertips back and forth across the rug, something I'd read that some autistic children do. The look on that man's face still haunts me. His eyes were sunken like he hadn't slept well in quite some time. At the same time, he had a blank stare. It was a sad look of defeat. A look of someone who'd been under a constant state of pressure and was ready to surrender and give up. His pain was palpable, and I couldn't help but wonder if I was looking at my future self."

Jack stared straight ahead and said, "Thankfully, our marriage survived, but unfortunately, my depression returned with a vengeance."

It was now late afternoon, and a chilly breeze began to rise. The two men were walking faster now, and Jack turned up the collar of his jacket against the gusty wind, but to no avail. He could feel a chill run down his spine, but these days he was never quite sure if it were the weather or his tenuous predicament that chilled him to the bone.

***

Father Desmond pointed to a street sign with an arrow pointing to the right that read *Saint Lawrence Catholic Campus.* "That's home, Jack," he said. "We're about ten minutes away. I'm looking forward to getting indoors. That wind tells me it is going to be a cold night."

"Jack, tell me one thing. What role was faith playing in your ability to handle all of this adversity?"

"Regrettably, attending church was a casualty of the move we made to Virginia before Louis was born," Jack said with a grimace. "I tried visiting several churches but was unable to connect with any of them. Unlike the Methodist church I attended on Long Island, all these congregations were much larger, making developing personal connections with other parishioners challenging. When I returned to visit family on Long Island, I looked forward to going back to church, but the visits became less frequent as the years progressed. After Louis's diagnosis, they stopped altogether.

"I also admit that comparing the other ministers to my former minister, Reverend Miner was unfair," he continued. "None could measure up. He was special. His sermons were thought-provoking, and as a young man, I found myself drawn to his message. I remember he once compared Maverick leaving his wingman in the movie *Top Gun* to our denials of Christ. How we might think we are doing our best flying, but in reality, we'll end up dead without being Christ's wingman. He had the congregation close their eyes and repeat, just like Maverick did in the movie, 'I am not leaving my wingman. I am not leaving my wingman.'"

Father Desmond smiled. "The Catholic Church could perhaps use a little bit of that folksy style in our homilies too. It sounds like he is an exceptional man of God."

Jack nodded. "He is. At my grandmother's memorial service, he gave a special message to me during his eulogy. Before the service, I told him about visiting my grandparents and that on Easter Sunday, my grandmother would joyfully sing the hymn, 'Christ the Lord Is Risen Today.' He had that hymn played at her service. Before we sang it, he stated, *'I know one young man, in particular, who will find Easter more joyous because of his deep faith in God.'*" Jack gave a hollow laugh. "I'm glad that he's not here to see what I have become. I fear I would be a disappointment to him."

"Jack, I am sure he would not be disappointed."

Shaking his head, Jack said, "I'm not so sure. I spoke to Reverend Miner on the way here. I told him I was heading to Lawrence, Kansas, and without going into any details, that my family was in trouble. I'm sure he could tell I was evasive, but he told me he would pray for us."

"That does not sound like a disappointment to me, Jack."

"Reverend Miner said one more thing before we were disconnected. Despite the static, I'm sure I heard a change in the tone of his voice. It almost sounded like a warning. He said, 'Do not forget Proverbs, Jack. Many advisors bring success but be careful who you ask for help. Some advisors are better than others, and not all advice is good advice.'

"As a minister," Father Desmond said, "I am sure he is speaking from his own experiences. It is good counsel for both of us."

Jack stared at the ground, unsure of whether he should ask the question that had been on his mind for quite some time. Reasoning that if he did not survive this ordeal, he might never get an answer, he finally decided it was now or never.

"Father, do you believe that sometimes trouble follows a man?"

"What are you asking, Jack? Do I believe in curses?"

"The first year after Louis's diagnosis had its ups and downs. Eventually, after intense therapy, Louis started to communicate through pictures and finally began to use words. We were overjoyed. Later in the year, we started discussing having another child. While there was much to be happy about in terms of Louis's progress, there still were storm clouds gathering for me. About a year and a half after Louis's diagnosis, we discovered that Amanda was pregnant and due in December.

"On Thursday, June 14th, 2001, another event occurred which would significantly impact both of us. It was our first sonogram, and the technician started the procedure and almost immediately stopped it. She excused herself and left the room. We didn't think anything of it at the time. We thought she just stepped out for something. A few minutes later, she returned with another technician. The second technician proceeded to tell us that the sonogram revealed an abnormality. One of the fetus's arms appeared to be missing, and the technician explained there was a possibility that the arm was under the body. Still, a higher magnification sonogram would be necessary.

"A few days later, we were at Mary Washington Hospital receiving genetic counseling along with an enhanced sonogram. The sonogram confirmed that the left arm of our child was missing. They suspected something called an amniotic band, and even though the fetus looked normal, they couldn't rule out the potential for other genetic abnormalities. We discussed our options, including aborting the fetus, which we knew was not an option we could consider. When we'd discussed having another baby, our focus had been on what if the child was autistic. We knew the odds were overwhelmingly in our favor, but we accepted that risk. We knew that even though we hadn't contemplated something like this, we were going to accept this too."

Jack paused to wipe tears from his eyes. Father Desmond saw the hurt in Jack's face and wanted to comfort him but was unsure what to say.

"I was trying to be strong for Amanda, but I was struggling with all of this. I questioned God and asked why he would ask more of us when we were already wrestling with Louis's challenges." His voice grew angry. "Family and friends tried to be supportive by reminding me of God's love. They told me that God had a plan for all of us, and sometimes the answers come when we least expect them. My mother tried to console me by telling me that God never gives us more than we can handle. I know they all meant well, but all I could think of was that I was drowning. The water level was up to my chin, and if this was not more than I could handle, it was pretty close to it. I asked God what sin we had committed. I told God that I did not understand the plan and asked why this was happening to us. I begged him to reveal the plan to me, but no answers came."

Jack got up and paced the room as he continued, "As Amanda's due date approached, the stress and pressure continued to build. There were so many unknowns associated with the birth, and the September 11 attacks had a significant impact on the insurance industry. It made work even more demanding. It was hard to balance the responsibility of being the sole breadwinner and keeping Louis's treatment on track while a potentially difficult birth loomed. Amanda's condition was delicate, and I knew she was worried. I didn't want to burden her with all of my other troubles. It seemed like every song on the radio was about our situation, and everything felt like it was spiraling out of control. I was off on Monday, November 12th, for the Veteran's Day holiday. Early in the morning, I told Amanda that I was going out for coffee, but instead, I drove to a bridge that crosses Bull Run Creek in the Manassas battlefield."

Father Desmond interrupted and asked with trepidation, "Jack, why there?"

"This is a location I know well. I'd sometimes spend my lunch hour walking the trails along Bull Run. It's quiet, and I knew it was unlikely that I would encounter anyone. If you want to be alone to think, it's a good place to go. You're unlikely to be interrupted if you want to commit suicide."

Jack had stopped walking now and was nearly hyperventilating.

"I stood on the wall of the bridge and thought about jumping. Due to a significant rainstorm during the night, the usually calm waters were a raging torrent.

"The only thing that stopped me was the thought of Amanda having to deal with my death and clean up the mess that I'd be leaving her. I stepped off the wall, got into my car, and went home. The next day I called the employee assistance plan hotline provided by my employer and asked for help."

**

Before Father Desmond respond to Jack's admission, his cell phone rang. He glanced down at the number, brow furrowed.

"Jack, please forgive me. I must take this call. Excuse me for just a moment," he said, stepping away. "This is Mark Desmond," he answered.

"Father, we need to speak to you. It's urgent."

Chapter 3

957 BCE
Ancient Israel

"Get back to work, you demon scum!" the guard screamed.

The work crew did not move fast enough for the guard, and he cracked his whip, striking the heavily scarred back of a demon by the name of Ornias, who cried out in agony. Even his thick, reptilian-like skin could not protect him from the iron-tipped instrument of discipline that terrorized the slaves every day.

The late afternoon sun cast a long shadow over the walled city of Jerusalem. Their strength depleted after a long day of hard labor; Ornias and several other demons fought to push a massive stone column, the final roof support, into place.

Struggling to push the pillar, Ornias said weakly, "Lucius, I'm not sure I can hold on much longer."

"You can," Lucius Rofocale shot back. "It is your duty to the Master, and you will fulfill it."

Though bound in iron chains for years, Lucius never wavered in his belief in Lucifer. His chiseled physique and massive size enabled him to endure the taskmaster's whip even if he could not break his restraints. His intense hatred for his captors grew with each crack of the whip.

Pausing from the drudgery of his back-breaking stonework, Lucius stared at Ornias and asked, "Are we clear?"

"Crystal clear, Lucius."

"You two," the guard said to Ornias and Lucius. "Less talking and more working."

Lucius rose from his knees, glaring at the guard. He towered over his jailer, and he clenched his jaw with his large, protruding canines bared as a reminder to the guard of his superior size and strength. Only his iron fetters stopped him from murdering his tormenter on the spot.

"You know the penalty for confronting me," the guard said threateningly.

CRACK! The whip struck Lucius across the black, leather-like skin on his shoulders. He flinched slightly but did not cry out despite the intense plan inflicted by the lash of his taskmaster.

"Unlike your demon brethren, you hold your tongue," the guard said with surprise.

Lucius growled in a deep, guttural voice, "The day will come when you will hear the roar of all demons. On that day, you will most surely die."

"Today is not that day," the guard yelled, rearing back and striking Lucius with all of his might with the back of his hand.

Lucius's head snapped back, but he quickly recovered, smiling menacingly at the overseer.

"Get back to work!"

Lucius resumed chiseling and shaping the slab of marble in front of him. After being captured, building Solomon's temple to God was initially a painful punishment, but Lucius eventually came to see it as a form of purification, which at its end, would make him indispensable to the Master.

Azazel, a rare yellow-eyed demon, whispered to Lucius, "Human filth. What I would not give for just one chance to fight back."

"Oh, but you are fighting back, Azazel. With every word of Lucifer's Manifesto that we share with our brethren, we prepare for the day of liberation. A day and time of his choosing. He is testing our faith and courage. When we prove worthy, Lucifer will come to release us."

Azazel smiled wickedly. "Knowing that reading Lucifer's book is punishable by death makes me feel that much more rebellious."

Of all the parables in the book, Lucius enjoyed the legend of the compromised soul the most. He longed for the day when he would once again reap the souls of humans. He savored those of the most pious individuals. Their fall from grace was the sweetest victory of all.

Just then, the royal chariot appeared, and King Solomon himself dismounted. A scabbard on his hip carried the Sword of the Arch Angel Saint Michael. This unholy weapon gave Solomon his power over demons and enabled him to turn them all into slaves. Lucius eyed the sword as the monarch, dressed in his purple robe, approached.

"You demon dogs," a member of King Solomon's royal guard yelled. "Kneel! Bow your heads low in the presence of the King!"

While the other demons knelt and turned away from King Solomon as ordered, Lucius remained standing in defiance.

"I said kneel, you abomination!" The guard prepared to strike Lucius, but King Solomon raised his hand to stop him.

"Why do you not obey?" King Solomon asked, voice stern.

"I swore no allegiance to you, highness," Lucius said sarcastically. "Lucifer is the only king I recognize."

"I could have my guards compel you to comply," King Solomon countered.

Lucius sneered. "Do you think they could force me to do so, sire?"

King Solomon patted the sword at his side. "You know this sword can destroy you, do you not? Or do we need a demonstration?"

"No such demonstration is required," Lucius admitted. "I understand its power."

King Solomon reached into his cloak and threw a book on the ground in front of Lucius. "Do you know the punishment for reading this book?"

"Death," Lucius said boldly.

Pointing at Lucius, one of the guards said, "Sire, we found this book in this demon's belongings."

A hush fell over the demon legions as the magnitude of what was unfolding became clear. Lucius Rofocale, their de facto leader, had just been sentenced to die.

***

Standing on the gallows erected in the center of Jerusalem, Lucius watched the executioner release the trap door. The iron chain went taut, and the silent crowd assembled for the hanging heard an audible snap that echoed through the plaza. The links of the chain groaned from the weight of the executed party. Another demon, sentenced to die for a different offense, swung limply in the air with its neck broken. The crowd shouted its approval.

Trumpets sounded, and King Solomon appeared in the royal box. The throngs of people knelt before the King. The demon slaves, chained together, were led to the front of the gallows. They were to have a front-row seat to witness the price of sedition. Lucius looked upon it all without any fear or concern. On the contrary, he wore a self-assured smile on this face.

Several guards removed the dead demon from the gallows, and one of the executioners reset the trap door. A judge stepped forward to read the charge against Lucius.

"You are charged with reading from the evil book and, in so doing, inciting rebellion against our King and Israel. The only remedy for this blasphemy is death." Looking down at the demon hoards, he said harshly, "Let this be a warning to all demons about what fate awaits you for such treachery."

Lucius heard someone walking up the stairs and turned to see who was joining him on the scaffold.

"Do you remember me?" a voice asked.

Stepping in front of Lucius was the guard who had slapped him across the face.

Lucius smirked. "Come to see me off, have you? How kind."

"You told me I would hear the roar of demons before I died," the guard said mockingly. "Do you remember what I told you?"

Lucius, bound and chained, stood silently.

"Today is not that day," the guard said contemptuously.

"The day's not over yet," Lucius said, his confidence never wavering.

The guard laughed and shoved Lucius so that he was squarely on the trap door.

"No blindfold?" Lucius joked.

The guard roughly shoved Lucius's head into the iron chain links fashioned into a noose. He tightened the noose around Lucius's neck. Sharp pains began shooting through Lucius's body. He tightened his jaw but made no sound and gave no indication that he was suffering. Lucius would not provide his enemies any such satisfaction.

The crowd stirred in anticipation. The demon slaves looked up at Lucius with a mix of pity and despair. Many of them wondered to themselves, *what will become of us now?*

King Solomon rose, and Lucius stared at the sword still fastened to the ruler's side. He focused on the sword as a way to ignore the anguish he was going through. *Just a few more seconds,* he thought. The King nodded to the executioner, who prepared to release the trap door. An eerie silence fell over the plaza.

Then, a thunderous roar echoed through all of Jerusalem.

"I have heard the cries of my people," the voice boomed. "Your hour of liberation has arrived!"

Azazel closed his eyes and said, "Lucifer!"

Suddenly, the iron chains that bound every demon fell to the ground. The crowd was stunned at first but began to panic when they realized what was happening.

"Protect the King!" the leader of the royal guard shouted.

The guards surrounded the King and led him away into the now finished temple for this own protection.

Meanwhile, on the gallows, a loud thud signaled that Lucius's chains and the noose around his neck were gone. The guard who had taunted and tormented Lucius slowly turned around and, with a terrified look on his face, realized that Lucius was no longer bound.

Lucius grabbed the guard by the throat and hoisted him into the air. He pulled the guard closer, so they were face to face and let out a roar like a male lion.

"Here's a lesson you humans will need to learn," Lucius said to the horrified guard. "Payback is a bitch."

Lucius tore the guard in two and tossed the remains to the ground.

Chapter 4

Looking out Father Desmond's living room window, Jack could see the sun setting on the horizon. As he watched the yellow ball slowly fade from view, a curious contrast developed. The sky seemed to split in two, the upper part still a fiery mix of red and orange while the lower half was pitch black. Jack pondered the divergence and, as was his introspective nature, found a way to connect what he saw within his current state of mind.

A fire raged inside him, filled with angry determination to save his family. It manifested itself in his demand to speak with Amanda and the anger toward God he had just shared with Father Desmond. Unfortunately, that dark side of his personality was always there. Fear and doubt would engulf him like the darkness of the night, slowly overtaking the light of the day. This constant war with himself was not new, and when the dark would overwhelm him, it would drive Jack into a deep depression.

It could have been the games his mind played with him or the hours of sleep deprivation, but Jack was exhausted and found himself dozing off. Father Desmond had provided him with the keys to his apartment while he went to his office to take an important call. He'd told Jack to make himself at home, and he decided to do just that. Jack took his shoes off and lay down on the couch, closing his eyes. *Perhaps some rest will do me some good.*

***

Father Desmond sat behind the desk in his office, staring down at his calendar and restlessly shaking his leg. He tended to do this when he was thinking about a particularly troubling issue or problem, usually unaware that he was even doing it. The office was quiet, and all he could hear was the ticking of the pendulum in the clock on the wall. *Tick-Tock-Tick-Tock.*

Suddenly, the chime went off, causing him to jump up from his chair. He saw that the clock read 5:00 p.m. and immediately, his office phone rang.

Father Desmond picked up the receiver. "This is Mark Desmond."

"Mark, it is good to hear your voice again," the caller said. "It has been a long time. Too long."

"Yes. Too long, Father Danielson," Mark agreed. "What can I do for you, my friend?"

"Same old Mark. You always were one to get down to business."

"I know this is not a social call," Father Desmond said directly. "What's happened, and what has it got to do with me?"

"A member of the order has gone missing," said Father Danielson.

"What do you mean gone missing?"

"He was sent out on a mission and never came back."

"Who was it?" Father Desmond asked with trepidation.

"Brother Abraham."

"Isn't he fairly new in the order?" Father Desmond asked. "What about his partner?"

"He had no partner, Mark."

"What?" Father Desmond said, incredulous. "He was far too inexperienced to be out there on his own already. What is going on?"

"Unfortunately, recruits are hard to come by these days," Father Danielson explained. "Almost every mission now is a solo one."

"I have been on the sidelines for a while, haven't I?" Father Desmond said ruefully. "What was the assignment?"

"That's part of the reason I'm calling, Mark," Father Danielson said reluctantly. "He was on a mission to Culpeper."

Father Desmond could feel the blood instantly rush from his head and, luckily, fell back into the chair before he fainted. He stared down at his desk, not seeing the calendar.

"Mark... are you there? Mark!" Father Danielson yelled. "Are you alright?"

The intensity in Father Danielson's voice jolted Father Desmond back to reality. "I'm-I'm here," he said hesitantly. "Did you say—"

"Culpeper," Father Danielson answered before Father Desmond could finish. "Yes, I said Culpeper."

Father Desmond shook his head in disbelief. Culpeper was a quaint, small town in Northern Virginia, but its pastoral appearance hid deep dark secrets. Terrible secrets. Father Desmond had been there once and never wanted to go back again. When the subject of Culpeper came up, even amongst friends and colleagues he'd known for decades, Father Desmond refused to talk about his experiences there.

"Why in the name of all that is holy was he sent to Culpeper?" Father Desmond asked. "Who in their right mind sends a rookie there by himself? It's like leading a lamb to the slaughter."

"You're preaching to the choir, buddy," Father Danielson said. "That's why I'm calling you. Something big is going on there."

"What makes you say that?" Father Desmond asked.

"This is the third member of the order that has disappeared there in the last few months. We have someone permanently stationed in the area who is far more experienced, but the Council won't risk blowing their cover."

Father Desmond took a deep breath. He could not believe what he was hearing. "The Council must have lost its collective mind," Father Desmond muttered to himself. He cleared this throat. "So, what do you want from me?"

"We need you to confront the Council about what is going on," Father Danielson said emphatically.

"What?" Father Desmond said. "Are you crazy? Absolutely not!"

"Mark," Father Danielson pleaded, "you're the only one who can speak about Culpeper from experience."

"While that may be true, the Council has relieved me of my command. Why do you think I am here in Lawrence? They've put me on the sideline. They retired me, Oskar. No one on that Council is going to listen to a word I say."

"We'll back you up, Mark," Father Danielson countered. "You have more supporters than you think. We'll make them listen."

"Oskar, you should see the looks I get from people on this campus. It's like I am a leper. The finger-pointing. The whispers. I may as well be a side-show freak." Father Desmond paused. "I'm sorry, Oskar, but I'm not your man. I have no credibility or sway with the Council. I can't think of one person on that body who is a friend of mine."

"Please, Mark," Father Danielson begged. "You're our only hope."

"I'd like to help you, but I can't. There is nothing I can do or say that will make any difference."

"I'm sorry you feel that way," Father Danielson, voice filled with disappointment. "I think you're wrong, but I can tell there is no changing your mind on this."

"Oskar, if you ever find yourself in Lawrence, you come and see me," Father Desmond said.

"I will, Mark."

"Oskar, one more thing."

"What's that?"

"You be very careful," Mark implored. "And whatever you do, stay away from Culpeper if you can. You don't want to go there. Trust me."

"Copy that, Mark," Father Danielson said as he hung up the phone.

As Father Desmond replaced the receiver, something occurred to him. Didn't Jack say he lived in Virginia?

What has Jack gotten himself wrapped up in?

***

The aroma was undeniable—freshly baked chocolate chip cookies. Jack's favorite! He wandered into the kitchen and found a plate full of cookies hot from the oven. Jack bit into a golden-brown piece of heaven, savoring the gooey chocolate goodness. He grabbed another cookie and headed back to the living room.

It was then that Jack noticed something unusual. He was still lying on the couch, fast asleep.

Suddenly, Jack found himself in a sea of people. The sun was brightly shining. It was comfortably warm but not hot, and there was just a hint of a breeze. Perfect weather. Jack noticed a large stage, and among the seemingly endless rows of chairs, he spied Louis and Amanda and waved to them.

"Over here," he called.

Jack was sure he locked eyes with Amanda, but she didn't indicate that she recognized him. In truth, her demeanor suggested that she didn't even see him. It was as if he was invisible.

Amanda glanced down at her watch. "Where is your father? I know he doesn't want to miss this."

"He'll be here, Mom," Louis reassured. "Don't worry."

Amanda smiled. "You and David have no idea how proud we are of you both. My babies are now both college graduates."

"Coll-college graduates?" Jack stammered. Louis had only received a special education diploma. Last week, they'd had David's IEP meeting, and college was not an option.

"I still can't believe David's grade point average was higher than mine," Louis said, feigning disappointment. "The older brother is supposed to be the smarter one!"

Amanda elbowed Louis. "You have to let him win at something," she teased. "You were Homecoming King and an all-state track and field athlete."

"Dad was a great coach, Mom."

The band began to play 'Pomp and Circumstance,' and the processional started. Graduates in their crimson red gowns with black tassels on the caps marched into the arena. Jack searched for David in the crowd of students.

The dean called out the names of the graduates, and then Jack heard, "David George Aitken."

In the blink of an eye, Jack was back home, standing in his kitchen. Christmas decorations adorned the house. *But it's only October*, Jack thought to himself. Loud steps thundered down the stairs from the second floor, and David came down the hallway. Jack recognized him immediately, but something was very different about him.

"David, would you set the table for me?" Amanda asked.

"Sure, Mom."

David reached into the cabinet for plates and glasses. *David has two arms. His left arm is intact.* He watched David set the table.

"That smells so good, Mom."

Amanda reached into the oven with a baster. "You know that turkey is your dad's favorite. Hopefully, the aroma will get him to come home," she joked. "He's been out exercising for quite a while now."

"Save a leg for me!" David said with a smile.

Save a leg for me? David doesn't eat turkey; he eats chicken, fries, and pizza. That's it.

The door from the garage swung open, and three small children Jack had never seen before stormed into the room.

"Nana!" they cried.

Amanda threw open her arms and embraced the smiling children. "Merry Christmas, my loves!"

Jack observed it all in bewilderment. His jaw nearly hit the floor with what he saw next.

"Merry Christmas, Mom!" Louis said as he entered.

He hugged Amanda, and then Amanda embraced the woman who was with Louis. "Merry Christmas, Jennifer dear," she said.

"The house is beautiful," the woman said, beaming. "And it smells heavenly in here, Mom!"

Mom? Who is this woman?

Jack instinctively looked down and saw a diamond ring and wedding band on the woman's finger.

Louis is married and has children? That's not possible.

"Where's Dad?" Louis asked.

"I'm expecting him any minute. That must be him now."

Jack heard the garage door open.

He was at a restaurant. Erin and Andrew, two of Jack's colleagues from work, decorated the private room with balloons and a large banner read *Happy Retirement.*

"Erin, who's retiring?" Jack asked.

"Andrew, hand me some tape, please," she said, totally ignoring Jack.

Andrew broke off a piece of tape and handed it to Erin. "He's going to be completely surprised."

Jack chuckled. "Okay, what's the gag, guys?"

Erin and Andrew continued decorating, totally oblivious to Jack's presence.

One of the restaurant staff entered the room, carrying a rectangular box. "Where would you like me to put the cake?"

Erin pointed across the room. "On that table over there would be great."

Andrew removed the cake from the box. The icing on the cake spelled out, *All our Best Wishes for a Happy Retirement, Jack!*

Retirement? Jack thought. *It can't be. What's going on?*

Suddenly, the room was full of Jack's friends, clients, and business contacts.

"I remember when Jack first told me he wanted to retire when he was fifty-five," Erin said to one of Jack's clients. "I thought he was just dreaming, but I guess I should have known even thirty years ago that when Jack sets his mind to something, he gets it done."

"Even now, he's a key contributor to our company," Andrew added. "He is going to be difficult to replace. Do you think we can keep him on retainer or something, just in case we need him?"

Erin laughed. "I'm sure Jack wouldn't mind, but he might be hard to track down for the first few months. When Amanda mentioned that they wanted to take a trip out west, I looked into the cost of renting an RV," she said with a smile. "They're going to flip when they find out I convinced the company to rent them an RV for the summer as Jack's bonus!"

"Jack and Amanda are here!" a voice yelled.

"Quick!" Erin shouted. "Everyone hide!"

Jack heard them yell, "Surprise!"

Jack found himself standing on a gravel path surrounded by brick walls. It was as if he were in a theatre where the stage lights had faded to black, and he was standing in the spotlight. Silence, absolute and total silence, surrounded him.

He looked around, and after a moment, he finally realized where he was. He was standing on the stone bridge overlooking Bull Run Creek on the Manassas Civil War Battlefield. This spot was familiar to Jack. All too familiar.

Suddenly, a voice emanated from the darkness. "Hello, Jack." A Scottish accent that Jack was sure he'd heard before.

"Who's there?" Jack asked, straining to see through the blackness.

A man gradually appeared and stood at the end of the trail. "Do you recognize me, Jack?"

Jack was amazed.

"It can't be. Poppy Aitken?" he asked.

"Yes, Jack. It has been a lifetime since we last saw one another."

"I was nine." He stepped closer. "Do you know what all of this is about, Pop?"

"Righting wrongs, Jack," he replied. "You've endured a great deal. What you've witnessed is just a glimpse of what your life should have been ... and can still be."

Jack frowned at his grandfather in confusion. "I don't think I understand, Pop."

"Aren't you tired of watching life pass you by, Jack? You have a chance to change the trajectory of your fate and create a new destiny for your family."

The voice of Jack's grandfather changed. It became graver, almost ominous.

"But only if you fulfill your mission."

Jack took a step backward. "You're not my grandfather," he said.

"How perceptive of you, Jack. I am sure this is all very confusing, but it is, in reality, quite straightforward. The carrot and the stick, Jack."

"What are you talking about?" Jack asked skeptically.

"You already know all about the stick. You fail, your family dies. You are all damned for eternity. Simple. The carrot is an incentive. Fulfill the mission, and you get to hit the rewind button. Think about it, no autism or physical disabilities for your children. No financial difficulties. Every unrealized dream now fulfilled."

A white light emerged from the darkness around the bridge. It transformed right in front of Jack into his wife, Amanda.

"Jack, darling, listen to what he is offering," the apparition counseled. "This can all be over if you comply. Please do it for us. Do it for me."

"You're not real," Jack emphatically stated as he climbed the wall of the bridge. "Amanda would never ask me to do such a thing for her."

"Jack, don't be a fool," his phony grandfather said. "Haven't you heard about what can happen when you fall during a dream?"

Amanda's apparition answered, "You might not wake up at all."

A steely-eyed Jack looked at the two imposters. "I'll take my chances."

He leaned backward, closed his eyes, and flung himself into the dark void below him.

***

"Jack! Jack!" Father Desmond shouted as he shook him by the shoulders. "Jack, wake up!"

Jack jumped up from the couch, startled and glancing around the room to get his bearings. "W-what. W-where am I?" he babbled, still unsure of his surroundings.

"It's alright, Jack," Father Desmond reassured. "You were having a nightmare."

"I was falling." Jack placed his hand on his chest and felt his heart beating rapidly. He continued to gasp for air.

"Do you remember anything about your nightmare?" Father Desmond asked.

Jack took a deep, cleansing breath and collapsed back on the couch. "I remember a graduation ceremony. Then it was Christmas day." He grew calmer and looked up at Father Desmond. "My children were not autistic. I met my grandfather, who died when I was a kid."

"Anything else?"

Jack struggled to recall other details of the dream. "Y-yes. Ah, I was at a bridge over Bull Run Creek. Amanda was there. She and my grandfather. I don't remember the rest."

"Jack, does any of this have significance to you?"

"Well, the bridge is the spot where I planned to commit suicide twice," Jack said with regret in his voice.

Father Desmond sat down next to Jack. The two men sat pensively, silently contemplating the meaning of Jack's nightmare as the darkness of the night settled in.

***

After dinner, Jack found himself in Father Desmond's library. Shelves filled to their capacity with books lined the walls. Father Desmond entered the room and handed Jack a glass of bourbon.

"A nightcap," he said. Holding up his glass, he continued, "To pleasanter dreams."

Jack gulped down the alcohol.

"Tell me, Father," he asked. "Have you read all of these books? It's quite an impressive collection."

"Most of them. I'm not a fan of television."

One particular book caught Jack's eye. It was leather-bound and appeared to be quite old. He nodded to the tome. "May I?"

Father Desmond nodded, and Jack pulled out the book.

"*The Interpretation of Dreams*," Jack read out loud. "I guess that explains why you were so interested in the details of my nightmare."

"It's a first edition copy of Sigmund Freud's book," Father Desmond said. "I've got a degree in psychology."

"Do you think my falling in the dream means anything?" Jack asked curiously.

"Possibly. One interpretation is that it represents a feeling of being overwhelmed and losing control. The waking up symbolizes taking control of the situation."

"Let's hope that's the meaning," Jack said, attempting to sound optimistic. He hesitated, then asked, "Do you think a dream can become a lie if it doesn't come true?"

Father Desmond pondered Jack's question.

Jack continued, "What I mean is, if a dream you share with someone goes unrealized, is that similar to making a promise that you fail to keep?"

"I believe dreams represent idyllic scenarios, Jack," Father Desmond answered. "Real life seldom can live up to such ideals."

"Maybe you're right, Father," he said. "Or maybe they are something worse than a lie." He sighed. "Maybe they're just visions meant to tempt and taunt a person. Kind of like seeing the summit of the mountain but never being able to get to the top."

Father Desmond glanced at the clock on the wall. It was nearly midnight. "Jack, do you have a place to sleep tonight?"

"I have been catching some sleep in my car where and when I can."

"Not tonight. You can sleep on my couch. It has to be more comfortable than your car."

"Thank you, Father," Jack said gratefully. "That is very generous of you."

Father Desmond looked Jack squarely in the eye and, in a serious tone, said, "Tomorrow, you can finish your confession and explain why you need to go to Stull Cemetery."

After they'd polished off their bourbon, Jack lay on the couch in the darkness, trying to fall asleep. He was still exhausted, but every time he closed his eyes, all he could see was Amanda, and his sons huddled together, clinging to one another. The three of them encircled by fire, which prevented their escape, their faces frozen with fear.

David was tall, and his body had compensated for his missing limb by giving him the build of a linebacker. He usually had problems sitting still, but he hugged Amanda tightly and didn't move a muscle. Louis was thinner and was typically a chatterbox. Now he seemed incapable of uttering a single word. Amanda's mouth moved to reassure them both, but her eyes could not hide the terror she felt inside. The wind was howling, fanning the flames surrounding them. The only thing that Jack could hear, however, was that terrible laugh. As he lay in the darkness, it rang around him as loud as thunder.

Chapter 5

October 29th
Lawrence, Kansas
Several hours before sunrise

Jack's eyes opened wide, his mouth agape as if he was going to scream, but he made no sound. He was no longer dreaming, but Jack was sure he still saw the flames separating him from his family. Sweat seeped from every pore of his body as if he were standing next to an inferno. He looked at his arms, and the color of his skin was as red as a summer sunburn. It all felt so real. He looked over at the clock, which read 3:00 a.m. Jack's face dropped into his hands, and he began to sob. It was as if this man, if you could call him that, had found his way into his mind and was toying with him. Jack lay back down on the couch, but he knew it would be impossible to sleep now.

Jack quickly got dressed, quietly exited the apartment, and made his way across the dimly lit parking lot to his car, which he had retrieved from the café during Father Desmond's call. A light wind rustled through the autumn leaves, and Jack's sweat-soaked shirt caused him to shiver. He reached the car, then paused and looked around. He'd had a feeling of being watched several times yesterday, and the same uneasy sensation once again engulfed him. With the nightmare still fresh in his mind, he was admittedly a little jumpy, so he dismissed the feeling but was sure to lock the car door anyway.

Picking up Route 32 on the outskirts of the Lawrence, Jack headed east. This early, the road was deserted, and Jack could hear the road rushing underneath the car's wheels. He was spooked by his nightmare and overwhelmed by the seemingly no-win situation that confronted him. Jack had no idea where he was going and only knew that he wanted to escape.

How had he gotten in this mess? As he drove, his mind turned over the events of the past few years, searching for something, anything, that could provide answers.

"Come in, Jack," Dr. Colby said in the doorway of her office. "Go ahead and have a seat."

Despite having had several sessions with Dr. Kathleen Colby, a highly regarded psychiatrist, Jack was nervous as he entered her office, his eyes fixed down at the hardwood floor. He was still reeling from his second aborted suicide attempt and unsure how much the sessions were helping.

Dr. Colby sat across from Jack in a brown leather chair, the shelves behind her filled with books. She listened attentively but said very little. Finding the right words to explain how losing one dream after another was like being in a perpetual state of grieving was difficult for Jack, and his pain and the sense of loss never seemed to go away.

The revelations of Jack's past only led him to more second-guessing, leaving him mentally exhausted and physically spent. He was in a hole that felt so deep he thought he might never crawl out of it. Staring at the mint green walls of the office, Jack also wrestled with the fear that even if he somehow managed to do so, someone would be there to kick him back down.

Tears began to roll down Jack's face over the guilt and responsibility he felt for what was happening to his family, particularly for the additional worrying he was sure he was putting Amanda through. He knew it was irrational to believe he was at fault for Louis and David's disabilities, or somehow, he should have prevented them. Still, it remained heartbreaking to speak about, and Jack felt selfish for focusing so much on his pain.

"Jack, my approach with new patients, is to let them talk, and I listen. We've had several sessions together now, and I would like to share my observations with you."

Truthfully, Jack was pretty sure that he did not want to hear it. Dr. Colby's tone made him anxious about what she would say. Digging his fingers into the arm of the sofa, he braced himself.

"I've been a therapist for nearly twenty years, and I am hard-pressed to recall meeting a patient that has so much on their shoulders," Dr. Colby said compassionately. "Your pain is palpable and understandable given the circumstances and challenges that you face."

Dr. Colby paused to review her notes on the yellow legal pad in her lap, then continued. "You are haunted, Jack. Your mind is like a house of horrors. You tirelessly try burying your unfulfilled dreams, only to discover they are ghosts that return to haunt you. You live with persistent guilt and regret, but perhaps worst of all are your fears and anxieties. These are vampires sucking the life out of you, and unless you put a stake through their heart, they are going to bleed you to death."

Jack nodded slowly. "As gloomy as your description is, Doctor, it makes sense to me. Somehow, in five minutes, you have managed to completely summarize what I've been experiencing for nearly the past twenty years," he said. "Part of the problem I have run into with other therapists is their inability to help me find new tools to deal with my problems. I exercise five days a week, have meditated all that, and it hasn't been enough. What strategies are we going to follow that will change this dynamic?"

Dr. Colby leaned forward. "Jack, learning to live in the moment will not be easy. Mindfulness is a technique that requires a total shift in your way of thinking. It requires you to make a conscious decision to live in the present while learning not to give in to your fears about the future or hold on to perceived failures of the past."

The day had been primarily cloudy until this moment, but now sunlight flowed through the sheer curtains covering the office window, bathing the office in bright light. Letting Dr. Colby's comments sink in drove home the point to Jack that if he did not find a way to change his path, the consequences would be dire. In the end, all he wanted to do was to take care of his family, but that would not be possible if he were not around to do it.

At that moment, Jack decided that it was time to stop running.

***

Skerrt! Jack's tires screeched as he slammed on the brakes. Lost in his thoughts, Jack hadn't seen what darted in front of the car until the last second. The car had spun out and came to rest on the shoulder of the road. Jack's heart was beating a mile a minute, and his eyes darted left and right, searching the pre-dawn darkness for what caused the near-miss. He immediately saw the culprit.

Standing in the middle of the road was an eight-point buck staring right at Jack. Its black eyes shimmered in the car's headlights. Miraculously, Jack had missed the majestic animal entirely. After a few moments, the deer turned and quickly disappeared from view. Shaking his head, Jack took a deep gulp of air and placed his hand on his heart in a mocking gesture to assure himself that he hadn't had a heart attack.

As a precaution, he got out and started walking around, searching for damage to the car. Looking east, he could see the faint glow of the sun beginning to rise, but the crisp morning air sent a chill through his body. The water vapor visibly condensing with each breath he took hinted that the temperature was right around the freezing mark. He knelt and checked the tires and saw that they weren't flat. As he walked in front of the hood, something caught his eye.

Roughly fifty feet away stood a light-colored stone obelisk about ten feet tall, with what looked like a mushroom on top. *Good thing I didn't hit that,* Jack thought as he began to walk toward it. Jack's curiosity grew with each step.

Finally, he reached the object. Despite the darkness, the bright yellow letters made it easy to read the inscription on the plaque in front of the obelisk:

The Day After

The American television movie The Day After *aired on November 20th, 1983. Lawrence, Kansas, the geographic heartland of America, was selected as the primary location for the film, and many scenes took place in the fields surrounding this monument. The dark mushroom cloud prominently displayed atop this memorial serves as a grim reminder of the inherent dangers of nuclear war. With some fear and profound hope, we dedicate this statue and pray that the horrors of such an Armageddon will never be visited upon the Earth.*

Dedicated this 30th day of July 1985

Jack stood pondering the inscription.

Armageddon, he thought to himself. *Horrors of Armageddon.*

"What was it that I was thinking about?" Jack asked, rubbing the stubble on his chin.

Trying desperately to remember, Jack thought back to the time right before the near-collision with the deer.

"Running away. I was in Dr. Colby's office. I decided to stop running away."

Suddenly, Jack realized what he was doing and that trying to escape was pointless.

"There is no avoiding a tormenter whose powers include the ability to invade my dreams," Jack reasoned with himself. "You can't run and hide from Armageddon."

Then, he thought about his family.

Jack rushed to his car and raced back toward Lawrence, leaving a trail of dust and flying gravel.

***

On his knees in his bedroom, his head bowed, Father Desmond prayed, "In the name of the Father, the Son, and The Holy Ghost. God, our Father, please be with us this day. Grant us both courage and wisdom so that we can bear one another's burdens as Christ bore our sins on the cross."

Making the sign of the cross on his chest, he finished, "We pray this in your name. Amen."

"Good morning, Jack," Father Desmond announced, entering the living room. "I thought I would cook breakfast." The couch was empty, the blanket he'd offered the night before strewn on the floor. "Jack?" he called. "Are you in the kitchen?"

Silence.

"Maybe he went out and left me a note," he murmured to himself.

Father Desmond went from room to room in the small apartment, and within a few minutes, realized that Jack was gone without a trace.

Grabbing his jacket, Father Desmond hoped Jack might have gone out for coffee. There was a coffee shop across the street, but Jack was not there. Father Desmond then checked the parking lot, and to his dismay, Jack's car was gone. On his way back to the apartment, Father Desmond began questioning Jack's motives. *Why was he really here?*

As he sat at the kitchen table, Father Desmond thought about all that Jack had shared with him. Just the sheer mention of Stull Cemetery had made Father Desmond nervous, and it helped him understand the purpose of Jack's inquiry about evil. It also led Father Desmond to think about what Jack had said about the threats to destroy his family.

Father Desmond whispered, "Just what have you gotten caught up in, Jack?"

***

The door to the apartment slowly opened, and Jack stepped into the room.

"Jack, you're back." Glancing at his watch, which read 10:05 a.m., a relieved Father Desmond said, "Where have you been?"

"I'm sorry, Father, I should have knocked first. I was hoping that I would get back before you even knew I was gone." Jack rubbed his face. "Let's just say I went for a drive."

"Is that how you want to leave it, Jack?" Father Desmond asked. "Just a drive?"

"It is, for now."

"Tell me, were you able to get any rest?" Father Desmond asked, respecting Jack's wish not to discuss where he had gone.

Jack shook his head. "Your couch is comfortable enough, but I have found it difficult to sleep recently."

"Jack, yesterday you asked me about trouble following a person. I've thought about that a great deal since you asked, and I wanted to share a thought with you."

Jack sat down in the kitchen. Mark's now cold cup of coffee sat on the table.

"I believe that what Jesus went through is one answer to the mystery of suffering and evil in our lives. Some people seem to be a 'living crucifix.' Jesus tells his disciples that to follow him requires that a person deny themselves and take up their cross. It takes courage to accept Jesus' invitation. God does not hate you for questioning him. Every day he wants to bless you with his mercy and help you and Amanda bear the immense responsibility on both of your shoulders. I will be praying every day that things will go better for you both and that your situation will improve."

"I want to believe that's true, Father," Jack said sadly. "But it is hard to after what I have to say next." Jack gulped down a glass of water. "All this talking is making my voice raspy."

In the distance, the church bell chimed eleven times.

Father Desmond's level of concern for Jack's emotional state increased with every sentence he uttered. The look on Jack's face showed a level of pain that bordered on agony. Every word was like reopening a wound that was never quite able to heal. There was not only sorrow in his voice but also an underlying tone of anger and frustration.

"I guess I should pick up where I left off. After David was born missing his left arm, we found out that he was also autistic two years later. The financial strain from the boys' uncovered therapy bills was immense."

"Go on, Jack," Father Desmond said, placing his hand on Jack's shoulder.

"There are other events, but the meeting where we found out that Louis would be unable to get into college was the proverbial straw that broke the camel's back for me." He shifted in his chair. "At this point, the dam had finally burst, and I was in freefall. I once described this time in our lives to Amanda as one where I existed but was not living, and my day-to-day routine never changed. Never-ending reminders of lost dreams, my hopes torn to pieces, these thoughts tortured me relentlessly. The competitive side of me knew that I had not always won the battles in life, but I felt like for the first time, I was losing the war. I had poured everything I had into Louis going to college, and when that dream died, part of me seemed to die along with it."

A knock at the door startled both men.

"Father Desmond," the voice at the door said. "This is Officer Marshall."

Jack shot him a panicked look. Father Desmond motioned to Jack, who quietly headed to the bedroom, closing the door but leaving it slightly ajar.

Opening the apartment door, Father Desmond said, "Officer, nice to see you again. What can I do for you?"

"I am sorry to bother you, Father, but is Mr. Grieve staying with you?"

Father Desmond had a decision to make. As a priest, he made it a practice not to lie to anyone, let alone the police. His instincts told him, however, that protecting Jack was of paramount importance.

"No, Officer Marshall. I'm afraid not. Is something wrong?"

"With me, no, Father. It's my superiors. Do you know how we might get in touch with him?"

"I don't understand," said Father Desmond.

"We found the little boy late yesterday afternoon. Alive."

"That's wonderful!"

"He was in the park, by the lake, just as Mr. Grieve suggested."

"So, you want to thank Mr. Grieve, then."

"I do, Father, but my bosses want to ask him some questions. They are a little suspicious that he knew so much about where to find the child."

"But you said he was unharmed? Do they think Mr. Grieve is responsible for the other disappearances?"

Shaking his head, Officer Marshall said, "I tried to tell them that Mr. Grieve was nothing but helpful and a great resource. I guess that's why they get paid the big bucks. They must see something about this that I don't."

Father Desmond knew Jack had nothing to do with any of these unfortunate disappearances. However, exposing him to the authorities would lead to questions that would put Jack's family in even greater jeopardy. The police might identify his picture from a bulletin issued by Virginia law enforcement, and if detained for any reason, it would be game over for Jack and his family.

"Officer Marshall. Mr. Grieve was more of an acquaintance than a friend. Yesterday was the first time I had seen him in decades. He was just passing through town. He left last night, and I have no phone number or other contact information for him."

"That's good enough for me, Father. I am sorry to have troubled you. Have a good day."

"I'm sorry I couldn't be of more help, Officer."

Father Desmond shut the door and waited for a few moments before going to the bedroom to get Jack.

"Jack, the officer is gone. You can come out now."

Jack opened the bedroom door and peered around to make sure it was okay to come out. "Father, thank you. I know you went out on a limb for me." Jack paused, then said, "I'm sorry I put you in a position to lie for me. I know that has to make you more than just a little uncomfortable."

"I know this sounds wrong coming from a priest, but sometimes the ends justify the means." Father Desmond smiled at Jack and said, "Now, where were we?"

***

Back in the kitchen, Jack reached into his wallet and pulled out a worn, yellowed piece of paper. It had been unfolded and folded so many times it looked ready to fall to pieces. He handed it to Father Desmond.

"In the depths of my despair, I wrote this document and shared it with my therapist, Dr. Colby."

Father Desmond read the document silently to himself.

The 10 Truths About Life

- Hope is a dangerous thing; holding on to it is often more painful than having none at all.
- Dreams rarely come to fruition, and nightmares are not random fears; they are daily realities.
- Honesty is not the best policy; some things are better left unsaid, and some thoughts are best to keep to yourself.
- People who say they care about you are often the ones that let you down when you need them the most.
- Often, people that you think you can trust are the ones that lie to your face.
- Life is not about enjoyment; it is about how much you can endure.
- Ignorance is truly blissful. The more you learn about things, the more you are going to wish you did not know.
- Those who play by the rules ultimately find themselves screwed in the end.
- People who tell you to "suck it up" and "be of good cheer" probably never faced an ounce of adversity in their entire life.
- All our parents' promises about the benefits of working hard and behaving were just myths and fairy tales designed to keep us in line.

"I'm almost tempted to let you keep it. I can recite it from memory."

Father Desmond handed the paper back to Jack.

"Over and over, I asked myself what did I do wrong? All that Amanda and I had been through over the past 15 years had to mean something, but I could not see what that was. I felt that all I had proven was my ability to take a beating, but for what purpose?

What was the point of it all? We had tried to do the right things, such as putting money away for college, and what did it get us? We had played by the rules, but where was the payoff for doing so? We had become permanent spectators in the parade of life. Everyone else was moving forward, and we were going nowhere."

"Jack, there is no question that you and Amanda have suffered great hardship. I could search the depths of my being to try to find something meaningful to say in an attempt to comfort you, but anything I would say is just going to ring hollow. However, I will remind you that the Bible is full of stories of people who suffered only to receive a higher calling to perform an invaluable service to their fellow man and God. I'm not saying that you or Amanda are the next Moses, Elijah, or Naomi, but sometimes God's plan takes longer than we expect or want before it becomes clear."

Jack paused for a moment and looked at Father Desmond. "Finding Dr. Colby allowed me to hit the reset button. It was a second chance, and at that moment, I decided I would take it. It has not been easy, and I sometimes struggle to live in the moment. I still see her weekly, which is my way of reaffirming my commitment to change. It helped me alter the trajectory of my life, but it did not solve everything. I still felt like something was missing, a hole that I needed to fill. At the same time, I also failed to repair my relationship with God, and Jesus's parable of the Sower was always on my mind."

"Ah, yes." He nodded. "'A farmer went out to sow his seed. As he was scattering the seed, some fell along the path, and the birds came and ate it up. Some fell on rocky places, where it did not have much soil. It sprang up quickly because the soil was shallow. But when the sun came up, the plants were scorched, and they withered because they had no root…'"

"'Other seeds fell among thorns, which grew up and choked the plants,'" Jack finished. "I kept asking myself which type of soil I was. Regardless, the answer was that I had allowed my faith in God to decline to the extent that I could no longer find it. I guess I was still trying to show God I did not need his help. Unfortunately, my hubris was going to prove costly."

***

It was nearly noon, and Jack was famished. Father Desmond returned with a tray of sandwiches and handed Jack a beer. After taking a bite from his sandwich, Jack took a long sip from his bottle and continued his confession.

"This past July, Amanda surprised me with a weekend getaway for my fiftieth birthday. I had always wanted to visit Appomattox Courthouse, where General Grant accepted Lee's final surrender that ended the Civil War. Being the good sport she is, Amanda booked a hotel and packed our bags. We jumped in the car and headed out.

"Lee Highway merges with US Route 15, and then around the town of Warrenton, it turns south. We'd driven this route several times over the years when we traveled to Charlottesville. Just outside of Culpeper, there's a state road that veers right off of Lee Highway. The route number is 666."

Father Desmond immediately put his cup down and looked at Jack. "There is a state road with route number 666?" he asked incredulously.

Jack nodded. "Believe it or not, there is. Every time we drove past the highway sign, Amanda and I would comment on it. I wouldn't consider us to be superstitious, but suffice it to say we found it peculiar and joked about not wanting to take the chance of driving it."

Father Desmond shook his head. A moment of silence passed before Jack broke the silence.

"When we passed by it this time, I noticed something was different. The road now had barricades. It struck me as odd, and at the same time, I was intrigued. I couldn't recall seeing any state road permanently closed unless another thoroughfare replaced it. That was definitely not the case in this situation. I joked with Amanda about them closing it because it was the Devil's Highway or something like that, and we drove on to our destination."

Father Desmond had a stern look on his face. Just mentioning the number 666 seemed to trouble him. Jack gave him an apologetic grimace.

He shook his head. "I am sorry. I did not mean to appear upset," he said. "I just find it difficult to understand why our society seems to be so fascinated by the topic of evil, yet at the same time is so ignorant about it. As you might imagine, what I experienced as a boy has given me a healthy respect for what the forces of evil are capable of."

Jack lowered his head and thought to himself *if only this conversation had taken place months ago.*

Time was running out, and he needed to be direct.

"Father, not only have I allowed myself to become trapped in something very sinister, but my family is in mortal danger as a result of my actions. I am here in Lawrence to retrieve an artifact from Stull Cemetery. If I do not recover the object and bring it back to Virginia, the kidnapper will murder my family, and as I said yesterday, their souls will go to Hell. I know how this sounds, but I am not mad, and I could not be more serious."

Jack tried to speak, but he found it difficult to calm down. He was stammering and tried to breathe at the same time he was talking. "Father, I never meant for this to happen. The signs were there. Why didn't I pay attention? Why didn't I believe what my head and heart were telling me? Was it wrong to want something more for myself?"

Jack now trembled and wept uncontrollably. Father Desmond looked at Jack sympathetically and hugged him while he sobbed. He tried to calm Jack by reassuring him he would do everything he could to help him. Eventually, Jack quieted down enough to continue their conversation.

"Father, I'm sorry for breaking down like this. I've been trying to keep myself together, but the reality of what I have done is just more than I can bear."

"Jack, there is no need to apologize, but I need to know what happened and why. There is no question that you have had more than your share of life's challenges, but something else must have pushed you into this. What was it?"

"Even though I was getting better, I couldn't shake this feeling of failure. My self-confidence was gone. Doubt permeated every aspect of my life. Any positive thoughts or new goals constantly were challenged by concerns about whether I honestly had it in me to accomplish it. I was an empty vessel with a need to be filled.

"While Amanda and I were away, I remembered something that a respected business colleague had said when I turned down his job offer, 'How long is Jack Aitken going to stay on the sidelines?'" He shook his head. "I challenged myself: Was that what I was doing? Were my doubts and fears preventing me from accomplishing my goals?

"It was then that this thought came into my mind. A book! Friends and business colleagues had told me that my writing skills were good. I'd always thought about writing a book but never dared to follow through on it. The next thing that popped into my head was Route 666. There had to be a story there! The Devil's Highway or some title like that. I turned to Amanda and started to talk to her about it. Being the supportive spouse and best friend that Amanda is, she was very encouraging. The rest of that weekend, I started thinking about a story. I'd been searching for something that was missing and thought I had found it. I didn't realize that this dream was going to turn into a nightmare. Things had been bad, then they got worse, but now they were going to become something unthinkable."

Jack said in a voice pleading for understanding, "All I wanted was a second chance."

Father Desmond began to piece together what had happened to Jack. His own experience combating evil told him there is nothing Satan and his followers would not do to corrupt a person's soul. Jack's soul was compromised by what had happened up until now, but he was undoubtedly not corrupt. Despite his demanding life experiences and doubts about God's role in inflicting them on him, he had not renounced God entirely. Father Desmond could see that Jack was not too far gone, and he started to mentally prepare himself for what it would take to reclaim Jack's soul and help Jack save his family.

Chapter 6

Early August, approximately one month before meeting Jack Aitken
Office of Lucius Rofocale, Curator of the Museum of Culpeper
History

Joseph Rogers strolled through the Museum of Culpeper History. He acted as if he were interested in an exhibit about a lost Native American tribe, but the truth was he honestly didn't give a damn. All Joseph wanted to do was complete his business transaction with Lucius Rofocale, the museum curator, and get the hell out of town. Lucius gave him the creeps, and the sooner he was out of Joseph's life, the better.

"Are you Mr. Rogers?" one of the museum employees asked.

"Yes, I am, Miss."

"Mr. Rofocale is in a meeting with members of the board of directors. He told me to seat you in his office, and he will be with you shortly."

Joseph sat in Lucius's office and could not help but notice the musty odor. "Must be all of these old books and papers," Joseph muttered to himself.

There was almost a claustrophobic feel to the room, and Joseph shifted in the seat several times in an attempt to get comfortable.

While he waited, the events of the past twenty-four hours replayed in his mind.

***

Joseph dialed the number and waited for an answer. After a few rings, a voice came on the line.

"Hello, this is Father Mark Desmond."

"Mark, this is a blast from your past. It's Joseph Rogers."

"Joseph! How are you?"

"I'm good, Mark. Believe it or not, I'm here in Topeka."

That was what he wanted Mark to believe. His cover was an antique dealer looking to add something to his collection, but that was not true.

"Mark, would it be okay if I stop by for a visit?"

Mark gave him directions, and before leaving, Joseph pulled a piece of paper out of his pocket and studied it carefully. It was a drawing of a sword that Lucius was sure that Mark would own. A picture would have been better, but he could work with this and find what Lucius wanted. Joseph did not think about his friend. All he could think about was the money that Lucius had promised him. A whole lot of money.

Joseph hopped in a rental car for the thirty-minute drive to Lawrence and took the entrance ramp onto Route 70 West.

Arriving in Lawrence, Joseph parked the car in the visitors' lot at the college. Mark had suggested they meet at a local restaurant, but Joseph insisted they meet at Mark's apartment instead. He knocked on the door, and Mark Desmond answered.

"Joseph, it is great to see you! Please, come in."

Joseph and Mark had been friends in childhood, but Joseph wouldn't say they'd been incredibly close. Mark's religious fervor was a little too much for Joseph but to each his own. Mark went into the kitchen, and while he was gone, Joseph surveyed the apartment, looking for the sword.

Father Desmond returned and handed Joseph a glass. Joseph downed his scotch and continued to glance around the apartment. He noticed a few religious objects, including a carved wooden crucifix and a bronze statue of an angel carrying a harp, but nothing that looked like a sword.

"Joseph, what brings you to Kansas?"

"I was attending an antique show in Topeka. I'm looking for something for my collection. Are there any shops in town I should check out?"

"Do you specialize in any particular type of antiques?"

"Rare weapons."

"I actually might have something you would be interested in." Mark smiled and excused himself. A minute later, he re-entered the room with a sword.

Joseph grinned. *Too easy.*

Handing it to Joseph, Father Desmond said, "I do not know much about it beyond it having some religious significance. As a seminary student, I developed an interest in the Crusades and dabbled in collecting objects from that period. I think it might be from the 11th or 12th century, but it could be even older."

Joseph held the sword in his hand. It was ornate, shiny, and made from some sort of precious metal. The sword's top was straight and about 18 inches in length, but the blade's sharp end was curved. The sword's handle, the hilt, was inlaid with precious stones of red and green. The etched pattern on the handle probably improved the user's grip. He knew this was what Lucius was seeking.

Earlier, Joseph had fashioned a harness in his jacket. The harness would allow him to strap the sword inside his coat without it being easily detected. Now he needed just the right opportunity to swipe the weapon and tactfully make his exit. Mark had taken the sword and placed it on a chair near the door to the apartment.

Mark headed to his bedroom. "I think I have a card for a local antique shop owner, and if you give me a minute or two, I'm sure I can find it."

This was Joseph's chance. He got up from the sofa, took the sword from the chair, and secured it in the harness. As long as Mark didn't hug him goodbye, this was going to work.

Mark came back into the room and saw Joseph by the door.

"Joseph, do you have to leave so soon?" Mark asked, sounding disappointed.

"Sorry, Mark. I just remembered that there's going to be a by invitation only showing at the convention that I do not want to miss."

Mark nodded his understanding and went to hug Joseph. He quickly preempted Mark's attempt at a hug and stuck out his hand instead. The two men shook hands, said their goodbyes, and Joseph left the apartment and quickly made his way to the car. As he pulled out of the parking lot, he grabbed the bottle of vodka in a brown bag on the passenger seat and drank a mouthful.

***

"Mr. Rogers, it is a pleasure to see you again," Lucius said upon entering the room.

"Same here," Joseph replied, although he frankly didn't mean it.

"You have acquired the object as requested, then?"

Joseph nodded and handed Lucius a box.

Lucius looked down at the box, then looked at Joseph and said ominously, "I hope so, Joseph. I hope so."

Joseph anxiously watched as Lucius opened the box. Lucius unwrapped the object, and a look of triumph came across his ordinarily stoical face.

Joseph had indeed obtained the sword of Saint Michael, the awful instrument responsible for enslaving Lucius long ago and for closing the gate to Hell once open at Stull Cemetery. Lucius held the ornately adorned sword aloft, knowing that JESU would now be powerless to stop him.

Still beaming, Lucius said, "You have done well, Joseph. Excuse me while I retrieve your reward, but first, I have to close the museum for the night. So, it may be a few minutes before I return."

Lucius left the office, still cradling the sword in his hands. Joseph had a fleeting moment of guilt for stealing from a friend, but the allure of all that money quickly drove those thoughts from his mind. Instead, a feeling of happiness like he'd never felt before came over Joseph. While his friends had moved on to bigger and better things, he struggled to make ends meet. Joseph wanted to feel like they did. He wanted to be a success, and his measuring stick was money. Lucius promised him a lot of it for fulfilling his end of their deal.

While he waited for Lucius to return, Joseph looked around the musty-smelling office. The odor was pungent, and he was sure he detected an underlying scent of rotten eggs.

"Smells like Sulphur in here," Joseph said to himself.

A leather-bound book sat on Lucius's desk. It was like no other book he had seen before. Joseph picked it up and read the cover.

"*Pre 20th Century History* ... History of what?" Joseph asked out loud.

As he examined it, Joseph noted the book cover did not smell soothing like old leather. It didn't smell moldy like damaged leather either. Instead, it smelled like the remains of meat that had sat in a garbage pail for a few days. It was the aroma of decay.

Something about holding the book made Joseph uncomfortable, yet at the same time, he was curious to read it. Unable to resist the temptation, he opened the book and began to scan through it. The pages were yellowed, and the ink was red.

Looks like blood, Joseph thought to himself. He began to read.

In Principio (In the Beginning)
After being freed from bondage, many demons were recaptured and thrown into the bottomless pit and bound in Hell forever.

"Bottomless pit? Hell? What kind of book is this?"

Joseph told himself to put the book down, but he found it impossible to do so.

Even the Kings of Hell, the most powerful demons other than Lucifer himself, were exiled there. Soon, only Lucifer could continue to travel freely between Hell and the surface, but even he found himself trapped in the pit. Nevertheless, some demons managed to avoid such a fate and continued to corrupt souls to join the legions in Hell as their slaves.

Always in search of more souls to steal while at the same time keeping a low profile, a demon leader emerged and found his way to the New World. During colonial times, he built a network of covens throughout North America and educated his brothers on how to battle JESU and, of course, how to harvest more souls.

Joseph put the book down on the desk. "This thing is like some twisted history textbook," he muttered, but he couldn't bring himself to stop reading.

Now mesmerized by the book, Joseph never heard the footsteps that began slowly coming down the hallway.

The Master's handling of the fallout from the Salem Witch Trials brought him to Lucifer's attention. Lucifer immediately recognized his organizational skills and liked the initiative he showed in teaching the few demons who remained free to fight JESU. It was "the backdoor project," however that made our beloved leader indispensable. Lucifer explained to the demon legions how this plan could safeguard them against an attack by JESU and, ultimately, be their path to final victory. Only later would we find out how prophetic Lucifer's words indeed were.

Stull Cemetery in what is now modern-day Kansas was the site of the entrance gate to Hell.

"What? Wait a minute…" Joseph frantically used his phone to search the Internet for the location of Stull Cemetery. He was stunned by what he found out.

"Stull Cemetery is not far from Lawrence, Kansas? I was in Lawrence twenty-four hours ago. "Oh my God, what did I do?"

He flipped through the pages of the book wildly, unsure of quite what he was looking to find.

Lucifer had corrupted the local minister's soul and built the gate on a desecrated church, an intentional insult to his father, God. As a result of the continuing battles with JESU, notably the war fought around Stull Cemetery, our Master recognized the need for a back door. If JESU found a way to close the gate, Lucifer would have no way to send reinforcements to the surface. There needed to be another entrance to Hell, and our great leader found an ideal location for it.

The value of the project became apparent when JESU managed to steal the keys that King Zagan had manufactured and, using the sword of Saint Michael, sealed the gate at Stull Cemetery. In the aftermath of these events, Lucifer realized the vital role Lucius Rofocale played in constructing an alternate entrance to Hell and rewarded his foresight by naming him his Prime Minister.

Joseph's eyes opened wide, and his jaw hung open. He began to utter, "L-u-c-" but he was interrupted.

"Lucius. That is right, Joseph, you will find a great deal about me in that book."

"And the sword?" Joseph asked anxiously.

"At the moment, far more important than you realize."

Joseph's eyes betrayed his bewilderment, darting back and forth between Lucius and the book.

"It might interest you to know that the cover is unique. A true artisan made it from human skin."

Joseph dropped the book onto the desk with a look of horror on his face.

Lucius's eyes began to glow a fiery shade of red as he stared at Joseph and said, "You should be more careful with other people's things, Joseph. That book is not only ancient, but it is quite important to my kind."

"Your-your kind?" he stuttered.

"Come, come, Joseph. You are smarter than this. You know what I am."

Joseph looked down at the book and then up at Lucius. "Demon?"

"Excellent, Joseph. I knew my belief in your intellect was not misplaced. But now that you know part of our story, you must hear it all."

"I-I think I'd rather not," he stammered.

"Oh, but I insist, Joseph."

Lucius flipped his finger, and Joseph flew back into the chair, unable to move.

Lucius grinned. "I so enjoy a captive audience."

Chapter 7

Lucius gave Joseph Rogers a crash course on demon history for several hours, emphasizing his personal contributions. He boasted about his skill at evading capture because of his deal-making ability. He shared his favorite with Joseph, how he would grant the wish of a victim, and in exchange, he would own the right to inhabit their earthly body for up to fifty years at a time. With so many humans in his debt, Lucius could avoid his enemies by merely moving from body to body.

"Unfortunately, Joseph, I have no such offer to give you."

"What does that mean?" Joseph asked fearfully.

Lucius toyed with Joseph, pretending to think about his answer. "Mmm, I will get to that later. You see, Joseph, for centuries, this deception was necessary as events such as the Crusades, the Protestant Reformation, and the Great Awakening of the 18th and early 19th centuries boosted the ability of men to resist my temptations. Despite my efforts and those of my demon brethren, Christianity, Judaism, Islam, Hinduism, and Buddhism survived and flourished."

Lucius sighed disappointedly. "No matter how many tyrants I have put in power or plagues I released across the planet, there were just not enough demons to harvest the souls of individuals that such events might tempt to turn to Satan for answers."

Lucius's gaze darkened. "It did not help matters that the Justice Ecumenical Society United became a constant threat. These so-called religious leaders banded together to combat evil and save souls, their hunters relentless in their pursuit of demons. They killed many, and the ones they could not kill they condemned to lifetime imprisonment in Hell."

Fearful of what Lucius might do in such a state, Joseph tried to change the subject while constantly looking for a way out of his precarious position. He wanted to keep Lucius talking about himself, something Joseph could tell Lucius enjoyed immensely.

"The back door, Lucius. Why Culpeper?"

"You have been paying attention, Joseph," Lucius said, pleased. "Culpeper is an ordinary, idyllic place. A town filled with regular people who fail to realize the ancient evil that lives among them. No one would suspect such a place could serve as an entrance to Hell, but a network of underground caverns in the area now connect to Hell itself. Thus, it is an ideal place to hide from JESU, and its rural character provides a great refuge in today's modern society. In short, it is perfect."

Lucius beamed. "When I arrived, the only inhabitants of the area were a Native American Tribe, the Manahoac. Just as King Solomon had done to me, I enslaved the tribe and forced them to construct the entrance, using the same building techniques."

Joseph remembered the exhibit he'd seen in the museum earlier. "So… the tribe didn't just disappear?"

Lucius ignored the question.

"Once the connection to Hell was complete, similar to Stull Cemetery, King Zagan manufactured twenty keys, three of which would be needed to unlock the iron door."

Lucius hesitated, then said dismissively, "Upon completing the project, the few remaining Manahoac were sacrificed and buried in the mound around the gate. The exhibit explaining that they moved west over the Blue Ridge Mountains in search of bison provides, how shall I say it, a plausible explanation for their departure."

"You seem particularly interested in the Manahoac, Joseph. Let us take a brief detour before our time together ends. I think you should see their burial ground, up close and personal. Who knows, you may have something in common with a few of the recent visitors."

***

Later the same evening
Manahoac Burial Mound, woods outside of Culpeper, Virginia

The trek to the burial mound seemed like it took forever. The day had turned to night, but it was still sweltering hot. With his hands bound, drops of perspiration fell from Joseph's forehead, stinging his eyes, but Lucius didn't even break a sweat. Instead, he just continued his history lesson. He droned on about how the late 20th and early 21st centuries were a demon's perfect hunting environment.

"There is no need for us to live in the shadows any longer. The whole concept of evil has changed. It is now big business. Halloween is the second most significant retail holiday, and vile creatures such as vampires are romantic and sexy. People even pay money to be scared by movies about those things that 'go bump in the night.'"

Stopping for a moment, Lucius said incredulously, "Joseph, do you know that the practice of Satanism is a right protected under the United States Constitution?" He shook his head. "You humans are a bizarre species."

Joseph scanned his surroundings, but the dense forest allowed no chance for escape, no matter where he looked. If there was a feeling beyond panic, Joseph had arrived there. A sense of dread washed over him.

"Our most effective defense is the non-belief of others. What was once called possession is now called a mental illness. Even our sworn enemy, organized religion, fuels the loss of faith among its believers through its sex scandals and financial misconduct."

Joseph noticed an additional eerie phenomenon as they walked: the deeper into the forest they went, the quieter it became. No insects were buzzing, frogs croaking, or any other activity you would expect to hear in the woods at night. Just dead silence.

"Ah, we have finally arrived. I hope you did not mind taking the scenic tour to get here, Joseph. I thought you should see everything before the next step in your journey."

Joseph found himself standing in a clearing where a large mound rose from the forest floor. A rusted iron fence in disrepair surrounded it. There were several tombstones set into the grassy knoll, which gave it the look of a graveyard. The full moon overhead illuminated the location enough that Joseph could have seen his hand in front of his face if only he could free them from his bindings.

"Joseph, you are unaware of this, but we have interacted far earlier in your life than our most recent business dealings might suggest. Do you remember the Ouija board?" Lucius asked aggressively.

Joseph thought for a moment, then answered tentatively, "Vaguely. That was a long time ago."

"Ouija boards are like a beacon for a demon. I heard a message asking if anyone was there. A communication from a Ouija board often means that children are fooling around." In a critical tone, Lucius continued, "Playing with something that they should not, children are easy to manipulate, and because of their age, they make excellent vessels for demons. I responded to the outreach, informing the questioner that I was a demon and giving my name."

The fog and haze of the past began to lift from Joseph's memory.

"I remember that. It spelled out L-U-C-I-U-S! We all freaked out and didn't respond."

"Precisely. That made me angry."

"I remember the board flying up in the air and getting tossed into the fire. We were all accusing each other of pulling a prank."

"I decided I would teach all of you a lesson. One you all would never forget," Lucius said ominously. "I waited until 3:00 a.m., a time at which we demons are most powerful. Then, rather than maintain my human form, I morphed into my true self and attempted to enter the tent."

Joseph flinched, expecting Lucius to repeat his earlier transformation, but he continued speaking instead.

"When I pulled back the tent flap, a young man confronted me and pointed a crucifix in my face."

70

"Mark," Joseph said.

"Yes. Usually, this would have little effect on me, but it caused significant discomfort for some reason. Desmond's faith flowed strongly through the crucifix. While backing out of the tent, I saw one of you other boys cowering in fear in a sleeping bag."

"It wasn't me. I know I never saw you. Paul and Thomas never spoke about it. Paul seemed to get pretty messed up after that. I'm guessing it was him."

"Exactly, Joseph," Lucius said sarcastically, "and Mark Desmond became a member of JESU."

Joseph thought to himself, *That's no surprise. He always was a bit of a holy roller as far as I was concerned.*

"What has this got to do with me? Or Paul or Thomas, for that matter," Joseph said abruptly.

Suddenly, he felt out of breath. It was as if someone was grabbing him by the throat and slowly shutting his windpipe.

"I do not like the terse tone of your voice, Joseph. Do you get my point?"

Joseph nodded, and Lucius released him. Joseph rubbed his throat and gasped in an attempt to catch his breath.

"Over the past thirty years, I have encountered Mark Desmond numerous times, never forgetting the painful sensation I felt that day. Desmond became a fierce warrior and an influential member within JESU, and while killing him was always an option, this is something every JESU member prepares for, and it would not be without risk."

Facing Joseph, Lucius said bluntly, "I had to come up with something far more cunning. That's how your friends became pawns in my never-ending chess match with Desmond. Rather than kill him, I opted to make him suffer by causing his peers in JESU to doubt his judgment and lose faith in him."

A perverse grin came over Lucius's face. "I knew losing their trust would hurt worse than death itself, and I had just the plan to do it."

Joseph coughed, still trying to recover from Lucius's vice-like grip.

"Tell me, Joseph, are you familiar with the phrase, "When they come at you, they come at what you love'?"

"Yeah, Michael Corleone," Joseph answered hoarsely.

"Exactly. It is how I chose to break Mark Desmond's spirit. First, it would be his friends. Those young boys from the tent who were now grown men. I took no chances and tracked you all down myself. Paul Sullivan was first.

"As you guessed a few minutes ago, Paul had seen me that night, and when I finally found him in a homeless shelter in New York City, it was apparent he had never recovered from the experience. Paul was an alcoholic and a drug addict. He had been unable to hold down a job and had been living on the streets."

Despite the desperation of his current circumstances, Joseph could not help but feel sad about Paul. They'd lost contact long ago, but the sense of loss Joseph felt was real.

"There was no way Sullivan could be relied upon to carry out my plan, so I decided to put him out of his misery."

"What did you do?" Joseph asked nervously.

"I would have enjoyed torturing him, but I did not have the time. So, I simply revealed my identity to Paul, which caused him to flee in fear. The next day Paul was found floating in the East River. He had jumped from the Hell Gate Bridge." Lucius laughed. "Rather appropriate, do you not agree?"

Joseph flinched at Lucius's twisted attempt at humor and turned away, feeling sick to his stomach.

"You did not strike me as the squeamish type," Lucius said mockingly.

Looking up, Joseph was shocked not to see Lucius but someone who he had not thought about for decades.

"Father Coughlin? That's not possible. You haven't aged. Is that you?"

The figure snickered. "That is exactly how your friend Thomas Manning reacted upon seeing me."

"But how? Why?"

"The good Father was interested in far more than teaching mathematics at Chaminade High School, and we will leave it at that. I discovered that Thomas was a partner at one of the leading architectural firms in New York. He enjoyed the trappings that came with their success—a big house, fancy cars, vacations in exotic locations, and a beautiful family. It should have been enough, really, but it turned out that Thomas wanted more."

Joseph had always envied Thomas's success. Things always came effortlessly to Thomas in high school, while he had to struggle for everything.

"At first, his stock market investments were highly successful, but he soon found himself drawing money from the firm's equity to cover his losses."

"I thought Thomas was too smart to get caught, no matter what he did."

"Do not be so surprised, Joseph. The accountant for the firm just happened to owe one of my demons a favor and was quite willing to disclose Thomas's peccadillos," Lucius said. "One afternoon, disguised as Father Charles Coughlin, I went to the office to visit with Thomas. I informed him of the unfortunate news about Paul Sullivan.

"Thomas admitted that he had not seen Paul for years. While he was shocked, he admitted to not being surprised. He'd tried to help Paul and felt terrible that he was dead, but long ago, he accepted that nothing he did would have changed this outcome.

"I then asked Thomas if he could do me a favor and go to Lawrence, Kansas, to share the news of Paul's unfortunate demise with Mark Desmond. Thomas said that he and Mark remained close, but he had a project with a tight deadline. He offered to call Mark to break the news."

The tone of Lucius's voice changed and became far more malevolent as he discussed what happened next.

"I explained that a phone call would not do, and before Thomas could reply, I showed him this."

Lucius, still appearing to be Father Coughlin, turned to Joseph with eyes as red as blood and returned to his demon form.

Joseph stepped back, still horrified by Lucius's appearance.

"Thomas changed his mind immediately and went to Lawrence to see Mark Desmond under the guise of informing him about Paul Sullivan's death. But he told Mark he had learned a terrible secret. One of his partners had approached Thomas and shared a blackmail plot by a demon who informed the partner he needed to find and bring to him three keys that would open the door to Hell. The partner had three days to deliver the keys to Culpeper, Virginia, or the demon threatened to expose that the partner had been embezzling funds from the firm, ruining him and his family."

On the surface, it sounded unbelievable, but Joseph recalled the incident in the woods and knew that Mark had always had a soft spot for his friends.

"Just as I anticipated, Father Desmond assured Thomas that he not only believed him, but he revealed that he was a member of an organization that fought evil."

Lucius paused and, sounding like a giddy schoolboy, said, "In other words, he took the bait.

"Desmond told Thomas that JESU had heard a rumor about a back door to Hell but had not confirmed its existence or location. Thomas's disclosure now presented an opportunity to seal Satan and his legions in Hell once and for all. Mark instructed Thomas to go back home and have the partner tell the demon that he would find the keys and bring them as ordered. Once Thomas was told by the partner where the actual meeting place would be, he should relay those coordinates to Mark, and he would arrange to have a full contingent of his brothers and sisters in position to ambush the demons and seal the door forever."

"You were setting Mark up," Joseph interrupted. "As you said before, you were using Mark's friends to make him suffer."

Lucius smiled smugly and continued, "Thomas reassured me that he told Desmond nothing about my involvement, but I made sure that he did not have a change of heart. After all, he was betraying one of his closest friends. I always thought that loyalty and friendship were highly overrated." Lucius sneered.

"After keeping Thomas under lock and key, I stood beside him while he called Mark to divulge where and what time the meeting would occur. All that remained now was to spring the trap."

Lucius never got tired of reliving this great triumph, and the only thing that bested it was the knowledge that the final humiliation of Mark Desmond was soon to come, thanks, in part to Joseph Rogers.

"Two days later, Mark Desmond and other JESU members approached a clearing in the woods near Culpeper, Virginia." Pointing at the burial mound, Lucius said, "The JESU forces found this hill, surrounded by tombstones encircled with a wrote-iron fence, just as Thomas had described it and as you see it now."

"And you killed them all," Joseph said, finishing Lucius's sentence.

Relishing the moment, Lucius bragged, "The shots rang out, and Hindu Pundits, Jewish Rabbis, Catholic Priests, Muslim Imams, Protestant Ministers, and Buddhist Monks began falling left and right. Mark Desmond had to know that they had walked into an ambush right away and that Thomas Manning, one of his closest friends, had betrayed him. My demon legions could have used other weapons, but guns were the most efficient way to ensure they killed as many JESU members as possible. It turned out to be a wise and deadly choice. Of the more than 100 holy men and women that entered the Virginia woods thinking they were closing the gate to Hell, less than ten made it out alive."

His massive ego on full display, Lucius crowed, "I made sure that Father Desmond was, purposely, one of the survivors, and his disgrace was complete." Looking at Joseph, Lucius declared, "Being posted to Lawrence is like being sent to Siberia in the former Soviet Union."

"What happened to Thomas?" Joseph asked fearfully.

A bolt of lightning struck the mound, sending Joseph reeling.

Lucius pointed to a tombstone embedded in the burial mound. The grave marker read, *Here lies Thomas Manning, a true friend... until the end.*

With a sinking heart, Joseph noticed that Paul Sullivan's grave was just to the right of Thomas's.

Lucius's voice thundered, "Thomas Manning died by my hand as the human sacrifice during an incredibly painful black mass."

Joseph suddenly found himself unable to move, and as he struggled to get free, two figures emerged from the woods and slowly made their way toward him. He never saw them coming.

Another bolt of lightning struck the burial mound. As the smoke cleared, it revealed an open grave.

Joseph looked toward the spot where the lighting hit and then heard moaning. Turning to his right, Joseph saw zombie-like beings approaching. Pieces of tissue and skin fell from the creatures, leaving a trail of flesh across the clearing.

"Please, NO, PLEASE!"

"Unlike your friends Sullivan and Manning, who betrayed their friend due to my coercion, your treachery was voluntary. You sold Mark Desmond out for money. I think your friends would like a word with you, Joseph."

The creatures, who in life had been Paul Sullivan and Thomas Manning, grabbed the screaming Joseph Rogers and began pulling him toward the burial mound.

"Paul, wait! Thomas, don't!"

Joseph Rogers begged and pleaded for his childhood friends to release him, but the appeals went unanswered. They hauled him along the ground with Joseph kicking and screaming until they pushed him into the empty grave. Joseph lay paralyzed, his eyes bulging as layer after layer of dirt fell upon him. He coughed and spat out the soil, but it piled up until it covered his face.

Paul Sullivan and Thomas Manning lumbered back to their final resting places, where the earth opened and absorbed them back into their eternal tombs, and Joseph Rogers now joined them in eternal damnation.

"The theft of King Zagan's keys by JESU prevented this gate from being opened for centuries," Lucius declared.

Raising Saint Michael's sword to the sky, he shouted, "Not only have I the location of the final key, but more importantly, I now hold in my hand the only instrument capable of closing Hell's gate. JESU will not be able to stop me this time!"

***

October 28thth
Culpeper, Virginia
Approximately 10:00 a.m.

Lucius ended the call abruptly and shut off his cell phone. He grinned, a smile more sinister than happy. He enjoyed toying with people like Jack Aitken, but it was often like a cat playing with a mouse. There was almost no sport in it. It was far too easy to manipulate humans, but Lucius delighted in it anyway.

"Mr. Abraham, could you hear the fear in Mr. Aitken's voice?" Lucius asked gleefully. "And the way he tucked his tail between his legs when I warned him about the fate of his family?"

Jesse Abraham sat motionless, strapped in a chair. He was barely alive. Lucius had been torturing him for days. He had been repeatedly beaten and then allowed to recover, only so Lucius could assault him some more. Jesse could no longer tell if he was still under interrogation or if this was just Lucius's perverse idea of fun.

"You should have seen the look on Jack's face when I first revealed my true identity. Here, let me show you."

Lucius morphed into his demon form. His fingers became elongated and turned into claws, and his lower jaw jutted forward, displaying his prominent canine teeth. Through his one eye that remained open, Jesse saw Lucius grow several feet taller and become a hunk of solid muscle.

"What do you think, Jesse?" Lucius said in a deep, menacing voice.

Grabbing Jesse by the hair on his head, Lucius demanded, "Take a good look, boy. Have you ever seen the likes of me?"

Jesse was astonished and frightened by Lucius's appearance. Even his bruised and battered face could not hide his fear.

Lucius laughed, and while doing so, transformed back to appearing human.

"Of course, you have not. You are still wet behind the ears."

Lucius dropped Jesse's head and walked away. He turned around suddenly, looked at Jesse, and said, "You know, I am genuinely insulted that JESU would send someone so inexperienced after me. They must be in worse shape than I thought to allow a rookie like you to confront me."

Jesse had been a member of JESU, the Justice Ecumenical Society United, for less than a year. He had joined the group out of a sincere desire to combat evil, but none of his training prepared him for this. Jesse had to admit that Lucius was right. Jesse was in way over his head, and he and Lucius knew it.

"I have been corrupting the souls of men for more than a millennium, but I never tire of breaking their will and then their spirit. That includes individuals like you, Mr. Abraham. But, you pitiful fool, you fail to realize that doing my master's work is not a job; it is an absolute pleasure."

Lucius slapped Jesse's cheeks. "You are not dead yet, are you?"

Jesse moaned as his eyes rolled back in his head. Lucius's pompous boasting made him wish that he were dead already.

"Why don't you kill me already?"

"Tsk, Tsk. Mr. Abraham. You are not a gracious guest, are you? You have been here only a few days, and now you want to leave. Did JESU teach you any manners?"

"Well, no matter, before you depart this world for Hell."

Jesse's life force was fading, but he said to Lucius, "Heaven. Going to Heaven."

"Oh, Jesse, I am sorry to be the one to tell you this, but you are heading in the other direction."

Jesse shook his head. "No. No."

"I'm afraid so, Jesse. Do you remember the young woman you slept with the other day in Culpeper?"

Jesse could scarcely remember anything at this point, but the image of a woman did appear in his mind.

"She was a succubus. I sent her to corrupt you and well, let us just say she succeeded. Your soul has the mark of Lucifer on it, and when you reach the pearly gates, I am sorry to say, but they will reject you."

Lucius laughed and said gloatingly, "You give my regards to Asmodeus, Alastair, and the rest of the demons."

Jesse's eyelid closed and as he took his final breath, a tear of sorrow slid slowly down his cheek.

***

Jesse Abraham's body was still warm when the phone in Lucius's pocket vibrated. He glanced down at the number and answered it,

"Yes, Nadia. I see. It is just as I planned. Keep an eye on them and let me know when they leave town." Lucius laughed. "Did Jack think that a cloaking spell would work on me? So naïve."

As he had suspected, Jack had contacted Mark Desmond. Precisely what he had hoped he would do.

Lucius tossed his cell phone up and down in his hand as if it were a ball. He could not help but gloat. After the massacre and in conjunction with the decline of the church's influence in society as a whole, JESU's ranks dramatically declined. Along with this went their offensive capabilities. To some degree, they were still a force to be respected, but the harvesting of souls for the Master began to escalate quickly.

The Internet was another gift to the forces of evil. It enabled the distribution of the book of Lucifer around the world in seconds. It also encouraged all manner of debauchery of a violent and sexual nature. Every form of temptation was at a person's fingertips, and while some people paid money for it, others paid with their souls. As he referred to it, his business was booming, but it still was not enough to tip the scales sufficiently in Satan's favor.

Putting the cell phone in his pocket, Lucius thought to himself,

Technology may have given people a means to stay in touch with one another, but it did nothing to improve their

communication or social skills. Life in front of a computer screen often left people longing and searching for something.

A wicked grin came across Lucius's face, "I am happy to help them find it, for a price."

Due to JESU's deteriorating force levels, they could not aggressively repel his demons, who located the first two of King Zagan's keys rather quickly. He knew that finding the final key was going to be more challenging. Then Jack Aitken walked through his door.

A legend from the book of Lucifer, Lucius's favorite story, predicted that a compromised soul would provide the final key that would unlock the gate. Aitken's arrival was even more than Lucius could have hoped for; the souls of Jack and his family were only the appetizer.

Destroying his adversary Mark Desmond and JESU once and for all would ordinarily be the sweetest of victories. However, the fulfillment of the prophecy and freeing the Kings of Hell in time to harvest all of those unredeemed souls on All Souls Day no less, well, that should be worthy of a new chapter in the book of Lucifer.

Chapter 8

October 29th
Lawrence, Kansas
Mid-morning

Jack sat up groggily on the couch. Father Desmond had left to attend to a few church matters and suggested Jack try to lie down and get some rest. He felt drained, but he could not fall asleep no matter how hard he tried.

He had left his jacket hanging on the arm of the couch, and reaching into an interior pocket, he pulled out a small notebook. Jack had used it when he initially started researching Route 666 for his novel, but now it served as a journal. There was no way to forget what had occurred over the past few months. It remained seared in his brain forever. However, he knew he needed a written record of what had happened. If Jack were to die, he wanted someone to understand what had occurred and warn others not to follow in his footsteps.

Jack opened the journal intending to update it but instead found himself re-reading his notes and previous entries. He flipped to the first page, and as he read, he realized how innocently this whole nightmare had started.

The state highway system of Virginia essentially began with the Byrd Act of 1932, a bill enacted in response to the great depression. Route 666 is one of these roads. Route 666 winds its way through the Virginia countryside for nearly seven miles outside Culpeper, surrounded by thick woods and the occasional farm. Maybe it's the existence of almost a dozen cemeteries along that short stretch of road, or perhaps the menacing route number, that has made it the subject of urban legends and ghost stories. Many locals say an ominous feeling comes over one when they travel this highway. Its recent closure to vehicular traffic heightens that eerie sensation and raises more questions about the route and its unique history.

In the beginning, Jack believed he could weave a compelling supernatural horror story just based on the route number alone. He had no actual knowledge of anything particularly odd about Culpeper or the road itself at the outset. Still, once the research started, it didn't take long to see a pattern of bizarre occurrences and downright weird stories. As Jack continued to flip through the pages of the journal, this became even clearer.

Notes from Library Research

Ghost stories about this region are numerous. Locals tell tales of seeing apparitions of railroad workers who haunt the area. There are no records of derailments or accidents, but the accounts all tell a similar story. Workers hold lanterns like they are searching for something but then seemingly disappear into thin air. Travelers have told of vanishing hitchhikers and picking up a young woman who vanishes before the route ends near Route 663. The young woman's description is almost always the same: a white dress, a face with a sorrowful appearance, and never a word spoken. Not surprisingly, there are also Civil War soldiers' appearances, some without heads, who march through a field in a northeasterly direction as if they are heading into battle.

Jack always found the next section to be both intriguing and more than a little unnerving. In addition to ghost stories, several paranormal researchers, none of whom would provide their name, shared experiences with Jack that they had while investigating these cases.

Several investigators, independently of one another, mentioned seeing green, glowing lights along the roadside. When they'd get to the spot where they were sure they had seen the illuminations, there would be nothing there. Violent screams and cries of intense anguish seemed to originate from the woods along sections of the highway, but there was nothing there when flashlights illuminated these areas. Some of these screams turned up on recording devices. Even in the heat and humidity of a steamy Virginia summer evening, there would be sections of the road where frost would develop on cars' windshields. The cooler temperatures are considered to be a sign of paranormal or ghostly activity.

One thing came across consistently in talking to these researchers: they all sensed what they described as a real evil presence. It was such a scary feeling that all of them decided never to go back again.

Jack put the journal down for a minute. He'd almost forgotten the tapes. He closed his eyes, and he could hear the screams. They were primordial, otherworldly. The anguish that emanated from those recordings was something that even Jack, with all of his personal pain, had difficulty comprehending.

At the same time, the dread these seasoned paranormal investigators expressed was unsettling. These were not individuals that scared easily. They had been a part of hundreds of investigations, and separately from each other, they all confided in Jack that this was the one investigation in particular that gave them nightmares. It should have been a warning to Jack, but he failed to heed it.

If he were truthful, it had intrigued him even more.

Jack headed to the kitchen and placed the journal on the table. He took a glass from the cabinet and sat down. Seeing the bourbon bottle still on the table from the night before, Jack poured it until the glass was full. Though never a drinker before all of this, he found that the more he read his notes, the more he needed the alcohol to steady his nerves. Putting the bottle down, he began to read from the journal once more.

Notes on Local Lore

There is a lot of unexplained phenomena associated with the highway. Local motorists have reported radio static all along the route, unable to tune in to a station. Mechanical and equipment failures also seem to occur routinely. There are numerous accounts of vehicles stalling, becoming inoperable, and requiring towing. An employee of Rusty's Towing Service on Brandy Station Road reported that when the road was still open to vehicular traffic, they would tow several vehicles a week from Route 666. He indicated it was not unusual for these vehicles to start without difficulty once they were back at the repair shop.

Rusty's offers 24-hour service, and the employee volunteered, "By the way. Despite the plentiful work we received from breakdowns on Route 666, none of us were too unhappy when they closed the road. No one was ever thrilled with the prospect of being on call overnight and having to do a job on Route 666 after dark. Something about that road just never felt right. It kind of made the hair on the back of your neck stand up."

The paranormal researchers had also told Jack they'd often have problems with their equipment during their investigations on the road. Fully charged batteries would drain almost instantaneously. When it came time to review the evidence from video recorders that were functional before a case, researchers often found blank screens.

Jack put the empty glass back down on the table. When he first took these notes, he did so with skepticism; however, he was no longer a skeptic, not after what Jack had experienced. Flipping through the journal revealed a page with the phrase "Urban Legends" written at the top.

Not surprisingly, there are many urban legends associated with the road. One such tale was that a figure would appear if you sat at the intersection of Route 666 and Route 29 and counted to twenty-nine six times.

"Tested that one myself, and nothing happened," Jack said out loud.

Another legend told the story of motorists followed by a black vehicle. It comes up behind them at a high rate of speed, and when they move onto the shoulder to allow it to pass, the car disappears. Yet another story centers on the witching hour of 3:00 a.m. Reports are that if you drive Route 666 alone at this time, an evil spirit will appear in the passenger seat of your car and attempt to steal your soul and drag you to Hell.

Hands tremoring, Jack dropped the journal and pushed away from the table. When he first wrote down the details of this last urban legend, he hadn't given any consideration to the potential authenticity of it, but now it was all too real to him.

Something happened that day Jack visited the road. He wanted to remember every detail, but the incident only came back to him in bits and pieces. Jack had fixated on it for weeks but just could not be sure of the details. The one thing he knew for sure was that this was no piece of folklore. It was not fictitious, nor a hallucination. It was horribly true.

Jack was about to walk away from the journal when the title "The Gates of Hell" caught his eye.

Notes from a story that I found on the Internet. Not specific to Culpeper itself, but it could be helpful to the story anyway.

Multiple stories exist which say Route 666 is an entrance to the Gate of Hell itself. The exact location remains a mystery. Many accounts describe a road turning into the driveway of a house located on a hill. Seven iron gates lead to the home, where a family supposedly went insane and committed unspeakable but undefined atrocities. Legends say that strange phenomena occur after passing through each gate, including unusual sounds, dogs growling, and howling of an unknown origin.

Further up the hill, people feel the sensation of being touched, and floating orbs surround them. Children's voices are said to whisper a warning about proceeding further, and in the distance, a woman's scream will echo through the night. At the fifth gate, electronic devices fail, and cameras take pictures that show no images. One tale says that no one really knows what lies beyond this fifth gate because no one has been courageous enough to continue the journey, but a few stories indicate that anyone who found such courage was never seen or heard from again.

There was no doubt in Jack's mind about the existence of the gates or their location. He knew all too well that they were indeed real, and they were located just outside of Culpeper. When the idea of writing a story about Route 666 popped into his head, he never thought that he would be writing anything other than a piece of fiction. Reading his journal now confirmed that what had happened was anything but fictional.

While all of these ghost stories, unexplained occurrences, and urban legends were undoubtedly interesting, what had really gotten Jack's attention were the events associated with the road that had actually taken place. It was the real-life incidents that told him he was indeed onto something. The first obvious question was, why had the highway been permanently closed?

Culpeper County has one of the highest rates of accidents per number of drivers in all of Northern Virginia, even though it has fewer drivers and vehicles when compared to more densely populated adjacent counties, such as Fairfax and Prince William. Route 666 had an unusually high number of fatalities compared to roads with similar traffic flow. Interestingly, highways numbered 666 throughout the United States were shown to have higher than average fatality rates. A coincidence? After several particularly gruesome accidents, Culpeper County authorities, with the support of the state, determined that the road was not only inherently dangerous, but it was a redundant thoroughfare, so the road got shut down permanently.

On the surface, the explanation for the closure made sense, but it still seemed unusual to Jack. Typically, when a road is closed, another route is built in its place. It perfectly fit the plot of the novel that was coming together in his mind. Of course, for purposes of his story, these numerous deaths were because of some ancient and malevolent evil.

If I had only known how close to the truth I really was, perhaps I could have stopped all of this before it went too far.

But he knew there was no way to change the past. Jack wanted to put the journal down, but he found himself continuing to read. Of course, the fatalities bothered him, but what he found out next was even more unsettling. While a good horror movie or a novel could be scary, there was something about real-life horror stories that Jack found even more frightening.

For nearly 75 years, Route 666, and the land adjacent to it, have been the site of numerous unfortunate deaths and unsolved crimes as well as suicides, unidentified bodies, and mutilated animals. It is not a stretch to say that it is quite literally a dumping ground for the dead. The local police, citing confidentiality concerns and the fact that some of these unsolved cases remain active, were unable or unwilling to discuss this information. However, back issues of a local paper, The Culpeper Exponent, appear to confirm it. Anonymous law enforcement sources cited in several articles suggested that the animal mutilations appeared to be ritualistic.

Route 666 and the Culpeper area turned out to have a very real and rather gory story to tell. Jack decided to look further back into the history of the region, and he continued to find accounts of other unexpected events that were disturbing but at the same time piqued Jack's curiosity and interest.

While Salem, Massachusetts, held the most famous witch trial in the new world, more than thirty such trials in Virginia from the 1600s until the final court proceeding in 1733. The fear of witchcraft was a common concern for settlers in Colonial America. In terms of its size, current-day Culpeper County is just a shadow of what it was back in the 17th and 18th centuries. Although hysteria surrounding witchcraft did not reach the heights of what occurred in Salem, the penalties for being found guilty of such an offense in the Virginia colony were equally as severe, including death.

Accusations of witchcraft were not just limited to women. In 1656, William Harding was found guilty of practicing witchcraft and received thirteen lashes for his alleged offense. People often fear what they do not understand, and searching for explanations for the hardships they faced led them to believe it resulted from evil in their midst.

One particular group looked upon with suspicion was the Native Americans, discovered when the settlers arrived. The culture of the Native Americans was foreign to the settlers, and their beliefs and practices were so unusual that the settlers concluded that they must be devil worshippers.

Jack stopped reading, removed his glasses, and rubbed his tired eyes. He needed some fresh air, so he got up from the table and left the journal there.

Shrugging on his coat, he closed the apartment door behind him. At the end of the corridor, a door opened into a courtyard. He headed down a paved path toward a gazebo and saw a bench set off in a cozy corner. The sun was shining, and the morning air was brisk and crisp. A light breeze stirred the leaves in the trees, and birds were singing, but neither of these noises was enough to break the silence in Jack's mind. Meditation had become a way for Jack to deal with his inner demons, and he enjoyed the solitude of not thinking about anything in particular. He sat down on the bench, closed his eyes, and tried to clear his mind.

For a brief moment, he felt a calm come over him, but that respite was quickly interrupted by thoughts of his family and the dangers they were now facing. There was not a moment that he was not thinking about them and how high the stakes had become. It was indeed life or death. For now, he knew they were okay physically, but mentally and emotionally had to be a different story. Ritual is important to people with autism, and all of this had to be difficult for David and Louis. Taking care of the two of them was always a challenge that Amanda seemed to manage with indescribable grace, but this took things to a place that neither could ever have imagined.

Jack bowed his head, placed his face in his hands, and began to sob. At the same time, he did something he had not done in quite some time; he began to pray.

It was begging and pleading with God, unlike anything Jack had ever done before. However, his prayer was not for himself; his prayer was that God would watch over Amanda, Louis, and David. Jack asked God to help him find a way out of the mess he created, not for his own sake but theirs. The one thing Jack had been preparing himself for was accepting the punishment that would and should come with their current situation. He couldn't imagine what that might be, or maybe he just did not want to think about it.

While the consequences of his actions were unintended, Jack had willingly bound himself with the chains that he now wore. As Marley's ghost stated, "*I wear the chain, I forged in life. I made it link by link and yard by yard. I girded it on of my own free will, and of my own free will, I wore it.*" There was no way to get around it, and the more he thought about it, the angrier he became. Jack's tears of woe turned into tears of hatred, a hatred of himself for creating the situation they were in, but more for the bastard behind all of it.

Jack's thoughts turned back to his journal. He didn't even need the book to recall what had happened next.

The Manahoac, also known as the Mahock, were a Native American tribe indigenous to the Piedmont region of Northern Virginia. Near current-day Culpeper, archeologists discovered stone tools and weapons that indicated they hunted and fished in support of a village of approximately 1,000 persons. That is until 1728 when they disappeared from the historical records.

It was the disappearance of this Indian tribe that intrigued Jack the most. How did a village of 1,000 people simply vanish? Even an epidemic would not cause an entire tribe to die off all at once.

This tribe quite literally appeared to be here one day and then gone the next. Jack sensed there was something more to this, but searching the Internet gave him very little information. During one of those searches, he'd come across an exhibit of Manahoac culture at the Museum of Culpeper History and decided to visit.

***

September 9th
Route 29 South in route to Museum of Culpeper History

"It was great that your mom and dad could stay with Louis and David today," Jack said excitedly in the passenger seat. "This is a win-win for me. I get to spend some time with you and do some research for the book too."

"It's so good to see you excited about something like this, Jack." Amanda smiled. Reaching out her hand for his, she said, "These times together like this are too few, so let's make sure we enjoy it."

When Jack had decided to become an author, he would speak with Amanda about how things were progressing. During their evening walks, Jack bounced ideas off her regarding the storyline and its possible sequence. Maybe she was just happy to see him so energized by something, but she at least appeared to be interested, if not enthusiastic, about the subject.

"Thanks for driving, Amanda. I'm just taking notes on the names of the small towns and crossroads."

"Route 666 is coming up on the right," Amanda said spookily.

Jack laughed and glanced to see if anything was visible beyond the barricade, but it wasn't easy to see much of anything at fifty-five miles per hour. *I'm probably going to have to get beyond that barricade at some point,* he thought.

About forty minutes into the drive, they took the Business Route 15 South exit for Brandy Road. About three miles down the road, they entered a traffic circle.

"Take the third exit from the circle onto North Main Street," he directed.

"I see it, Jack. What's next?"

"Take your next left on East Davis Street, and at the second intersection, take another left. It should be right there."

Jack pointed at a building on the right and said, "Look, there it is." He glanced at his watch. "It's 10:00 a.m. Perfect timing."

The $5 entrance fee per adult was more than reasonable. The museum was established in 1977 as the Culpeper Cavalry Museum. It took on a broader mission in 2000 and renamed itself the Museum of Culpeper History. The museum moved several times until it arrived at its present location, a former train depot, in 2014. Amanda and Jack held hands as they took in the multiple exhibits in the museum.

Jack had been very into dinosaurs as a child, so he found the Triassic Culpeper exhibit particularly interesting. At a local stone quarry in 1989, workers had uncovered nearly 5,000 dinosaur tracks of a large carnivore. There also were exhibits on Culpeper's role in the American Revolution and the Civil War.

"Amanda, look, there's the exhibit on the Manahoac," Jack said eagerly. "Let's check it out."

The presentation confirmed much of what Jack had seen on the Internet, but it also offered an explanation for their disappearance. The exhibit suggested the tribe left the Piedmont area to pursue one of their primary food sources, bison. This explanation certainly seemed believable, but in some way, it was not exactly what Jack had been hoping to find. He noticed the museum brochure said there were tours available by appointment. He wondered if the exhibit curator might be open to the possibility of providing some additional information about the Manahoac.

"Amanda, the brochure mentions the possibility of a private tour. I'm going to inquire about it."

Amanda continued to study the exhibit while Jack headed to the information desk, manned by a woman whose badge indicated she was a volunteer.

"Sir, you're in luck," the volunteer said. "The exhibit curator is here today. Let me see if he might be available to speak with you."

A few minutes passed, and a middle-aged man approached them. He had salt and pepper hair and appeared to be in his early to mid-40s. His skin was tan as if he'd been working outside all summer, and he had very dark brown eyes. He stuck out his hand to Jack and introduced himself.

"Good morning, sir. My name is Lucius Rofocale. I understand you have some interest in learning more about the Manahoac exhibit?"

Jack shook Lucius's hand. "Nice to meet you, Lucius. I appreciate you taking the time to speak with me. My name is Jack Aitken, and this is my wife, Amanda."

"Good day to you, Mrs. Aitken."

Amanda smiled back, but it didn't quite meet her eyes.

Jack continued, "I am doing some research for a book I'm writing, and the disappearance of the Manahoac is potentially an interesting storyline for the novel. I was wondering if you might be able to tell me more about them."

"Tell me, what type of book are you writing?"

Jack could not quite place the accent. It sounded like he might be from Great Britain. He certainly had the politeness and mannerisms of an English gentleman.

"It is going to be a book with a supernatural angle."

"That is very interesting, Mr. Aitken. I am not sure how helpful I can be, but I would be happy to assist you in any way possible." Lucius thought for a moment. "Do you have a deadline to meet? If you can give me a little time, I could look over some documents I have in my office and at home to see if there might be any useful information for you."

Jack's enthusiasm grew. "I don't want to impose on you, Lucius, but I would certainly appreciate that."

Lucius rubbed his chin. "If I can find anything useful, I should have it by next week. How about we meet a week from today at around noon. The Frost Café on the corner of Davis Street would be convenient for me if that would work for you."

"That would be great." Jack eagerly shook Lucius's hand. "Thank you, and I will see you next week."

"Very good. Goodbye, Mrs. Aitken."

Amanda weakly smiled and nodded.

Lucius departed, and Jack turned to Amanda. "Well, that sounds promising."

Amanda's smile disappeared. "If you say so, Jack." He held the door open for Amanda, and they walked to the car and drove home.

Jack remembered Amanda didn't say much on the way home or the week before he met with Lucius. After nearly thirty years of marriage, he knew when something was troubling her. Over the years, he'd joked with her that when she got this way, he would ask her three questions:

Are you hungry?

Are you tired?

What did I do?

That week, she was in no mood for jokes. The night before he met with Lucius, they were taking their usual evening walk, and Amanda finally told him what was troubling her.

"Jack, I don't want to sound unsupportive of your book. I know how much this means to you, but I do not have a good feeling about this meeting tomorrow."

Jack wasn't surprised. Since the visit to the museum, he'd sensed she was upset about something related to his book. "Okay, Amanda. I am listening. What are you concerned about?"

They walked a little further. "It's Lucius. There's something about that man that I do not like. You've always told me that I am a good judge of character, and there is something very wrong with him. I've got a terrible feeling about this."

Jack frowned. "Come on, Amanda. Don't you think you might be overreacting a little?"

Amanda shook her head. "Jack, please listen to me. Do not do this. You don't necessarily have to give up writing the book, but maybe you can choose a different angle for it."

Jack started to become agitated. He took a deep breath. "Amanda. It is just a meeting. What bad things could happen because of a meeting?"

"Jack, it's a feeling I have. Lucius… he makes my skin crawl."

***

A Blue Jay landed on the edge of the birdbath, startling Jack from his thoughts. He thought to himself, *what a beautiful bird but such a noisy song*. He remembered what happened next. It was something that didn't occur very often. Amanda and Jack had fought intensely. He probably could count on one hand the number of times they'd argued in the nearly forty years they'd known one another, and this one was the worst of them all.

He recalled trying to choose his words carefully. He'd listened to what Amanda said, then told her he was going to the meeting anyway. Of the many regrets about their situation, this was perhaps the worst of all. The one person who loved him more than life itself was trying one last time to save him from himself. Why didn't he listen?

That Saturday morning, Jack and Amanda took David and Louis to Panera for a bagel and coffee, just like they did every Saturday. What made this Saturday different was that Amanda and Jack did not say a word to one another. The boys could sense something was wrong, but both Jack and Amanda assured them everything was fine. Around 11:00 a.m., Jack pulled out of the driveway and headed to the Frost Café to meet with Lucius.

He arrived at the café and found Lucius already seated in a booth. Thinking about Lucius now made Jack want to cringe, but he'd been keenly interested in what he had to share with him at this meeting.

"Mr. Aitken," he said as Jack took the seat across from him. "I think I have located some information that might be of interest to you. I found some documents at the Culpeper Library, where they store historical documents about the County. I came across a document I had never seen before. It discussed some archeological excavations conducted during the 1750s on some burial mounds found in the local area."

"That is interesting," Jack said, pouring himself a coffee. "Please go on."

"An unverified account describing the mounds indicates them being six feet tall with hundreds of thousands of corpses. Unfortunately, over time, these mounds have been destroyed by farm plows, floods, and erosion. I have been here in Culpeper for most of my life, and I have seen no such evidence of these mounds."

This was precisely the information he'd wanted. He was sure that he could use this for his novel.

"Lucius, I'm very appreciative of the research you did. This information is beneficial."

Lucius put his hand up. "Wait, Jack, there is more. While there is no recent evidence that these mounds existed, I did come across this."

Lucius handed Jack a document. Based on the look of the paper and its texture, it appeared to be very old. Jack moved the glasses out of the way and unfolded the document on the table. He was surprised to see that it was a map of the Culpeper area.

Jack looked at Lucius and asked, "Does any of this look familiar to you?"

Lucius had studied the map for a few moments and then started to point landmarks out to him. He read the map as if he'd seen it before, although Lucius insisted this was the first time he had laid eyes upon it.

They had poured over the map for nearly an hour when Jack asked, "What is this symbol over here, the one in the upper right-hand portion of the map?"

Lucius looked at the symbol. "I believe it is a symbol for a cemetery that appears to be in the shape of a mound. Perhaps one of the Manahoac burial mounds. If I am reading this map properly, it appears that it might be in the vicinity of Route 666. Are you familiar with it? Route 666 is the road the state closed awhile back."

Jack tried to contain his enthusiasm, but he was sure that Lucius must have seen it. A cemetery near Route 666 and the possibility of it being a Native American burial mound! After all of the challenges he'd faced in his life, something finally appeared to be going his way.

"Actually, I am familiar with it. It has something to do with the book that I'm writing."

Lucius smiled, revealing perfectly straight teeth. "Well, isn't that fortuitous? Jack, do you see this mark over here? This line appears to be a trail, and these symbols along the trail seem to be markers of some sort. While it is not leading directly to the cemetery, it certainly appears to be going in that direction. The entrance to the trail seems to be marked by two large rocks. If you can find these rocks, you may be able to follow the trail and find the cemetery."

Jack realized now that Lucius had been leading him into a trap, but at the time, his excitement and perceived good fortune blinded him to what was truly happening. He thought about Lucius and remembered what Albert Speer had said when someone questioned how he could follow a man like Adolf Hitler: "One seldom sees the Devil when he puts his hand on your shoulder."

Perhaps he should have asked why Lucius would allow him to keep what appeared to be such a potentially important document, but he told Jack that he would need the map if he intended to find the cemetery. Lucius suggested he might try searching for the entrance off of Route 666, as it appeared that it might not be too far from the road. Jack checked his watch and was surprised to see that it was nearly five o'clock.

"Lucius, I can't thank you enough. How can I ever repay you for your kindness?"

Lucius smiled. "No thanks are necessary. It was my pleasure to be in a position to assist you with what sounds like a fascinating project. If I can be of any additional service to you, please feel free to contact me again. You know where to find me. I won't say goodbye—something tells me we are going to see each other again."

Jack got up from the table, shook hands with Lucius, and headed for the door. As he passed the road sign for Route 666 on the drive home, he glanced toward the barricade, and an AC/DC song came on the radio. *"I'm on the Highway to Hell."*

Jack laughed. "That's it! The name of the book, Route 666: Highway to Hell."

Chapter 9

Father Desmond returned from his errands and found Jack sitting in the gazebo in the meditation garden. Jack saw him approach and waved him over. He joined Jack on the bench, and the two men sat together for a minute or two.

"Jack, I see you found our meditation garden. I often come here myself. I hope I am not intruding."

Jack smiled. "Not at all, Father. I'm happy to have the company. This garden is a beautiful spot. I can see why you would spend a lot of time here."

Looking across the courtyard, Jack saw several students pointing in his direction and whispering to one another. It made him uncomfortable, but Father Desmond seemed not to notice.

"I guess you were not able to get any rest."

Jack took in a deep breath and sighed. "Unfortunately, no. Every time I try to lie down, I can't clear my mind. My thoughts just keep racing. I was just reviewing some of my journal entries."

He shared some of the contents of the journal with Father Desmond. When he told him about his meeting with Lucius, Father Desmond felt something in his gut—it reminded him of being punched in the stomach—but he remained silent and allowed Jack to finish. Jack then showed him the map that Lucius had given him. It obviously was historical by its appearance and was challenging to interpret.

Jack gulped then found the courage to say, "I am sure you have figured out by now that I used the map." Jack stared at the map he was holding in his trembling hands. "I am still shocked about how the journey I took to get to this point started with such a heady sense of adventure."

He held up the map and shook it angrily. "I set out that day eager to solve the mystery of Route 666 and unlock this map's secrets. Now I live in a constant state of fear of the evil that I have unleashed. How could an excursion that started so innocently go so terribly wrong?"

***

September 21st
Culpeper, Virginia
11:00 AM

Jack burst through the front door and quickly made his way into the kitchen to let Amanda know he was home. His half-day of work was over, and he found Amanda preparing a sandwich for him to take on his afternoon "adventure." He kissed her hello and then dashed upstairs to change. Over the past two weeks, Amanda had continued to express her concerns about Lucius and this whole "crusade," but she could tell how important it was to him. She could also see that fire in his eyes and a level of drive and determination that she had not witnessed in many years. While she still expressed reservations about this project and today's trip, in particular, she was supportive for Jack's sake.

Amanda finished the sandwich, wrapped it in plastic wrap, and put it in the knapsack on the counter. She had also added two protein bars and two bottles of water along with some sunscreen. Although it was officially the first day of fall, the Autumnal Equinox, it was pretty warm, and the sun was still powerful enough to give a person quite a burn. As a young man, Jack had spent a few too many summers in the sun as a lifeguard for Amanda's taste, and she was always making sure he protected himself accordingly.

Jack came back downstairs dressed in jeans, a white T-shirt, hiking boots, and a baseball hat. He reached into the knapsack, opened the sunscreen bottle, and started applying it to his face, neck, and arms. He smiled at Amanda, knowing that she knew he was doing this to make her happy. She grinned and watched Jack add mosquito repellant, a compass, and that map that Lucius had given him to the knapsack. That map, she thought to herself. It was all that Jack could seem to talk about these last few weeks. She watched him zip up the knapsack, and they made their way to the cars in the garage.

Louis and David were already in Amanda's car, waiting for her. Jack's plan was for Amanda to follow him to the barricade on Route 666, closest to Route 29. Jack would park his car in a commuter lot adjacent to the wall that closed off the road, and then Amanda would drive Jack to another barricade on the Southwestern side of the road. Jack would then walk the seven miles of Route 666 and, along the way, try to find the entrance indicated on the map, which would mark the trail that could lead to the Manahoac burial mound. Just what Jack would do if he found the path was something that Amanda hoped they could discuss on the way to the drop-off point.

Jack pulled his car out first, and Amanda followed him out of their subdivision with the boys in tow. As he turned onto Lee Highway toward Culpeper, Jack was excited to be setting out on this quest. At the same time, he thought to himself about how fortunate he was to have the family he had. Despite their differences over this project, Amanda vowed to act supportive, even if she was not overly encouraging.

If there were a poster child for an angel on Earth, it would be Amanda. She was not only his spouse; they'd been best friends since they first met nearly forty years ago. Jack had never met someone so genuine. No one ever had a negative word to say about Amanda, and with good reason. She was kind, gracious, and always knew what to say—and, equally important when saying nothing was appropriate. She was quiet and reserved; when she spoke, her words had a significant impact. A trait she had learned from her grandfather.

Her even-keeled disposition was the perfect fit for their family, relying on her steadiness and "Rock of Gibraltar" qualities. She was the love of his life and the only person he ever really worried about disappointing. She was the only person who could have put a stop to what he was doing today, but she understood why he needed to go. Amanda knew Jack's confidence and ability to believe in himself again were at stake, and if he did not write this book, he might never be able to find that sense of self he had lost so long ago.

As they drove southwest, they passed numerous antique shops and self-storage units. They crossed the Rappahannock River into Culpeper County, and forty minutes later, they arrived at the commuter lot. Jack pulled into a parking space, got out of the car, and hit the button on his key chain to lock it. He then hopped into the back seat of Amanda's car and sat next to David. As they began to pull away from the lot, David caught sight of the Route 666 sign. He called out that this was a bad number.

Some might have referred to David as a savant. Before he was even speaking in sentences, he demonstrated an aptitude for math. He could walk through a neighborhood one time and memorize the five-digit house numbers on both sides of the street, with no pattern to the sequence of numbers. If you asked David what day of the week September 29th, 1990, was, he'd be able to tell you it was a Saturday.

As soon as David mentioned 666, Louis began doing what he did best: ask twenty questions. He was prone to bouts of anxiety, which often led to rapid-fire questions directed at Amanda. Both Amanda and Jack attempted to calm the boys down, but it wasn't working. They asked David to explain why he said this was not a good number, but he would not answer them. David had not gone to church since his baptism. The chances that he knew about the book of Revelation and what 666 stood for were remote at best.

Driving to the other side of Route 666 took nearly thirty minutes. By the time they arrived at the drop-off point, the boys were still agitated but had calmed down sufficiently that Jack felt it would be okay for him to leave. They protested when he went to leave the car, but he assured them everything would be fine. He leaned through the window to kiss Amanda goodbye, and he told her he would see her later.

Before he could leave, Amanda grabbed his arm. "Jack, wait." She leaned closer. "Please be careful. If you find the trail entrance, please think about what we've been talking about before you decide to take it."

"I will," Jack said to reassure her. "Please don't worry. Everything will be okay."

The last thing Amanda had said to Jack before he got out of the car was, "Remember, don't bring anything home with you."

As she drove off with David and Louis, Jack chuckled to himself. The paranormal shows they watched together suggested that objects could have spirits and demons attached to them. It was one reason they agreed never to go antiquing or shop at garage sales.

After Amanda and the boys were out of sight, he turned to face the concrete barricade, which was in place to prevent vehicular traffic from entering the road. He swung the knapsack over his shoulder and started walking.

***

September 21st
Culpeper, Virginia
1:00 PM

Jack had certainly picked a beautiful day for his expedition. There was not a cloud in the sky, and the sun was bright and warm. The calendar might have said it was the first day of fall, but it still felt like summer in Northern Virginia, hot and humid, just the way he liked it. He joked with Amanda that the older he got, the more reptilian he became. The sun's warmth eased the chronic neck pain he had developed over the years, and it made his muscles feel free and loose.

His knee surgery nearly twenty years ago had ended the competitive running that he enjoyed, but he still was in excellent shape for being almost fifty-five years of age. Jack even weighed the same as he did when he'd graduated from college, and he took pride in keeping himself fit. While physical fitness would benefit him today, it was his attitude that gave him confidence for what might lie ahead. Frankly, he hadn't felt this energized in years. He certainly hoped to find a lot of interesting information for his book today, but the truth was it felt great just being out here. Many times in the past, he would have talked himself out of doing this, made excuses, and found reasons not to follow through. But not this day.

Jack estimated that the road was approximately seven miles long and that if he kept a three-mile-per-hour pace, it would leave plenty of time to look for the two large boulders on the map that marked the trail entrance. If he were reading the map correctly, the boulders would be around the five-mile mark, so a brisk pace, in the beginning, would save time to find the trail later and possibly follow the map to the burial mound, if it was really there.

Although the road had been closed for less than two years, it was shocking how much Mother Nature had started reclaiming her territory. Weeds were growing in the cracks in the asphalt, and plants, including wild mustard and even tree seedlings, were already beginning to take root. The grasses along the road's shoulders were thigh-high in places, and their seed heads danced in the light breeze. The same breeze gently rolled through the leaves of the trees, which would, in a month, be shades of yellow, red, and orange.

Cornfields dominated the surrounding land, and the stalks were visible for what seemed liked miles around him. Stacked stone walls subdivided the farmland, and most of the fields had large trees that seemed to rise out of the corn. It was a clear day, and when he looked westward toward the horizon, he could see the outline of the Blue Ridge Mountains. He was close enough to see vineyards at the base and on the slopes of the mountain foothills.

As Jack walked, he took in the scenery and the solitude. Were it not for the flapping wings of the flocks of birds rising out of the corn and the wind blowing through the cornstalks and leaves in the trees, virtually the only thing he might have heard was the sound his boots made as they hit the pavement. Not too much further down the road, he came across a high school, and the outline of the football, soccer, and baseball fields was still visible despite being abandoned.

He took out his pad and started to make notes about what he saw to remember all of it when he sat down to write the book. While he was enjoying himself, the quiet felt eerie at times. No car horns, school buses, or people. It was certainly not what Jack was expecting. The further down the road he went, he began to see more evidence of the road closure's impact on the area. Farms that must have been thriving at one time now had weathered signs offering acreage for sale, and the state completely blocked the rear entrance to Mountain Brooks Estates. He stopped to read a remaining historical marker that informed the reader about the Civil War Battle of Brandy Station, which had occurred in the area more than one hundred fifty years ago.

After walking for nearly an hour, he came across train tracks that ran across the road. The rails were not rusty, which indicated that they were still in use. Jack thought to himself that perhaps this was the source of the railroad worker sightings. He saw a steel pole with some signal lights on it about thirty yards up the track. Jack went to look at it and saw the light was red, meaning there was no train coming. David was fascinated by trains and had taught Jack that a green or yellow signal light meant a train was coming, but red indicated the track was clear. He headed back to the road and kept walking.

After nearly an hour and a half, he started to come across abandoned industrial buildings. The silo of the Comet Concrete Company plant came into view. The painted company logo on the silo was beginning to flake and fade, but the company's name was quite clear. He also saw an empty building that appeared to have been an auto parts store. Jack found broken windows on many of the buildings, and there were empty beer bottles on the ground. Clearly, some kids had been here for a little late-night partying. *Who knows, maybe they were doing some ghost hunting of their own*, he thought.

The next building Jack came across was Jordan's Feed and Seed store. Jack was an avid gardener and thought he would take a brief break and check it out. He drank about half a bottle of water and bit into a protein bar as he peered through the window. A desk and chair were visible, and Jack turned the knob on the door. The door opened, and he stepped into the store. Jack looked around and walked through the aisles. The shelves were all empty, but as he turned to go down the last aisle, his boot stepped on something which skidded under the sole of his shoe, almost causing him to twist an ankle.

Regaining his balance, he looked down at his feet. There was an object on the floor, but it was hard to make out due to the building's lack of light. He leaned over to pick up the object, but he took a step backward before he did so. He then knelt to get a closer look and realized it was a bone. He pulled the flashlight from his knapsack and pointed it down the aisle. The floor was littered with bones that were blackened as if they had been in a fire.

He stood and glanced around to see if he could find any animal activity in the building. He did not see droppings or anything else that would indicate an animal had been there. Nor did Jack see any obvious evidence of a fire. As he stood looking around, he recalled the researchers' stories about ritual sacrifice in the area. Jack was trying not to spook himself, but it was hard not to be concerned about what seemed to be happening in this building.

He still had plenty of ground to cover, so he went back to the road and continued walking, trying to push what he had seen out of his thoughts.

***

September 21st
Culpeper, Virginia
4:00 PM

As Jack passed Mile Marker Four, he took the map out of his knapsack. Based on what Lucius had shown him, the two boulders that would mark the trail could be anywhere in the next mile or so. His pace slowed as he studied the map and scanned the tree line for any sign of the path. Nearing Mile Marker Five, he grew slightly frustrated as he saw no evidence of the large boulders.

Jack saw a church to the left and decided to survey the property around the building to see if there might be any clues that led to the trail entrance. Glass from the smashed windows of the vandalized building littered the ground. All of the doors to the structure were left wide open. He walked around the building's side and then to the church's rear but saw nothing except overgrown grass waving in the breeze. He returned to the front of the building and peered in through the front doors.

Inside the church, it was pretty dark, but enough light came through the windows to reveal a thoroughly trashed sanctuary. All of the pews and the cross that had once hung over the altar were gone. Jack slowly entered the sanctuary and found a few benches that remained intact. They appeared to have brass plates on the end of the pew, and he took out his flashlight to read one of them. There was a name engraved on the plate: *The Bradford Family.*

That name was familiar to him. While researching the Culpeper area, he'd found several references to William Bradford, a large landowner from the late 1700s. It seemed likely that the Bradford family had been members of the church and had dedicated the pew. When he was a child, Jack's family had vacationed in places like Colonial Williamsburg and Boston, Massachusetts, and he recalled that this was not an unusual practice during those times. The building did not seem too old, so perhaps the pew had been transported here from another location. Jack left the church and continued his search.

After walking for another ten minutes, Jack came across what appeared to be a gravel road partially hidden by the overgrown vegetation. He was reluctant to go into the grass due to fears about ticks and snakes; he debated whether it was worth the effort, but he knew time was becoming a concern, so he decided to take the risk. Jack parted the grass with his hands to make a path and began moving through it. It was tough going initially, but after getting a few feet in, the grass opened up, and he was on what had once been a driveway.

Jack removed the map from the knapsack and quickly took a look at it. At first glance, he didn't see anything identifiable but thought it would be worth walking up the road a little further. Jack glanced up at the sky and saw that the sun was beginning its downward trajectory toward sunset. He started up the driveway, which became quickly covered by a canopy of trees that made it appear much darker than it was. The foliage along both sides of the road was dense, and it wasn't easy to see what was in the woods beyond it.

Looking ahead, he thought he saw some daylight, which might be a clearing in the woods. He walked toward the light, and the woods did indeed open up. To his right was a small cemetery, a familiar sight to him, as small cemeteries seemed to dot the Northern Virginia landscape. They also showed up in some of the most unusual places. In fact, there was one in the middle of the giant shopping center near his home, and the subdivision across the street actually had one in between two of the houses. He decided to take a look.

The grass leading to the cemetery entrance was tall and thick, which made walking difficult. As Jack got closer to the opening, he found a metal sign propped up against the stone wall that encircled the graveyard. He carefully brushed aside the foliage and saw that the sign read "Bradford." He stepped into the cemetery to see if he could read anything on the tombstones, but time and the elements had erased most of the names. There was no doubt this was an old graveyard. He read "William Bradford" on one marker and "Abigail Bradford" on another.

Something caught Jack's eye in the back corner of the graveyard along the stone fence line. He moved in that direction and peered over the fence. He saw two green mounds, which were about five feet apart. Jack looked for a safe place to climb over the stone wall, and once clear of it; he made his way to the two mounds. The ground under his feet was soft, and the surface of the green knolls was actually moss. Pressing his fingers and palm on the moss, he found it wasn't spongy or soft but hard.

Jack tried to pry off the moss with his fingernails, but he found it difficult to do so. He picked up a stone and started scratching it off instead. It didn't take long for him to see a gray surface. It was a stone! He quickly moved over to the other mound and scratched at the moss. It was another rock. The distance between them left no doubt in Jack's mind that this had to be the entrance to the trail.

He looked through the underbrush and trees and thought he saw the outline of a path leading into the woods. He tried to use a compass to verify what direction the trail seemed to go, but the compass wouldn't work. At the time, it seemed odd. Could metals in the rock be influencing it? The stones were facing toward the Blue Ridge Mountains, which he knew should be west of his position.

Now Jack faced a difficult decision. He looked up at the late afternoon sun shining through the white cotton clouds and checked his watch. It was almost five o'clock. He knew he would have several hours of sunlight left, but he was unsure how long it might take to follow the map. Regardless, it was clear that if he decided to proceed, he would have to find his way to the car in the dark. It was supposed to be a full moon tonight, which would help, and he did have a flashlight with him, which he thought should provide him with enough light to find his way back.

He unzipped his knapsack and pulled out the small orange flags he used to mark the sprinkler heads in his lawn. He'd taken them as a means by which he could identify the trail and more easily find his way back. Jack's thoughts went back to Amanda. He knew she would be worried if he were not home before dark. He pulled out his cell phone, but there was no service. He also noticed that the battery was down to 38%, which did not make sense since he had fully charged it before leaving. Had the phone's screen been left on accidentally? He made sure he shut it off this time.

Now that he had found the trail entrance, perhaps he could come back another day to walk it. The biggest obstacle to this was the situation with the boys. He'd already taken the half-day today, precisely because trying to do something on the weekend was difficult. Louis had his social activities, such as going to the movies and club meetings, while David had his own routine of going to store after store with Amanda. Rituals and routines were vital to them due to their disability, and he knew that changing it could result in tantrums and other potentially undesirable outcomes.

What free time he did have on the weekend was filled with chores and home repair projects. Trying to get a block of time that would allow him to drive back here and spend the day walking the trail was not going to be easy. He had no vacation time left, so another half day was out of the question. None of these alternatives considered other variables, such as the weather on any given day.

While Jack weighed his options, he downed the last protein bar and emptied the water bottle he'd opened earlier. He took note that he had one bottle of water left. Watching the leaves rustle in the wind reminded Jack that today was the first day of fall. When he had decided that today was the day he would walk the road, he'd done a quick search on the Internet to see if this day had any particular association with evil. If there was, he thought he might use this information as part of the book at some point, but what he found was just the opposite.

Most of the material he found about this day was positive. In the Jewish faith, holy days such as Sukkoth, Rosh Hashanah, and the most sacred of all such days, Yom Kippur, all at one time or another, had fallen on September 21st. Other cultures celebrated it as a day of thanks for a bountiful harvest. The United Nations had declared it the International Day of Peace, where light and dark are in harmony.

Pondering this, Jack also looked upon this day as one of renewal for himself. He had arrived here in a positive frame of mind, and his real goal was right in front of him. His hard work had brought him here, and it felt good. The more he debated all of this in his mind, the clearer the decision was becoming. He had come too far to turn back now. It had been far too long since he'd felt this way; the chance he had wished for was here, and he was going to take it. Today was the day that he would conquer his demons once and for all.

He confidently stepped through the space between the rocks and started down the trail.

Chapter 10

October 29th
Lawrence, Kansas
3:00 p.m.

It was a little early in the day to be drinking, but Jack knew he would need some liquid courage to get through the next part of his story. Set 'Em Up was a dive bar near the college campus, and the two men settled into a quiet corner table. When the waitress brought the glasses of whisky Father Desmond told her, "Leave the bottle, please."

She set the Jack Daniels on the table and shot the priest a surprised look before leaving.

He filled a glass and slid it across the table to Jack. "I think I am going to need this too."

Jack gulped down the whisky and quickly poured another glass. He hoped to feel the effects of the alcohol soon but feared his adrenaline would counteract it. Jack was already feeling afraid, and he wondered how he was possibly going to get through this.

"Father, you told me about your camping trip in the woods. Have you been camping since?"

"I have been to the woods since, but not as a camper. I have not spent another night in the woods since then."

"I see. Based on what you told me, I certainly understand why. Tell me, Father, your life-altering experience notwithstanding, what is it specifically about the woods that scares you?"

Father Desmond rubbed his forehead. "For me, it is the darkness of the night. You know, when there is no moon in the sky. The pitch blackness hides so many things that we have a reason to fear, and not just those things that creep, crawl, or fly. What I mean to say is, when we go to the woods, we are generally only there for a particular purpose, such as camping or hiking, and for a limited time. We are blind to the fact that the woods existed for thousands of years before we ever entered them. There is no way to know what evil resides in those woods, when it arrived there, what forms it can take, and how potent it might be. They are things we take for granted and that we really ought not to seek out."

Jack took another sip of whisky and leaned back in his chair. "For me, it's what the woods do to your senses that scare me. It amplifies them; what you smell, hear, see, and feel. I have experienced what I call the 'clean woods,' as well as, most recently, the darkness. When I was a boy scout, I'd go away to camp for two weeks each summer. The campground was in upstate New York, in the Catskill Mountains in a town named Livingston Manor. The camp's name was Onteora, which means 'Land in the Sky,' and it remains the 'cleanest' woods I have ever visited."

"I never thought about the woods that way, Jack."

"Let me give you an example. I can still recall how the woods at Camp Onteora smelled. It's nearly forty years since I was a scout, but I can remember that scent like it was yesterday. They say that the rain will deaden the senses, but I found it intensified while at Onteora. It was fresh and clean. The fragrance of the evergreens and pine trees was like a Christmas wreath in July. Christmas has always been my favorite time of year, and this made two weeks in the camp like an early Christmas gift. It was beautiful, and I never felt unsafe or scared there. Even in the darkest night, I felt no fear. I guess to know the evil; you also need to know goodness. Onteora was goodness to me."

Father Desmond leaned forward and said, "I think I understand what you are saying."

Jack laughed. "You know, I think I might be the only Eagle Scout who hated camping. I loved the merit badge work, but there were certain badges that you really could only complete while you were at camp."

Father Desmond grinned. "There had to be something about it that you enjoyed, right?"

"Yes, getting in the car Sunday afternoon to go home! Seriously, I liked the hikes we would go on and some of the historical places we'd visit, such as Gettysburg. I didn't particularly care for sleeping on the ground in a tent. It was bumpy, and even with an insulated sleeping bag, it was cold."

Father Desmond shook his head in agreement. "I did not enjoy that either, but I did like starting a fire and cooking over an open flame. The food always tasted better."

"We called ourselves The Pyro Patrol! That was always the first thing we seemed to do when we got to camp. We didn't even pitch the tent until after we made a fire."

After swapping camping stories for a bit longer, Jack suddenly got quiet. He squirmed in the chair, trying to find a comfortable position. "Father, I think what I'm about to tell you won't do anything to help your fear of the woods. Candidly, it turned the woods into a horror show for me."

***

September 21st
Culpeper, Virginia
Late afternoon into the early evening

Jack found walking the path, if you could call it that, a real challenge. At times it was difficult to see where the trail was due to the dense undergrowth. The wild raspberry canes with their thorns were particularly problematic, as they not only scratched any exposed areas of skin but also got caught on his shirt sleeves, pants, and his knapsack. Vines on the lower portions of the path grabbed at his boots and caused him to stumble. He even fell twice.

"I hope I don't end up with a bad case of poison ivy or poison oak," Jack muttered to himself. He'd had both as a kid, and it would be just as unpleasant this time around.

He heard the distinctive call of ravens and crows; disembodied voices of the dead according to legends he had come across. Otherwise, the only sound he heard was his own movements through the brush and his profanity as he struggled. He made sure to place an orange flag in the ground periodically. Due to the dense undergrowth, it did take time to find suitable places for the flags. For some reason, his watch wasn't correctly functioning, so he was unsure of the time. He estimated he had been walking for maybe a half-hour or so. The path started to take a curve to the left, and Jack noticed something along the trail about 100 feet ahead of him.

He stopped and reached into the knapsack for the last bottle of water. He took it out, and before he opened it, he wiped the sweat from his brow with his forearm. He was filthy and was going to need a nice hot shower when he got home. He opened the bottle and mentally told himself not to drink too much water as he needed to make it last. He put the bottle back in the knapsack and continued to make his way up the footpath.

As Jack neared the object, he could see brick through the English Ivy that engulfed it. Jack was not a Master Gardener, but he knew English Ivy was not indigenous to Virginia. Someone had to have planted it there. He got closer and saw something that appeared to be sticking out from the brickwork—a gate. He finally got close enough to see it was wrought iron, and at one time, there had been a matching gate on the other side of the path. The missing gate stuck out from the underbrush; the brick column it had attached to had crumbled and was in pieces strewn across the path and into the woods.

Jack closely examined the brick column and gate that was still relatively intact. There appeared to be something inset into the brick, but the ivy mostly obscured it. He pulled the ivy off it and saw it was an iron disc. It was rusty, but the symbol on it was unmistakable: a pentagram. His thoughts immediately turned to the Seven Gates of Hell legend he discovered while researching the book. The hair on the back of his neck stood up, his feelings straddling the line between excitement and fear.

Jack felt the mosquito bite his neck and swatted at it. He opened his knapsack and took out the repellant that he had made sure to pack earlier. Jack sprayed repellant around his neck as well as his ears and cheeks. He squirted some more of it on both arms and then returned the bottle to his knapsack. It had a pleasant, citrus-like smell. A smile came to Jack's face as he recalled wearing it in the garden once, and Amanda asking him if he was wearing a new aftershave lotion. Jack chuckled to himself as he thought about it, but he stopped laughing when he realized it was getting near dark, and Amanda was sure to worry about where he was.

Although the trail had moved into some heavily wooded territory, he could still see rays of sun shining through the canopy of leaves. However, the dappled light was weak, and it barely illuminated the forest floor. The fading light, along with the increasing insect activity, told Jack that it was nearly dusk. He saw a deer in the woods; it was the first sign of life Jack had seen, except for the insects, since he had left the road. The deer turned and ran into the forest.

The soil had become increasingly damp, and the trail was muddy. Jack deduced he was entering into densely wooded marshland, and he could hear the sucking sound that his boots made as he pulled his foot out of the muck. He struggled to step forward. There was a putrid smell in the air, an odor you would associate with decomposing organic matter found in a swamp.

As Jack moved down the path, it did not surprise him when he came upon a creek. The water was still and murky, with no hint of current. The trail ahead led to a small bridge's remnants. The wooden walking surface was missing, appearing to render it unusable. Upon further examination, however, what remained of the bridge was reasonably stable, so it would have taken a significant rise in the creek level to have damaged it. Jack looked across the creek and was stunned by what he saw. Just beyond where the bridge pilings sank into the creek bank was another gate.

Jack searched up and down the creek for an area where he might cross. In the distance, he heard a train whistle. His thoughts immediately went to David and then Amanda and Louis. What was he doing out here? He should be home right now playing NFL Monopoly or some other game with his family.

A noise took his thoughts back to the present. The air was absolutely still with not even the hint of a breeze, but he heard what sounded like leaves rustling. He glanced around him but saw nothing. Then he listened to the snap of a branch like someone or something had stepped on it. Jack was sure that it was right behind him. He quickly turned around, but all he saw were more trees.

He told himself that it must be an animal, perhaps another deer. After all, dusk was the time that many animals ventured out, looking for food. He saw that vegetation covered the riverbank, so he looked to the right and started walking along the edge of the creek. About 100 feet from the bridge, he came to a bend in the stream where the water level was much lower. He jumped down off the bank onto an exposed area of the creek bed and began stepping from rock to rock, slowly making his way across the creek.

The light was fading fast, and it was becoming increasingly difficult to see where he was stepping. 2/3 of the way across the creek, he came to a sudden stop. There were no longer any rocks above the waterline where he could take his next step. It also became too dark now to trace his steps back. Knowing he had no choice, Jack stepped into the water. His boot sank into the mud up to his ankle, and it became hard going. He finally made his way to the other side of the creek, but the bank was steep. The mud was slippery like grease, and he struggled to find something to hold. Eventually, he found some exposed tree roots and managed to pull himself up the bank onto the firmer ground.

Jack pulled the flashlight from his knapsack and made his way along the bank back to the bridge. He examined the gate and found it to be intact but tremendously weathered. The iron gates were quite heavy, but they would still swing back and forth, and they made a loud creaking sound that echoed through the woods. It was a screech, but it could have been a scream if Jack did not know better. He found similar brickwork to the first gate but no pentagram on either of the two columns. The effort it took to get across the creek made him thirsty, so Jack took another sip of water. He marked the trail with an orange flag and made a mental note that it would take some time to find a way back across the creek when he returned.

***

Father Desmond sat at the table, absorbed in Jack's narrative about the gates and the Culpeper woods. He was all too familiar with the area surrounding the burial mound. However, on the day of the massacre, his forces approached from a much different direction than Jack described. He felt like he was actually there with Jack, walking the trail with him. He could smell the woods and hear the gate groaning as it opened and closed. The hair on the back of his neck began to stand up at the thought of what might have happened next.

Just then, Jack spoke, "Father, are you hungry? Let's order a pizza, okay?

Father Desmond nodded. "That sounds like a plan. My treat. I insist." He waved over a waitress and ordered a traditional cheese pizza.

"The pizza will be out in about twenty minutes," the waitress said.

Father Desmond looked at Jack and said, "Let's continue with your story while we wait."

***

September 21st
Culpeper, Virginia
Just after nightfall

Once the sun went down, the "night sounds," as Jack called them, quickly took hold of the woods. As the chirping of the crickets and croaking of the tree frogs increased, so did Jack's uneasiness and anxiety. He couldn't help but feel vulnerable to the woods' real dangers, such as snakes, but it was the perceived dangers that were the worst. What person or thing did he not see enter the woods that was now following him? The boogeyman was behind every tree, and he thought, *just what might cross my path as I come up around the bend?* The idea of being beyond rescue and those scary things the human mind could conjure up when a person was alone in the woods could paralyze even the most self-confident outdoorsman.

117

Jack was wrestling with the games his mind was playing, and he was losing.

Fortunately, there was a full moon this evening. As a matter of fact, the moon appeared so close to him that he felt like he could reach out and touch it. It made following the footpath easier, and it was bright enough that using the flashlight was unnecessary. Jack walked a while, then came across a massive tree next to the path with the moon in full view behind it.

He looked the tree up and down. *If it were Halloween, I would expect to see a hangman's noose suspended from those branches.*

Looking forward, the path narrowed. The woods felt like they were closing in. The brambles were so deep and dark that he felt like he was looking into pure blackness. The vines were everywhere and so thick he wasn't sure he would even make it through. He sensed them around his feet and tugging at his legs and arms. At times he thought he might have to crawl under them to make any headway. It was creepy and reminded him of a Vincent Price horror film, the scene right before the vines strangled their victim. An even more terrifying image was Jason Vorhees from *Friday the Thirteenth*. If there were something or someone in the patches of undergrowth with him, he would never know it. Jack felt defenseless, and there was nowhere to run or hide. He tried to put the thought out of his mind and hoped that as he pushed forward, the thickets would relent.

About 100 feet further up the trail, he came to a small clearing where the woods opened up, and the path did not feel so claustrophobic. He paused for a moment to drink some more water but then felt something tug at his shirt sleeve. Startled, he jumped away, then spun around quickly to see what might have grabbed him.

There was nothing there.

Not even a vine, shrub, or tree branch. Not one thing that Jack could have snagged himself on or gotten tangled up in. He was sure that something had grabbed him and knew his imagination was not playing tricks on him. There was no other way to say it. Jack was officially scared and wanted to get out of there, but instead, he found a suitable spot for another marker and shoved it into the grass. His heart was pounding out of his chest as he saw the path again and quickly moved on.

It could have been ten minutes or ten hours; Jack had lost total track of time at this point. The trail ahead began to curve slightly, and he couldn't really see what was around the next bend. This change in the route made him uneasy, and Jack slowed down, thinking it would make it less likely to run into something unexpected. The moonlight caused the tall trees to cast shadows on the path, and Jack saw what he thought might be another gate ahead of him. As he got closer, he saw more brick columns, one on each side of the path. The heavy vegetation around them almost entirely consumed them. The iron gates themselves were not there. He took out the flashlight to see if he might locate them and scanned the woods and the forest floor to his right. He saw nothing unusual.

He turned and flashed the light into the forest on his left. He didn't see a gate, but he did see what looked to be a house deep in the woods.

Who would build a house out here? He tried to get a better look.

Suddenly, the flashlight stopped working. Jack tried turning it on and off, but it would not light up.

"Great. Just great," Jack muttered.

Jack put the flashlight back in the knapsack and questioned if he'd put fresh batteries in before he had left. He knew that he had, which made this seem even eerier.

He should have packed a few extra batteries just in case, but who'd think brand new batteries would suddenly stop working? Jack's thoughts went back to stories the paranormal investigators had told him about the batteries on their equipment draining almost instantaneously. He also thought about his compass that would not work correctly and the cell phone that went dead. These events all felt way too coincidental, but there was nothing he could do about it now. Unless, of course, he wanted to turn back.

He quickly dismissed that idea and stared into the woods toward the house. His eyes adjusted to the darkness, and the moon illuminated the structure enough for him to make out a colonial-style home with three dormers and two chimneys ascending from the rooftop. It was like something he'd seen at the village restoration in Colonial Williamsburg.

Jack's gaze moved away from the roof. He saw what looked like green lights floating either in front of or actually inside the house. They didn't move much and had no shape that he could make out. What he was seeing was definitely odd, but there was no path through the woods to get to the house from his position, and he decided it would be best if he kept moving forward. He walked through the brick columns and continued up the path.

A light breeze had begun stirring, and when it hit the sweat on Jack's body, it caused him to shiver. The air temperature had cooled, and while the moon was still bright, it was now partially obscured by some cloud cover that had moved into the area. The night noises were not as loud in this part of the woods, making it easier to hear the knocking. It sounded like someone had picked up a stick and was striking a tree with it. It echoed through the woods and continued for several minutes. Jack looked around the trail, but all he saw on either side of the path were trees without end.

The density of the woods told him he was deep into the forest now. Interestingly, as he walked, he realized the path seemed a little easier to navigate. It was almost as if someone had been on it recently. He wasn't much of a tracker, but there were no signs of broken branches, footprints, or other indications that would support this conclusion. It was weird.

When he scanned the woods on either side of the trail, any light from the moon quickly dissipated, and it was pitch black. However, he'd occasionally see balls of light floating in the surrounding thickets, but he did not know if they were orbs or not. Sometimes they seemed to hover in one spot for a while, and then it was as if they disappeared entirely. Jack pushed one more orange flag into the ground and continued walking on the portion of the footpath that the moon was still illuminating despite the cloud cover.

He hadn't progressed too much further down the trail when he came upon a fourth gate. He could see the outline of the bricks, but without the benefit of the flashlight, there was no way to examine them thoroughly. It was impossible to tell what type of foliage was clinging to the columns, and Jack decided not to explore the bricks with his hands. The last thing he needed right now was to get bitten by something or end up with thorns in his fingers. It probably was just as well because he knew if he found another pentagram on the columns, it would have freaked him out.

He pushed open the heavy iron gates, which groaned as if they were unused for many years. Stacked about waist high was a ring of flat rocks on the ground in front of him. He instantly recognized that he was standing in front of a well. It seemed to be a long way from the house he'd seen earlier, but he did not notice any other structures in the area. He leaned over the wall of the well and stared into the darkness below. Unable to see anything, he felt around on the ground for a stone and dropped it in. He expected to hear a splash, but there was none. He then listened for the thud you would get if the well were dry, but he heard nothing other than the leaves rustling in the wind.

He backed away from the well and took a step toward the trail when he heard a moan. He froze, trying to determine if his mind was playing tricks on him. Then, he heard it again. He was sure he heard something this time, He scanned the clearing, but there was nothing in sight. Looking up at the tree canopy, he expected to see an owl or another animal making the sound, but nothing was there.

All of Jack's senses were on high alert when he heard what sounded like a voice, whispering,

"Go back."

Jack's eyes opened wide, his heart beating faster with every breath he took. He expected to see an apparition or possibly something worse, but all he saw were the shadows cast by trees, which were beginning to look more like people with every second that passed. He turned around to see if the wind might have moved the gate, but it was in the same position where he had left it.

"Go back."

Jack heard the voice clearly, this time in a tone that sounded like someone was pleading with him to leave.

"Who is that?" Jack asked, sure that he didn't really want an answer. It sounded like the voice of a child, and it seemed to be emanating from the well. He leaned over the edge again and peered down into the darkness. As before, he saw nothing.

Jack did a 360-degree turn, scanning the forest, desperately looking for answers. "If someone's there, show yourself, damn it!" he demanded.

This time, the voice was more assertive.

"Go back!"

Jack quickly turned his head and was stunned to see a spirit hovering over the well. It had the face of a child wearing a Native American headdress.

The apparition began floating toward him, and Jack stepped sideways to move away from it. In front of his eyes, the spirit began to change form. Curved horns emerged on the side of its head and a shaggy beard on its chin. Fiery red eyes appeared as if somebody flipped on a light switch. Its nostrils flared, filling the air with a fine mist.

"A buffalo?" Jack whispered.

The head charged.

Jack stumbled backward. The next thing he knew, he was on the ground. Jack could smell the dampness of the grass and feel the moisture on his skin. He jumped back up, frantically looking around for his knapsack. Jack found it lying in the grass and grabbed it. Instinctively, he ran up the path away from the well, too afraid to look back.

The buffalo stopped and transformed back into the spirit of the Native American girl. Unable to follow Jack up the path, the now visible shackles on the ghost's ankles revealed it to be chained to the well. Alsoomse's head dropped in resignation. As she slowly disappeared, Alsoomse wept for her failure to convince the man to leave and for the unfortunate destiny she knew awaited him at the end of the trail.

***

September 21st
Culpeper, Virginia
Time Unknown

Jack wasn't sure how far he had run, but he felt safe enough to stop for a moment. The path was beginning to take a turn to the right, becoming difficult to follow and forcing him to slow down to ensure he didn't stray off it altogether. The full moon seemed even more prominent now, and it had taken on a yellow hue. He found it difficult not to think about what he had just experienced, but he managed to convince himself it was nothing more than his overactive imagination. His thoughts turned to Amanda, and she was likely to be growing concerned right now, but something inside of him that he could not explain kept driving him forward.

The narrowing trail caused Jack to recognize that they would've had to walk single file if he had brought company with him on this adventure. The trees clumped closely together, created a claustrophobic feeling. He tried to pick up the pace to get through this area as fast as possible. He felt like something was watching him. Truthfully, if something or someone wanted to grab him, he'd never see them coming.

He'd heard continuous noises from the woods almost since he'd passed the fourth gate. They sounded like growls. He was continually surveying the forest for evidence of an animal, but nothing moved, at least nothing that he could see. The noises didn't sound like they were near him, but he couldn't figure out what might be making them. A dog seemed highly unlikely, and he was unsure what other animals might be in these woods that would make such sounds.

The path straightened out once more, and the moonlight revealed a structure on the left side of the trail. As Jack got closer, he could see it was a small cabin—and yet another gate. The gate was open, the columns devoid of vegetation, unlike the previous gates. He stopped to examine the brickwork and ran his hands around the columns, searching for an embedded iron disc. He found one on the side of the column that the moon could not illuminate. It felt like it had something etched on it, but he couldn't determine if it was a symbol of a pentagram or not.

Jack walked through the gate and made his way over to the cabin. The door was ajar, and he slowly pushed it open and stuck his head in the doorway. He paused for a minute, allowing his eyes to adjust to the darkness inside the building, then stepped in.

The cabin was small. It was only one room, and the wall on the right side had an intact but dusty window. A table stood in the middle of the room, with nothing on it. Jack looked past the table to the far wall and saw several objects piled against it.

He stepped around the table toward the wall and knelt on the floor. The objects were shoes and clothing. The clothing was in a pile about four to five feet tall, but the boots were all neatly stored on the floor. He estimated there could be up to fifty pairs of shoes, maybe more. Jack was trying to process this when he looked to his left and saw an even more unsettling sight: bars and an iron door. It looked like a prison cell. He got back on his feet and went over to investigate it further.

As he approached the iron door, he saw something on the floor in the right rear corner of the cell. He tried to open the door but found it locked. His hands gripped the bars as he tried to find a way to get a closer look at what was in the corner. He moved to his right and peered inside the compartment.

It was a skeleton.

Stepping backward, he almost knocked over the table. Jack knew he should be running out of the cabin, but instead, he found himself searching for a key or some other way to open the door to the cell.

Jack looked around the entire cabin before finding a set of keys hanging on the wall opposite the cell. He removed the keys from their hook and made his way over to the door. Jack placed a key in the lock, carefully turned it back and forth, and heard a click. He stepped into the cell and slowly went over to the body in the corner. Jack had never seen a real skeleton before. Perhaps this could have been a leftover from some teenage stunt, but that seemed highly unlikely based on what he'd already witnessed this evening.

The skeleton had no skin or hair and was still clothed, although the pants and shirts were more rags than clothes. Jack suspected whoever this was had been here for some time. He started looking around the cell for anything that might give him some information about the identity of this person. Scanning the wall of the cell, Jack came across scratches above the shoulder of the skeleton. He tried to sound out what he saw. *"Diabolus Enim Hic,"* and then *"Porta Inferi."* It appeared to be a language of some sort, but it was nothing with which Jack was familiar.

Jack backed out of the cell and shut the door, although he was unsure why he did so. He made his way out of the cabin and stood by the gate. He waited for a moment, thinking about the entirety of what he had seen thus far.

What had started as a research project for a book appeared to be evolving into something much more. Jack recalled what he'd read about no one ever going past the fifth gate, or at least no one ever returning to tell about it. Jack was very uneasy about what he experienced thus far. The problem was he couldn't be sure if he were more afraid of the darkness that permeated the surrounding landscape or what might be lurking in it.

He took a deep breath, and as he walked, tried not to worry about what he might find ahead.

***

Father Desmond studied Jack over his pizza, taking in everything he said.

"The language is Latin, Jack," he said finally. "I studied it while I was in seminary. Up until modern times, Latin was the language used by priests to perform a Catholic mass. In English, *'Diabolus Enim Hic'* translates to 'Devil is here,' and *'Porta Inferi'* means 'Gate of Hell.'"

"I'm not surprised," Jack replied. "Once I finish, I know you'll understand."

Father Desmond sat back in his chair. "What I have heard already tells me that this is an unholy place, so I am not surprised either."

His gaze drifted down to the table. What Father Desmond did not tell Jack was his fear that this prisoner was someone he once knew and that he may have been responsible for their death.

Chapter 11

Jack was sure that he smelled smoke, but there was no sign of a fire anywhere. The last few weeks had seen plenty of rainfall, so it was unlikely to be a brush fire. Jack was feeling jittery. He didn't know what to expect, and if the legend of the seven gates of Hell were correct—so far, things sure seemed to be following the script pretty closely—he had reason to be on edge.

The ground began to turn soft and muddy, and he heard the sound of water. As he neared another bend in the trail, he saw a fast-running stream that was clearly much deeper than the previous one. The sound of the water tumbling over the rocks was somehow soothing and helped to steady his nerves. The trail ran parallel to the stream for a short distance, and eventually, the two merged at a bridge. In front of the bridge was another gate.

Despite its age, the bridge appeared to be passable. At least Jack wouldn't have to run the risk of getting wet, which was a relief as the wind was continuing to pick up. There was little tree cover around the bridge, allowing the moonlight to illuminate Jack's location. The gate was open, and Jack inspected it closely. It was precisely like the others he'd encountered, right down to the brick columns to which it was attached. He studied the pillars and found another inset iron circle, and this time he could easily make out the shape of a pentagram.

Hurriedly started over the bridge before he lost his nerve. When he reached the other side, he instantly wished he hadn't made the crossing. To his right, skeletal remains littered the grass. There were piles of bones everywhere, as well as some intact skeletons. Whoever these poor souls were, they had died where they fell. Jack recalled the shoes and the clothing in the cabin and wondered if it were possible that he had stumbled across an undiscovered Civil War battlefield. He knelt to inspect some of the remains and found, however, that the clothing was modern.

Jack stood and turned to see if there might be more bodies behind him. The bodies were scary enough, but now he was staring at church pews, arranged in rows as if they were ready for a religious service. An aisle led to an altar set up in a small, open-faced structure. Above the altar was a cross hanging in an upside-down position.

His mouth dropped open. *What the hell is going on here?*

Jack started down the aisle. In some of the pews sat skeletons. It appeared someone had taken the dead and assembled them in the pews as witnesses of a ceremony of some kind. Arriving at the altar, he found it was constructed of stacked stones and covered in a dark substance. Jack reached out to touch it, and it was tacky. He brought his fingers up to his eyes to get a better look, and he could swear that it looked like blood.

Every instinct told him to run. However, he was concerned about stepping on the remains that littered the ground. A twisted ankle was a real possibility, and it felt disrespectful to step among the dead haphazardly. Cautiously, he made his way back down the aisle to the path.

A screech broke the silence, and he flinched. Frantically, he looked around the woods for an explanation. Jack finally realized, with a flood of relief, that it was an owl.

In that instant, Jack decided that this book was not worth all this, and it was time to go home. He'd seen more than he ever imagined or wanted to see. Much of it would stick with him forever. At that moment, a bone-chilling scream pierced the night air. It was a cry of anguish, unlike anything he'd heard before. He instantly turned in the direction the cry had originated from and noticed a bright glow in the distance. Instinctively, Jack hurriedly began running toward the sound he'd heard.

Jack ran as quickly as the terrain would allow. The undergrowth made that problematic, but if someone were hurt or needed help, he wanted to find them as soon as possible. Further up the path, the smoke got thicker and the smell of it more pungent. He'd checked the weather forecast before he left, and it had made no mention of a storm, but the moon had disappeared behind heavy cloud cover, and the wind was whistling through the trees as if a storm were approaching.

Perhaps fortuitously, the path was illuminated by whatever was happening ahead. The trail began to turn slightly to the left, and when the wind would die down enough, Jack could hear noises in the air. He could not quite make out what the noises were, but it was repetitive, the same beat and volume over and over again. While Jack was running, he constantly scanned for any sign of an injured person. The only thing he saw was more skeletal remains in the woods, scattered among the trees.

For the first time in a while, the path became devoid of vegetation, and he could move freely. The route was more dirt than grass, and the ground was hard under his feet, indicating routine foot traffic in this area. Until now, the path had a slight incline, but it had flattened out. As a result, he had a clearer view of what was ahead of him. The smell in the air confirmed that a fire was burning, and through the smoky haze, he saw a large hill. *Could this be the Manahoac ground?*

The noises were becoming louder and more precise. It sounded like monks chanting. He was sure he overheard these phrases *"Ave Satanas, Pater de Tenebris"* repeated over and over again.

The pitch of the voices never changed. There was no vocal variation, and it droned on, almost hypnotically. If Jack were home, it was the type of monotone sound that could put him to sleep. But Jack knew he was not home, and he was feeling very much like he did not belong here.

Jack had not forgotten there was an injured party somewhere in the area, but he found it odd that there was no trace of blood or anything else that indicated someone was injured. He wanted to act with a sense of urgency, but he deliberately slowed his pace as he was just not sure what he might see. His mouth was dry, and he longed for another bottle of water. The tree canopy surrounding the path opened up, and in front of him was a sizeable treeless hill covered with grass. An iron fence encircled it, and from Jack's vantage point, looked to be of the same metal as the gates he had encountered along the way.

Several stone markers lay beyond the fence. They were tombstones, and Jack was able to read the names on two of them.

Thomas Manning
Here Lies Thomas Manning, a true friend... until the end.

The next marker just had the name *Paul Sullivan* inscribed on it. There was no epitaph. The final grave marker was blank, and it sat in front of an open hole.

Every second, things were getting more and more bizarre. Jack had officially moved from frightened to scared out of his mind. Several questions, in rapid succession, were going through his head.

What are tombstones doing in what's supposed to be a Native American burial ground?

Who are the people buried there? Those names are certainly not Native American... but they're somehow familiar to me.

Why is there an open grave?

Where is the person who screamed?

Who is chanting?

Why in the name of all that is holy am I still out here?

Jack really didn't want to know the answers. The chanting had grown louder, and it sounded like it was coming from the right side of the mound. He crept into the woods, seemingly unnoticed. Slowly, he moved through the brush, trying not to make a sound.

It took only a few minutes, but it seemed like hours before Jack could find a place where he could observe the chanters. Everything he'd seen so far was shocking, but none of it prepared him for what he witnessed.

There were six figures in brown robes. Their hoods hung in such a way that their facial features were not visible. One of them held open a book for the tallest individual, who read and recited something from the text. What the leader said was inaudible, but the other figures were walking in a circle, continuing to chant, *"Ave Satanas, Pater de Tenebris."*

As Jack processed what he was watching, he looked to the ground and saw a circle with a pentagram embedded in it. At the end of each point of the pentagram were large torches. That explained the smoke, but Jack now saw the source of the screaming, a figure secured tightly to the pentagram. He was blindfolded, gagged, and thrashing around in an attempt to free himself.

During his research, Jack had come across descriptions of a black mass. The rite intended to mock God and the church, right down to using the consecrated host/wafers as part of the ceremony. There were numerous variations of the ritual, dating back to medieval times, but it likely went back as far as Lucifer's fall from heaven itself. What Jack was witnessing seemed to qualify as a black mass, but he thought this ceremony always took place around 3:00 to 3:15 a.m. There was no way it could be that late.

Suddenly, the four hooded figures stopped moving and chanting. The tallest participant, the leader, read from the book. *"In nomine magni dei nostri Satanas, introibo ad altare Domini Inferi."*

All five of the participants replied in unison, *"Rege Satanas."*

A flash of lightning lit up the sky, and the thunder rolled. The wind roared through the trees, causing them to creak. Jack thought they'd snap from the gusts' intensity, which fanned the fire in the torches, increasing the flames' size and strength. He searched the sky warily. Meanwhile, he tried to develop a plan to rescue the person tied to the pentagram, who had to be beyond terrified at this point.

The leader pulled out what appeared to be a knife. What emerged from under the robe looked like a claw and not a human hand. Jack observed in horror as the figure raised the knife above his head, ready to plunge it into the person tied to the pentagram.

Jack could sit back no longer. "NOOO!" he screamed.

The leader immediately stopped and, along with the other participants, looked in Jack's direction.

The figure locked eyes with Jack. Jack stepped back when he saw that they were blood red. The leader and his followers all pulled back the hoods on their robes.

All had red eyes like the leader. Their skin, if you could call it that, was black and looked reptilian, with raised bumps similar to that of an alligator. Their hands had fingers, but they were elongated and had claw-like fingernails. Their faces were dominated by the oversized canines that emerged prominently from their lower jaw.

Their heads were hairless and their ears large and pointed as you might see on a Doberman. While the leader was the tallest of them, Jack estimated that each figure was taller than six feet. Jack started to backpedal and fell onto the ground. He quickly got to his feet and retreated into the woods. Whatever these things were, they just kept staring at him and made no move in his direction.

After what seemed like an eternity, the leader let out a howl, not unlike a coyote. Immediately, two animals appeared on either side of the leader, one part dog, and another wolf. Their size rivaled that of a Great Dane, and the hair on both animals was jet black. Their glowing red eyes matched those of their master. The beasts bared their teeth, and saliva dripped from their jaws as they growled and snarled. Their muscles tensed as they waited for instructions from the leader.

Now paralyzed with fear, Jack couldn't figure out what the leader was doing. Then the figure began to laugh. It had a menacing and malevolent tone to it.

That was enough for Jack. He began to back further into the woods and glanced around for the trail. The leader spoke and motioned toward Jack with his hand. The two animals moved forward, growling loudly. Jack found the path, and while he recalled that it was best to stand your ground when confronted by wild animals, he wasn't sure that mantra applied to supernatural beasts. He started to run, the animals in pursuit.

As Jack fled, all he could hear was that horrific laugh echoing through the trees.

Jack ran toward the bridge. He knew the two Hell Hounds were right behind him, but he didn't want to turn around and find out just how close they might be. He heard footsteps, but there was no way to know if they were the beings he saw at the burial mound or the beasts. The wind had picked up significantly, and the trees groaned as it tore at the leaves and branches. At least that terrible laughing had stopped, but now he could hear the sound of drums, Native American drums.

As he passed the church pews, he saw that the altar was now bathed in a red light that wasn't there earlier, and the benches were full of figures. Jack continued running and tried not to bring any attention to himself. Whatever or whoever was in the pews, however, turned to look at him. There were no faces on any of the attendees of the perverse ceremony. Their yellow eyes staring at him, Jack raced across the bridge as quickly as his feet would take him.

After carefully navigating the muddy path next to the creek, the overgrowth forced Jack to slow down. The temperature had dropped, and the sweat on his body caused him to shiver. The woods were now alive, and every manner of creepy crawler seemed to be at his feet or flying around his head. Jack heard a howl that sounded like it was right behind him, and he was on the verge of panicking. He struggled to keep his wits about him and focus on making his way through the brush.

He was closing in on the cabin where he'd found the skeleton in the cell. The weather was getting worse. It had started to rain, and the wind was blowing it sideways into his face. Visibility was almost nil now, and he was equally scared about what might be ahead in addition to what was chasing him. Near the cabin, he saw two red eyes ahead of him on the trail. The entity snarled.

How did this monster get ahead of me? Shouldn't this underbrush slow up the "Hell Hounds" as much as it's impacting me?

Jack stopped in his tracks and looked around for an alternative route. There, to his left. He never stopped looking at the red eyes glaring at him as he carefully stepped into the trees next to the path.

The storm was now immediately overhead, and the lightning illuminated the sky, followed by claps of thunder that shook the ground beneath him.

There was no sign that the animal that crossed his path had followed him, so Jack slowed his pace to catch his breath. The rain was coming down harder now, and the ground was turning to muck. He slipped and fell in the mud several times. It smelled putrid, and he was thankful the rain helped keep the odor down as he thought it might make him vomit. He ran to a small clearing among the trees and found a camp with several tents. The flaps were open, but there was no one in them. He was thankful for that as he was terror-stricken already. As he passed by the tents, he saw holes in them, suggesting that this abandoned camp had been here for some time and the tents would not provide any substantial shelter from the storm.

Just then, a loud clap of thunder caused Jack to jump. A bolt of lightning struck a tree in front of him. He looked at the tree, and it was engulfed in flames but was not burning. Something was oozing from the bark. He couldn't get too close to the tree itself due to the fire, but the substance oozing from it was dark and congealed, like blood.

The thunder continued to rumble, and another burst of lightning illuminated the night sky. Jack used it to reorient himself and headed away from the campsite in a direction that he thought would take him back to the trail and, hopefully, to his car.

The rain began to let up as Jack slogged his way through the woods. He was moving as quickly as he could despite the terrain, but it wasn't fast enough as far as Jack was concerned. He just hoped he was heading in the right direction, but there really was no way to know for sure. The rain had masked the forest noises, but they were as loud as ever now that the rain was tapering off. Yet, the screams and wails reverberating through the trees were even more deafening. The cries were from souls in agonizing pain. It took all the strength that Jack could muster to bear the sounds of their torture.

Suddenly, the woods took on a greenish, yellow hue, and dozens of apparitions appeared and surrounded Jack. They looked like Civil War soldiers and were marching in formation. Seemingly unaware of his presence, the headless soldiers kept moving forward until they eventually disappeared into thin air. As one group would fade, another would appear at the end of the formation to replace them.

Jack decided to move in a direction that took him away from the decapitated specters. The storm was still circling the woods, and a mist hung in the air. A few minutes later, he saw an orange flag. He'd found the trail again! He was still scared, but there was a sense of relief as the area looked familiar, and he thought he saw the mansion in the woods, which he had seen earlier. The massive oak tree he'd noticed previously loomed ahead.

He'd made a joke about a hangman's noose when he'd seen the tree, but a flash of lightning told him this was no longer a laughing matter. The tree was now dead, and the upper branches were full of crows. From its thickest limb hung a noose. Every lightning flash revealed a body whose tattered clothing blew in the breeze as it swayed back and forth at the end of the rope. Jack couldn't believe his eyes, and a scream died in his throat when he heard the growls. He turned to see both Hell Hounds staring at him with their blood-red eyes.

Too spent to think straight, Jack instinctively took off. He was beyond exhausted, but his body was pumping massive amounts of adrenaline through his system. The hounds were closing in on him, and at one point, he was sure he felt their breath on his neck. As he neared the first bridge, he ran into a large patch of ground fog hovering around his waist. He slowed his pace and tried to use the mist as a cover so that he might be less easy to track.

While getting wet had concerned him earlier, he wasn't worried about that now. He arrived at the creek and jumped into the water. It was up to his knees as he staggered across the stream to the opposite side. He crawled up the bank and paused briefly to listen for the hounds. He heard nothing but the crickets and tree frogs. He spun around and immediately started to sink. Before he could react, he was waist-deep in a bog, and suddenly his fatigue seemed to catch up with him. He was pulled down further into the muck, and the more he struggled to extricate himself, the deeper he sank.

Jack tried not to panic as he knew losing control of his emotions would be deadly. He kept still and looked around to see what he might be able to use to pull himself free from the mire. Fortunately, his arms were free, and Jack started to feel around for solid ground. He found some behind him and slowly turned himself around. His right hand found what felt like a tree root. He grabbed it with his fingers to see if it would give him enough leverage to pull himself out. Slowly, he began to move toward solid ground. Bit by bit, he pulled to extricate himself and finally rolled out of the muck onto the creek bank.

Lying on his back, Jack tried to rest long enough to gather his strength. He knew he was a goner if the hounds or any other ghost, ghoul, or monster were to show up at that moment. It was raining again, and he opened his mouth in an attempt to quench the intense thirst that was permeating his body. He was drenched and smelled of rotting and decomposing filth. He knew he needed to get to his feet and find the path as soon as possible. With just a little luck, he would be back on the road and on his way to the car. He got up off the ground and stumbled forward.

Just as it had done earlier, the thick undergrowth slowed his progress. The thorns surrounding the path scratched his arms and face, and his muscles ached. Providentially, he was finding the orange flags he'd left for himself, and eventually, he found his way back to the two large rocks and the Bradford Family Cemetery.

Jack leaned against the rocks. The wind was still gusting, but the rain had stopped. The clouds had dissipated, and the full moon was once again dominating the night sky. The storm appeared to be over, and for a minute, he thought his ordeal might finally be coming to an end, but then he heard it again.

That laugh. That spine-chilling, evil laugh. It echoed all around. Jack pushed off the rock he was leaning against and made his way past the cemetery. He found the gravel road and the high grass that he'd carved his way through near Route 666. Finally, he was back on the road.

He was ready to make his move toward the car when he caught something out of the corner of his eye, stepping out of the brush. The figure he had encountered at the burial mound was on the road, staring at him. Then, two other entities stepped out from behind the figure—those damn Hell Hounds that had been pursuing him all night.

Jack was both perplexed and terrified. He kept hoping he'd suddenly wake up in his bed and realize this was all a terrible nightmare, but it was the most realistic nightmare he had ever experienced. This hideous creature was intensely staring Jack down. After what seemed like an eternity, the figure said something to the two animals, who slowly walked in Jack's direction. Their red eyes glared at him, and they each let out a low growl as they continued to move forward. Jack knew all along that attempting to fight them off was not an option, so he took off running at full speed. The hounds immediately took off in pursuit.

Jack felt like his chest was going to explode, and if he did not find his car soon, then to say this was going to end badly would be an understatement. He could hear the beasts barking, which meant they were closing in on him. Still running as fast as possible, Jack checked his pockets and was relieved to find his car keys. He found the button that could open the door remotely. Jack took a chance that the car was within range and pressed the button. A short distance away, he saw the white headlights and red taillights blink. Then the barricade came into view. He quickly glanced behind him to see how close his adversaries were and raced to the wall. Just as he pulled himself over the top, the two hounds slammed into the barricade, snapping and clawing at his feet.

Jack dropped to the ground and could hear the frantic barking and growling. He was pretty sure these two beasts could have made it over the barricade, but for some reason, they made no effort to do so. Regardless, Jack was thankful they didn't follow him. As he scrambled to get up, he hit the button on the key again and heard the door locks release. He stumbled to the car, flung the driver's side door open, and sat behind the wheel.

Slamming the door, his nerves completely frayed; Jack fumbled to get the key into the ignition. The engine turned over immediately, and he put the car in reverse and hit the gas. He then put the car into drive and floored the pedal. The rear wheels spun rapidly, kicking up sand and gravel from the road surface. The car's rear fishtailed as he sped away from the barricade, making his way back to Lee Highway.

Jack started to calm down when he looked in his rearview mirror and saw nothing following him. He was approaching the intersection with Lee Highway and saw the red light turn to green. *Something finally went right tonight.*

As he made the left turn, at a high rate of speed, he glanced at the clock. The time read 3:00 a.m.

"That's not possible," he muttered. "There's no way I was in the woods for more than ten hours!"

Just then, the radio turned itself on, and harsh static came out of the speakers. Jack jumped, nearly losing control of the car. He reached the bridge over the Rappahannock River, and as soon as he was over it, saw red lights in his rearview mirror. He was never so relieved to see a police car in his life, and this was one ticket he was going to be happy to pay.

He pulled the car over to the shoulder of the road, and the police car parked behind him. A friend had taught him that if a police officer pulled him over to keep his hands on top of the steering wheel, so they were visible to the officer. He hit the button to lower his window and placed his hands on the wheel.

In his side-view mirror, Jack watched the police officer exit his vehicle, shut his door, and start towards him. There were no other vehicles on the road, and the night was quiet now. He heard the officer's footsteps approaching the window. The footsteps stopped, and Jack turned to acknowledge the officer. At the same time, the officer leaned through the window.

Jack came face to face with one of the hideous beings he had seen at the burial mound. It placed its long fingers on the door and reached for the handle to open it. He screamed, hit the gas pedal, and took off down the highway.

Jack pushed his car to its limits. He continued to search for the police car, sure that it would follow him, but there were no signs of it anywhere. Jack now had the entire road to himself. All he wanted to do was to get home, and nothing was going to get in his way. Exhausted, Jack pressed the button to open the passenger side window, hoping the fresh air would keep him awake. He kept pushing the button, but nothing was happening. He looked toward the passenger side window, and Lucius Rofocale, the museum curator, was in the seat next to him.

"Lucius, is that you? It cannot be you, can it?"

Lucius, or whatever this being was, did not respond.

Jack rubbed his eyes and made sure to focus on the road. He glanced over to the seat again, and it was empty. *Did I see what I thought I saw?* It had to be fatigue, he thought. He tried to open the window again, but it wouldn't budge. He glanced at the passenger side once more, and he almost lost control of the car.

In a split second, they somehow switched positions, and the leader from the burial mound was now driving the vehicle, Jack in the passenger seat next to him. Jack could feel the pure evil emanating from this figure. Its red eyes felt like they were drilling a hole right through him.

"WHAT THE HELL ARE YOU?" he yelled.

The entity started to laugh at him in that same menacing tone. The laughing grew louder and began to hurt Jack's ears. Simultaneously, the figure was causing the car to weave in and out of its lane.

Finally, the sound of the laughter became too intense. Despite his instinct to grab the wheel and restore control over the vehicle, Jack's hands instead covered his ears in an attempt to relieve the agony. Closing his eyes, he said a silent prayer as the car spun out of control.

Jack screamed, but it was as if he made no sound. All he heard was that horrible laugh echoing in his head.

Chapter 12

Jack swallowed the last mouthful of his beer and set the empty bottle on the table. The plate before him contained a half-eaten slice of pizza. Father Desmond had been correct—the pizza was excellent—but as Jack continued to pour his soul out to Father Desmond, he'd lost his appetite. At least he'd eaten enough to ensure the beers and shots he'd downed wouldn't result in a headache in the morning, but he was hoping they might deaden some of the pain that came with telling his story.

Father Desmond finished his beer. "How about some coffee? I could use a cup."

"Sure, Father. The pizza was delicious. I'm just sorry I didn't have much of an appetite."

"I understand. I know all of this is hard to talk about, but it can be cathartic to share your burdens with someone else. Sometimes just knowing that you are not bearing the weight of such a load on your own can help."

As Jack listened, his thoughts drifted back to Amanda and the boys. Where were they? Were they okay? There were so many fears and concerns running through his head at the moment. He was acutely aware that every minute that passed was precious time he was losing in his efforts to save Amanda and his sons.

During his bouts of depression, he'd often search the Internet looking for answers to the questions troubling his mind. He recalled a quote he came across from the author Laura Wiess:

"Time is not your friend. It doesn't care if you live fast or die slow, if you are or if you aren't. It was here before you arrived, and it will go on after you leave."

Jack couldn't help but make the connection between Ms. Wiess's description of time and its similarity to Lucius himself. Time, like Lucius, was his enemy, yet he still had so much to tell Father Desmond. He knew this was going to be another long and sleepless night.

"Father, I just wish that I had a crystal ball so I could see Amanda and the boys and make sure they are okay. I have assurances that if I comply with Lucius's demand, they will remain unharmed, but I don't have to tell you that taking the word of a demon is not very reassuring."

"I know this seems cliché, but you must keep your faith. There is a reason that you got in touch with me. I don't think it was a coincidence, and I am going to do all that I can to help you and your family."

Jack looked down at the table. "Thank you, Father."

***

September 23rd
Bristow, Virginia, 30 miles west of Washington, DC
10:00 a.m.

Jack awoke bewildered and found Amanda with her hands on his shoulders, shaking him. She was shouting his name to get his attention. She kept saying everything was okay and he needed to calm down. His eyes darted around the room. It felt like his heart was beating out of his chest.

"What? What's going on? Where am I?"

Amanda wrapped him in a hug to soothe his concerns. He continued looking around and finally realized he was in his bedroom. Closing his eyes, he held Amanda tightly.

A few moments later, he asked, "I know this will sound crazy, but am I really here? Is this real, or am I dreaming?"

Amanda continued to hold him. "Jack, everything is okay. You're home, in our bed. Trust me. You are not in a dream. I'm so relieved that you are okay."

Jack gently pushed her back so he could look into her eyes. "Amanda, how did I get into bed? The last thing I remember was almost crashing on Route 29."

"What? Jack, the boys, and I found your car in the driveway, and you passed out in the driver's seat. When we opened the door, you started muttering something. It sounded like '*Diablo*' or something similar to that. The boys helped me carry you into the house and up the stairs. I put your car in the garage and opened the windows. Jack, the smell when we opened the car door was indescribable. Like Sulphur, but more intense than anything I've ever smelled before. It was like dozens of rotten eggs had been baking in the summer heat in your back seat for a year."

Jack pulled the sheets back and sat on the edge of the bed. He was about to get up when Amanda said, "Jack, you have been asleep for nearly two days."

He shook his head and looked at her, incredulous. "What? That cannot be possible."

"I called the office and told them you weren't feeling well. They were shocked. Did you know this is the first time you've called in sick in the fifteen years you've been working at the agency?"

Jack continued to shake his head, trying to make sense of what Amanda was telling him. *How could I have been asleep for two days?*

The two of them sat together for several minutes until Amanda broke the silence. "Jack, what happened? I was so worried that night when you did not come home. When we found you in the car in the morning, I was relieved, but the state you were in was alarming. You were incoherent. I gave serious consideration to taking you to the emergency room but decided against it since I wouldn't have been able to explain your condition or how you got that way."

Jack tried to recall what had occurred, but he struggled with the details. He remembered walking on Route 666 and finding the two rocks that marked the path on the map. Things after that were hazy. He questioned if what he remembered was real or if it had been a nightmare. He closed his eyes, and images of a body hanging in a tree, a cabin with a prison cell, and other strange events flooded his thoughts.

It was difficult separating what might have been fact versus what may or may not have been fiction. Thinking about it gave Jack a headache. He just wanted to take a shower and clean up. He saw the scratches on his arms, his back hurt, and his legs were sore. He glanced into the bathroom and saw a pair of dirty jeans.

Amanda saw him looking at the pants. "I kept the jeans, but I have no idea how I'll get them clean. I don't know what you got yourself into out there, but your clothes were an absolute mess. I have washed them repeatedly, but that smell from the car must have embedded itself in the fabric. If it's okay with you, I would like just to throw them out."

Jack nodded. "I'm sorry for making you worry. I'm going to take a shower."

"Good idea, Jack. Are you hungry? I could fix you something to eat. It's almost noon. Maybe we can talk a little more after that?"

Jack smiled weakly. "Thanks. I am a little hungry. I'll clean up and be down in a few minutes. Just a sandwich and a few Tylenol will be fine."

Amanda went downstairs and Jack headed into the bathroom. As he stood in the shower, more and more details of what happened in the woods began to come back to him. He remembered finding the burial mound and a person tied down on a pentagram. All at once, memories of hooded figures, Hell Hounds, and worst of all, that horrible laugh came flooding back to him.

Trembling, he slumped down in the corner of the shower. As the water cascaded over him, he sat, paralyzed with fear.

"Jack, lunch is ready."

He jerked back to reality at the sound of Amanda's voice. He needed to compose himself before he went downstairs. Amanda could read him like a book, and she'd know something was wrong. He finished his shower, dressed, and went downstairs.

"Your food is on the table out on the deck. I thought it might be easier for us to talk out there."

Jack sat at the table and stared at the sandwich in front of him.

Amanda sat across from him. "So, Jack, what happened?"

For one of the few times in his life, Jack decided to hide the truth from Amanda.

"I got lost in the woods and probably got disoriented from dehydration. I should've taken a few more bottles of water with me."

"You didn't find anything out there?" she asked, disbelief in her voice. Jack needed to be more convincing.

"Just some empty buildings and a lot of overgrowth."

Showing Amanda his arms, he said, "That's how I got all of these scratches." He picked up his sandwich. "No trace of a Native American burial ground." Taking a small bite, he continued, "Or anything else for that matter."

Finally, Jack looked Amanda straight in the eyes and told her what he knew she wanted to hear.

"I've decided to give up writing the book."

"Not that I'm too upset about that, but why, Jack?"

"There's no story to tell and, therefore, no book to write."

Amanda smiled and appeared to be relieved.

He stared at the deep blue sky over Amanda's shoulder and slowly ate his sandwich. At that moment, he felt not relief but a sense of foreboding. He just hoped that somehow, he would be able to forget the horror of what he'd experienced.

Mark's voice drifted in, "What happened after you spoke with Amanda?"

Jack took a breath, exhaled, and said, "Actually, for the first few days after, things were quiet and seemed to go back to normal. I took the rest of that week off, my first extended vacation in years. I worked outside cleaning up my garden, and soon, the events of September 21st began to fade, at least during the day anyway."

Father Desmond raised a questioning eyebrow.

Jack fidgeted in his chair. "I could handle the daytime, but the nighttime would come around way too soon. I've never had problems sleeping. I have slept through earthquakes, fire alarms outside my dorm room, and even gunshots, but I started having difficulty falling asleep, and once I did, staying that way. Even after I thought I slept through the night, I'd wake up in the morning totally exhausted. It was not normal, at least for me."

Father Desmond rubbed his chin, considering what Jack told him. "Were you having any nightmares or flashbacks?"

Jack shook his head. "That may have been the strangest part of all. I couldn't remember anything. I knew that something was impacting my sleep patterns, but I wasn't able to articulate what it was."

He was perplexed. He was not sure that Jack's inability to remember had any real significance, but it was odd. He conceded that the human mind was a complicated thing, and perhaps this was a defense mechanism to protect Jack from the trauma he had experienced.

"However," Jack continued, "it didn't take long for everything to start to change. It started slowly, but things began to escalate, and eventually, they reached an alarming level. It got to the point that I began to wish that I would go back to not being able to remember anything."

***

October 1st–October 8th
Bristow, Virginia, 30 miles west of Washington, DC

Jack sat on the couch in the family room, watching the football game. Amanda and the boys had gone to Walmart, and he was enjoying a respite from the usual excitement and chaos that came with raising two teenage boys. Typically, he would've put his feet up on the ottoman and gotten comfortable, but Ivy, the family cat, had claimed that spot and was sprawled out on it fast asleep.

Several years ago, Ivy had gotten David's attention at the animal shelter, and she turned out to be the perfect fit for their household. She had the ideal disposition and was highly tolerant of the boys, particularly David, who could be a little rough with her. Ivy never scratched or tried to bite and purred continuously. As a matter of fact, she seemed to be a glutton for punishment. Regardless of where Ivy was, if she saw or heard David sit on the floor, she'd immediately come to lay down next to him. There was little doubt that she was David's cat.

Ivy had been asleep for some time, and her twitching was generally an indication that she was in a deep sleep. So, it was unusual when she quickly jumped up and turned to stare into the far corner of the room. She started to hiss, and her fur stood up on end. Jack's experience was that only two things could provoke Ivy in this way, and that was another cat or a dog. Jack got up to look out the sliding glass doors, and there was no evidence that either of these two animals was creeping around outside.

Jack called out to Ivy, "What's the matter, girl?"

But she just continued to stare into the corner. Jack looked in the same direction, and he saw nothing. Then he heard the garage door open. Ivy bolted from the ottoman and ran down the hallway and up the stairs. Jack got up and opened the door to the garage. He'd seen Ivy act crazy in the past, so he didn't think anything of it. Perhaps hearing the garage door had just startled her. He helped Amanda unload the groceries and sat down to finish watching the game.

A few days later, Jack was at work, and the boys were at school. Amanda, who worked part-time from home when she was not a substitute teacher at the high school, was upstairs on her computer. She turned the television on so she would have something to listen to while she was working. Amanda flexed her fingers and stretched. She'd been working for a few hours and needed a break. She glanced over at Jack's desk and saw that the clock was showing

3:00 a.m. Obviously, something was wrong with it. Not only was it the middle of the day, but it also was a digital clock with a battery backup. She checked, and it shared the same surge protector as her computer.

Amanda thought this was strange, but then she heard a noise that caught her attention. She sat still in the chair and heard it again. She got up and turned down the volume on the television. Then, Amanda heard it a third time. It sounded like someone was playing the piano in the living room. Amanda's grandmother had bequeathed it to her, and Amanda herself had learned to play the piano on it. It was something she cherished.

Amanda walked through the bedroom to the hall and started down the stairs. She heard the musical note again. Amanda stepped onto the landing and went into the living room, and found the space was empty. She looked out the window to see if the boys' bus had arrived early, but it was nowhere in sight.

She looked toward the ceiling. "Grandma, is that you? You promised if you were to visit after you were gone that you wouldn't frighten me."

There was nothing but silence, and she didn't hear any other musical notes for the rest of the afternoon.

During dinner that evening, Amanda mentioned to Jack what had occurred earlier that day. After they finished eating, Jack researched the Internet, which provided several potential explanations for this incident, ranging from hammers sitting on the piano strings to fluctuations in the room's humidity levels. Having lived in their Virginia home for over twenty years, Jack did not doubt that the transition from summer to fall could and likely did impact the house's humidity levels.

Jack went upstairs and shared this information with Amanda. He then asked her, "When was the last time we had the piano tuned?"

She thought for a minute. "That must be it, Jack. I haven't had it tuned since it was delivered to us after Grandma passed away. That was more than ten years ago."

Satisfied with that explanation, Jack went back downstairs to pay some bills, and Amanda went back to work. About an hour later, when he was signing the last check, Jack put down his pen and started sniffing the air. The odor was familiar. It smelled like the fireplace was in use, but they hadn't even had the chimney sweep come to the house yet. After a while, though, the smell became more robust, and it was as if something were burning. It smelled like food had been left in the toaster oven too long and was charred to a crisp. As a precaution, he checked the kitchen and then the furnace in the basement, but he smelled nothing down there. When he came back upstairs, the odor was gone.

A few days later, Jack was at work, eating his lunch in his office. He had to admit he was surprised that his book and experiences on Route 666 had not been on his mind more frequently. There were even a few days during the week when he hadn't even thought about it at all. Things seemed to be going back to normal. A sense of relief washed over him, but it was to be short-lived.

That night Jack had a challenging time falling asleep. He was often exhausted by the end of the week, and this one was no exception. Usually, this meant he would fall asleep rather quickly. However, this night he just kept tossing and turning.

Amanda rolled over. "Is something wrong, honey?" she asked. "Are you having trouble falling asleep?"

"Sorry if I'm keeping you up," he said. "I just cannot seem to fall asleep."

Amanda rubbed his back. "How about a sleeping pill? Maybe that will help."

Ordinarily, Jack would have declined, but he decided maybe he should try it. A restful night's sleep was going to do him a world of good. Jack took the pill and faded off to sleep. Unfortunately, pleasant dreams were not what he was about to experience. A real-life nightmare was beginning to unfold.

***

October 29th
Lawrence, Kansas
10:00 PM

Jack shook his head and admonished himself. "I should've seen what was coming next. The nightmare I had that night was like reliving September 21st all over again, but even worse. I woke up just at the point I had seen that being—no, that monster—in my car, but I couldn't move. I was awake but could not scream."

Father Desmond had heard stories like this before. The paranormal community documented a similar condition called sleeping sickness.

He looked at Jack and said, "I know this had to be traumatic, but there is no way you could have known what was going to happen."

Jack became animated. "Father, there were other things that happened that week before the nightmare. There were picture frames turned backward. One morning I couldn't find my car keys."

Father Desmond interjected, "Losing your car keys is not unusual, Jack."

Jack, voice growing increasingly frustrated, continued, "My keys are on the table in the hall all the time. I remember specifically putting them there as I had done every night for years. The next morning, I looked for them for over an hour before I found them. The keys were sitting on the driver's seat as if they had fallen out of my pocket. I never put my keys in my pocket when I come home as I need the key chain control to lock the doors."

Several patrons in the bar glanced over at Jack.

He slumped back in his chair. "I'm sorry, Father. I didn't mean to get upset. It's just frustrating when I look back at it because maybe I could have done something about all of this before it got to where it is now."

Father Desmond put his hands up. "Jack, take it easy. I realize you are under a great deal of pressure. You do not have to apologize to me, but you need to try to stay calm. Mistakes get made when we lose control of our emotions."

Jack took a deep breath, acknowledging Father Desmond's counsel. "You're right, Father. I know you are right. If Amanda, Louis, and David are going to survive this, I have to keep my cool." He stood. "Some fresh air might do me some good. Would you mind if we took this conversation outside and walked around the block or something?"

Father Desmond got up from the table right away. "Let me get my coat."

***

October 9th–October 16th
Bristow, Virginia, 30 miles west of Washington, DC

Jack found himself in bumper-to-bumper traffic on his way to the office. Washington, DC, had a reputation of having some of the country's worst traffic, but having been raised on Long Island, it was like second nature to Jack. He flipped through the radio stations and yawned. Jack had not been sleeping particularly well, and last night's nightmare didn't help. He was still trying to process what had happened. He'd had nightmares before, but not one where he felt like he couldn't get up from the bed or speak.

At that moment, 'Enter Sandman' by Metallica came on the radio. Jack started to laugh as he heard, *"Sleep with one eye open, gripping your pillow tight."* As he pulled into the parking lot at work, he began to think of the day ahead, and the nightmare slipped from his mind.

Later that same night, Amanda and Jack were watching television. David and Louis were downstairs in the basement, playing video games. The lights began to flicker on and off, which was odd, but it was an unusually windy night. Jack had barely clicked the television back on when there was a scream from the basement, and the boys came charging up the stairs.

"What's going on?" Amanda asked.

"Some-some someone in the closet," David stammered.

"Who? What did you see, boys?" Jack asked.

150

"A dark figure," Louis said, eyes wide.

David began hitting his head with his fist. His outburst was not an uncommon reaction in stressful situations. Still, the frequency and level of intensity with which he was self-injuring was a concern to Jack and Amanda.

While trying to comfort David and Louis, Amanda looked at Jack. "They're talking about the unfinished part of the basement. Where the furnace and water heater are located."

"Got it," he acknowledged as he headed down into the basement to check things out.

Jack slowly went down the stairs and looked around the room. The lights were on, and everything appeared to be in order. He then checked the closet. Jack pulled the string that turned on the lights, and he saw nothing. He made his way back upstairs.

"There's nothing down there."

Amanda had managed to calm David down, but both he and Louis refused to go back into the basement, and they decided to go to bed instead.

The following two days were quiet, but Jack was still not sleeping well. He was grateful that he was not having the same nightmare, but he woke up between 3:00 and 3:15 a.m. every night. Jack was not unaware of this time's significance; adherents of the occult referred to it as the witching hour. He had to admit it was spooking him a little. Each night was quiet, but it was almost too silent. He tossed and turned, trying to get comfortable, but it was elusive.

***

On Thursday morning, Amanda was upstairs working. The incident with Louis and David was still on her mind. It was always upsetting to her when David hit his head. Over the years, Amanda, Louis, and David had been through a great deal together, but it was this one behavior of David's that always got to her. If the basement incident were the only thing that had happened recently, she would've found it easier to let David's outburst go, but other things bothered her.

She hadn't said anything to Jack, but she'd had a feeling of being watched for the last several days. It was an uncomfortable feeling like someone was staring at her constantly. However, when she turned around, there was never anything there. Then there were the noises. It sounded like someone was scratching on the wall, and she was sure she heard doors slamming too. She tried not to think about it as she typed, but this was easier said than done.

A few hours later, Amanda was in the kitchen preparing lunch for herself. As she did so, she thought she heard a voice. It sounded like somebody was calling her name.

Then she heard it again. "*Amanda.*"

The voice seemed to be emanating from the basement. Amanda went over to the basement door and slowly opened it.

"*Amanda.*"

The stairs leading down to the basement were dark. Amanda reached for the light switch and flicked it up, but the light did not come on. She continued to gaze down the stairs, and as her eyes adjusted to the darkness, she thought she saw someone or something at the bottom of the stairs.

She asked, "Is anyone there?"

There was silence. Amanda was unable to make out what she saw, but something was moving. Before she could utter another word, whatever she saw suddenly charged up the stairs, knocking her over.

Amanda found herself on the floor, stunned. *What the hell was that?* She looked around the room, and nothing was there. She quickly got to her feet and slammed the basement door shut. She then pushed the latch to lock the door. Her heart was racing. She opened the door that led into the garage, hit the button to open the garage door, and ran out of the house.

Shortly, the boys would be home from school, so she sat down on the front stoop and dialed Jack's work number. It rang several times and went to his voicemail. She left him a message.

"Jack, please call me on my cell phone as soon as possible. I'm alright, but something just happened to me here at the house. I think it might be related to the other things happening over the last two weeks. I know this sounds crazy, but I think the house is...well...haunted."

A few minutes later, Jack returned her call and told her he was on his way. Just then, the bus pulled up, and the boys got out of it. Amanda immediately put them in the car and drove to her mother's house. She left them there and returned home to wait for Jack.

* * *

October 29th
Lawrence, Kansas
11:00 PM

Despite the late hour, the University of Kansas campus was rocking. The men's basketball team, a perennial contender for the national championship, had held its season-opener against Emporia State College in the Allen Fieldhouse. Father Desmond and Jack walked through the campus for nearly an hour, but neither paid attention to the time or the commotion connected to the basketball game. They just continued walking across the university grounds, wrestling with the weight of the burden brought to bear upon both men by Jack's story.

The noise from the basketball game was behind them when Jack began to speak once again,

"When I got home that afternoon, Amanda and I went into the house so she could show me where the most recent activity had occurred. I went to flip the light switch to the basement, and Amanda tried to tell me it was not working, but I flipped it before she could finish her sentence, and the light bulb came on. We looked at one another, and she described for me again what had happened to her earlier that day. I carefully went down the stairs, with Amanda following right behind me. Of course, we found nothing out of place and no sign of whatever it was that had charged at Amanda from the bottom of the stairs."

Jack continued, "We knew we weren't imagining things and decided we needed to get help. The boys stayed with their grandparents, and we contacted a paranormal research group to investigate what was happening. They came to the house on the afternoon of October 17th to set up their equipment. The fall has been unseasonably warm in our area, and that night we had one of the most intense thunder and lightning storms that I can remember. A research team member was a medium, and he told us that he sensed an evil presence in the home. He attempted to communicate with it, and just as he did so, a flash of lightning illuminated the room, and standing there was the outline of a hulking figure with red eyes."

Based on the entity's description, Father Desmond knew it was almost certainly a demonic presence. He shared his insight with Jack then asked him, "What happened next?"

Jack answered, "Honestly, things quickly got out of control."

***

"GET OUT! THEY BELONG TO ME!"

The entity let out a guttural scream, and the whole house shook.

The medium forcefully said, "I demand that you tell us your name, and you must leave this house immediately!"

The entity just laughed.

In a shower of sparks, all of the equipment shorted out, and the smell of Sulfur engulfed the room. The medium was then picked up by an unseen force and violently thrown across the room.

Coming to the medium's aid, the team asked, "Are you alright?"

As they helped him get to his feet, every object in the room, including the furniture, became suspended in mid-air.

"DEATH WILL COME TO ANY WHO REMAIN HERE," the entity thundered.

The medium slowly backed out of the room. "Demon. Only the most powerful of demons have this level of strength and capability," he muttered.

The rest of the paranormal team followed the medium out of the house.

***

"That's how the investigation ended. We never heard from the team after that, and we still had lots of questions and no apparent solutions."

"When did you make the connection between what was happening in your home with Route 666?"

"Looking back on it, I know I should've made the connection when the nightmares started, but I was hoping I was wrong and kept trying to convince myself that I imagined it all. Seeing that figure during the paranormal investigation was the moment I stopped denying it. Something had come home with me the night of September 21st, and we were about to find out what it wanted from us."

***

Night of October 17th
Bristow, Virginia, 30 miles west of Washington, DC

The paranormal investigation had given Jack and Amanda very few answers, and it appeared to worsen an already deteriorating situation. After seeing the entity, it was clearly unsafe to remain in their home, so Jack, Amanda, and the boys stayed in a hotel. That night Jack had a different dream than those he'd been experiencing. He was sitting in his living room, and Lucius Rofocale was in the chair across from him.

Jack looked at him and thought to himself, *I'm dreaming, aren't I?* He then asked, "What are we doing here, Lucius?"

Lucius smiled ominously. "You are a very busy man these days, Jack. It has been challenging to get, shall we say, a personal appointment with you. Your dreams seemed like the most practical way for us to get a little one on one time. I thought you might be more comfortable speaking here. After all, it is your home. I do appreciate your hospitality and allowing my brothers to stay here with you and your family. I hope they have not been too much trouble."

Jack glared at Lucius. "So that was you at the burial mound. I assume then that the entity we saw tonight was one of your brothers. Neither you nor your so-called brothers are welcome here. I want you all out, and I want you to leave my family alone."

Lucius smirked. "How perceptive of you. Yes, Jack. That was me. Your visit was a little unexpected. If I had known you were going to be attending my little gathering, I would have *dressed* more appropriately for the occasion."

Lucius continued, "You are a most inconsiderate host, Jack. After all, you are the one who invited us here."

"I extended no such invitation!"

Lucius shook his head back and forth. "Jack, Jack, Jack. Of course, you did. You even chauffeured us alright to your front door."

Jack growled, "Well, then I un-invite all of you."

Lucius laughed. "Oh, Jack, I am afraid it just is not that simple. I have some work for you to do."

Jack scowled. "Work for you? I'm not going to do anything for you!"

Lucius's demeanor suddenly changed, and he stared Jack down. "Mr. Aitken. You will find that I am not someone to be trifled with, and I do not take well to threats. Well, I think you will find that out soon enough. We will see each other again…soon."

Before he could utter another word, Jack woke up and found himself on the floor—of his living room. It was morning, and the sun was streaming through the windows. He went to sleep last night in a hotel room, so how is it possible he could be back in his own home? He struggled to understand what had happened last night, but he knew it was not just a dream. The odor of Sulphur still hung in the air, and black footprints leading to the door, seared into the carpet, confirmed Lucius had indeed been there. Jack wanted to keep things as normal as possible, so he went upstairs, took a shower, and got ready for work, but Lucius's words continued to echo in Jack's head.

***

October 25th
Route 66 E, Centreville, Virginia
8:00 AM

As Jack drove to work, he wondered if he might be losing his sanity. Every night since the paranormal investigation, he'd been visited by Lucius in his dreams. He incessantly taunted Jack about a face-to-face meeting they'd be having shortly, "in the flesh," as Lucius put it. Of course, Jack reiterated he had no intention of ever meeting Lucius again, but Lucius would laugh, that horrible menacing laugh that turned Jack's blood cold.

He really needed someone to talk to about his nightmares. As he pulled into a parking space, he thought to himself; *I'm sure it would go over well with Dr. Colby if I told her I was having midnight meetings with a demon.*

He reached to open the office door, shook his head, and muttered, "She would have me committed before the appointment was even over." Jack stepped inside and headed down the corridor to the kitchen and put up a pot of coffee. He was going to need it this morning.

The rest of the morning was uneventful, and Jack found himself alone. Usually, his colleagues would be in the office by this time, but it wasn't out of the ordinary for him to be there by himself. He just assumed they were out on sales calls or perhaps had some other matters to handle. It was nearly noon, and he went back to the kitchen to get his lunch out of the microwave. He stepped out for less than a minute, but when he returned, he stopped dead in his tracks. His mouth fell open, and the sound of his soup bowl shattering as it hit the floor echoed through the office.

"Oh my God," he said slowly.

Sitting on the table in his office was a knapsack, the same one he'd lost during his odyssey through the woods. He had forgotten about it until this moment. Jack looked around his office in a panic.

"How is this possible?" he whispered.

The bell that rang if someone entered the office had not gone off. Jack opened the knapsack, and everything, including his cellphone, appeared to be there. He checked the rest of the suite, but there was no one there. The lights that would immediately come on when someone entered any room in the building were dark.

Jack sprinted back to his office and picked up the phone to call Amanda. He was unsure if she was at the school as a substitute teacher today or working from home, so he tried the home number first. The phone rang and rang until the answering machine came on. Jack then called her cell phone. It rang twice and then a voice answered. It was familiar but not the voice he was expecting.

"Good afternoon, Jack," the voice said. "I take it you found your knapsack."

Jack did not need to ask who it was.

"Lucius! Where is Amanda? What have you done to her?"

"Jack, where are your manners? Aren't you going to thank me for returning your property to you?"

Jack slammed his fist down on the desk. "If you have done anything to her, I will—"

"You will what, Jack? What have I told you about making threats? You know, I like you, Jack, but having to repeat myself, well, it irritates me. Now, Amanda is fine…for the moment. If you successfully play your part in the drama that is about to unfold, she will stay that way."

"I am going to kill you, Lucius!" Jack said through gritted teeth. "I am going to rip your heart out if you even have one!"

"Jack, you have tried my patience for the last time. I warned you there were going to be consequences for irritating me. I suggest you make haste and get home, but remember that what you find there is your responsibility."

Jack heard a click, and the line went dead.

Chapter 13

October 25th
Bristow, Virginia, 30 miles west of Washington, DC
12:30 p.m.

The ride home should've only taken Jack twenty-five minutes, but it felt like he would never arrive. Finally, he made the right turn into their subdivision and pulled up in front of the house. He hit the button to open the garage door and sprinted up the driveway. Throwing open the door that led from the garage to the family room, he found the house was silent. He looked around the room, relieved that nothing appeared to be out of place. Jack hit the button to close the garage door, but a ghastly sight met him as he stepped into the kitchen.

A wooden cutting board, embedded with spikes to hold meat in place for carving, was on the kitchen island. An eviscerated animal with gray fur lay upon it, the spikes protruding through its body. The organs were placed neatly on a platter next to the board. Jack stared at the sight in horror.

"Oh, no, it can't be."

As Jack stepped closer to the island, his worst fears were realized.

It was Ivy, the family cat. He stood staring at the beloved pet, trying to compose himself, and the phone suddenly rang. Jack checked the caller ID, recognizing the number immediately.

"So, Jack, do we need to review the code of conduct again, or are we clear on how one should behave?"

Jack took a deep breath before he replied. "Crystal clear."

Lucius's tone darkened. "Crystal clear, what, Mr. Aitken?"

"Crystal clear... sir."

"That is better, Jack. Now, just to be sure we understand one another, I would like you to open an envelope I have left for you on the kitchen table."

He turned and looked at the table. He saw a plain white envelope with his name on it propped up against the Lazy Susan. Jack grabbed the envelope.

"I have it."

"Good, Jack. Now open the envelope."

Inside were pictures of David and Louis being escorted to and forced into the back seat of a dark sedan. Jack was beyond furious now. He was nearly insane with rage. It took every ounce of self-control he could muster not to let Lucius detect even a hint of anger in his voice.

"Lucius, are Amanda and the boys okay?"

Jack could hear the conceit dripping from Lucius's lips. "Yes, Jack. I am pleased that you are able to keep your temper in check. I intended to leave your children out of this affair, but you left me little choice, and I had to take them into custody to ensure your compliance. Poor Ivy, on the other hand, her fate was totally your responsibility."

Jack's head slumped. He was relieved to hear Amanda and the boys were okay, but he dreaded the thought of telling David and Louis about Ivy. Under the current circumstances, it seemed surreal that he would be thinking about such a thing, but Ivy was family, and her loss would be difficult to bear. Jack's thought was interrupted by Lucius's voice.

"Jack, now that we are on the same page, we have some important matters to discuss. The sun will set around 6:30 p.m. this evening. I will be expecting you at the burial mound. Please try to be on time. We have a great deal of ground to cover."

Before Jack could respond, the line went dead. He sat down at the kitchen table, staring at the pictures of David and Louis. His thoughts raced from their well-being to this meeting with Lucius. What did he want? Why was all of this happening to his family? There were many questions but no answers. Jack was in turmoil, and he could feel the darkness washing over him. He knew he needed to be focused, calm, and act confidently if he, Amanda, and the boys were going to make it through all of this. Yet, those old feelings of doubt and desperation, something that he knew all too well, were creeping into his subconscious, and once they took hold of his soul, they were difficult to shake.

He knew that sitting there obsessing over all of this for the next four to five hours was going to be counterproductive. Jack got up from the table and headed to the garage. He grabbed a shovel, went to the backyard, and started to dig a hole.

As he pushed the shovel into the grass, the sky clouded over and darkened. A rumble of thunder echoed in the distance. The ground consisted of heavy clay and rock. Jack's fingers were throbbing, and blisters began to rise on the palm of his hands from gripping the shovel so tightly and repetitively hitting the hard soil. Bathed in sweat, Jack finished digging the hole and went back into the house. He carefully wrapped Ivy's remains in a towel, then tenderly placed the remains in the bottom of the hole.

A light rain began to fall as Jack slowly started to fill in the grave. Once he finished, Jack stood over the gravesite with a heavy heart and closed his eyes, saying a silent prayer and thanking Ivy for the love she had given to his family. He was sure that Ivy's ability to keep David and Louis calm would've been of great value at the moment for Amanda. He hoped Ivy's spirit might be with all of them. After finishing his prayer, Jack walked away from the grave, went back into the house, and got ready to meet Lucius.

It was only a few hours, but the rest of the afternoon felt like an eternity. Jack spent it at the kitchen table, staring at pictures of his family. While he certainly did not trust Lucius, something in his gut told him that his family was physically unharmed, at least for the moment. Their emotional wellbeing, on the other hand, was another matter. Amanda had to have her hands full right now, trying to calm David and Louis down. A change in any part of their daily routine inevitably threw them for a loop, and if they sensed any worry or concern on Amanda's part, it would only increase their agitation.

As he entered his car, Jack didn't even want to think about what seeing Lucius's demon appearance would do to them.

As he crossed the Rappahannock River into Culpeper County, Jack thought about what had happened the last time he'd made this journey. Over the last month, more and more of his memories of that night had returned, and they scared him to death. He warily looked toward the passenger seat of the car, almost expecting to see Lucius there. Jack was sure he could find his way back to the burial mound if the orange flags he had left behind were still in place but worried about what he might see along the way.

One of Jack's favorite songs by the rock group Styx, Crystal Ball, popped into his head.

The thought of having a crystal ball at the moment felt like a double-edged sword. It would enable him to confirm that Amanda and the boys were okay, but it might also reveal what he would have to face to save them. He knew he needed to be resilient, but could he be strong enough? He wanted to be self-assured, but he had to admit there were doubts in his mind about any of them getting out of this alive. That reality cut him like a knife. He gritted his teeth and clutched the steering wheel tighter.

As he neared the right turn he'd need to make to get back to Route 666; Jack considered what Lucius might want from him. What was this "work" he was going to be required to do? Jack's imagination began to run wild, and he worried it might mean he would have to participate in one of Lucius's rituals, like the one he witnessed at the burial mound last month. Jack shuddered at the thought of assisting Lucius with something like this, or anything else for that matter. Yet he knew in his heart that he would do anything to save his family, including losing his soul, if that were the price he'd have to pay.

Jack made the turn onto what was formerly Route 666. He parked at the barrier and said another silent prayer before he exited the vehicle. As he arrived at the barricade, he took a deep breath, then scaled the wall and started down the road toward the trail entrance.

Jack took the path that led past the Bradford family cemetery and arrived at the trail entrance. He glanced again at his watch to see what time it was. Jack had roughly an hour to get to the burial mound. Spotting an orange flag in the woods, Jack felt reassured that he could make it on time as long as the other flags remained in place. The last thing he wanted was to be late, as he was confident that would piss Lucius off. Jack thought for a moment about Ivy and what Lucius had done to her. Being late was a risk he was unwilling to take, so he quickly started down the trail.

As Jack made his way through the underbrush and brambles toward the First Gate, he noticed one significant difference between this trip on the trail and the one he'd made last month. The silence. No birds were singing, and no insect sounds. The only noise that Jack heard was the crunch of his footsteps as he walked up the trail. It felt eerie and unnatural, but Jack moved forward as swiftly up the path as he possibly could.

Although the vegetation at the First Gate appeared to have gotten thicker in the past month, he was able to find another orange flag that showed the way forward. The creek he had to cross to get to the Second Gate had risen from the recent storms, which he feared would mean that the way he had crossed the bridge previously would not be an option. Jack arrived at the bridge, at least the spot where the bridge used to be. The remains of the bridge had washed away. Jack faced the challenge of finding a way across the creek.

Glancing at his watch, he knew he had to find a solution quickly. The creek's current made wading a dangerous option, even at the point where the creek banks narrowed. It occurred to Jack that if he could not wade across the stream, perhaps he could find a way to jump it. A running jump was impossible due to the distance involved and slippery mud along the creek's edges. However, Jack had been a pole vaulter in high school and thought he might be able to get across the torrent if he could find a "pole" that was long enough.

Jack left the trail and searched the nearby woods for a branch or tree limb that would be long enough and strong enough to enable him to make the jump. After a few minutes, he found what he thought would be a suitable substitute for a pole. Jack grabbed it and headed back to the creek. He searched for an area that would allow him to get a running start before placing the branch's end into the stream. There were no ideal spots, but Jack chose one that would give him the best chance to make the jump. He backed up several paces, took a breath, and started running toward the creek bank.

As he reached the creek, he felt his footing start to give out, but it was too late to turn back now. He began to skid toward the bank but maintained his balance sufficiently to plant the branch in the middle of the creek bed. Jack pushed the limb downward as hard as possible and allowed his momentum to carry him across the water. However, the weight on the branch was too great, and it snapped while he was halfway across the creek. Jack found himself floating through the air and instinctively allowed the energy generated from his leap to carry him across the stream. He hit the creek bank on the other side with a loud thud and then rolled through the brush, which helped cushion some of his fall.

Once he stopped rolling, Jack threw away the broken branch that he'd somehow managed to hold on to during the vault. He looked back toward the creek, amazed he'd somehow successfully made it across. He saw the other half of the broken branch embedded in the creek bed's mud and standing up vertically in the fast-running stream. Jack realized that the fabricated pole had become stuck in the stream bed, which caused it to lose any flexibility that it might have had, and as a result, it had merely broken in half.

Jack got up off the ground and looked at his watch. He'd lost precious minutes and knew he needed to pick up the pace.

To make up for the time lost at the creek, Jack ran up the path. He was thankful it was still daylight to avoid stones and other obstacles on the trail. Jack stumbled several times when his shoe got caught on a vine growing across the path but managed not to fall. He quickly passed the Third Gate and saw that the house, dark during his first visit, was now fully illuminated. Jack could see figures through the windows moving from room to room. While he was curious about the activity, Jack knew this was no time to find out exactly what was going on in the house, and he turned his attention back to the trail.

Next, Jack came to the clearing in the woods, the spot where he had felt something touch him. He had seen many strange and horrific things during his first trip to the burial mound, but this touching may have made him feel the most uncomfortable. Jack did not pause or stop for even a moment in the clearing. He just kept right on moving. However, he couldn't help but notice that the wind was picking up. Leaves had already started falling from many of the trees, and the breeze blowing through the leafless branches sounded like someone whispering or moaning. These were the first noises from the woods that Jack had heard all evening.

Gate Number Four and the well where he'd seen the vision of the Native American child and heard the voice telling him to *"Go back"* was just ahead. Jack preferred not to repeat this experience, but he was a little out of breath after so much running. He stopped and leaned on the wall of the well to rest for a moment. Jack checked his watch and saw that time was no longer a concern. He didn't recall this area as being particularly wet or damp, but his shoes sank slightly into the saturated ground this time. He looked down, and to his right, there was a patch of mud. In the soil was the outline of tracks, as if something had recently walked through the area.

From the position Jack was in, he could not make out precisely what had left the footprints. He knelt to get a closer look and noted they had a cloven imprint like a pig might have. Jack wasn't sure if wild pigs were living in this area or not, but he realized it did not really matter. *There are only two hoof marks.* Whatever made the prints did not walk on all fours but walked upright. Jack knew that hideous beasts already roamed these woods. He just hoped that he would not run into whatever had recently been there and left these tracks.

The light was fading, and even without checking his watch, Jack knew the sun was beginning to set. He continued his journey toward Gate Number Five and the cabin with the skeleton chained in the prison cell. As Jack approached the area, a red light appeared in the distance. He advanced slowly toward the now illuminated cabin and peered through the door. The skeleton was still in the cell, but there were now several items on the table. He looked down and saw they were photographs. He picked up the pictures; they were of Amanda, David, and Louis. It seemed as if someone was sending him a reminder about who held the upper hand. Jack looked at his family longingly and put the photographs in his pocket.

Jack reached Gate Number Six and found the church pews in the same position they were in previously. Unburied remains still littered the ground surrounding the path. Jack glanced in the direction of the altar and saw that there was something different about it. He went down the aisle of the profane sanctuary and found a leather-bound book, open as if someone had recently been reading from it or writing something in it. It was apparent that the book was ancient and written in a language Jack could not understand. There was one entry, however, that he could read without any difficulty. His name, "Jack Aitken," appeared to be written in red ink or possibly blood.

It was no mistake. The pictures and the book were purposely left out for Jack to find, a not-so-subtle reminder of what was at stake tonight. Jack sprinted to the bridge, which took him over the stream toward the burial mound. He arrived at the hill and saw Lucius, thankfully in human form, standing next to it with a boiling cauldron in front of him. He was flanked on each side by tall, menacing-looking men.

Lucius smiled smugly. "Right on time, Jack. I never had a doubt. I know our relationship got off to a rocky start, but I think we are going to be able to put that behind us and work well together."

As Jack approached the cauldron, the two men morphed into the gruesome Hell Hounds that had previously chased Jack all the way to the barrier. Their red eyes fixed on Jack. Saliva dripping down their lips, they growled at his appearance.

Lucius turned to the animals and admonished them. "Barghest, Gwyllgi, where are your manners? Jack is our friend. He is going to be working for us."

The two animals immediately were quiet and lay down at Lucius's feet.

Jack stood in front of Lucius. "Are Amanda and my boys alright?" he said, trying to keep his voice steady.

Lucius started to pace back and forth in front of the cauldron, his hands clasped behind his back. "Of course, they are, Jack. Come look in the cauldron and see for yourself."

Jack moved slowly, keeping his eyes fixed on the Hell Hounds, then stared down into the cauldron. A roaring fire had brought the liquid inside the kettle to a rolling boil. The steam cleared, and the black contents of the pot transformed into a picture. Amanda and the boys huddled together inside a room. The boys had blank stares on their faces. They were in shock. Amanda was speaking to them, embracing them both. Jack could tell she was trying to comfort and reassure them.

Jack glared at Lucius. "Where are they being held, Lucius?"

Lucius's face lost its smile immediately, and the tenor of his voice once again became more threatening. "Jack, I do not care for the tone of your voice, and I do not answer your questions. Never forget this, or your family will suffer the consequences. Are we clear?"

Jack replied immediately, "Yes. I'm sorry. I'm worried about my family, and while you may not care about them, surely you can understand why I am concerned."

"Jack, Jack, Jack. I understand your concern, but you have no cause for alarm. I am concerned about your family as well. Do you not see that? You need not worry as long as you do what I ask you to do. Remain civil, and they will continue to be unharmed. As I have said before, all of this is in your hands. It is all up to you to decide how this will work itself out."

Jack was ready to explode but managed to keep his cool. His family's life depended upon it.

"Okay, Lucius. I understand. What is it that you need me to do?"

"Good. I thought you might want to get right down to business, Jack."

Lucius walked past the cauldron toward Jack. The two Hell Hounds immediately got up and followed him. They walked around, circling Jack.

"Now, Jack, pay careful attention to what I am about to tell you. I will likely share more information with you than you want to hear but indulge me. Your fate and that of your family will depend on it."

Jack stood still, not wanting to provoke the two animals.

"Jack, tell me, did you go to church when you were a boy? You know, Sunday school and that sort of thing?"

"Yes. I attended a Methodist church."

Lucius chuckled. "Well, then I should not have to explain the whole concept of good versus evil to you, should I? I am sure you heard all kinds of stories about this epic battle of ideas, but of course, you know by now that this is not some hypothetical discussion or metaphor. No, this war is truly the real thing."

While Lucius continued to pontificate about the topic, Jack remembered Reverend Miner and his sermons. He wished that he were here now. The confidence with which he would speak from the pulpit would have been a far better weapon to debate Lucius than anything Jack would be able to say.

"Well, enough about that for now. Jack, your mission is a simple one. There is an object I need you to retrieve for me."

Lucius reached into his pocket and pulled out a photograph, which he handed to Jack. Jack looked at the picture carefully. The object appeared to have a polish to it that was similar to silver. It was not unlike an ice pick, but the top was in the shape of a ball. The ornately adorned ball had detailed engravings, one of which appeared to be a woman riding on the back of a seven-headed animal. The animal looked very similar to Lucius's Hell Hounds.

Some letters formed words, but they were a language that Jack could not identify. The other end of the object had a flat end like a screwdriver. Even Jack could tell a highly-skilled metallurgist made the item. As evil as he knew this artifact had to be, there was no denying its craftsmanship. He couldn't help but think that this was something you might see in an Indiana Jones film. Lucius held out his hand, and Jack placed the photo back into it. He had only seen the object for a minute or two, but he knew he would never forget its appearance.

"The object in the photo is an ancient artifact made from, shall we say, otherworldly materials."

Jack looked cautiously at Lucius and asked, "Is it okay for me to ask you what it is?"

Lucius grinned smugly. "You see, Jack, we are getting along splendidly! Since you have asked me so courteously, the artifact is a key. This burial mound behind us is actually a doorway. It is an entrance to Hell itself. Like any doorway, it may be locked or unlocked, and this key is needed to open it."

Jack was stunned. Did he really hear "*doorway to Hell*"? Jack felt like an actor in a horror film, but this was no movie. Amanda, Louis, and David's kidnapping felt like a horrible nightmare, but this nightmare was all too real.

"While I have great confidence in you and your ability to fulfill this mission," Lucius continued, "I need to retain the photograph as if you were to suffer some sort of mishap, I will need to show it to your replacement. Of course, that would have serious consequences for your family, so I know you are going to give this mission, shall we say, your all."

The two Hell Hounds continued to watch him closely. Listening to Lucius talk about opening a portal to Hell while these two monsters continuously stared at him was highly unsettling. Jack fought hard to concentrate on what he was going to have to do. He knew there could be no mistakes or slip-ups.

Jack eyed the Hell Hounds warily and asked, "Where do I find the artifact, and how long do I have to recover it?"

"Very perceptive of you, Jack. I knew the first time we met that you were the right person for this mission. Your intense interest in finding out more about the burial mound told me you had the determination required to succeed. This mission is quite simple. The artifact resides in a burial plot in Stull Cemetery, a graveyard about fifteen miles outside Lawrence, Kansas. You will bring the artifact to me right here at the burial mound at midnight on November 1st. This is a straightforward task, is it not? Not too complicated at all."

Jack was slightly surprised by the date that he needed to return with the artifact. He would have suspected Halloween due to its relationship with the occult, but he wasn't sure that he wanted to know what the significance of November 1st really was either. Jack also had no idea where Stull Cemetery was, nor its importance. As he contemplated this, he heard thunder rumbling above him then saw a flash of lightning in the distance behind the burial mound. The treetops bent over due to the force of the wind pushing through them. Another storm was coming.

Suddenly, Lucius transformed from his human appearance to that of his demon self. Jack didn't want to look at him. He was scared enough already. The Hell Hounds howled at the sound of the storm which was approaching.

Lucius spoke once more in a resonant, menacing voice. "Okay, Jack. Our question-and-answer session is over. It is time that you got to work, but one last thing before you go."

As he spoke, Lucius reached inside his cloak and pulled out an object. It was a sword with tremendously elaborate handiwork, made of gold or some other kind of precious metal.

"Just in case you get ideas in your head about a daring family rescue, you should know that the key you seek is made from a virtually indestructible metal. The only thing capable of destroying it is this sword. It is the sword of Saint Michael, the Archangel, and as you see, it is in my possession. There is no other way to save your family than to deliver the key to me as planned. You have already witnessed the consequences that come with making me irate."

Jack cringed at the thought of his family and Ivy's death. While his anger was running hot and deep, he would not run the risk of showing it to Lucius. At the same time, he tried not to let his fear show either.

"I understand, Lucius."

"Time for you to leave, Jack. Barghest and Gwyllgi will escort you out."

Lucius disappeared before Jack's eyes, and he was alone now with the two Hell Hounds. The animals growled, and their jaws snapped in Jack's direction as they ushered him back down the path.

Chapter 14

Amanda Aitken sat on the cell floor, trying to assure her children that things would be alright, but inside her heart, she had her doubts. She was struggling to keep them calm while maintaining her composure. Just then, the door opened, and a tall shadow stretched across the floor. Their tormenter entered the room.

"Good evening, Mrs. Aitken," Lucius said. "You will be pleased to know that I just met with your husband, and he is well. Of course, he is concerned about you and the children, but I have assured him that you are all in good health."

"I suppose you expect me to thank you."

Lucius smirked. "You and your boys will continue to remain unharmed as long as Jack keeps to the script and follows instructions. He is on his way back home right now and will be heading to Kansas in the morning to retrieve the artifact that I have mentioned to you previously."

Amanda recalled the initial conversation she had with Lucius after the kidnapping. He described to her the need for a key to open a doorway to Hell. She had difficulty following everything he was telling her as she was more concerned about the boys. It all sounded so surreal, and yet she could not help but believe it. After watching Lucius transform into that hideous demon entity, she knew it was all too real. She was just thankful that he had not done so in front of Louis and David as that almost certainly would have been more than the two of them could take.

"I will keep you informed as to Jack's progress, Mrs. Aitken." Lucius turned to one of the guards. "Go get Nadia for me. I have a job for her."

The guard left to fetch Nadia, and Lucius went to an adjacent room. A few minutes later, Nadia, one of Lucius's aides, entered the room.

"Nadia, I have a job for you. Shadow Jack Aitken while he is on his mission to retrieve the key. I expect that you will keep me informed as to his movements and his progress. That is all."

Nadia nodded, acknowledging that she understood his orders, and left to catch up with Jack. Lucius leaned back in his chair and grinned. Things were going just as he had planned.

***

October 25th
Bristow, Virginia, 30 miles west of Washington, DC
11:00 p.m.

Jack parked his car in the driveway and entered the code to open the garage door. The walk through the woods back to the car had been surprisingly uneventful. Except for being escorted by two hounds from Hell, he experienced no other paranormal phenomena. While the storm clouds swirled and raged in the sky above him, no rain fell until he entered his car and pulled away from the barricade. The woods themselves had been quiet; as if Lucius had commanded, they remain silent. Even the Hell Hounds had remained mute.

He thought of one thing the entire ride home. Where were Amanda and the boys being held, and how were they coping with this terrifying experience? Jack was riding an emotional roller coaster, alternating between regret and fear and eventually ending in unparalleled anger. Worst of all, however, was the self-doubt that began to creep into his mind. He questioned himself over and over again. *How do I fight something that I cannot even define? Are demons just a supernatural phenomenon, or are they something otherworldly, such as an alien presence?*

He'd seen plenty of horror movies and read scary novels, but would weapons such as holy water, garlic, wooden stakes, or

173

crucifixes have any effect on Lucius? Were they the thing of myths and legends, their origins rooted in some truth located deep in the past? Where were the answers to these questions, and would he be able to find them in time to save Amanda and the boys?

He was sure of just one thing: Lucius was going to kill them all, regardless if he delivered that key or not.

It was nearly midnight by the time Jack arrived home and cleaned himself up. His adrenaline was in high gear, and while he needed it, sleeping was not an option at the moment. Hunger pangs reminded Jack he had not eaten since early in the morning. He turned on his laptop and went to the refrigerator, searching for something to eat. He sat at the kitchen table with two bottles of beer and a bag of pretzels, then started searching the Internet for answers to the questions dominating his thoughts.

Jack typed "Lucius Rofocale" in his search engine, and it provided nothing he didn't already know. It confirmed his employment at the museum and the background of his research on the Manahoac tribe. Jack scrutinized every page linked to the search, but it turned out to be a dead end. He finished the second beer and wrestled with the disappointment that was creeping into his soul.

Next, Jack searched for information on how to defend oneself against a demon. This search was much more productive. In fact, it was information overkill. The sheer volume of information was overwhelming, and the contradictory nature of it was frustrating. What was he to believe? Some publications highlighted the Catholic Church's capabilities in such matters, while others mocked them as outdated or useless. Eventually, Jack concluded he needed to find someone who had expertise in this area.

Jack then entered Stull Cemetery into his search engine. He found it was a rural location, with the nearest significant population center being the city of Lawrence. It was steeped in legends referring to it as being a gateway to Hell. Jack wondered, *with all of Lucius's apparent strength and power, why would he need me to retrieve the key? Why didn't he simply send one of his subordinates to recover it, or due to its apparent importance, why not simply do it himself?* Jack sensed something potentially significant surrounding this question, but he needed to locate someone who might know the answer, and he needed to find them quickly.

Lawrence was a city of nearly 100,000 people, and Jack was sure they would have a Catholic Church. While he knew there were potentially other religious sects that might help him, the Catholic faith seemed to have the most recognized experience in the area of battling demons. His initial search located Saint John, the Evangelist Catholic Parish. Jack perused their website and found a great deal of social outreach information, but not a word about good versus evil.

The following listing was for the Saint Lawrence Catholic Campus. Jack reviewed their upcoming events, and a seminar on reconciling science with faith caught his eye. He noticed the name of the presenter was Father Mark Desmond. The name was familiar, but possibly because of his fatigue, Jack could not figure out why. He returned to the home page and clicked on the staff directory. Jack found that Father Mark Desmond was the director of the organization. He clicked on Father Desmond's bio and was stunned by what he read.

It turned out Father Desmond had been an ordained priest at Saint Aiden's Church in Willison Park, New York. The church was in the next town over from where Jack had grown up. Saint Aiden's was in the parish that sponsored the Catholic Youth Organization, which ran sports leagues on Long Island, including the club where Jack and his brother learned to play soccer.

He was sure this was no coincidence, but he could not confirm any additional information about Father Desmond's background from the website. Jack found an e-mail at the bottom of the page and decided he had nothing to lose.

Dear Father Desmond:

I read your bio online and wondered if you might be the Mark Desmond I knew in my childhood. I played soccer through Saint Aiden's Catholic Youth Organization when I was a teenager, and one of my teammates was Mark Desmond. If you are indeed that same Mark Desmond, I would very much like to hear back from you.

Best regards,
Jack Aitken

After sending the e-mail, Jack continued his research. He came across a document that discussed a theory known as cloaking. It was a ritual that, once performed, provided a person the ability to move freely without being tracked by others. Jack recalled something Mary Boynton had told him. Mary was Jack's massage therapist, and they had come to know each other well over the years that she had treated his neck problems. They had discussed religion in the context of some of the trying circumstances that Jack had experienced. It turned out that Mary practiced Wicca.

Jack had not put too much stock in what Mary shared about being a Wiccan, but when he shared with her that he was researching a book about evil, she grew quite concerned. She cautioned Jack that there was a risk associated with what he was doing and that stirring up the forces of evil could have significant consequences. Jack shook his head. Here was an example of another person who tried to warn him, but he failed to listen to her the same way he had ignored Amanda. While silently rebuking himself one more time, Jack recalled she had talked about the use of spells and incantations during one of their conversations. He wondered if she might perform the cloaking spell discussed in the document he was reading.

As Jack began to e-mail Mary about arranging a meeting, he received a notification that he had just received a new e-mail. Jack pulled up his messages and saw that it was a response from Father Mark Desmond. Jack anxiously opened the e-mail.

Jack:

It is a pleasant surprise to hear from you after all of these years! I am indeed Mark Desmond, who you played soccer with years ago. I would very much enjoy catching up with you when your schedule permits.

All the best,
Mark Desmond

For the first time in a while, Jack felt a slight sense of hope. Perhaps Mark could help him or, if nothing else, put him in touch with someone who could. He finished up the e-mail to Mary about meeting the following day and decided he should try to get a few hours of sleep.

Jack went upstairs and slipped into bed. He closed his eyes and silently prayed to God, asking him to protect Amanda and the boys. Jack was tired. Sleep should have come quickly, but he found himself tossing and turning. As hard as he tried to relax and calm his mind, he knew rest would not come easily.

***

October 26th
Bristow, Virginia, 30 miles west of Washington, DC
9:00 a.m.

Jack closed his journal and slumped back in his chair. He had tried to sleep but found himself unable to do so. Since dawn, Jack re-read his journal entries and had a hard time believing the words entered in the notebook. Did he really write about Hell Hounds and demons? If Jack had not experienced all of it himself, there would have been no believing what was in the journal. Unfortunately, reading it felt like he was experiencing the ordeal repeatedly and only served to reinforce how desperate the situation had become.

Mary was not able to meet with him until around lunchtime. He went upstairs to pack a bag for the trip to Stull Cemetery. Jack had checked and found it would take nearly eighteen hours to drive there. He figured he would meet with Mary and then leave immediately after that to retrieve the key. Jack decided that while he was on his way there, he would reach out again to Mark Desmond and see if he would meet with him. He hoped that perhaps his old friend might be able in some way to help him.

Just as he finished packing his bag, he heard the doorbell ring. Jack went down the stairs and saw a woman standing at the front door. He unlocked the door and opened it.

"Good morning. Can I help you with something?"

"Are you Jack Aitken?" the woman asked.

"Yes, I am Jack Aitken. What can I do for you?"

The woman reached into her coat pocket and pulled out a badge.

"Mr. Aitken, I am Detective Anne Bishop of the Prince William County Police Department. Are you aware that your wife and children did not show up at school yesterday?"

Jack was not prepared to be questioned about their disappearance and struggled to think of a reasonable response. After all, he could not tell her that demons kidnapped his family.

He paused for a moment, then said, "Detective, I am very concerned. They did not come home last night."

Detective Bishop looked at Jack quizzically. "Has this ever happened before?"

Jack quickly said, "No, Detective. Never."

"Mr. Aitken, do I have your permission to come in and look around?"

"Certainly. Please come in."

Detective Bishop entered the house and turned her head, searching each room as she headed for the basement. She flipped the basement light on and went down the stairs. She looked around and found nothing.

As she headed back upstairs, she asked, "Mr. Aitken, is it okay if I go upstairs too?"

"Absolutely, Detective," Jack replied. "The stairs are down the hall and to the left."

Jack watched the detective pause at the top of the stairs, then head down the hallway. She checked the boy's rooms, then came back down the hall and entered Jack and Amanda's room. She saw the knapsack on the bed.

Detective Bishop turned toward Jack and stared him down.

"Mr. Aitken, are you going somewhere?"

Jack began to panic. He did not want to appear to hesitate in responding, but he didn't know what to say without bringing additional suspicion upon himself. After all, based on every real crime show he ever saw, it was only logical that he would be the primary suspect in his family's disappearance.

Jack responded emphatically, "Actually, Detective, I just got back into town. I haven't had time to unpack yet." It was the best explanation he could come up with at the moment.

The detective looked at Jack side-eyed with suspicion. "Oh. Where were you?"

Jack looked Detective Bishop directly in the eyes and said, "I was meeting with a client in Virginia Beach. His name is Michael Mancini, and he's the Chief Financial Officer for the National Gardening Association. Here's his business card in case you need to contact him."

At least part of what Jack said was correct. Michael was his client and did work with the NGA. Jack knew he was on vacation in Hawaii for the next two weeks. It would take some time for the detective to make contact with Michael to confirm their meeting. Of course, this meeting had been more than a month ago, but he hoped this would buy him enough time to get to Kansas and back before anyone would know he was gone.

As they made their way back to the front door, Detective Bishop handed Jack her card.

"This has my contact information. Please call me if you think of anything that might help me find your family or if your family returns home. Just so you know, Mr. Aitken, I will be checking out your story."

Jack nodded. "I understand, detective. Thank you for your time and concern."

He closed the door and locked it. He went upstairs to gather his things and got ready to leave to meet with Mary.

***

Jack pulled into the parking lot, removed the key from the ignition, and leaned his head against the steering wheel. It seemed just when he thought things couldn't get any worse; something else would arise that complicated the situation further. Jack was not only at the mercy of a demon, but the police considered him the prime suspect in his family's disappearance, a disappearance orchestrated by this same demon.

This cannot be happening. Jack thought to himself.

Not only was it happening, but he had less than a week to retrieve the artifact demanded by the demon, or his family would be subjected to torture, murdered, and who knew what else might happen. Jack also had to consider what other consequences might arise if Lucius got his hands on the artifact. Opening the door to Hell sounded terrible enough, but what other catastrophes would Jack be unleashing by complying with his demand? All of this weighed heavily on his mind as he opened the door to Mary's suite.

Mary greeted him at the door. "Good morning, Jack. Come on in."

Jack had known Mary for many years. They had met in a business networking group, and when Jack mentioned chronic neck pain, she suggested that he give deep tissue massage a try. Nearly ten years later, she was still keeping his neck muscles loose, and they had become good friends.

They had grown comfortable discussing almost any topic with one another, and that included religious faith. Mary once told Jack she had been a practicing Catholic but had become disillusioned with some of their teachings and had become a Wiccan. Jack was curious about the tenets of her faith, even if he didn't put much stock in them. Now, he was hoping his skepticism was misplaced, and Mary would be able to help him.

"Hi, Mary. Thank you for seeing me on such short notice."

Mary removed her glasses and rubbed her hazel eyes. Putting her glasses back on, she gathered her buttery blonde hair into a ponytail and smiled. "Any time, Jack. I was able to clear my schedule for the next two hours. How can I help you? I'm pretty sure you are not here for a massage."

Jack laughed weakly. "I wish. I could probably use one. I'm here to see if you can help me with a big problem that has developed from my research for the book. You remember...the one we discussed a few months ago."

Mary's expression changed immediately, and she frowned. "Jack, I am not telling you I told you so, but I warned you about stirring up something that was better left alone." She paused for a moment, took a deep breath, and said, "Tell me what's going on."

Jack's eyes lowered. He recalled Mary had been alarmed when he had told her about the book. She'd cautioned him to be very careful, and frankly, he remembered her advising him to forget about the project altogether. It was an understatement to say that he should have heeded her warnings.

Jack raised his head and looked Mary in the eye with a tear rolling down his cheek. "To anyone else, what I'm going to say would sound absolutely insane, but I know it won't sound crazy to you. I found the Native American burial mound that we had discussed outside of Culpeper. During the expedition, I stumbled upon a group of people in robes performing a ritual. It appeared to be a human sacrifice. I fled through the woods and somehow made it home. I immediately gave up on the project, but something followed me home that night. A demonic presence."

Mary sat stoically. "Okay, Jack. I follow what you are saying, but what else has happened? I know that there's more to the story."

Jack continued, "I wish I could tell you that you were wrong, Mary, but the story gets worse. Do you remember when I told you about the historian at the Culpeper Museum?"

Mary nodded. "His name was something like Lucian, wasn't it?

"Lucius. His name is Lucius Rofocale. Well, it turns out he's a demon."

Mary was startled. "Jack, are you sure? How do you know that?"

"Believe me. I am certain. Right in front of my eyes, Lucius transformed from his human form into a monster. I cannot even begin to describe his appearance to you. It's beyond hideous."

Jack could see the fear in Mary's eyes. It made him feel even more uneasy. Before she could ask another question, he dropped the biggest bombshell of all. "Mary, Lucius has kidnapped my family."

Mary's jaw opened. "Jack, I am sorry. Can you repeat that? He *what*?"

"Mary, he kidnapped Amanda and the boys. He's holding them hostage. If I don't retrieve an artifact, a key of some sort, he will kill them. If I want to have any chance of saving them, I have to bring the key back to the burial ground by Midnight on November 1st."

The two friends sat together in silence. After what seemed like forever, Mary spoke. "Jack, I am so sorry. I wish I knew some way to help you. I know we talked about my being a Wiccan, and while I have some basic understanding of demonology, this is far beyond anything that I could even begin to assist with."

"Mary, I understand. There's one thing I was hoping you might be able to do for me. Do you know anything about cloaking?"

Mary bit her lip. "I am familiar with the concept. Cloaking involves a spell capable of hiding a person's aura, their life force, if you will. It prevents supernatural entities from detecting or tracking a mortal person."

"Do you know how to perform a cloaking spell?" Jack asked. "I plan to contact an old friend in Kansas who is a priest. I hope he can help me, but I don't want Lucius to know about it."

Mary paced around the room. "I don't know, Jack. There's a cloaking incantation in my spellbook, but I've never performed the ritual before. I'm not even sure that it will work."

"Mary, please give it a try," he pleaded. "My family is living on the edge of the knife right now, and I need any potential advantage that I can get."

Mary felt Jack's desperation. His agony and fear were palpable. She did not know how to tell him that even if he were to survive this nightmare, it was very likely that even a positive outcome would come at a high cost. Mary was familiar with the challenges Jack had faced in his life, and she was not sure that he could bear the losses that might result from this ordeal. She knew that if she could, she had to help him.

Mary reached for her spellbook. "Okay, Jack. Let's get started."

***

October 27th
Rest stop, U.S. Route 50 W, somewhere in Ohio
11:58 PM

Jack pulled into the rest area and searched for a place to park. Eventually, he located a spot that was not so isolated as to draw attention to his vehicle but with just a few cars in his vicinity. He was exhausted and hoped to get a few hours of sleep. As he tried to relax, the events of the day raced through his head.

After leaving Mary's office, he'd immediately gotten on the road to Lawrence. He took the precaution of periodically getting off the interstate highways and driving secondary roads, hoping this might help him evade the authorities. He was concerned the detective who had visited him yesterday might become suspicious if she discovered he'd left town, and she just might put an all-points bulletin out for his vehicle. At this point, he wouldn't be taking any chances of being stopped, so he made sure to signal his lane changes and kept his speed at the posted limit.

He stopped in a secluded area he had found in West Virginia and changed his car's license plates. As he had done so, he thought about whether events happened randomly or if they were somehow predetermined. Months ago, he'd taken Louis to an appointment.

On one of the grassy islands in the parking lot were a set of license plates. He'd attempted to turn them into the building's management office, but there were no reports of anyone missing plates. He was not quite sure why, but he took the license plates home. If nothing else, this tactic could possibly confuse anyone who might be looking for him.

Jack's thoughts turned to tomorrow. If he maintained his current progress, he estimated he would arrive in Lawrence around 2:00 a.m. on the 28th. During one of his breaks, he had e-mailed Mark Desmond to see if he would be available to meet for breakfast. He hadn't received a reply as of yet but would check during the day tomorrow. Jack closed his eyes and tried to sleep, hoping that Mark would help him and Mary's cloaking spell would prevent Lucius from knowing his exact whereabouts.

***

October 27th
Lawrence, KS
Late Afternoon

Nadia sat in a car outside the St. Lawrence Catholic Center. She glanced around in all directions, hoping to get a glimpse of Jack Aitken. Lucius had assigned her the task of keeping an eye on Jack's movements and whereabouts, and Nadia had blown it big time. She had tracked him to that massage therapist's office, but after he left there, something had changed. It was as if a switch had turned off, and Nadia could no longer feel his presence anywhere around her. She immediately knew that this was going to be a problem.

Having to make that call to Lucius and confess to him that she had lost his trail was the most challenging thing she had ever had to do. She was surprised that his reaction was not one of fury. Indeed, Lucius seemed amused by it all and instructed her to catch a plane for Lawrence, Kansas. Upon her arrival, she needed to find Jack, and he suggested that locating Mark Desmond's whereabouts might help her with this task.

Nadia knew better than to ask questions, but Mark Desmond was one of the most feared adversaries demons faced. He had developed a reputation as someone to avoid, not someone a demon would want to trail, let alone meet. Lucius had cautioned every demon that they should never underestimate Mark Desmond even after the massacre at the Manahoac burial mound.

Lucius had been quite forthright that she should not confront or engage Desmond in any way. She intended to follow that particular order to the letter. She had been waiting for hours without a sign of Jack or Desmond. Just then, a figure crossed the street and headed toward the front door of the St. Lawrence Center. Nadia looked closely at the photograph in her hand and then back at the man entering the Center. IT WAS DESMOND! She sat back in the seat, and a sense of relief washed over her. She had located him, and now she was going to make sure he did not give her the slip! She was to check in with Lucius on the morning of October 28th, and she was pleased that she would have good news to tell him. The only thing that could be better would be if she could say to him that she had located Jack again.

***

October 28th
Lawrence, Kansas
2:00 a.m.

Jack had been driving for hours and exited the car to stretch his legs. He was stiff all over, and his neck, in particular, was sore. Just holding the steering wheel had become uncomfortable, and Jack shrugged his shoulders in an effort to release the muscles in his upper body. He'd heard from Mark Desmond, and they had arranged to meet at the Cosmic Café. Jack had taken the time to locate it and was now looking for a place that he might park his car and try to take a nap.

While the entirety of the mess he had created was enough to prevent him from getting any significant rest, it was the thoughts of Amanda, Louis, and David that were really getting to him. They were never out of his thoughts, and his anxiety about their current condition increased by the second. Jack found a parking lot at a local park that was not too far from the café and crawled into the backseat. He tried to tell himself tomorrow was going to be a better day. Jack wanted to believe Mark would be able to help him and his family. After all, he was a Catholic priest. Who would know more than a priest about combating evil? No matter how hard he tried to convince himself, the feelings of doubt and desperation were simply too powerful to overcome.

Chapter 15

October 30th
Lawrence, Kansas
12:01 AM

Jack and Father Desmond sat together on a bench outside the Danforth Chapel. The nondenominational chapel was constructed and dedicated to the University of Kansas in 1946, but the ornate exterior stonework and stained-glass windows made it seem far older. Its purpose was to serve as a place of prayer and silent reflection. Father Desmond had visited the chapel frequently over his ten-plus years living in Lawrence. It was quiet and peaceful, and it seemed an appropriate place for Jack to finish his confession. After all, Father Desmond had silently confessed many of his own sins in this same place.

Off in the distance, the church bells chimed, and just as Jack spoke the final word of his declaration of guilt, they went silent. It was midnight. October 30th had arrived, and, depending on what area of the country you were from, after nightfall, Devil's Night, Mischief Night, Trick Night, or Devil's Eve would rule the darkness. There really was no real significance to the date. It was just an excuse for egging houses and sometimes not so minor hijinks, but Father Desmond knew this October 30th was likely to lead to something more than just run-of-the-mill vandalism. He knew all of this led back to Stull Cemetery and eventually back to the woods of Culpeper, Virginia. A chill ran down his spine.

After a moment of silence between the two men, Father Desmond heard Jack speak again. "There are a few things I don't understand, Father. What does all of this have to do with my family and me?" he asked plaintively. "How did we get here?"

Father Desmond hesitated. He knew what all of this was about, but he needed some time to think it all through. Unfortunately, Jack was not going to like the answers that Father Desmond would reveal to him. The answers, he knew, lay in his collection of books.

"Jack, let us head back to my apartment. I have some information I can share with you on the way back, and there are resources in my library that will also shed some light on all of this."

***

It took about thirty minutes to walk from the chapel to Father Desmond's apartment. During their walk, Father Desmond told Jack a story that days ago would have seemed surreal. Not too long ago, the concept of a secret society within the world's religious hierarchy, whose purpose was to combat evil, would have sounded like something out of a Hollywood movie script or an end of the world religious novel. After all that Jack had experienced in the last few weeks, it was not a shocking revelation, nor did it sound implausible.

Father Desmond shared with Jack that JESU was Pope Gregory VII's brainchild. During early January in 1077 AD, the Holy Roman Emperor Henry IV traveled to meet with Pope Gregory VII in Canossa, a town in Northern Italy. History has written that Henry IV came to Canossa seeking forgiveness and reinstatement from the Catholic Church's excommunication. Even today, scholars continued to debate whether Henry IV's act was a great embarrassment to him or a brilliant move on his part to assert that the Germanic peoples would not be subject to the rule of outside parties. However, according to Father Desmond, the event's real impact might be the best-kept secret in human history.

The price of Henry IV's reinstatement was his support for the creation of JESU. Pope Gregory VII had grown concerned about the rise of secularism and the influence of evil amongst the rulers of Europe. He attributed this to the supernatural temptations of the Devil and his demons. Fearing the example these rulers were setting would lead the people away from the church, the Pope concluded the world needed an exceptional order of monastics, an order trained not only in liturgy but in the art of war as it relates to the destruction of all forms of evil. They were to be real warriors for God, and Henry IV would provide the men as well as the financial means by which they would be recruited, trained, and set to the task of protecting the world from the "Snares of the Devil." JESU would guard the world against the things the world would find incomprehensible.

"Father, is this where the role of exorcists originates from?"

"Good question," said Father Desmond. "Exorcism, as a formal ritual, was first written by the Catholic Church in the early 17th century. The basic doctrine surrounding this ritual came from JESU's experiences in the centuries before the ceremony's formal parameters could be established. In some respects, you might even consider exorcism to be a 'red herring,' so to speak. It is perhaps the most well-known and obvious ritual surrounding the impact of evil on our society today, but not every exorcist is a member of JESU. Giving the faithful something like this ritual to focus on, the real work of fighting demons and the Devil can go on in the shadows without their knowledge. It serves as a rather valuable distraction since what JESU does is something most people would not be able to wrap their minds around."

"I think I understand, Father."

"While it began as an instrument of the Catholic Church, JESU expanded over the centuries to meet the evolving risks presented by its enemy. After the Crusades ended in 1291 the order realized that the world beyond Europe was also a battleground. For example, JESU discovered that Muslims were fighting demons, which they referred to as Shaitan. Muslim Imams shared the Quran with JESU and showed them how reciting the Surah-Al-Bagarraa could be used to defeat demons. Both JESU and the Imams had to keep their newly created coalition a secret as the running narrative was that Catholics and Muslims were at each other's throats, not allies in a great crusade against evil. Even today, the friction among religious sects helps JESU maintain its secrecy. The media's love of negative stories means JESU's positive work goes unnoticed."

Everything that Father Desmond told Jack was as fascinating as it was frightening. He described how the release of the Black Death by demons led faith in the church to suffer, causing the institution to tremble to its very foundation. The Black Death began as a spell that a witch or warlock would invoke against a singular enemy. Lucius's demon legions weaponized the magic, and before JESU could figure out what was happening, the plague ran rampant throughout the world. It took centuries for JESU to develop an antidote. JESU's soldiers' willingness to treat the sick even at the risk of their own lives helped save the Church as an institution, but the attrition caused by this nearly brought JESU to its knees. It took hundreds of years to rebuild the organization, and JESU began bringing women into the order in an attempt to overcome the losses. In the meantime, the civilized world plunged into the Dark Ages.

JESU recruited Joan of Arc and thousands of women to its service, but demons infiltrated the Burgundian Faction, which turned Joan over to the English, who burned her at the stake. Martin Luther's ninety-five Theses publicly challenged the church's authority, but it allowed JESU to expand its numbers as Lutheran Reverends swelled its ranks. The Age of Enlightenment and the Great Awakening movements of the 17th and 18th centuries brought Methodist Reverends, Anglican bishops, and Baptist ministers to JESU. The rise of Protestantism influenced Judaism, and the Rabbi's role evolved to include representing the congregation to the community at large. This exposed Jewish leaders to a broader understanding of demonology and the forms evil could assume. In turn, the Talmud expanded JESU's knowledge of demons, including their role in building the temple in Jerusalem.

"Finally, as knowledge of Buddhism and Hinduism expanded in the 20th century," Father Desmond said, "the awareness of the impact of demons in Asia grew. Along with this came new concepts of how to view what is evil. Good and evil are simple concepts, which makes them easy to understand. The danger in keeping things simple is that it may prevent people from looking for the deeper causes of evil."

Father Desmond paused, looked Jack directly in the eye, and said, "Once one can confirm evil's existence, there is no need to explain it. The only requirement is to fight and destroy it."

The two men entered Father Desmond's apartment. Father Desmond headed toward the library and called out, "Hey, Jack, could you get me a beer?"

Jack went to the kitchen, opened the refrigerator door, and grabbed two bottles of beer. He removed the caps from the bottles as he entered the library.

He handed one bottle to Father Desmond and then took a long mouthful from his own. He placed the bottle on the table, removed his jacket, and tossed it on the couch. Father Desmond took a sip from the bottle as his eyes scanned the bookshelves.

"Father, can I help you look?"

Father Desmond turned to Jack. "It's a hardcover book. It appears to be new, a recent publication, but it is ancient. I do this to all of my rare texts to disguise their appearance. Not every book I have here is considered acceptable reading material for a priest. I will explain what I mean once we find it."

Father Desmond's cryptic statement instantly aroused Jack's curiosity. He was not sure if he was genuinely interested or just plain nervous about finding this book. However, he did trust Father Desmond completely. Jack was sure whatever this book was, Father Desmond had a good reason for having it.

"Okay, Father. How will I know it's the book we are looking for? All of the covers look the same."

"You will recognize it when you touch it," Father Desmond said. "It will make you feel the same way you do when you speak to Lucius."

Jack quickly turned to Father Desmond, blood draining from his face.

Father Desmond looked apologetic. "Jack, I am sorry. I should have been more sensitive than that."

"No offense taken. I know I need to be stronger than this. It is just that I got a glimpse of what Lucius is capable of when I threatened him after he kidnapped Amanda. He was furious. He mutilated our cat and took my children hostage as well. I'm terrified of what he's going to do next."

Father Desmond's face lost all expression. "Jack, Lucius is a far greater evil than you realize. The reason I even have the book we are looking for is because of him. I won't lie to you. Your fear is totally justified." Before Jack could react, Father Desmond continued, "Lucius is not an ordinary demon. He is the most powerful evil entity that walks the planet. Perhaps only Satan himself may be more powerful, but since his entrapment in Hell, at least at the moment, Lucius takes the title of most evil. He has walked among men for more than a millennium. His origins date back to the enslavement of demons by Solomon to build the holy temple in Jerusalem. He is as intelligent as he is cunning. He is as a brilliant strategist as he is a ruthless adversary. It can be lethal to underestimate Lucius, and your crossing paths with him was no accident."

Despite what he had already experienced, Jack was still stunned by what Father Desmond had told him. He had started out to write a book. How could all of this be anything but coincidental? What did he mean that meeting Lucius was no accident? Jack's head was spinning. He instinctively raised the beer bottle to his mouth and swallowed the remainder of its contents.

"Jack, I found it!"

Father Desmond quickly sat down on the couch and placed the book on the coffee table in front of them. He opened the book and then picked up an object from the table. It looked like a rock. If Jack recalled his high school geology, it was rose quartz. Jack watched as Father Desmond took the stone, placed it on the text in the book, and started moving it from right to left on the page. Father Desmond never took his eyes from the rock as he moved it across the page.

"Jack, have you ever heard of Cuneiform?"

"Yes. It's an ancient Egyptian language, isn't it?

Father Desmond continued reading. "Mesopotamian, actually. It is unique, and you read the language from the right side of the page to the left, which is the exact opposite of how we read today. This book is in a language that is related to Cuneiform. The rock I am using is made of quartz and is actually a translator. When you move it across the letters, they appear in English."

"What does the book say?"

Father Desmond stopped reading and looked up at Jack. "Are you familiar with Sun Tzu?"

Jack quickly replied, "Actually, yes. He was responsible for writing the *Art of War*. What does this have to do with this book?"

"I realize that a priest who knows about the *Art of War* sounds strange, but hear me out. One of Sun Tzu's truisms was, 'If you know neither your enemy nor yourself, you will succumb in every battle.' This book allows me to know my enemy. The *Codex Giga* is also called the Devil's Bible. Ironically, a 13th-century monk wrote it. The *Codex Giga* is a book of evil, an unholy bible, if you will. Its contents include spells, demon lore, and legends. While you were sharing your confession with me, I recalled reading several passages during my study of the text about a devout soul manipulated into opening a gate to Hell. I thought it was a myth, but I am convinced that Lucius believes he has found that soul. It is you, Jack."

Jack sat down on the couch. Assuming he was not frightened before, he indeed was now. His family was being held hostage by someone or something nearly as powerful as the Devil himself. He was charged by this agent of evil with the task of retrieving an object, a key that he had only seen in a picture one time, from one of the most sinister places on Earth. It was not too far of a leap from there to see that if he failed, his family was dead, and if he succeeded, he would free the Devil from the pit and all that came with that. Of course, his family would still be dead or, even worse, damned, and he along with them.

Jack shook his head and covered his face with his hands. "This cannot be happening." He began to sob.

Father Desmond put his arm around Jack's shoulder. He knew the truth was difficult to accept, but it was the only way Jack would be able to come to grips with what they were going to have to do.

Sun Tzu called the situation they faced *"Desperate Ground."* When an army was in a place where there was no way out, the only choice was to fight. It was human instinct to want to survive, and an army faced with this single option will fight with fierce determination; to win the battle or inflict the maximum amount of punishment on the enemy. Sun Tzu put it this way, *"If you fight with all your might, there is a chance of life, whereas death is certain if you cling to your corner."* Father Desmond knew the sooner Jack accepted this the better.

As Jack composed himself, Father Desmond reiterated the difference between a compromised and a corrupted soul.

"Jack, do you recall my description of a compromised soul? Someone who had gone down the wrong path, but there still was a chance to change the road that they were on. For this individual, redemption is a real possibility. On the other hand, a corrupted soul is so far down a chosen path that it's too late to make amends. Damnation is the only thing awaiting this sinner."

Father Desmond looked Jack in the eye. "Jack, you may be compromised but are far from corrupt. The key, however, will be defeating Lucius."

Father Desmond continued to leaf through the book. "A task far easier said than done." Another passage caught his attention. He turned and asked, "Jack, didn't you mention Lucius requested that you bring the key at midnight on November 1st?"

"Yes. Lucius was precise about that time and date. As I was driving here to see you, I thought about why he did not ask me to deliver the key on Halloween. Perhaps it was the haunting at my home that influenced my thinking. Poltergeist activity, the visits from Lucius in my dreams, and the slaughter of our cat all seemed to point to October 31st as a more appropriate date. I really can't figure out what the significance of November 1st might be."

"November 1st is All Saints Day," Father Desmond stated. He rubbed the stubble on his chin, then leaned forward to reread the passage in the book. "The text, however, references the Day of the Dead. That is actually November 2nd and is known as All Souls Day."

What is Lucius's end game here? Father Desmond wondered. *He never does anything without a purpose. Opening the door to*

Hell seems too obvious of a goal. Lucius needs something more significant than that. The ritual is as much about his ego as it is about releasing Satan from the pit. Why All Souls Day?

"What is All Souls Day, Father? Why is it celebrated?"

"Jack, that's it!" Father Desmond exclaimed. "It is not All Saints Day that matters here. It is All Souls Day. All Souls Day is what Lucius is really interested in."

Before Jack could speak, Father Desmond continued, "Opening the pit is not about letting something out. It is about bringing something into the pit. It is the souls! Don't you see? Lucius wants to harvest the souls."

"I am afraid I do not understand, Father."

Still excited, Father Desmond responded, "All Souls Day is a day of prayer. The faithful pray for the departed souls still caught in purgatory. The prayers help to release the souls, which then make their way to the gate of heaven for their final judgment. These souls are waiting for beatification, which means when the doors to Hell open, they can be swept into the pit in massive numbers."

"I see what you are saying. An army of slave labor and demons in the making."

"Precisely, but there is more to it than that. Part of JESU's mission has been to fight evil. For various reasons, this has come to mean preserving a delicate balance between JESU and Lucius's legions regarding the number of saved souls versus damned souls. If all of those souls from purgatory end up in Hell, it would dramatically upset that balance, which would plunge the world into a period of devastation that it has not witnessed since the Dark Ages. Suffice it to say; this would make events such as the Black Death look like just a common cold. To say that humanity is unprepared, spiritually and otherwise, for what is likely to happen is a total understatement. It might not be the apocalypse as forecasted in the Bible, but it would be pretty damn close."

"And there stands Lucius with his arms folded, smugly overseeing it all."

Father Desmond nodded. "Exactly."

Jack looked at Father Desmond quizzically. "Father, I know it's late, and we have got another long day ahead of us, but I have a question that I want to ask you. How is it that you have come to know so much about Lucius? I'm not a detective, but I sense that you know him far more, shall we say, intimately than a person might from just reading all of these books."

Father Desmond bowed his head. "You are a better detective than you think. I have come to know more about Lucius Rofocale than I really ever wanted to. Not unlike you, he started as the thing of nightmares to me. In many ways, he still is. He's been a relentless adversary and an enemy to all that I believe and hold true. When you first mentioned his name in the diner, I am sure that you saw my reaction. The fear you saw on my face was genuine. It has been more than ten years since my last encounter with Lucius, but I remember it like it happened yesterday. That encounter changed my life and the lives of many of my friends forever.

"Jack," Father Desmond said softly, "I have heard your confession. Now it is time you heard mine."

Jack was shocked. "Father, I can't hear your confession. Isn't there another priest or JESU member we can contact?"

"It has to be you, Jack," Father Desmond said pleadingly. "Once you hear it, you will understand why."

"Okay, Father. The circumstances being what they are and for your willingness to listen to my story without having me committed to an asylum, I will be more than glad to return the favor."

Father Desmond got up from the couch and finished off his beer. He placed the bottle back down on the table and started to speak.

"While it was unknown to me at the time, I first met Lucius Rofocale during the camping trip that I told you about previously. He was the demon that my friends and I summoned through the Ouija board more than forty years ago. As I mentioned, this event led me to become a priest, but it also led to the death of my friends."

Father Desmond took a deep breath and said mournfully, "You see, Jack, you are not the only person who participated in a seemingly harmless activity that ended up destroying the lives of people close to them."

"I am sorry, Mark. After all, I have told you, I know what this sounds like coming from me, but you have to know that it is not all on you. Those boys participated along with you."

Father Desmond sighed. "That's true, I guess. They participated, but it was my board, and I was the one who really wanted to use it. As far as I know, Thomas Manning and Joseph Rogers managed to sleep through Lucius's visit, but Paul Sullivan, like me, saw Lucius in his true form that night. Paul never wanted to use the board in the first place. He was pressured by his friends, mostly by me, to participate."

Father Desmond paused to clear his throat and wipe a tear from his eye. "After the trip and Lucius's appearance, Paul was terrified and became a nervous wreck. He never was the same after that. Paul began to have problems in school, and eventually, his downward spiral led to taking drugs and becoming an alcoholic. When I became a priest, I tried to help Paul, but he stopped coming to the homeless shelter we ran, and I lost track of his whereabouts. That was until I found out that he had committed suicide by jumping from a bridge. I am not sure why, but my instincts tell me that Lucius went to see Paul, and all of those nightmares came rushing back. However, even if that is not the case, I am the one who brought Lucius into Paul's life, and it killed him. Either way, I have to live with it."

After a few seconds, Jack said, "I did not know Paul that well. I do not think he was on the soccer team. Obviously, I knew Thomas and Joseph, but I lost touch with them after soccer ended as we did not go to the same school. Do you know what happened to them?"

Father Desmond heard Jack's question but side-stepped it. "As I said, this incident led me to become a priest, but it also led to me becoming part of JESU."

"How so?"

"While the incident did not bother me anywhere as negatively as it did, Paul, it did continue to have an impact on me. Lucius would come to visit me in my dreams."

Jack had been listening intently, but this certainly got his attention. "So that happened to you too."

"One minute Lucius tried to recruit me; the next he mocked me for my beliefs. Sometimes they were horrible nightmares about the future. I finally confessed what was happening to a fellow priest. I thought he would think I was unhinged, but he listened intently and without judgment. Shortly after that, I had lunch with a different priest. He spoke with me about my dreams and my experience with Lucius. He assured me that he believed everything I said, and he asked if I would like help in putting an end to Lucius's visits. I told him I was interested."

Father Desmond excused himself to get another beer. When he returned, he handed one to Jack and picked up where he had left off.

"I was desperate to have Lucius's intrusions end, and this priest put me in touch with others who taught me what I had to do to stop it. It worked. Clearly, these were not your typical priests. I asked them who they really were. They shared the story of JESU and invited me to join them."

"I'd sure like to learn what you did to get Lucius out of your head. Every time it happens, I end up feeling dirty, violated, if you will."

"I know the feeling, Jack," Desmond whispered, almost inaudibly. "I can help you with that. Remind me later, and I will teach you the incantation you need to speak to block him from your dreams."

Father Desmond tapped his beer bottle with his fingertips. "I accepted their invitation. I was all in. It turned out that I was particularly good at research, which was critically important to JESU's mission. I guess my library bears witness to my success. It helped me climb to the upper echelons of JESU's hierarchy. The rumor was that I was up for consideration for an appointment to the Grand Council, which sets the organization's policy. It is the highest responsibility a JESU member can assume."

Jack interrupted, "Father, for someone who's in such an important position, there's not one iota of arrogance that emanates from you. Your humility is admirable. I guess it comes with your profession, but I still wanted you to hear it from me."

Father Desmond smiled slightly and said, "Thanks. You are very kind for saying so."

His facial expression quickly became somber once again. "While Lucius was out of my head, he never seemed to be far from my thoughts. As the years went by, we crossed paths numerous times. At times it was like we were playing chess. In retrospect, I believe he was just probing my defenses. He was searching for my weaknesses, evaluating my faults and flaws to find an edge. Eventually, he found it."

As Father Desmond continued his confession, Jack noticed a tautness and tension in his face. As much as Father Desmond admitted to his fear of and respect for Lucius Rofocale as an adversary, it was evident to Jack that Lucius had gotten under Father Desmond's skin. Although he was a priest, it was apparent that Father Desmond totally loathed Lucius and hated the evil that Lucius represented, but it was more than that. He despised Lucius's tactics and detested his insufferable arrogance.

"I do not believe you ever asked me how I ended up here in Lawrence. Have you wondered why a priest from Long Island would end up in the Midwest? A priest on the fast track, so to speak, in the most secret organization, possibly in the world. Does not seem to make a lot of sense, does it?"

Jack thought he detected almost a cynical tone in Father Desmond's voice, but before he could respond, Father Desmond answered his own question. "I am on probation, Jack." He took a deep breath and swigged his beer. He spoke again, but the tone of his voice was now remorseful. "I am on probation, and I deserve it. This punishment is probably better than I deserve. I am about to share something with you that very few people on this planet have ever heard. Unfortunately, one of them happens to be Lucius Rofocale."

Father Desmond walked over to the desk in his library and opened the lower drawer. Despite the alcohol they'd both consumed, he pulled out a half-finished bottle of Jack Daniels and grabbed two glasses from the top of the desk. Filling them both, he handed one of them to Jack. The room got eerily quiet as the two men drank whiskey together. It seemed like an eternity before Father Desmond finally broke the silence.

"Jack, a little while ago, you asked me about what happened to Thomas. A little over ten years ago, I received a call from him. We had always been close friends and had kept in touch. Whenever I went back home, Thomas and I would have dinner and catch up. Thomas said he needed to see me and would be flying out to Lawrence the next day as the matter was urgent. When he got here, he told me that Paul had jumped to his death, but I could tell something else was bothering him. Thomas had never really thought of me as a priest and did not confide in me that way, but that day was different. He shared a story that is very familiar to both of us."

Jack's eyes opened wide. "Let me guess. A demon needed him to obtain a key to open the door to Hell, or his family would die."

"While not the same exact story, it was pretty close. Thomas told me that one of the partners in his architecture firm had confided in him that he was a victim of blackmail. A demon had informed the partner that he was to obtain three keys that would open a gate to Hell, or he would expose that the partner was embezzling funds and would ruin him and his family. While Thomas admitted it sounded unbelievable at first, he remembered our experience in the woods and offered to help the partner by reaching out to me."

Father Desmond paused and poured more whiskey. Jack took a swig and encouraged him to continue.

"I assured Thomas that I believed him," Father Desmond said. "I also shared with him that I worked with a society dedicated to fighting evil. Based on my research, JESU had become aware of a second entrance to Hell, but we could never confirm its existence or location. I convinced Thomas that the best way to help him would be to work together to seal this gate permanently. The plan was that he would go back home and have the partner assure the demon he would obtain the key. He just needed to know where and when the keys should be delivered.

Thomas would then share that information with me, and I would arrange with my associates from JESU to ambush the demon, locate the gate, and ensure it would be closed permanently."

"So, what happened next?" Jack asked.

"A day after Thomas left, I received a call from him giving the location of the gate. GPS confirmed the coordinates as a forested area of Culpeper, Virginia. It made sense. As you are now aware, Jack, this part of Culpeper is very remote. It was basically out in the middle of nowhere. He indicated that the meeting would be two days later."

Father Desmond scratched his temple and blinked several times. Despite his fatigue and the effect of the alcohol, he continued. "This did not leave much time. I had to move quickly. I presented my findings to the leadership council of JESU. I needed their permission to act. There was quite a bit of debate, and not everyone on the council believed that we had enough information to commit the significant resources required for such an operation."

As he spoke, Father Desmond recalled the meeting in his mind. He flew to the Vatican, where the Grand Council would meet to discuss policy and strategy.

"Father Desmond," The Chairman of the Grand Council had said, "you realize that assuming we agree you are correct, we are putting a lot of our resources on the line for your operation?"

"Yes, sir. I understand what our organization is risking, but I also want to emphasize what would be at risk if we don't. If this demon were able to open this gate, all Hell would break loose, literally."

The Chairman responded firmly, "We can live without the metaphors. The Council is fully aware of what is at stake here. You are asking us to rely almost entirely on the word of your friend. We have not vetted this individual ourselves and know nothing about him."

"I am asking the Council to trust me," Father Desmond said, raising his voice. "Indeed, you do not know Thomas Manning, but I do. I can assure you that what he is telling me is the truth. There is also my research on the existence of gates leading to Hell."

"Watch your tone, Father," the Chairman interrupted. "We are not calling into question your credentials or reputation. We are, however, less inclined to act based on the myths and legends in your research materials. Some of these are otherworldly, and their authenticity is in question."

Father Desmond had to bite his tongue. He knew losing his temper would not be effective now, even if he thought the Grand Council was composed of close-minded, old-fashioned clerics.

"Alright. Let us put this to a vote. Rabbi Shlomo Tannenbaum, what say you?"

Rabbi Tannenbaum was the father of modern Christian-Jewish relations and strongly supported Father Desmond's role within JESU.

"It is my opinion that Father Desmond has provided us with enough information to move forward with this operation. I vote yes."

"Hindu Swami Aghamkar. As the leader of the Hindu Institute," the chairman asked, "what say you?

The Hindu Swami responded, "I am uneasy about moving forward so quickly. I must say no."

The vote continued, and the Chairman turned to the Buddhist representative Kelsang Gyatso. "Master Gyatso, what is your vote?

Master Gyatso paused for a moment. "I have been unable to obtain any clear direction from the Dalai Lama on how to proceed. As a result, I, too, must vote no."

The Chairman moved next to the Catholic representative. Cardinal Francesco Borghese was newly appointed, and over the years, Father Desmond had interacted very infrequently with him.

"Cardinal Borghese. I realize you have not had much time to get acclimated to your role on the Council. I know you are in a difficult position, but what is your vote?"

Cardinal Borghese rose to address the Council. "Father Desmond. I know your reputation within the society and respect your knowledge. However, I do have concerns about our ability to pull off this operation. I believe we should wait until our forces are far more concentrated and success is more certain. I, therefore, must say no to this mission."

Father Desmond was concerned about how the vote was proceeding. There were already three 'no' votes, and a fourth would prevent the operation from moving forward. The Chairman turned to the Protestant representative next.

Reverend Derek Prince was the senior representative on the Council, having served on it for more than 25 years. He was well-liked and known to have great wisdom.

"Fellow Council members," he said. "I have been a member of this body for many years. I have watched our numbers and influence decrease over the past few years, particularly, and I believe our organization will face significant challenges moving forward. I ask myself this question. 'If we do not react to this threat now, then when will we?' I do not see any other alternative but to act. I vote yes."

"Thank you for your perspective, Reverend Prince," the Chairman said. "Imam Kamil Mufti. Our Islamic representative on this body. What say you?"

Imam Mufti stood. "It is my opinion that we have not had a better scenario for us to strike our enemy in many years. The element of surprise is on our side. I vote yes!"

The vote was tied three to three, with the Chairman now responsible for casting the deciding vote. Father Desmond had butted heads with him many times but believed him to be a fair-minded individual. The Chairman rose to address the Council.

"My friends, never before have I faced such a monumental decision. I share many of the same concerns that you have just articulated. It also is not lost on me that, at this time, the balance of power between ourselves and our enemy is quite tenuous. My decision comes down to one factor."

Looking directly at Father Desmond, the Chairman said, "I believe in you, Father Desmond, even if I have reservations about the operation and its timing. I vote yes. The Council authorizes your operation. I ask that the Council Secretary record the vote as four to three in favor of action."

"I'm sorry, Jack," Father Desmond said now, jolted from his reverie. "Where was I? Oh, yes, JESU's present situation.

"While JESU is a worldwide organization, our numbers have been dwindling over the decades. Since I joined the society, the average age of our members has increased. Conversely, recent religious scandals are shrinking our pool of recruits. Being a religious leader is not viewed with the same respect as it once had been. There is no ignoring that we, as religious leaders, have to shoulder the blame for this. Still, governmental policies have usurped the role that faith-based organizations once played in people's lives. It used to be that when people needed assistance, they would turn to their religious institution. Now they go to the welfare office and seek out food stamps. While these policies may be well-intentioned, the money and power that go hand in hand with them help promote secularism, humanism, and consumerism. All of these philosophies are tailor-made for Lucius's devious schemes, and his demons have no problem keeping their numbers up. Anyway, I put my reputation on the line and convinced the Council to back the operation, and I agreed to lead it. Preparations began immediately, and more than one hundred JESU members were under my command. That night I flew into Dulles Airport, and I met with local JESU members to finalize our plans."

Jack downed the rest of his whiskey and looked at Father Desmond. He saw the pain on his face and the dread in his eyes. Jack had a pretty good idea about what Father Desmond would tell him next. He remembered all of the unburied remains, all of those bones. During his initial visit to the burial mound, Jack knew something terrible had happened there but could not figure out just what it was. Before he could utter the word in his mind, he heard it from Father Desmond.

"Massacre. It was a massacre," Father Desmond said as he sat staring at the floor. His voice was quivering, and his body was trembling. "We were, um, we were ambushed. It was a trap." He muttered to himself, "I led a coalition of the faithful into a slaughter. All those men and women. My friends. I got them all killed."

Father Desmond began to sob. He tried to speak, but what he said was inaudible. Jack slid off the couch and knelt in front of him. He reached out and embraced the Father as he wept bitterly. Jack found himself crying along with him. He searched for words that could comfort him, but Jack could not find any. The two men just hugged one another.

Eventually, Father Desmond was able to pull himself together. Jack poured the final contents of the whiskey bottle into each of their glasses, then said, "I think we can both use this right now."

Father Desmond nodded and gulped down the whiskey. "Thank you. I am sorry for losing my composure."

"Father, there is nothing for which you need to apologize. I'm the one that dragged you back into this business and should be saying sorry to you. I cannot imagine the pain you are in now and the suffering you have been through all of these years."

Father Desmond stared straight ahead at the wall. "I walked off that plane, not realizing that forty-eight hours later, my future would never be the same. There were less than twenty survivors that day. There was talk of dismissing me from the order entirely, but instead, I was given this post here in Lawrence. Oh, they talked about the importance of guarding Stull Cemetery, but I am merely a sentry. I have not been on another mission since then. No one trusts me anymore."

"I trust you, Mark. I would not be here if I didn't."

Father Desmond smiled sadly.

"Thanks, Jack. I know that you mean it. However, please do not forget that I underestimated Lucius. The Society and I have paid a tremendous price for my failure."

Rising from the couch, Father Desmond began to pace around the library. "I have suffered from some variation of PTSD since then. It is why I reacted with fright in the diner when you asked me about evil, and you mentioned Stull Cemetery. After the massacre, I had days where I went from dropping to my knees to beg forgiveness and pray for the souls of my departed friends one minute to cursing myself for my failure the next. I also had to come to grips with the fact that Thomas, one of my best friends, had betrayed me. I suspect that he probably was blackmailed in some way. I really don't know what happened to him. I received a call from his wife, telling me that he had gone missing. To this day, his body has never appeared. I do not anticipate that it ever will."

Jack jumped up from the couch. "Father, I'm sorry to interrupt you, but I know what happened to Thomas. Let me get my notebook."

He retrieved his notebook from his jacket and started leafing through the pages. He pointed. "Here it is. When I reviewed my notes, I recalled writing something down about a tombstone in the graveyard around the burial mound. I wrote down a name, Thomas Manning. The epitaph read, 'Here lies Thomas Manning, a true friend...until the end.'" Jack looked up. "I am sorry, Father," he said quietly. "But I think Thomas is dead."

Father Desmond's head dropped. "I assumed that he was dead. It was likely to have been a torturous death at that. I forgave Thomas a long time ago and prayed he found some peace in the afterlife. I know now that it was not a partner in the firm that was in trouble. It was Thomas."

Father Desmond walked over to the bookshelves and started glancing at the book titles. "After I recovered from my injuries and was sent here to Lawrence, there was nowhere I could go to hide from what happened. I felt like an outcast and spent most of my time alone here in the apartment. At least I had my books to keep me company. That first winter may have been the toughest. It was bitterly cold, but I would wake up every night covered in sweat. It has been ten years now, and things have gotten better, but I still find myself reliving what happened. All the sounds and everything that happened that day will always be with me. Worst of all are the nights I lay in my bed and hear the screams of the wounded. After a while, it grows quiet, and then I lie there in the silence and think about the dead."

Father Desmond turned to face Jack again. "Even today, when I pass colleagues in the courtyard, I still hear them whispering to one another about me."

At that moment, Jack remembered the students pointing and whispering while they were in the courtyard together.

"Sometimes, they talk about me being a murderer loud enough so that I hear it. I go so long without speaking with another human being I think I might go insane. To say that I have lost confidence in myself is an understatement. I still feel shame for my role in all of this. When I look in the mirror, I do not recognize myself. I look for the man I once was, but I do not see him staring back at me. Between what I know people think about me and my own self-loathing, I am damned if I know who I am anymore."

"I'm pretty sure I know how you feel, Father," Jack said. "At least on some level. I understand what it feels like to lose who you are and to be unable to regain your self-confidence."

"I know you do, Jack. I know it is very late, but I have one last thing that you need to know."

While it seemed like an eternity, in ten minutes, the carnage was over. After the gunfire stopped, Mark lay on the ground, trying to make sense of what had just happened. The wounds in his arm and leg were painful enough, but when he heard someone or something walking among the dead and dying, he tried to remain motionless, hoping whoever or whatever it was would pass by. Then he heard that voice.

"Mark, you can roll over. I know you are not deceased. If I wished it, you would already be dead."

Rolling over, Mark came face to face with Lucius Rofocale in his demon form, the way Mark had seen him when he was a teenager. Lucius was every bit as hideous as Mark remembered him to be.

"Father Desmond," Lucius said gloatingly. "You are alive because that is how I wish it to be. You see, this ambush was not just about extinguishing JESU. No, it was more about destroying you. You have been a thorn in my side since our first encounter.

While slaughtering you would certainly be satisfying; it will give me even greater satisfaction knowing that your reputation within JESU is now going to be permanently in ruins. After news of this incident reaches JESU headquarters, it will be evident to the leadership that their faith in you has been, shall we say, misguided. The few of your associates that I allow to live will surely help see to that. While I suspect that the leadership's collective conscience will not allow them to excommunicate you, you will most certainly be a pariah for the rest of your life and beyond. History will not be kind to you or your reputation. For you, a man driven with such ambition, that is a fate worse than death itself."

Father Desmond, who had been pacing the room incessantly, sat back down on the couch and said, "Lucius did his work well. He must be proud of what he accomplished. He broke me, and while he said it was not his primary objective, he wounded JESU grievously. It is ten years later, and we not only have not recovered, but the limited information with which I have access tells me we are losing ground to Lucius and his legions. Lucius is more powerful than ever, and JESU is now so weak they are unable to mount an effective offensive."

Jack sat in silence, trying to absorb what he had just heard.

"Jack, it is nearly 4:00 a.m.," Father Desmond said, standing. "The sun will be rising in just a few hours, and we have some serious work yet to do. I suggest we try to get a few hours of sleep. I have the map with the location of the key, and I will fill you in on Stull Cemetery while we drive there in the morning."

Father Desmond left the library, and Jack lay down on the couch, taking his cell phone from his pocket. He flipped through his saved messages and slid his finger across one from a few months ago. Amanda's voice came on, and he could hear the boys laughing about something in the background. She reminded him of an upcoming appointment, and then he listened to the words, "I love you, Jack."

Jack smiled and promised himself that tonight, he would try to dream of happier times.

Chapter 16

Jack woke on the couch, his throat on fire from screaming. His eyes darted quickly around the room, and it took a minute for him to realize exactly where he was. The apartment was quiet, and he was stunned that his screams had not awakened Father Desmond. Thanks to Father Desmond, Lucius could no longer invade his dreams, but this did not stop Jack from having the same nightmare he seemed to have night after night. Was it his mind playing tricks on him or, worse yet, was it a premonition of things to come?

Occasionally, he would wake up in the middle of this nightmarish scenario, but when he would fall back asleep, he would pick up the horrible dream right where he'd left off. It was always the same ending. Amanda, Louis, and David lay on the ground, defiled by satanic symbols carved into their lifeless bodies. The blood still draining from their bodies, transforming the once-green landscape around them to a sickening crimson red. It seemed so real, and it always concluded with Jack kneeling next to their bodies, screaming in agony.

Pushing the nightmare from his mind, Jack made his way to the kitchen and stood before the stove. Once the coffee pot finished percolating, he poured himself a cup. He placed the mug under his nose, closed his eyes, and deeply inhaled the aroma. The vapors from the hot, black liquid began to lift the shroud of fatigue that dominated his mind and body. He pulled out a chair, sat down at the table, and took a sip from the cup. Rubbing the stubble on his chin, Jack started to think about what he and Father Desmond had discussed last night, as well as the challenge they faced today. A sense of fear and dread began to dominate his thoughts.

While he had faced unspeakable challenges in the woods around Culpeper, somehow, he sensed that Stull Cemetery presented risks far beyond what he might be able to imagine. It was less than reassuring to see that Father Desmond was anxious about going there. Jack also wondered what state of mind Father Desmond was going to be in after his confession. The pain on his face had been intense, and even though the events he had shared occurred ten years ago, the wounds appeared to be still very fresh. Jack wanted to be there for him, but at the same time, he selfishly wondered if Father Desmond could be on his game so soon after what they discussed. A few hours seemed like it might not be enough time to process it all, and Jack needed him to be at his absolute best. Any concerns that Jack had instantly faded when he saw him.

Father Desmond entered the kitchen. He wore a brown camouflage jacket with denim jeans. He placed a canvas knapsack on the table with two pairs of insulated, weather-proof gloves sticking out of one of the pockets. Heavy-duty hiking boots completed the ensemble. It was clear Father Desmond was ready for this mission.

"Good morning, Jack. I see you made coffee. How about some breakfast?"

Jack found another mug and poured some coffee into it. He handed the cup to Father Desmond and slid a plate of eggs across the table. Both men ate quickly, and Jack poured another cup of coffee while Father Desmond took something out of his bag.

"Jack, this is a map of the area around Stull Cemetery. I wanted to show it to you so we could go over the plan for today."

The document Father Desmond placed on the table appeared to be in immaculate condition.

"How old is this map?"

"It is from the late 19th century. You can tell by the weave of the paper. It has been updated several times since then."

"I'm amazed at the condition it's in."

"The Society preserves such documents in a room which is climate controlled. As the archivist, I have access to all of the documents related to the cemetery."

Father Desmond was stone-faced, his demeanor businesslike.

"Jack, Stull Cemetery doesn't show up on any GPS or other navigation equipment. I have gone there only once, and after you have been there, you will never be able to forget it. It is the front line in the battle of good versus evil. You will find this out for yourself today. Route 40 West is a straight shot from Lawrence to an area around five miles from the cemetery. It is about a 25 to 30-minute drive. The road there ends abruptly for reasons that I will explain later."

Father Desmond began to trace what appeared to be a hiking trail. "From here, we will approach the cemetery on foot, moving in a northwest direction. Based on the terrain, it is roughly a two- to three-hour hike. We need to leave enough time to find the key. I have a document in the bag that provides the object's exact location, but this assumes I am interpreting it correctly. None of my books say who buried the key or why they interred it where they did. Some of the research materials suggest it is near the grave of the minister who led the people astray, but that is not something I can confidently confirm."

Father Desmond hesitated briefly. "We will want to keep close tabs on time and be sure to leave the cemetery no later than 4:00 p.m. The cemetery is ominous even during the day. Mist often hangs in the air, and you always feel like thousands of sets of eyes are staring at you. Millions and millions of years of evolution and biology condition us not to be afraid of the daylight, but if there were such a thing as a 'daymare,' Stull Cemetery would be the poster child for it."

Jack struggled to choke down the rest of his coffee as Father Desmond continued.

"At this time of year, sunset is around six-thirty, and we absolutely want to avoid the area after dark. Stull Cemetery at night is pitch black. Light from the moon or stars cannot seem to penetrate its darkness, and an aura of evil surrounds it. I heard moaning, groaning, and screams all around me when I was there, but no evidence of what caused them. I saw floating lights and shadowy figures that vanished into thin air."

Father Desmond rolled up the map and put it in his knapsack.

"Jack, do not forget that today is the day before Halloween. The barrier between the living and the dead is at its thinnest on this day, and we need to be aware of the potential for increased supernatural activity."

Looking Jack straight in the eye, Father Desmond warned, "I wish I could give you more specifics, but we need to be ready for just about anything. I would sooner predict the numbers for tomorrow's lottery drawing than try to predict anything surrounding Stull Cemetery."

If it was possible, this briefing made Jack even more nervous than he'd been previously. He glanced through the kitchen window and saw the sun beginning to rise. With trepidation, he said, "Okay, Father. I'll get my coat, and we can get going."

Father Desmond slung the knapsack over his shoulder, and the two men exited the apartment. Jack noticed that this time Father Desmond locked the door behind them. They headed to the parking lot and got into Father Desmond's car.

As they pulled away, neither man noticed the eyes that were watching them.

***

Nadia slid down in the front seat of the car, making every effort possible to remain undetected. She had followed Aitken and Desmond back to the apartment late last night and was waiting to see what they were going to be up to today. Once Nadia confirmed their movements, she would report back to Lucius. She was not exactly sure what was going on as Lucius had not filled her in on much, but the one thing he did tell her was that Jack would be heading to Stull Cemetery to "acquire something" for Lucius.

Within the demon community, Stull Cemetery was a place of both historical and spiritual significance. It was a beacon and a cautionary tale of what demons lost while serving as an inspiration for what they might once again achieve. A pilgrimage to this location was something that every demon wanted to make. Nadia had never had the privilege, but she had heard that the place had energy beyond description; it was something you had to experience. She was actually looking forward to the possibility that she might get to feel it for herself, but business before pleasure.

Just then, she saw Father Desmond and Jack emerge from the building and head to Father Desmond's car. She carefully observed Desmond opening the driver's side door and placing a knapsack he was carrying on the front seat. As he slid behind the wheel, Jack entered the passenger side and slammed the door. Desmond turned the ignition, and the car headed out of the parking lot.

Nadia watched them turn the corner, and she pulled her car out of her parking space to follow them. She tailed them closely but not in a way that would reveal her presence. Nadia followed them as they turned right on Massachusetts Avenue and then a left onto West 6th Street. She knew that West 6th Street would eventually become Route 40. Just as Lucius had said, they were heading in the direction of Stull Cemetery. Nadia picked up her phone and began to dial Lucius's number.

Jack looked out the window, admiring the historic homes and the fall foliage. The car quickly left the outskirts of Lawrence, and the geography took on a rural character. They passed a highway sign that indicated the road had become Route 40. Father Desmond began to speak, and the tone of his voice became very solemn.

"Jack, I have been searching for the words that will help you understand Stull Cemetery. My religious studies, and most other religions for that matter, feature some variation of Hell and describe it as a place of eternal punishment, torment, and suffering. But Stull Cemetery is much more than just a physical location, more than just a place located on the map I laid on the table. Even though the entrance has remained sealed for more than 100 years, it still radiates pure evil. There is an unnatural quiet that surrounds the place. Even the land around it is cursed. The landscape you see out the window will begin to change the closer that we get to it. Time has spawned many stories about Stull Cemetery. Hauntings and paranormal activity as well as witchcraft and a satanic cult. Some of these stories are true, and some are just legend, but there is one common theme to them all: Stull Cemetery is undeniably and inherently evil."

Father Desmond paused, and Jack just sat, listening intensely. He glanced out the window and noticed no trees or autumn colors like he'd been taking in only a few miles back. Some patches of green grass and small patches of undergrowth were evident in a sea of brown foliage. There was not much else.

"Stull is tucked away in the quiet, rural Kansas countryside. This most sinister piece of land, located in the least likely place, was settled by immigrants of German descent in the 1850s. An ornate church built in the heart of the town sat atop a hill that gave a panoramic view of the local area. It was the epicenter of the community. Unfortunately, a cemetery constructed adjacent to the church quickly filled up with bodies as the settlement suffered significant hardships, including harsh winters, disease outbreaks, and great famine. Everything about Stull and its inhabitants seemed to be cursed, and the remaining settlers wanted to leave. Still, they had no means to resettle elsewhere, and with Kansas being torn apart by violence between pro-slavery activists and abolitionists, there was no place for them to go."

Father Desmond quickly glanced at his watch, and Jack looked out the window again. He took note that where there had once been a significant, almost abnormal amount of roadkill earlier in the trip, now there was none. There were no signs of life anywhere. He sensed this meant they must be getting closer to their destination.

"I found a diary written by Josiah Bradford in the archives of JESU's research library, which indicated that a stranger arrived in Stull in the spring of 1857. He told them he was a minister sent to replace the one who had perished over the winter. He promised the settlers that he brought with him prosperity as they had never known before. They only needed to have faith in him. The minister carried with him a sack of what he said contained especially blessed wheat seed. Later that fall, it appeared to be just that as the settlers reaped a bumper crop."

Father Desmond continued, "The diary stated that as Halloween approached, the nightly sermons of the minister began evolving from recommendations to demands. The settlers worked long hours excavating the basement under the church. The minister addressed their questions in the form of threats that their lives would return to the poverty and difficult times they had previously experienced if they failed to obey. An ominous darkness took over Stull, and the settlers one by one fell under the spell of the minister."

"Sounds a lot like Lucius," Jack interjected. "Do the archives provide any further information on the minister? Also, did you say the name of the diarist was Bradford?"

"Yes. The Bradford's were a prominent family in JESU history. Josiah's diary has been the best source of information we have about Stull Cemetery. It is written in code, probably to protect Josiah from the wrath of the minister. While we are pretty certain about the details, some parts are either indecipherable or missing. The identity of this minister is unknown. We are not precisely sure what happened between 1857 and 1859, but we know that the land around Stull started to go sour. Nothing would grow, and large fissures began to show in the soil with steam venting out the cracks. Rumors began to circulate in the towns surrounding Stull of witchcraft and people abducted by shadow figures, never to return. No matter which way the wind would blow, it brought with it a scent of decay. An odor like burnt flesh. A smell of death surrounded Stull."

Jack did not notice until the car stopped that they had literally reached the end of the road. There was a 20-foot-high berm covering the highway and a stone barrier across the road covered in satanic symbols and other types of graffiti. To the left was a steep slope that no vehicle would be able to navigate. To the right was more of the browned-out landscape that Jack had seen along the way. While Jack surveyed their surroundings, Father Desmond pulled two flasks from his knapsack. Jack thought that a good stiff drink before they set out might be a good idea, but it turned out that Father Desmond had something else in mind.

"End of the road, Jack," Father Desmond said. "We will be walking from here."

Jack glanced up to the top of the berm. "Why the barricade?"

"The local government closed the road years ago," Father Desmond answered. Then he said ominously, "It seems that fire always burns under the ground around Stull. The road buckles, fractures, and cracks so frequently that it is not worth the effort to maintain them. The local government closed the road ahead years ago."

"A fire burning beneath the surface of the earth, continuously?" Jack asked in disbelief.

"Sounds like Hell, doesn't it," Father Desmond stated. "It causes steam and carbine monoxide gas to vent from fissures in the ground. You cannot see it or smell it, but I am certain you are aware that a high concentration of CO can kill you."

"Doesn't the fact that we would be outdoors eliminate this risk?"

"Jack, in some places here, the air is more poisonous than Venus's, whose atmosphere is a lethal combination of CO gas and Sulfuric Acid droplets. This mixture would poison or suffocate any living organism known to humankind."

"This all just keeps getting better and better," Jack said sarcastically. Staring at the graffiti on the wall, he said, "I can't believe the authorities allow this vile crap to remain here."

"The authorities do not patrol here anymore, Jack. Frankly, they act as if Stull does not even exist."

"I can see that. Anything else I need to know?"

"While I finish telling you the final part of the story of Stull Cemetery," he continued, "we need to drink the contents of these flasks. They contain holy water, herbs, and other protective minerals to shield us from any evil we might meet. When it comes to Stull Cemetery, it is best to take no chances."

Jack opened the flask and took a sip. It was surprisingly pleasant tasting, very similar to mineral water.

"Communication being what it was back then, it took time for the reports to reach the members of JESU. The archives indicate that in July 1859, several JESU investigators arrived in Stull to verify the locals' claims. Only one of them returned, and he painted a far more sinister picture. He confirmed that black masses involving many human sacrifices were ongoing, but he was equally troubled by what he saw at the church. He was sure that the church on the hill was a portal. His notes were very detailed, and he indicated that demons routinely traveled through the church, and the area was always heavily guarded.

"He positively identified one of Hell's princes, Dagon, who appeared to be playing a key role in what was occurring. Dagon held dominion over demon agricultural and fertility practices, and the use of the special wheat seed that I mentioned earlier confirmed his role here. At that time, JESU's archives had no definitive sightings of Dagon for more than a thousand years. It was clear that something very significant was occurring at Stull."

Jack and Father Desmond finished drinking the flasks' contents and exited the car.

"What's in the knapsack, Father?"

"Two additional canteens of water, a compass, the map, and another document that has a diagram of the cemetery itself, along with what I believe to be directions to the location of the final key. Here, Jack, clip this to your belt."

"What is it?

"I mentioned concerns about carbon monoxide, and this is a special CO detector."

"Is there anything you haven't thought of, Father?"

As he locked the vehicle, Father Desmond hoped that Jack was right and that he had not missed anything. At Stull Cemetery, even the simplest oversight could be lethal.

As the men headed to the right, Jack asked, "What happened after JESU discovered that something was going on at the cemetery?"

"We know the ultimate ending, but what really happened next is pure conjecture. The best we can tell is that JESU sent a significant force, perhaps nearly all of its warriors, to Stull, and the battle began in late September of 1859. Casualties were high, so firsthand accounts are rare, and we are unsure how accurate they may be. One thing the few accounts we do have all agree on is that the battle went badly for JESU."

As the men slowly walked the trail, Father Desmond continued, "One of my theories is that they rushed the force to Stull to ensure that they were in place before Halloween. For psychological and spiritual reasons, fighting evil when the veil between the supernatural and our world is thinnest might be problematic. Evil is at its most powerful then. If nothing else, it could create a morale issue. I think the battle may have begun before all of our warriors were actually assembled. We may have sent our forces in piecemeal rather than massing them, and we may not have done enough reconnaissance to probe the enemy for their weaknesses. Again, that is purely speculation on my part."

Jack thought to himself that Mark would be a great raconteur, giving guided tours.

"You speak very passionately about this subject," he said. "I understand why your research skills are held in such high regard. You clearly know your stuff."

"It's ironic, Jack. This epic battle, perhaps the most critical life and death struggle in history is one which the whole world is totally unaware ever took place."

Father Desmond continued with his analysis, "As I mentioned previously, the church's location dominates the top of a hill, which made it impossible to approach without being seen by the demon legions. In military terms, they held the high ground, and frontal assaults were suicidal. A lesson that the country at large would soon learn a few short years later during the Civil War. The battle raged on for several days until something significant changed the tide."

Jack was mesmerized, mouth slightly agape. He forgot where they were for the moment, totally caught up in the story that Father Desmond shared with him. Jack always found stories surrounding significant religious events fascinating. He loved movies like *The Ten Commandments*, *King of Kings*, *The Greatest Story Ever Told,* and the religious symbolism of films such as *Raiders of the Lost Ark* and *The Last Crusade*. He would always get caught up in the story and often wonder, *"What if there were scientific evidence that they were true?"*

He thought the same thing about the account that Father Desmond was now sharing. Jack looked down at the ground, carefully gauging each step that he took.

"Don't leave me hanging, Father."

"JESU's historical accounts say that with the battle appearing to be lost, the remaining soldiers dropped to their knees and prayed in unison for the intervention of the Archangel Saint Michael."

"And?" Jack asked in anticipation.

"Saint Michael appeared with his angel army and, assisted by the heavenly host, JESU routed Dagon's demons and banished Dagon back to Hell. The roof of the former church collapsed on itself, and the angels found that the basement entrance was opened and closed by a large door. The door, made of a material that appeared to be similar to iron, was a metal unknown to man. When the angels shut the door, they noticed several keys in the locks. They turned the keys to lock the door, and then Saint Michael raised his sword and slashed the keys with his blade. The intent was to seal the door by breaking the keys off in the locks and jamming them for eternity. Saint Michael was successful in doing so, but the sword shattered."

As Father Desmond finished speaking, Jack flinched. The sword! He remembered what Lucius had told him about the sword and what he had shown him. Jack stopped and said, "Father, as I mentioned the other day, Lucius had a sword. He told me it was the sword of Saint Michael. If it no longer exists, how is it possible that he had the sword? The sword I saw was intact."

Father Desmond put his hand on Jack's shoulder. "I remember, Jack. I have some information about that which I will share with you, but not here. There is always demon activity around the cemetery. Visiting Stull Cemetery to a demon is not dissimilar to how a Muslim might make an obligatory pilgrimage to Mecca. But it is an attraction to those whose dreams are evil and include reopening the gate. We never know who might be listening or who might be following us. The sword is a topic best revisited in a more secure setting."

Jack nodded his agreement. The men continued walking, and Jack asked, "Father, how do we reconcile what you just told me with religious texts such as the Bible? What I mean is that when I read the Bible, the only reference to Saint Michael is in the book of Revelation, surrounded by events related to the apocalypse. Stull, Kansas, is not the holy land, so what do you really make of all of this?"

Father Desmond thought carefully for a moment. "A few days ago, I shared with you my thoughts on good versus evil and the supernatural. What I told you then I believe to be true now. Jack, for me, these questions often come down to facts verse faith. I am a man of faith, but as a researcher, I have come across information that does not precisely match everything I learned in the seminary. As a JESU member, I have seen and experienced things that the average person would not fully comprehend. You have experienced some of those things yourself. Would you have believed them before all of this happened to you? Some might call me a skeptic, but I believe myself to be a realist. Perhaps I am scarred by the massacre and its aftermath, but I do remain open to the possibility of anything if there are facts to back it up. Do I believe every word in the Bible verbatim? I would be less than truthful if I told you that I did, but that does not mean I doubt the overarching premise that good and evil exist and are in perpetual conflict with one another. I have seen and experienced too much to doubt this."

Jack mused. "It's just a lot to take in, I guess."

The trail began to narrow, and Father Desmond took the lead. While they were walking, Jack pulled out the picture of Amanda and the boys he had found in the cabin. Jack wondered where they were and what they must be thinking right now. He knew Amanda would have her hands full trying to help David and Louis deal with what was happening. As he put the picture back in his pocket and his mental resolve stiffened, he knew he would need to dig deep to find the strength to see this through. Retrieving the key today was the first step in getting his family back. He said a prayer in his head, asking for the courage to accomplish this.

***

Nadia pulled her car off the road, and while there was not much material to work with, she managed to hide it behind some brush just off the highway. She took out her phone to check in with Lucius and was unable to get any cell service. Nadia could not text or e-mail either. She was going to have to do this the old-fashioned way. Nadia closed her eyes and began to chant:

"Igenti Domino Mio Volo Loqui Tecum. Dimitte Loqui Invicem."

After several minutes Nadia made a mental connection with Lucius.

"Nadia, my dear. No cell service, I see. What update do you have for me?"

"My Master. As you directed, I have followed the Priest and your bitch Aitken. They arrived at the highway barricade and started toward Stull Cemetery. They are probably about twenty to thirty minutes ahead of me. As you desired, I made no contact with them, nor are they aware of my presence."

"I see, just as I expected, Nadia. Tell me, were you able to get any sense of their state of mind? How did they present to you? Confident? Frightened?"

Nadia paused before she responded. She wanted to choose her words carefully. Lucius's reactions to her reports could be unpredictable.

"They appeared to be engaged in a very lengthy discussion, Master. Desmond was doing most of the talking, and Aitken was listening with great interest."

"I see, Nadia," said Lucius. "Go On."

"Desmond's face appeared to be very serious. I saw no fear from my vantage point. It was taut; I would say he had a look of determination. Aitken, on the other hand, had a deer in headlights appearance. I would not say he was afraid, but there was a profound sense of concern and perhaps some confusion on his face. Whatever Desmond was telling him, it was certainly making an impression."

Lucius considered Nadia's report, then asked, "Did Father Desmond have anything with him?"

"Yes, Master. He had a knapsack. Through my binoculars, I saw him hand a flask to Aitken, and then they both drank the entire contents of their containers. After they exited the vehicle, Desmond took out some papers and placed them within in a pocket on his jacket."

"Good Nadia, excellent," Lucius replied. "I expect that the papers are a map that will direct them to find the key which Mr. Aitken is going to return to me in the next twenty-four hours. You have done well, Nadia. So much better than on some of your previous assignments."

Nadia breathed a sigh of relief and said, "Thank you, Master. What are my orders?"

Lucius thought for a moment and said, "Nadia, I want you to continue to follow Father Desmond and Mr. Aitken. I do not want to hear back from you until you confirm that they have successfully retrieved the key. While my preference would be that they remain unaware of your presence, it also is imperative that their mission is successful. If you need to intervene to ensure this, you have my authorization to do so."

Lucius's voice grew firmer. "You are not to take Father Desmond lightly. While he may have been sitting on the sidelines for a decade, he is still more than a match for the likes of you."

Nadia flinched at Lucius's statement. While Lucius had given her more latitude on this mission than he had ever done before, this was far from a ringing endorsement of her work. She was well aware of what failing to follow Lucius's orders would mean. Failure was not an option for her, particularly on a mission of this importance. There would be no verbal assault or banishment back to Hell. Not even torture. With a snap of his fingers, she would cease to exist.

"Do we understand one another? Are we clear, Nadia?"

"Yes, Master, we are clear...crystal clear."

"Good. I will await your next report."

The mental connection between the two terminated instantly. Nadia collected herself and then took off down the trail after Father Desmond and Jack.

***

Jack and Father Desmond had been hiking for a little over an hour. As lush and overgrown as the forests of Culpeper, Virginia, had been, the trail to Stull Cemetery was nothing but utter desolation. As far as the eye could see, everything was brown as if it had not rained here in years. Grass, which Jack imagined had once been green, waving in the breeze. Black piles of ash from trees littered the landscape, incinerated where they once stood. Those trees not consumed by fire were twisted and bleached white, like charcoal after it has burned for hours. It was acre upon acre of ruin.

Outside of the boundaries of the trail were cracks and fissures in the ground. Steam and who knows what other types of gases seeped into the air, and the smoke hung around their knees, seemingly hugging the ground. Every so often, Jack would see what once were plastic bottles melted. Jack was sure he could feel the heat radiating from the ground into his shoes. He worried if he stood too long in one place, the soles of his shoes might melt.

There was one thing in common with Culpeper: the silence. Were it not for their footsteps breaking sticks on the ground or the whistling of the wind; there would have been no noise. No birds singing. No rustling of animals in the brush. No crickets or other insect noises. There were no signs of animal life anywhere, not even any bones. The area appeared to have an inability to sustain life of any kind.

The trail's incline began to increase, and the two men reached the top of a slight rise. Father Desmond removed a pair of binoculars from the knapsack and looked toward the west. Through the smoke and clouds, he was able to see the ruins of the church. He handed the binoculars to Jack and pointed toward what remained of the church. They were still about an hour from their destination, but finally, seeing the church brought home the reality of their mission and what was at stake. Jack saw it, and a new wave of fear came over him.

As the trail descended, Father Desmond told Jack about how the destruction they were seeing was slowly spreading across the countryside.

"Over the century since the battle at Stull, several towns have been erased from the landscape. First, the paved streets began to buckle and crack. Then, foul odors permeated basements, and the danger of asphyxiation from the poisonous gases created by whatever was happening under the ground led people to abandon their homes. The once vibrant neighborhoods became smoldering ghost towns. A picket fence here, an abandoned chair there, and driveways were disappearing into the craters and cracks that seemingly appeared out of nowhere. An eerie grid of what once were busy thoroughfares were now just abandoned roads."

Jack closed his eyes and shook his head. "That is unbelievable and tragic. I cannot imagine what those people were going through."

"I don't believe it made the national news, but a near catastrophe was averted in one town when the owner of a gas station happened to check the temperature in his underground tanks and found that they were nearly at the point of causing an explosion. Fortunately, the gasoline did not blow up, and the tanks were filled in before something terrible could happen. Unfortunately for the town, however, it eventually was evacuated and left to die."

"I wonder just what could generate enough heat to cause all of this to happen. I read an article once about the planet Mercury. Being the closest planet to the sun, surface temperatures there could climb as high as 800 degrees Fahrenheit during the day, and lead would be instantly liquefied there."

"Jack, let me show you something."

Father Desmond took out his phone and began showing a video

"This is footage from one of these towns. A mix of snow and rain is falling, and you can see the steam created as the water vaporizes on contact with the road."

Jack asked to see the video several times. He found it difficult to believe what he was watching.

"Look at that." Jack pointed to the video. "Even railroad cars were left where they stood. The tracks are all twisted."

"Scientists said the temperatures of the fires burning under the earth might exceed a thousand degrees. Attempts to relocate graves proved futile, as the bodies experienced cremation from below."

"My God, the smell must be horrific."

"It is, Jack. The smell of burning is everywhere."

Father Desmond stopped and pulled out a canteen from his knapsack. He tossed it to Jack and took another one out for himself. "Do not worry. It won't dilute the elixir I had you drink earlier."

Jack took a deep drink. He turned and looked at a tree stump that was just off the trail. It was smoking, steam rising out of the hollowed-out middle of the stump.

"So, you have been to one of these towns?" Jack asked as he moved in to take a closer look at the stump.

Before Father Desmond could respond, the ground gave out beneath Jack's feet, and the next thing he knew, he was suspended in mid-air, hanging on a tree root with one hand. His step off the trail had triggered the collapse of a sinkhole.

The hole was ten to fifteen feet across. It was dark and appeared to be very deep. As Jack swayed in space, his CO monitor slipped off his belt and fell into the black expanse below him. The next thing he heard was the piercing sound of the monitor. Jack knew he was in real trouble as he tried to reach the exposed root with his other hand.

"Jack, hold on!"

Father Desmond carefully made his way around the hole to take up a position that would enable him to reach out to Jack. He grabbed Jack's wrist on the arm, attempting to get to the exposed tree root.

"Gotcha!" he said.

Ten years ago, he would have had the strength to extricate Jack from this hole, but time had taken its toll on him, and he was concerned that he might not be able to pull him out.

Just then, a feminine voice said, "Well, gentlemen. It seems that you have run into a little difficulty, haven't you? Let us see if I can lend a hand."

The woman stood next to the tree stump. The heat from it had no impact on her at all. She moved around the hole toward Jack, using the side opposite of Father Desmond. The side he chose to avoid was due to the heat radiating out of the tree stump. She reached down to Jack and grabbed his shirt and jacket, then yanked him from the hole to safety with ease. Both men jumped to their feet as the ground was too hot to sit on. They turned to thank their rescuer, but she was gone. They frantically looked around, but there was no trace of her.

Jack panted. "I have never met a woman who would have the strength to do what she did."

"That was no woman. It was a demon. No human being has that type of strength. The question is not only who she was, but why did she save you?"

Jack looked Father Desmond in the eye and said, "Lucius. Lucius sent her."

"Had to be. What concerns me is normally, I would have recognized that she was following us. I am not sure how I missed it. Whoever she was, she was good, and I mean very good. Only Lucius would employ someone so skilled."

"So why, Father? Why would she intervene?"

"Remember the legend, Jack? You are the compromised soul that is going to bring the key to Lucius. He must have sent her to shadow us and ensure that you hold up your end of things."

"I guess I owe her a thank you. I never thought I would be happy to be saved by a demon. That hole scared the shit out of me."

Father Desmond nodded. "Right. We are losing time, Jack. Let us get going. I do not want to be around here when it gets dark."

Jack shook his head in agreement. The two men continued up the trail toward the cemetery but with a heightened level of caution.

Jack flexed his shoulder. The area that his rescuer had grabbed felt sore as well as unnaturally warm. It was an eerie feeling. Jack glanced behind him. He was sure they were being watched, but he saw nothing but the hole in the ground that almost swallowed him up. Jack reasoned that the landscape was so barren that it left no place for someone to hide. The demon must be far away by now. He chalked up his wariness to nearly losing his life and picked up his pace to catch up with Father Desmond.

Chapter 17

October 30th
Stull Cemetery, Stull, Kansas
11:00 a.m.

Despite Jack's brush with death, the two men tried to pick up the pace. He found it challenging to keep up and concentrate as along the trail were dozens of altars and remains of sacrificed animals and humans. The few trees he saw had inverted crosses nailed to them or strange-looking symbols fastened from branches hanging off the limbs.

"Did you hear that?" Jack asked nervously. "It sounded like someone was whispering my name."

Father Desmond stopped to listen. "I don't hear anything at the moment, but don't forget, Jack, Stull Cemetery is highly symbolic to demons and an inspiration for all those who worship evil. These entities frequently explore the area, searching for an entry point."

Jack looked around but saw no one.

"Forgive me, Father, but that explanation is less than comforting."

"No matter how closely JESU patrols the area, these incidents are almost inevitable. If it isn't demons or occultists, the local kids are always looking for a thrill on a Saturday night. It doesn't help that the police and politicians want nothing to do with Stull and do nothing to help secure the area."

Jack recalled Father Desmond had told him that no demon could access the site once they hit the road. Angels buried an iron chain encircling the area after the 1857 battle, preventing access to the cemetery by demons. For some unknown reason, iron had a repelling effect on such monsters. Rituals, including the sprinkling of holy water to sanctify the ground around the defiled church, were performed annually to reinforce the warding. Jack took at least some reassurance from all this but hoped they would reach the road soon.

It was not long before the trail intersected with the remains of a gravel road. No words passed between Jack and Father Desmond, but at the same time, the sky took on a menacing dark gray hue. Both men could not help but notice that nature did nothing to reclaim what belonged to her despite the location having no inhabitants for more than a century. The shoulders of the path had more of the browned-out foliage that had lined the trail. No grasses or any other vegetation grew in the crevices of the gravel road itself. It was as if time had stood still, and the road looked just as it might have when the battle occurred there more than a century ago.

As the men looked left, they saw that the road meandered downhill and disappeared into a burnt-out tree line. Jack looked at the dead forest through a pair of binoculars. He got the feeling that something was staring back at him. *Even the lifeless woods around here seem to have eyes.*

In front of them was an open field with a steady incline toward the top of the hill. Scattered in the area were clumps of dead scrub brush. The field eventually ended at a twisted fence that outlined the graveyard's boundaries. The cemetery was full of graves whose tombstones were in various stages of upset. Some were leaning over, others lying on the ground. There was a space in the wrought iron fence line encircling the cemetery where an entrance gate that was ten to fifteen feet tall still stood, and on top of which were letters that clearly spelled out: Stull Cemetery. Father Desmond took a deep breath and pulled the map out of his knapsack.

The two men reviewed the map closely, and Father Desmond pointed out that the first stop on the map was the church's front steps. The two men visually followed the gravel road, which wound its way up the hillside and ended at the building entrance. The structure before them dominated the summit of the hill upon which it sat. Father Desmond folded the map and placed it back in the knapsack. The two men started walking on the road in the church's direction when several individuals emerged behind them.

They heard a voice say, "Do not go any further and listen to me carefully. When I tell you to do so, you will put your hands up and away from your person and turn and face me. You will do this very slowly." A pause. "Okay. Turn around. Slowly."

Father Desmond and Jack complied with the request and turned around to face the person. They found themselves facing three armed men, who had their weapons drawn and stood in a defensive posture.

Father Desmond was about to speak when one of the men held up his hand and said, "Please. Do not speak. I will be asking the questions, and you are going to answer them. Understood?"

Both Jack and Father Desmond continued to hold their hands in the air and nodded.

The leader then spoke once more. "What are you are doing here?"

Before Jack or Father Desmond could answer, the man said, "Father Desmond, is that you?"

"Yes, Isaac. It is me."

Rabbi Isaac Geller had been recruited and trained by Father Desmond years ago. He was one of the few people who would still speak to him these days, although they had not seen one another in some time.

"Father, why are you here? You know that Stull is off limits unless there is prior approval from the Council. I have received no such clearance."

"Isaac, may we put our hands down and approach you and your team?"

Turning to the other members of his security team, he told them to put their weapons away. Father Desmond and Jack put their hands down and moved toward the security team.

"Isaac, it is good to see you. How have you been?"

He frowned, and deep creases appeared on his forehead. "Father, I am fine," he said abruptly. "I need to know right now who this person is and why you are here."

Staring intensely at Father Desmond, Isaac continued, "You know you do not belong here, and bringing a third party with you is strictly forbidden."

Father Desmond raised his hands to his chest with his palms facing out, and in a reassuring voice, said, "Isaac, I understand." Pointing toward Jack, he persisted, "This is my friend Jack Aitken. He has delivered an artifact to me related to Stull Cemetery, and we are here to put it back where it belongs."

Father Desmond glanced at Jack, hoping that he would play along. He knew he was lying to Isaac, but Father Desmond reasoned that sometimes the ends justify the means. He had tried to prepare for this contingency, and he hoped he would be able to pull it off.

Isaac looked at Jack and then back at Father Desmond. "What artifact?" he asked suspiciously. "And why wasn't this cleared with the Council? Unscheduled visits are not the protocol, Father, and you know it."

"I know, Isaac. I know."

Father Desmond pulled an object from his knapsack and held it up.

"The artifact is this bell. Jack just delivered it to me last night, and it is a supplement to the ritual we do each year that prevents demons from accessing the area. It is a replica of the bell that hung in the steeple of the church. This bell is from remnants of the very bell left behind after the battle in 1859."

Father Desmond reached into his knapsack once more and pulled out the map he and Jack had just studied.

"We need to bury this object at the tomb of the minister who led the congregation astray. This map tells us where his secret grave is, and this ritual will be a backstop if we find ourselves in a position where we cannot do the annual warding ceremony. This object will prevent demons from entering this site forever."

Father Desmond made sure to look Isaac directly in the eye. He knew this would help sell Isaac that this was a valid reason to be here. Over the years, Father Desmond had become particularly good at reading faces and had sensed that he won Isaac over.

He considered what Father Desmond said and then replied in a far less confrontational tone, "Okay, Father, but why haven't you informed the Council? You know how important it is for you to do that."

Father Desmond shook his head in affirmation and said, "You are right, Isaac. Unfortunately, there was not much time left to perform the ritual. I have to bury the object before midnight tonight, or I would have to wait an entire year before I could perform it again. I know my reputation within JESU is not the greatest, but I felt it was in the best interest of all of us to do this. I fully intend to file a report with the Council tomorrow morning."

Isaac rubbed his lips with his finger as he considered Father Desmond's explanation. He gave Jack another once-over and looked back at Father Desmond. After a few seconds, he finally responded, "Father, please make sure you file that report ASAP. I will be checking in with the Council Secretary to ensure that they receive it. Be careful out here. We have been tracking demon activities in the area all day. Naturally, it picks up around Halloween. If you take my advice, you will be out of the area before dark. The activity picks up significantly when the sun goes down. Good luck with your mission, Father."

"I will be sure to do that, Isaac. Thank you for your good wishes and your service to the Society."

Isaac and the other patrol members turned and soon disappeared down the trail.

Once the security team was out of sight, Father Desmond turned to Jack. "Forgive me for lying. I anticipated that this could happen and had that story prepared on the chance that we encountered resistance. Sometimes the best story is the one not shared with everyone. I thought it better not to put you in a position of having to explain things. I just needed you to play along, and you did just as I anticipated you would."

Jack smiled and said, "No problem. I understand what you did and why you did it. No apologies are needed. I just want to get Amanda and the boys back safe. I will do whatever it takes to make that happen."

The duo set off for the ruins of the church at the top of the hill. Jack felt the wind blow across his face and detected an overpowering stench in his nose. He remembered that Father Desmond had talked about the smell of death surrounding Stull. Suddenly, it seemed to be all around them.

The two men finally reached the top of the hill and approached the remains of the desecrated church. The walls of the red brick and stone structure were crumbling but mainly remained intact. The roof was gone, and frames where stained-glass windows once existed were still evident. The doorway was blocked by debris, and an outline of a cross was visible above the entrance. However, all that remained of the cross was a charred imprint of the symbol. Its location was typical of most churches in rural areas of the United States, but there was one significant deviation: the outline showed that the cross had been hung upside down. This prominent symbol of devil worship, while perhaps not surprising, was intimidating. Despite the successful closing of this gate to Hell, the site still felt infested by evil.

While Father Desmond used the map to get his bearings, Jack could not help himself and went to one of the empty window openings to peer inside the structure. He was not sure what he expected to see, but when he peered inside, there was a large hole where the pews and altar had once been. When he looked down, all he could see was darkness. It was pitch black with no visible signs of a bottom. He looked down toward his shoes and found a stone that was about the size of his fist. Out of curiosity, he threw the stone into the hole. He expected to hear an echo or some sound to indicate that the rock hit bottom. He waited for a minute and heard absolutely nothing. Jack nervously stepped back from the structure and rejoined Father Desmond.

"I am beginning to understand why you find this place so frightening," he said. "I cannot find the right words to tell you how eerie it really feels. All I can say is I want to find this key and, if you forgive the expression, get the hell out of here as soon as possible."

Father Desmond continued to review the map. "I do not think I told you this before, but this place is so repugnant to the Catholic Church that when the Pope visits the United States, he refuses to even fly over the site. He insists that the pilot plot a course that comes nowhere near here."

"Is that really true?" Jack asked.

Father Desmond paused his review of the map for a moment and turned to look at Jack. "While the Church says it is an urban legend, my sources tell me that it is absolutely, 100% true."

"If I was not scared already, I am now."

"Jack, do not forget that the strength of the warding in this area is so strong, even Lucius cannot walk in here and get the key himself. I think I found the starting point on the map. If I am interpreting it correctly, I believe we will start over there. At the corner of the front steps of the church."

Father Desmond moved toward the stone steps in front of the barricaded doorway. They walked over to a spot in front of the steps and took another look at the map.

Pointing to a spot on the map, he said, "I think we start at the front left corner of the steps. We would then take thirty-one steps forward into the cemetery."

"That is an unusual number. What is its association with evil? Wouldn't it be 666 or some number like that?"

"You are actually right that it is associated with 666. It is the total you arrive at when you add Revelation Chapter 13 and its 18th verse, the passage where 666, the number of the beast, is actually mentioned in the Bible."

Jack wanted to spit on the ground in a symbolic act of defiance toward Lucius and the evil he represented. Unfortunately, Jack was so nervous that his mouth was too dry to produce any saliva. The two men walked thirty-one steps into the cemetery.

Father Desmond had not bothered to check the weather before they left. The weather forecast for Stull Cemetery was always the same, ominous. As he glanced around, double-checking the instructions on the map, he saw storm clouds gathering. They were as black as he had ever seen. There were rolls of thunder that got louder as the storm approached their position, and the wind began to pick up as well. Something wicked was coming, and the exposed location where the men stood would be a dangerous spot. They needed to hurry.

Jack could not help but notice the developing storm himself. His growing apprehension about it amplified the nagging doubts he harbored about his ability to rescue Amanda and the boys. Jack was just an average, ordinary man and a flawed one at that. His faith in God had eroded, and he felt like a hypocrite turning to him now when he had abandoned him so many years ago. He recalled a sermon that Reverend Miner had preached when Jack was still a teenager. The moral that Jack took from it was that you could not just "break glass" and pull God out only for those times that you were in trouble. Jack prayed silently anyway and pleaded for God's protection for Amanda, Louis, and David, as well as strength and courage for himself.

As Jack finished his silent prayer, he saw Father Desmond pull out a book from a pocket inside his jacket. The book was the size of a paperback novel that you would buy at a drug store. It had to be old by its appearance as the pages' edges were yellow and brown, while the leather cover was cracked and faded. Jack glanced at the cover to try to read it, but the words were in a language that was unfamiliar to him.

"Father, what are you looking at, or should I be asking what you are looking for?"

Father Desmond's eyes never left the book. "This is a book of Numerology. Numbers have connotations in the occult, and when added together or combined into another number, they have specific meanings to those who follow Satan. For example, the number thirteen stands for rebellion, while the number eighteen stands for bondage. Added together, they make thirty-one, which stands for offspring or branch. Every number on this map is going to have some meaning to it. The number thirty-one, I think, indicates that the key we are looking for is from a branch of Satan. Satanic lore says that King Zagan made the key. He is the leader of a sect, a branch, if you will, of Satanism. Dagon, who I mentioned earlier, was Zagan's apprentice."

"Father, aren't you uncomfortable holding that book?" Jack asked apprehensively.

"It does not hurt physically to hold it, but knowing its true purpose is unsettling. Honestly, knowing what happened here at Stull makes holding it kind of creepy. This book has power in it no matter where it resides or who is reading it. Even more than a century later, despite JESU's warding and spells, the evil committed here helps amplify that power. I can feel its malevolence."

"How do you stop it from negatively influencing you?"

"Suffice it to say; this is not a book that my superiors would really want me to have. I try to reassure myself by saying it is a tool for fighting evil. Even the saintliest person is not immune to the influence of dark forces. Some say that Mother Teresa once underwent an exorcism. If that is true and it can happen to her, then it can happen to anyone. That includes someone handling this book. The elixir we both drank earlier was a precaution taken to protect both of us from the influence of evil, whether from the book or Stull Cemetery itself."

Father Desmond pointed at the map. "Look, Jack. The next clue lists number eleven and number seven. Number eleven in numerology stands for chaos. Seven represents the curse of Satan. These numbers point west and suggest that at the end of the path would be a grave marker. I am adding these numbers together, and it only nets eighteen. This number has already appeared before, and I see no repetition of any other numbers on the map. The map suggests the marker is much further away than what we had walked previously. I think the numbers need to be combined rather than added. Let us walk 117 steps to the west."

This task was easier said than done. The path, choked with dead grass and weeds, grabbed their shoes with each step that they took. There were also dead tree branches to contend with, and several times they almost twisted an ankle stepping in a hole where a grave marker had once stood. Large pieces of the tombstones, possibly damaged in the battle or broken by vandals, littered the ground. A few intact gravestones remained upright or tilted over but, weathered by the elements, were illegible. These obstacles made it difficult to stay on course, and it took more than an hour to walk the 117 steps.

When they arrived at the spot, there was no marker to be found.

"It should be here. It has to be here!" Father Desmond was desperate. "The debris on the trail probably sent us slightly off course. Let us look around here for a marker. There are no tombstones in this area, so look for something embedded in the ground."

Jack glanced at his watch. "It's four-thirty."

A soft shower had started to fall about fifteen minutes earlier, but the thunder continued to rumble, which suggested heavier rainfall could arrive any minute. Both men were now on their knees, frantically feeling around in the wet grass for evidence of the marker.

Finally, Jack exclaimed, "I think I've got something here!"

He pulled the grass away from the object and used his fingertips to find the edges. It had a rectangular shape that Jack knew was evidence that this had been placed here by someone or something. There was no way this could be a natural occurrence; it had to be made by people. Father Desmond quickly made his way over and knelt next to Jack. He removed the map from his pocket and began to review it once more. He did his best to keep the rain from getting on the map, fearing that water might make it illegible or destroy it. To his surprise, the water beaded and dripped off of the paper, which remained dry.

Jack looked at Father Desmond. "Have you ever seen anything like this before? The paper is not getting wet."

Father Desmond shook his head. "No, but it is helpful to our cause. I will wonder about how it is possible some other time."

The men tried to read the marker, but there were no letters. However, they quickly saw three numbers carved into the stone. Six, six, six in succession.

Jack said, "I guess 'X' marks the spot."

Father Desmond nodded and said, "The map suggests that the key might be under the marker."

He reached into the pack and took out two hand shovels. He handed one to Jack, and the men started to dig around the edges of the marker. The sky released an enormous clap of thunder as they did so, which caused both men to look upward. A bolt of lightning immediately followed the thunder, hitting the iron fence that circled the cemetery, illuminating it with an eerie greenish glow. It seemed as if the closer they got to finding the key, the more intense the storm was getting. Was it a sign that what they were seeking was not meant to be disturbed?

However, they were beyond the point of no return. It was too late to turn back now.

The men glanced at each other and got back to digging. The fence remained aglow while they did so. The intensity of the rain picked up, and the wind blew it sideways. Jack and Father Desmond were soaked to the bone, but they did not seem to notice as they finally found the bottom of the marker, which was about a foot deep. It was too heavy to lift, and Jack grabbed two of the dead tree branches as levers to push the marker out of the ground. The two men struggled to pry the gravestone marker from its hole. It took some time, but the heavy rainfall loosened the soil sufficiently for them to rock the stone marker back and forth. This motion allowed them to slip the branches further under the stone object and push it up and out of the ground.

Together they bent over the hole that remained. It was filling up with water due to the torrent of rain falling from the sky. They both put their hands in the hole and felt around for the bottom. Simultaneously, they felt something that they knew was not a stone. It felt rough, but whatever they were feeling could be traced with a fingertip. It had a pattern with straight lines and curves. Jack and Father Desmond ran their fingers around the edges of the object and then slowly lifted it from the muck in the bottom of the hole. A sound could be heard, like that of removing a suction cup from a glass window, and the object finally emerged.

The object sat on the ground between the two men. The falling rain removed the mud that was on its surface and revealed a rectangular metal object. It was shiny and gray, like silver or pewter. The exterior was ornately etched. These etchings were the rough surface they'd felt when the object was in the hole. It was about one foot long and eight inches wide. It looked similar to a jewelry box. The four corners of the box had carved feet, identical to that found on an armoire or another piece of classic furniture. This feature elevated the bottom of the object slightly off the ground. There was enough clearance for Jack to put his hand under the box.

Jack leaned over and yelled to Father Desmond over the storm, "Have you ever seen anything like this before? Do the etchings on the box have any significance?"

Father Desmond yelled back, "I have seen pieces similar to this in Europe. It looks like the work of a silversmith. Paul Revere was a silversmith and did work similar to this. I recall seeing his work when I visited a museum in Boston years ago. The etchings do not mean anything to me, but I have reference materials in my library that probably could tell us more about them."

"I think that we should open it. What Lucius showed me was so unique I know that I can identify if what is inside is the key or not."

Father Desmond nodded. "Ordinarily, I would not open something like this until I was in a place that had been thoroughly blessed. You cannot really ever be sure what may be released when you remove the top. However, under the circumstances, I agree with you that we have no choice. We cannot leave here without the key, and whatever daylight is left will soon be gone. Let's open it up, and if it is what we are looking for, we need to get out of here."

Jack fumbled with the clasp that held it shut. It was dark enough that he could not see the fastener clearly, so he had to use his fingertips to figure out how to open it. Jack grabbed the clasp and was able to pull it up. He glanced back at Father Desmond and looked down again as he raised the top of the box. The box's interior had a red felt lining, and a silver object lay nestled in the padding at the bottom of the box. There was now no doubt in Jack's mind—it was the object Lucius had shown him.

Jack looked at Father Desmond and said excitedly, "This is it, Father! It's definitely the object that Lucius showed me! Absolutely no question in my mind!"

Father Desmond's response was far less enthusiastic. "Let's get going."

He slipped the box into his knapsack. They carefully made their way out of the cemetery and back to the gravel road. They took one last look over their shoulder at the church's ruins, shrouded by storm clouds and the cemetery fence, which still illuminated the graveyard in that eerie green hue.

Nadia stood behind some brush, soaked to the bone. It had indeed been an exciting afternoon. First, she had to save Jack Aitken from a sinkhole. It took some time for her to confirm that she had done so without giving her identity away to Father Desmond. She then spent the rest of the afternoon playing cat and mouse with a JESU patrol while at the same time keeping an eye on Aitken and Desmond to be sure they recovered the key. A second sigh of relief washed over her, similar to the one she felt earlier when she knew she would not have to tell Lucius of a possible problem with her mission.

She tried to phone and text Lucius again but still had no service in the area. The storm had not helped things either. She finally found she could tap into the consciousness line Lucius set up with her earlier that day to give him the good news.

"What is it, Nadia?"

"Good news, Master." Nadia went on, "I can confirm that Aitken and Desmond have retrieved the key and are heading back from the cemetery to their car."

"Excellent, Nadia. Have you remained undetected?"

Nadia paused for a moment, then said, "Yes, Master, but it was not without some difficulty."

Nadia proceeded to share with Lucius what had occurred at the sinkhole and how she intervened to save Jack's life. Lucius actually sounded impressed.

"Nadia, you surprise me," Lucius said. "I did not know that you had such heroics in you. You have done well. The next time I want to hear from you is to confirm that Jack is on his way back here. I expect that Father Desmond will accompany him, and you should make sure to account for his whereabouts as well."

Nadia smiled cunningly and said, "Yes, Master. I understand and will obey."

Lucius finished his consciousness call with Nadia and went to see Amanda Aitken. As Lucius entered the basement of the Bradford house, the two guards came to attention.

Lucius approached the cell. "Mrs. Aitken, I have good news for you. Your husband was able to retrieve the object that I mentioned to you previously."

Amanda knelt on the floor, both sons at her side. She continued to console Louis while David watched Lucius fearfully. "Good news for you, I suppose," she said. "I'm pretty sure it does not really mean good news to the rest of us."

Lucius smiled mockingly. "Come, come, Mrs. Aitken. Have I not been a man of my word? No harm has come to you or your family, has it?"

As Lucius finished his sentence, David leapt from the floor and tried to reach through the prison cell bars to strike Lucius with his fist.

Lucius instantly grabbed his hand and said tersely, "Mrs. Aitken. You really must teach your children better manners." Pulling David closer to the bars, Lucius transformed into his true self. "David, I would suggest you refrain from such activity in the future," he roared. "Let me know you understand me by nodding."

While he was speaking, he'd picked David up off the ground. David struggled to get free while suspended in mid-air. David finally shook his head, and Lucius dropped him to the ground and transformed back into his human appearance.

Amanda rushed to David's side, then looked up at Lucius and screamed, "You bastard! If you ever touch my children again, I will—"

"You will what, Mrs. Aitken? Hmm?" Lucius sneered. "Do you really believe you can protect your children or even yourself from me?"

David began to sob, and Amanda cradled him in her arms. She softly whispered to him, "David, it is going to be okay."

Amanda led him to the rear of the prison cell and had him lie down on a cot. During the altercation, Louis had darted into the far rear corner of the jail cell, where he rocked himself back and forth in an effort to calm down.

Amanda looked back over her shoulder at Lucius with an icy stare. Lucius responded with an evil smirk and said, "Good evening, Mrs. Aitken." As he headed to the door, he said, "Do not go anywhere. I will be back."

Amanda muttered under her breath, "I am going to kill you."

The guards resumed their positions guarding the cell, and Lucius laughed as he exited the room.

A coyote wailed, and a blood-curdling howl answered its call. Jack looked around fearfully, and his eyes quickly dropped back down to the trail in front of him. He and Father Desmond had been walking for nearly an hour. On the way back, they made sure to steer clear of the sinkhole Jack had fallen into earlier. As they passed by it, Jack leaned over to look into the hole, and all he saw was pitch darkness. Jack shuddered at the thought of what nearly happened. Even if it were a demon that had helped save him, he was still thankful to be alive. The weather had cleared, and the sun was setting. Unfortunately, this meant that at least part of the hike back to the car would be in darkness.

The two men took turns carrying the knapsack weighed down by the metal box they retrieved from the cemetery. Jack could not stop thinking about the box and the time by which Lucius had instructed him to return with it. Midnight November 1st was a little over twenty-four hours away. They still had to get back to Virginia and had yet to discuss how they would save Amanda and the boys. *So much to do and so little time,* Jack thought to himself. He picked up the pace and could not wait to get back to Father Desmond's apartment.

Up until now, the hike back had been relatively uneventful except for one thing: the terrible putrid smell of death continued to hover around them. Suddenly, Jack stopped. He felt the wind blow and thought he heard a whisper. He looked around but saw nothing.

The breeze picked up once more, and he was sure he heard a voice saying in a drawn-out, melancholy tone, "J-A-C-K."

Father Desmond was ahead of him, and he had continued walking as if he had not heard anything.

Jack listened to the voice once again. "J-A-C-K."

Up ahead, Father Desmond suddenly stopped and began looking around.

Jack called, "You heard that, too, didn't you?"

Father Desmond nodded at Jack, then they listened to the voice for the third time, but in a deeper and more menacing tone, "J-A-C-K, I know you are here."

After the voice stopped, Jack heard a twig snap behind him. He turned and saw a figure. It was tall, well over eight feet, with a muscular build. It appeared as a silhouette, and its head was that of a goat with two large, curved horns protruding from the sides of its head. Jack slowly began to back up toward Father Desmond.

He muttered to himself, "That cannot be possible."

"Jack, did you say something?"

He pointed at the figure. "I was saying that this could not be possible. While we were walking, I was thinking about where we were and what happened today. A thought entered my head about a television show I once saw with a demonic figure that terrorized a family. It looked exactly like that thing back there."

Father Desmond said, "It is a Skinwalker."

Jack whispered, "What? What did you say?"

"It is a Skinwalker, a very gruesome myth from the Navajo culture that, unfortunately, is all too real. Its appearance was what I was concerned about when I cautioned you this morning about the thinning veil between the living and the dead around this time of year. Normally, it would never approach two people like this. The weakness of the barrier allows entities like this to channel power from the dead and, as a result, become more aggressive. A Skinwalker reads your thoughts and appears to you in a vision that matches what your brain was picturing. It knows what scares you and uses it. If it catches you, it will possess your physical body and eventually devour your soul."

"So…So… what do we do? Can we chase it off or kill it?"

Both men slowly backed down the trail, never taking their eyes off the figure, which started to approach them.

Father Desmond shook his head. "Not likely. I did not prepare for this. Killing a Skinwalker requires magic that I have not studied. Our only hope is to outrun it. It cannot transfer itself through a physical object. I mean, it cannot get into the car if we are in it and lock the doors. If we can just get to the car…"

Just as Father Desmond was about to finish, the figure picked up speed toward them.

"Jack, we have got to go. RUN!"

The two men raced down the trail as fast as they could with the figure in hot pursuit. Jack instinctively held the knapsack tightly while trying to keep up with Father Desmond. After running for a few minutes, he looked over his shoulder for the figure but saw nothing.

"Father, it's gone. It has disappeared."

Both men slowed down but continued walking at a brisk pace. Before Father Desmond could respond to Jack, they heard a different voice. It was all too familiar to Father Desmond. He looked behind him and saw Paul Sullivan standing on the trail. His body mangled; what you might expect to look like after jumping off a bridge.

Father Desmond knew it was the Skinwalker but stopped to face the figure. It spoke directly to him.

"Mark, why did you stop looking for me? You knew what happened in the woods destroyed my life, and you gave up on me. How could you do it?"

Father Desmond mumbled, "I am sorry, Paul. I did not mean to..."

As the men watched, the figure morphed into someone else. It was Thomas Manning.

"Father, it's not real. Thomas is dead."

Father Desmond knew it was not Thomas but listened as the figure spoke.

"Mark, how could you have sent me back home without something to protect me from Lucius?"

"No. Thomas, it was not like that. You betrayed me—"

The figure then changed once again.

Father Desmond gasped. "Joseph Rogers?"

The figure that appeared as Joseph spoke to Father Desmond. "Mark, you used me to get back at Lucius. You allowed me to leave with the sword. You knew I had it, but you let me go anyway." The figure then screamed, "He tortured me, Mark!"

Father Desmond felt a tug on his sleeve. It was Jack trying to pull him away. The figure started moving closer and changed once again. Father Desmond's jaw fell open as he tried to speak.

"Mark," the figure said, "don't you recognize me?"

Father Desmond could not bring himself to respond. He stared at the figure. Finally, he was able to mutter, "Father Jose Ramos. It cannot be?"

"So, you do remember me, Mark? At least you remember me now. You led us into that massacre, and then you left me there. You did not even check to see if I was alive. Do you know what Lucius did to me, Mark?"

Jack was now pulling Father Desmond's arm and dragging him.

"I am so sorry, Jose."

"Mark, sorry is not going to make up for the fact that Lucius chained me in that cabin. He slowly bled me until I was nearly dead, just for the sheer pleasure of it. Then, he left me there, and I died from starvation and my wounds." The figure shouted, "You went on with your life while I lost mine!"

Father Desmond was startled when he felt a hard slap across his face.

"Father, they're not real. You know what you're seeing is not real!"

All this time, the figure had continued to advance toward them.

Jack continued to drag Father Desmond until he came to his senses. The two men then took off running again with the figure right behind them, screaming, "MARKKKKK! Do not leave me here!"

They made it to the car, and Father Desmond fumbled for the keys. The men got in and closed the doors as the Skinwalker slammed into the vehicle, almost overturning it. Father Desmond dropped the keys and felt around for them on the floor. The Skinwalker circled the car and continually morphed from one figure into the other while screaming, "Let me in."

Father Desmond found the keys and said, "Got them! Let's get the hell out of here."

He placed the keys in the ignition and tried to start the car, but it would not turn over.

Jack was pleading with him, "Start the car, Mark! Start the car!"

Father Desmond started yelling at the vehicle, "COME ON! COME ON! GODDAMMIT!"

Finally, the engine roared to life, and Father Desmond floored the accelerator. The tires smoked as they gained traction on the road surface, and the car sped down the highway with the Skinwalker trying to follow them. Each man breathed a sigh of relief as they raced back to Father Desmond's apartment, leaving the Skinwalker far behind. Neither of them noticed Nadia's car trailing them once again.

Chapter 18

After finally leaving Stull Cemetery and the Skinwalker behind them, Father Desmond and Jack had little to say to one another the rest of the way back to the apartment. Both men remained edgy and continued nervously checking the mirrors to ensure that the Skin-Walker was gone and nothing else was behind them. Upon reaching the apartment, Father Desmond excused himself to make a phone call, then retrieved a whiskey bottle from one of the kitchen cabinets. Jack and Father Desmond drank in silence with the knapsack containing the key on the kitchen table between them.

A knock at the door broke the quiet in the apartment. Jack was spooked by the noise and quickly looked at Father Desmond. Father Desmond put down his glass and signaled that Jack should remain calm. He rose from the chair and exited the kitchen. Jack turned to watch him.

Father Desmond leaned in toward the door and asked, "Who is it?"

The voice on the other side of the door quickly replied, "Mark, it's Father Mathias."

Father Desmond glanced toward Jack. "Do not worry. Father Mathias is who I called a few minutes ago."

Jack, who had been holding his breath, sighed in relief.

Father Mathias stepped in and embraced Father Desmond. Jack surmised that Father Mathias was likely to be in his early to mid-forties. His brown hair was starting to gray at the temples. He looked to be about the same height as Jack. His clerical collar was recognizable under the jacket he was wearing.

"I came over as soon as you called, Mark." He removed his jacket and handed it to Father Desmond.

"Jason, thank you for coming over so quickly."

Father Desmond ushered Father Mathias into the kitchen and introduced him to Jack.

"Jason Mathias," Father Desmond said, "please meet Jack Aitken. Jack is the old friend that I mentioned to you on the phone."

Jack got up from the table and shook hands with Father Mathias. "It's a pleasure to meet you, Father."

Jack moved over to the next chair so that Father Mathias could sit down at the table. Father Desmond went to the cabinet and got another glass. He filled it with whiskey and topped off his glass as well as Jack's. The three men sipped whiskey and made small talk. Father Desmond and Jack shared stories of their childhood exploits on the soccer field. Father Mathias told Jack about his youth and how he came to be a priest.

The mood was light, but that changed as they ran out of small talk. The night suddenly grew quiet, and Father Desmond's face became expressionless.

"Jack, Father Mathias is a member of JESU. I recruited him into the order, and he is one of my most trusted friends. Candidly, he's one of the few members of the order that still maintains a relationship with me. There is not a person in the society more reliable than Jason. He has paid the price for his loyalty to me, including recently being sent here to Lawrence. If you have not figured it out already, this post is like being sent to purgatory. A place to pay your debts to JESU. It is supposed to be where our souls are purified, but few people who come here ever leave."

Jack was somewhat surprised at Father Desmond's candor. He looked at Father Mathias to gauge his reaction. If Father Mathias disagreed, Jack was unable to tell.

Father Mathias said, "Let us hope we change that someday, Mark." He then pointed to the knapsack on the table and asked, "Is the key in there?"

"Jack, when I called Father Mathias, I briefly filled him in on what transpired today. We will need his help, and for him to give it effectively, he needs to know everything going on. I know that I should have discussed this with you first."

"I trust you, Father," he said. "I understand that time is of the essence. It took eighteen hours to drive here, and we are running out of time to get back to Virginia and meet Lucius's deadline."

"That is part of why we need Father Mathias's help," Father Desmond said. "There are several things we have got to do before we leave. These include filing a report with the Council about our activities today. We also need to ascertain if there are any bulletins out for your arrest. If there are, we have to make the appropriate travel arrangements to avoid the authorities. Finally, I have placed a call already to begin the preparations for the Michaelmas, but we need to be sure that there will be enough time to hold it when we get to Virginia."

Father Desmond continued, "Jack, please do not misunderstand what I am about to say. I know your family is your primary concern, and rightfully so. They are my concern too. However, I have to consider the bigger picture here. There are grave ramifications that go along with Lucius getting his hands on that key. If we fail, you and your family will not be alone in your sentence to damnation. The entire planet will plunge into darkness. Natural disasters, pestilence, famine, wars, and other devastating consequences beyond human comprehension will occur. Satan has been waiting for this moment, and the Book of Revelation outlines what he will do when he gets his opportunity to control the world. It will tear itself apart before our eyes, and life as we know it will come to an end."

Jack suddenly felt like the weight of the world was now squarely on his shoulders. His hands began to tremble, and he slid them under the table to hide his anxiety from Father Desmond and Father Mathias. Father Desmond's pronouncement was forcing Jack to confront a reality far greater than losing his family. Jack could be responsible for setting in motion events that would lead to the destruction of the world.

"Father, I do understand. I know the burden that I have brought down upon you. I want to save my family more than any words can express, but I also realize the magnitude of what we face. I recognize failure is not an option here. I also know that Amanda would expect me to do the right thing for the greater good. She has always put the needs of others ahead of her own and would expect that I would do the same thing. What was it that Mr. Spock said at the end of the Star Trek movie *The Wrath of Khan*? 'Logic clearly dictates that the needs of the many outweigh the needs of the few.' And Father Mathias said, "Then Captain Kirk responds, 'Or the one.'"

Jack looked down to hide the tears welling up in his eyes and said in a trembling voice, "I am with you on this, Father. I am with you."

He knew they were all in for a long night.

Across the courtyard, the church bell tower chimed twelve times. It was midnight. Halloween had arrived, and the lights were still on in Father Desmond's apartment. The three men had been working diligently through the night. Father Desmond and Father Mathias sat at the kitchen table, working on the report that Father Mathias would deliver to the Council later in the morning. Jack was in the library on a laptop, researching what was going on back home.

Earlier in the evening, he did find a Prince William County police bulletin published on October 29th that referenced Amanda, Louis, and David's disappearance. A few hours later, he went back to the page and found that an October 30th update now included a BOLO/APB for him. The authorities wanted to question Jack, and anyone with information about his whereabouts was to contact Detective Anne Bishop.

He got up from the couch and headed toward the kitchen to inform Father Desmond. As he entered the room, he saw that Father Desmond and Father Mathias appeared to be finishing up the Council's report. He heard Father Desmond tell Father Mathias, "Jason, are you sure you still want to be a part of this? If you want out, I will understand."

Father Mathias leaned back in his chair and said, "Mark, I am all in. You are doing the right thing, and you can count on me. I will do all I can to sell your story to the Council. At least some of what is in the report is true. Abraham will confirm that you were on your way to the Cemetery and that Jack was with you. I have a picture of the bell, which he should be able to identify. While the documents that support the story about the bell are forgeries, they are highly sophisticated, and I do not believe anyone on the Council will be able to tell they are fakes."

"I hope you are right, Jason. I confess I have my doubts."

"Regardless of what your reputation might be with the Council, they know your research skills are still unrivaled. I think the biggest obstacle is explaining why you're not submitting the report in person. I am certain I can convince them you are visiting a mutual friend with Jack in Abilene, but I wanted to file the report right away to avoid any problems with the Council. Ministering to others is still our calling, after all. I am confident they will buy it."

"Thanks, Jason. I will be forever indebted to you."

Jack interjected, "I am sorry to interrupt. I just found something online that I wanted to share with you."

Father Desmond nodded and motioned for Jack to join them. "What do you have?"

"It was only a local bulletin, posted within the last hour. The detective I mentioned to you is looking to speak with me about my family's disappearance."

He rubbed his chin, considering. "It may be local now, but it is likely only a matter of time before it gets picked up nationally."

Father Desmond went back to the table and picked up a pad of paper with their travel arrangements on it. He turned to Father Mathias and Jack, then said, "We will have to change our plan. Originally, Jack and I were to catch a flight out of Kansas City at 6:30 a.m. and then take a connecting flight at 9:30 a.m. from Chicago to Charlottesville, Virginia. From there, we would catch a train to Union Station in Washington, DC."

He looked up from the pad. "Jason, do you know if Tracy Guidry is still supporting the Kansas State University parachute club out of the Abilene Municipal Airport?"

Father Mathias quickly responded, "She is, Mark. I actually spoke with her a few days ago to arrange a flight for Bishop McNamara to go home for Thanksgiving."

Father Desmond excused himself to make a phone call. He returned to the kitchen a few minutes later and stated, "We are a go. I spoke with Tracy, and she is filing the flight plan with the FAA as we speak. She can fly us out at 8:00 a.m. We will fly directly into the Manassas, Virginia Regional Airport and arrive around 1:00 p.m. This schedule will allow time for the Michaelmas I mentioned earlier."

Father Desmond turned to Jack. "I hope you won't mind flying in a small single-propeller plane. It only seats four people, including the pilot. Tracy is not a JESU member but has provided transportation and logistical support for other missions from time to time. She is reliable and very supportive of the Church. She is also very trustworthy and can keep a confidence."

"Candidly, flying is not my preferred mode of transportation, but it all makes sense. Manassas is also less than an hour from Culpeper."

Father Desmond sat back down at the table and took another gulp of whiskey from his glass.

"Jason, as I mentioned to you on the phone, Jack and I had someone following us today. After you submit your report to the Council and we leave for Abilene, I would like you to stay here at my apartment. I want to give the appearance that I have remained behind. I am hoping we might gain some element of surprise if we can sell that ruse to whoever is tailing us."

Father Mathias nodded his agreement. "It would be a good idea to leave the paper with your prior travel information out in the open. On the off chance that someone was to break into your apartment and discover our trick, this information may throw them off your trail. The paper has the flight numbers, flight times, and airlines listed on it."

Father Desmond nodded affirmatively. "That is a good idea. Leave it here on the table."

Jack was mesmerized by the quick thinking and expertise of both priests. The ability to adjust the plan and change direction quickly in light of new circumstances was awe-inspiring. There was no doubt that both men were well trained and worked well together.

Father Desmond reached for the knapsack on the table and removed the container. He placed it in the middle of the table, and the three men began to examine it.

Father Mathias said, "It is safe to say that I have never seen anything like this, Mark. I cannot get over the artistry. Demon or not, this was made by a real craftsman. Do you know what materials they used to make this key?"

Father Desmond shook his head. "I am guessing it is silver or a similar metal, but I am really not certain. I have looked through some of the reference books in my library, but I cannot find anything like it. It is in extraordinary condition, considering how old it may be. There is no rusting or fading whatsoever. We could not tell in the dark what the embossed designs were on the box, but now I see they are clearly Satanic."

Pointing to the designs, he said, "This is a reproduction of an inverted pentagram used in rituals to conjure up evil spirits. The other symbol is a satanic cross. This one is a variation of the symbol for Sulphur and stands for fire and brimstone. You will often see this symbol on the Satanic Bible."

Jack said nervously, "I think this box makes me even more uneasy now that we are looking at it in the light. Should we open it to look at the key?"

Father Desmond excused himself and returned with gloves and a bottle of holy water. He sprinkled the box with holy water and led the men in prayer for strength and protection.

"Lord God, heavenly Father, you know that we are in the midst of so many great dangers that because of the frailty of our nature, we cannot always stand upright. Grant us such strength and protection, support us in all danger, and carry us through all temptations, through your Son, Jesus Christ our Lord. Amen."

Father Desmond and Father Mathias made the sign of the cross on their chests, and Father Desmond slowly opened the box, revealing the luxurious red velvet lining. The key, nestled in the middle, appeared made of the same metal as the box. On one end of the object was the bit, which seemed to be typical of most antique skeleton keys except for the number 666 punched through it. This part of the item was the end inserted in the locking mechanism. The other end was a circle with a skull set inside of it. The head had no lower mandible, and two femurs were crisscrossing one another. Embedded in the eyes were two red gemstones. It quite literally was a skeleton key. A skeleton key stamped with the number of the beast to honor Satan.

Father Desmond carefully picked up the key to examine it further. It had weight to it and felt quite substantial. Father Desmond pondered how an item, a key, seemingly innocuous, could be so inherently evil. Then he remembered how the bite of a simple apple had caused the fall of man and banishment from the Garden of Eden, and the key took on an even more menacing feel. This key had the power to release forces that could exterminate the human race. Father Desmond knew this was not hyperbole; it was a fact. He put the key back in the box.

He turned to the other two men and said, "I am going to close this up unless one of you would like to inspect it."

Father Mathias shook his head, and with a somber tone, said, "No, thank you. I am here to help both of you, but I do not want to touch anything so profane. I understand why you needed to retrieve it, but it strikes me as something that will only have death associated with it. I fear that this wicked object is cursed, and we will come to discover that it should not have been disturbed."

Jack's facial expression showed that he agreed with Father Mathias. "Based on the situation I'm in at the moment, I'd be naïve to say that I do not want to touch it. I know that I am going to have to, but I'd prefer to wait until that required time actually arrives."

Father Desmond shut the box and put the latch down.

"Gentlemen, it is a little after one in the morning. I think we should try to get some sleep. Jason, it will take us nearly two hours to get to the airport in Abilene. Jack and I are going to leave around 6:00 a.m. You will need to meet with the Council first thing in the morning. Why don't you sleep in my room and I will sleep on the recliner here in the library? Jack, you can sleep again on the couch. I will set the alarm for five. We can have breakfast and go over our plan one more time."

Lucius entered the study and locked the door behind him. The lavishly furnished Bradford family study had an array of 18th-century French furniture, including a Louis XV Style Rosewood desk with a matching leather upholstered armchair. The furnishings were most appropriate for someone of Lucius's prominence. He reveled in the luxury of the surroundings and the adoration of his underlings. His every whim fulfilled. His every word law. His every order obeyed without question.

Power, limitless and unconstrained power.

Lucius sat down in the chair behind the desk and prepared for his consciousness call, but this call was not like the ones he held with his minions seemingly all day long. No, this call was quite different. Despite his bravado and immense self-confidence, speaking with the boss made even Lucius nervous. Lucifer was beyond arrogant, and he was indescribably condescending as well as savagely ruthless. The lord of Hell was cruel and merciless. He had zero tolerance for excuses and was indiscriminate in his punishment. In aggregate, he made even Lucius look benevolent.

However, even Lucifer had limitations. While he was still in Hell itself, the only time his stream of consciousness was powerful enough to connect with Lucius was at 3:15 a.m. on Halloween, the date and time of the year when evil was at its zenith and Lucifer was at his most potent.

Lucius fidgeted in his chair like a small child might do at a restaurant table while waiting for their meal. Patience was never one of his strengths. After all, as powerful as he was, he did not have to wait for anyone or anything. He did not have much reason to practice this so-called virtue. Finally, he felt the signal in his brain confirming someone was reaching out to him, and the connection was complete.

"Greetings, Omnipotent One," Lucius fawned. "It is indeed my pleasure to be of one mind with you again. It has been far too long."

"Enough with the platitudes, Lucius," Lucifer thundered. "Just tell me we are ready to open the damn gate finally. I have been locked down here for more than two thousand years. That is one thousand years longer than in the Book of Revelation. So much for Saint John's math!"

Lucius's voice quivered slightly. "Yes... yes, my Master. All is going as planned, and everything is on its proper schedule. The key will be in my hands and the gate unlocked shortly after midnight tomorrow. You will be free, and the soul harvest will be ready to proceed immediately after that. Just as you have instructed me."

Lucifer scoffed. "We will see, Lucius. I have my doubts. It could just be your turn to fail me like all of your predecessors."

Lucius quickly interjected, "Master, did I not build this second gate which has proven to be of great potential value to our cause? Did I not effectively plant disinformation and urban legends about other gates and portals to Hell which has successfully misled and hidden this one from JESU for centuries?"

Lucifer swiftly responded with a tone suggesting significant irritation, "And you were handsomely rewarded for your efforts."

Lucius responded, "Yes, Master. You have been most generous."

"I know, Lucius," Lucifer said. "There is no need to thank me again for the thousandth time. However, if you succeed where others have failed me, you will join my Seraphim, the highest order of demons. You will be the fourth most powerful demon behind me, Asmodeus and Beelzebub."

Lucius listened to Lucifer with great interest. What he was offering was an absolute honor. He attempted to sound modest when he responded, "I am profoundly flattered, Master."

"Now, tell me about this Jack Aitken. Just what makes you think he can deliver the goods?"

Lucius paused, then calmly said, "He fits the profile of the compromised soul in the legend, my Master. His relationship with God, your Father, has been diminished over the years. He once attended religious services but has not done so in many years. The legend also indicated that he would approach us rather than have us search him out. In my surreptitious role as Museum Curator, he came to me seeking information about the Manahoac tribe."

Lucifer listened without interruption. Lucius took this as an encouraging sign.

He continued in a voice far more confident than before, "He is also easily manipulated and controlled. I have his family in custody as well to guarantee his compliance. He has already obtained the key and should be on his way here within the next several hours."

Lucifer's tone became somewhat less aggressive, "And what of JESU?"

"Master, this current world is perfect for us. Sex scandals and financial malfeasance among religious leaders have led to a decline in moral authority, accelerating JESU's demise. As I anticipated, Aitken did reach out to Father Mark Desmond. He was the leader that led JESU into the massacre ten years ago."

Lucifer said, "I remember. Go on, Lucius."

"Desmond is finished. He has been on lockdown by JESU. They have posted him to watch over Stull Cemetery. It is where they send associates to wither and die. There has been no sign of him or his influence in any JESU operation ever since. Just in case, however, I have had him under surveillance for years. I am taking every precaution to make certain that he is no threat to our plan. He and Aitken are under surveillance now. All of our surveillance indicates no one else from JESU has mobilized. All signs are that they are unaware of what is currently unfolding."

Lucifer responded in a severe tone of voice. "Do not underestimate JESU or Desmond, Lucius. I do not want any slip-ups or mistakes. Am I understood?"

Lucius answered, "Yes, my Master. I understand."

Lucifer terminated the thought connection between them. Lucius knew he had done well, even if Lucifer would not acknowledge it. He pulled out his phone to make a call. Now leaning back in his chair, his lips curled into a smug smile, Lucius laughed out loud and said, "Gotcha, boss!"

Chapter 19

Jack sat up on the couch and stared at the container on the table in front of him. He had moved it from the kitchen last night, not wanting to let it out of his sight, but wondered if the key inside had somehow been responsible for the nightmare that shattered the sleep he so desperately needed. Most of the dream details had faded from his memory, but he couldn't shake the feeling that this key would either lead to his salvation or eternal damnation.

Over the past several days, he'd considered how he could leverage the object to obtain his family's freedom as well as, hopefully, to save himself. As Father Desmond had so forcefully pointed out last night, turning over the key to Lucius was unthinkable, but Jack's heart and soul knew that not doing so, for him, would be unforgivable. Unfortunately, he had come up with no solution to the dilemma he faced and could not stop asking himself, *what happens if I fail?*

He found Father Desmond at the stove cooking and Father Mathias sipping coffee at the table. Jack bid them both good morning and joined Father Mathias at the table. Father Mathias poured Jack a cup, and as he blew on the hot liquid, Father Desmond came to the table with a platter of bacon and eggs. The three men ate eagerly and cleared the dishes from the table.

Father Desmond glanced at his watch. "Jason, it is almost time for us to get going. There are a few additional details that I thought about this morning. In the *Art of War*, Sun Tzu said, 'In conflict, direct confrontation will lead to engagement, and surprise will lead to victory. Those who are skilled in producing surprises will win.' Based on what happened at Stull Cemetery, it is evident that Jack

259

and I are under surveillance. Last night we discussed leaving the phony travel itinerary on the table. I wrote up a second copy of the itinerary that I would like you to take to the Council meeting. Along the way, I would let the paper drop to the ground. If someone is watching us, maybe they will take the bait and fall for the ruse."

Father Desmond continued, "While it should still be dark when you leave for the Council meeting, I would also suggest that you turn the collar of your coat up to shield your face. You and I wear the same uniform each day, and perhaps, they will think you are me. After the meeting is over, come back to my apartment and stay here. On the off chance that they do not identify you, your presence here in my apartment might convince them that I have not left Lawrence."

Father Mathias nodded. "Understood, Mark. Consider it done."

Father Desmond then turned to Jack and said, "Jack, do you remember the route we took yesterday to go to the Cemetery?"

Jack quickly responded, "Yes. I remember it."

"Good. You are going to your car alone. Take the knapsack with the container inside and follow the same route we took yesterday morning. You are going to pick me up on West 6th Street."

Jack looked at Father Desmond, puzzled. "Mark, how are we going to make that happen? If someone is watching us, isn't that going to be suspicious?"

Father Desmond looked at Jack and Father Mathias and said, "Follow me into the library."

The three men entered the library. "This is how this will work. You two are going to leave at the same time. Jack, you are going to the car, and Jason will head to the Council meeting."

Father Desmond stepped toward one of the bookcases in his library and searched the shelves as if he were looking for a particular book. He pulled one from the bookshelf, and the entire case slid to the left, revealing a stairwell. Jack and Father Mathias glanced over at one another with surprise and then looked back at Father Desmond.

"These stairs lead to the basement, where there is a tunnel entrance running under the streets of the city. The tunnel has an exit at West 6th Street that will allow me to meet Jack. If this works as planned, Lucius's spy will see you, Jack, and Jason looking like me, leaving at the same time."

Jack nodded his understanding, and Father Mathias said, "Okay, Mark. I think we are following you. What's next?"

"If I know Lucius as well as I think I do, his main concern at the moment is not you, Jack; it is me. By now, his spy will have informed him that you have contacted me and that we have retrieved the key. Lucius has your family, so he knows you will be heading back with it. What he does not know is whether or not I am coming with you. I anticipate that the spy will let you go, Jack, but pay particular attention to you, Jason. If we are fortunate, the spy will see the paper fall from your folder, and after you are out of sight, they will retrieve it. If not, perhaps they will attempt to break into my apartment and find the itinerary there. In the meantime, Jack will pick me up, and we will head to Abilene. Hopefully, the spy will see Jason, return to my apartment, and think I have remained behind. They will then report all of this, including the fake travel itinerary, to Lucius. It may be a longshot, but if it works, then the element of surprise will be on our side."

Jack enthusiastically said, "Let's do it!"

Father Desmond turned and headed through the entrance in the library wall. He pressed a button, and the bookshelf slowly slid back into place as Jack and Father Mathias watched him start walking down the stairs to the basement.

Father Mathias pulled up the collar on his jacket as Father Desmond had suggested, picked up the documents from the table, and said, "Okay. Now it is our turn. Let's go, Jack."

Jack and Father Mathias left the apartment, leaving the door unlocked. They headed down the stairs and out the front door of the building. They briefly walked together in the pre-dawn darkness before Jack shook hands with Father Mathias and made his way across the parking lot. Father Mathias headed toward the building where the Council meeting was taking place. He tried his best to make it look accidental and let the paper with the fake travel information fall to the ground behind him. Father Mathias never looked back as he entered the building, nor did Jack as he drove out of the parking lot and turned toward West 6th Street.

As a result, neither man saw a figure emerging from the shadows, walking across the courtyard and picking up the fallen paper from the ground.

Nadia's phone vibrated. She quickly picked it up to read the text. It was Lucius's number. It read, "Verify Father Desmond's presence and wait for my instructions."

Nadia put away her phone. The campus was silent, but there were lights on in a few apartments and the Council building. It was still dark as the sun had yet to rise. She was anxious, waiting for Desmond to emerge from the Council meeting. When Aitken and Desmond split up, she had to make a choice. Did she follow Aitken or Desmond? Her first instinct was to follow Jack Aitken, but Nadia saw a paper fall from Desmond's folder. After both men were out of sight, she made her move and collected the paper. After reading it, she knew she had made the correct decision.

The paper listed travel plans, including times and flight numbers, precisely the type of information Lucius would want to have. When she relayed the news to him, she sensed some glee in his voice, but he also cautioned her that it could be a trick. He wanted to know what Desmond was doing. Nadia scouted the building's exterior several times and saw nothing that indicated Desmond was anywhere other than in the building he had entered. After what seemed like an eternity, Nadia saw the door of the building begin to open.

The figure exiting the building looked familiar to Nadia. He wore the same priestly vestments, the same black jacket, and held a folder in his hand. The sky was becoming lighter as she watched him walk back across the campus, the collar of his coat turned upward against the cold. There was little doubt in her mind that it was Desmond. Rather than walk to his car, however, the figure headed back in the direction of the apartment. Nadia was surprised, but it was not her job to think. That was Lucius's responsibility. Her role was to report, and she dialed the number and got Lucius on the phone.

"Yes, Nadia. What is it?"

"Master, Desmond has emerged from the building and appears headed back to his apartment."

Lucius sounded surprised. "Really? Interesting. I take it that there is no sign of Jack Aitken. He has not returned, has he?"

"No, Master. Aitken has not returned."

Lucius was thinking out loud when he said, "Fascinating. It is not like Desmond to shy away from a confrontation, particularly one with me. He has to have figured out that I am behind all of this. Yet, he appears to do nothing. Why?"

There were a few moments of silence as Lucius pondered his next move. Finally, he spoke once more. "Nadia, my dear, are you familiar with the works of Sir Arthur Conan Doyle?"

"No, Master."

"I thought not. Doyle once wrote, 'Once you eliminate the impossible, whatever remains, no matter how improbable, must be the truth.' Well, I think of myself as more of a believer in the so-called Reagan doctrine, 'Trust, but verify.' I take it you are not familiar with that either?"

"No, Master," Nadia responded.

On his side of the phone connection, Lucius was shaking his head. He thought to himself, *sometimes, I wonder how I accomplish anything with the lack of intellectual resources I have at my disposal. It is a testimony to the remarkable abilities that I have taken this organization so far. I wonder if Lucifer really understands and appreciates all that I do for him.*

"Perhaps Father Desmond has indeed decided to sit this one out, in a manner of speaking, but just in case he changes his mind, you, Nadia, my dear, will be my eyes. To that end, you will stay just where you are and monitor our friend, Father Desmond. If you see anyone coming in or going out of that apartment, you will inform me immediately. Do you understand?"

"Yes, Master. Consider it done."

"Excellent, Nadia." Lucius terminated the call.

Nadia put her phone away and continued watching the figure as he went back to the apartment. She was just about to head back to her car to continue her surveillance when she noticed that the person she had been watching started to turn away from the apartment and head in her direction. As the figure closed the distance between the two of them and the sky began to lighten, she was able to get a clear view of the figure's face. This individual was of Korean descent! This Priest was not Father Desmond at all.

Nadia realized the error she had made and reached for her phone to contact Lucius. As she began to punch in the number, she heard a voice.

"Miss, please drop the phone," the voice said. "Put your hands up where we can see them."

Nadia looked up and saw two men approaching her. She immediately recognized them as a JESU security patrol. Nadia had managed to evade them until now, but detection meant serious trouble, both from the patrol and worse yet, from Lucius. She needed to move quickly.

She put her hands up and began to back away from the patrol. She was ready to make a run for it when she started to feel dizzy and unsteady. Then she could not move and found herself falling to her knees. Finally, she felt intense pain rush through her entire being.

As she fell to the ground, Nadia realized the patrol had shot her with a taser. Then, everything went black.

As he did every morning, Reverend Harold "Hal" Wallace called the Council briefing to order. Over the years, the daily briefing had become nothing more than a formality as the war with the demon hoards had evolved into an uncomfortable but stable stalemate. It was not unlike the demilitarized zone between North and South Korea, where two forces with the means to annihilate one another stared each other down daily. However, today's meeting held the promise of a respite from the boredom of mutually assured destruction. After all, Father Mark Desmond's name was on the schedule.

Reverend Wallace had met Father Desmond several times over the last ten years that Desmond had resided at the Campus. His reputation within JESU was beyond rehabilitation, but he had always found Mark professional and pleasant. If nothing else, the discussion of Mark Desmond ought to be far more exciting and entertaining than the five-minute official charade that substituted for an update each morning.

The minutes of yesterday's meeting was quickly read and unanimously accepted by the Council representatives. Reverend Wallace then said, "Shall we move onto the business at hand? Father Desmond, please step forward."

Father Mathias approached the podium. "Good morning, Reverend Wallace. I am here in Father Desmond's stead."

Reverend Wallace was surprised and disappointed at the same time. "Father Mathias, why isn't Father Desmond here? Where is he?"

"Called away to Abilene on personal business, sir."

He held up a copy of Father Desmond's written report. "Father Desmond gave this report to me to give to the Council with his apologies. As the report indicates, he has a childhood friend in town, and they jointly have gone to see a mutual acquaintance in Abilene who is very ill."

Father Mathias approached the dais and handed the report to Reverend Wallace. As he returned to the podium, Rabbi Isaac Geller entered the Council chamber.

Reverend Wallace began scanning Father Desmond's report and said, "Rabbi Geller. Thank you for joining us."

Father Mathias stepped aside and allowed Rabbi Geller to take the podium.

Rabbi Geller passed his written report of the previous day's events to Reverend Wallace and said, "Good morning. The report I provided Reverend Wallace has my summary of yesterday's brief encounter with Father Desmond at Stull Cemetery."

Reverend Wallace said, "Very good. The Council will take a recess so that it can thoroughly review both reports."

The Council left the dais and retreated to an anteroom to review the reports. Father Mathias and Rabbi Geller sat and chatted while they waited for the Council briefing to resume. Thirty minutes later, the Council members returned, and their faces appeared to be very serious.

Reverend Wallace asked the scribe to note the time in the meeting minutes, specifically. It was now 7:00 a.m. He asked Rabbi Geller to step forward.

"Rabbi." Reverend Wallace continued, "why didn't you reach out to the head of the security team when you found Father Desmond and Mr. Aitken on the trail near Stull Cemetery?"

Rabbi Geller responded, "Cell phone reception is a problem in that area, Reverend. There is an inability to text or make phone calls when one is that close to the cemetery. My understanding is that this has always been a problem."

Reverend Wallace probed further, "Okay. So why didn't you inform someone as soon as you were in cell range? It is not typical to find people at the cemetery in this fashion, is it?"

"I confess to initially finding it more than surprising. Encountering demons and teenagers is routine at this time of year. I normally do not meet JESU members near the Cemetery unless it is time for the annual warding ceremony. I did inform Father Desmond that I would be here at the Council meeting to provide my report."

"So, you were not alarmed in any way?"

"No. Father Desmond answered all of my questions and had what I ultimately considered to be a plausible explanation for being there. I know what his reputation within JESU is, but he has never, to the best of my knowledge, ever had an accusation of deception leveled at him. Despite his debatable record as a tactician, my understanding is that his research skills are still an asset to JESU. What he wanted to do with the artifact seemed logical to me, and while the timing could be considered questionable by some, I had no reason not to believe him. Furthermore, I told him I would file this report, and he promised to do the same. Unless you find a discrepancy between the two reports, I would say the documentation provided supports my conclusion."

Suddenly, the doors to the Council chamber flew open, and a woman held up by security personnel was dragged into the room and thrown to the floor. She was unconscious.

Reverend Wallace briefly huddled with the other Council representatives. He then turned to Rabbi Geller and said, "Rabbi, do you know this woman?"

Rabbi Geller looked at the woman on the floor. "She looks familiar to me. I am pretty sure I may have seen her around the cemetery yesterday. My security detail and I did pursue someone for several hours, but we were not able to catch up with them."

Reverend Wallace turned to Father Mathias and asked him the same question. Father Mathias responded, "I have never seen this woman before in my life."

Reverend Wallace continued, "This woman is a demon. We captured her creeping around the campus this morning. Under interrogation, she told us a very troubling story."

Father Mathias and Rabbi Geller were both stunned.

Reverend Wallace stared at Father Mathias and said, "Father Mathias, what is the nature of your relationship with Father Desmond?"

Still reeling from the sight of the demon, Father Mathias said, "Father Desmond recruited me into JESU. We have known each other for years."

Reverend Wallace then asked, "So would you say that if Father Desmond asked for your help with anything that you would provide it to him?"

"Mark is my friend. If he asked for my help, I would give it to him. He has never given me any reason not to stand by him."

Reverend Wallace continued the inquiry about Father Mathias's relationship with Father Desmond. He then asked, "Father Mathias, I assume you are aware of Father Desmond's history with JESU?"

Father Mathias became defensive. "I am aware that Mark has dedicated his life to faithfully serving JESU. I have heard about the massacre that occurred ten years ago, and Mark never tried to evade responsibility for what happened."

Reverend Wallace's face became even more somber as he said, "Father, I want you to take your time and think before you respond to my next question. What do you know about a key that Father Desmond recovered from Stull Cemetery yesterday?"

Rabbi Geller interjected, "Key? What key? Father Desmond told me he was burying an object, a bell. It was to provide additional warding protection for the cemetery."

Reverend Wallace interrupted the Rabbi. "This woman, this demon, tells a far different story. She says that Father Desmond and his friend were there to recover a key and remove it from the cemetery, not to bury something there. So, Father Mathias, I will ask you once more. What do you know about this key?"

Father Mathias tried to stay calm as he considered how to respond to the question. After what seemed like an eternity, he said, "Father Desmond called me last night, indicating that he needed my assistance. He told me that his friend had gotten into serious trouble and that the key needed to be found to help him."

Imam Banu Daws, another member of the Council, interjected, "Father Mathias, who is Jack Aitken?"

Father Mathias quickly responded, "Jack Aitken is Father Desmond's friend."

Imam Daws interjected, "Father Mathias, you told us you were aware of Father Desmond's role in the massacre that occurred in Virginia ten years ago. Did it occur to you at all that Father Desmond's friends had betrayed him ten years ago, which led to the deaths of a large number of JESU members? How do you know that this so-called friend was trustworthy?"

"I met the man, Imam Daws," Father Mathias said. "If you had met him, I believe you would be able to tell that Jack is genuine and truthful. The man is suffering from a heavy burden."

Imam Daws shook his head. "Given Father Desmond's history, I am flabbergasted that you would just accept all of this at face value, and it would not concern you enough to contact the Council immediately."

Father Mathias grew angry at the Council members' insinuation that he should have been warier of Mark's motives. Before he could respond, Reverend Wallace spoke once again and asked, "Father Mathias, what were Father Desmond and Jack going to do with that key?"

"I am not sure, Reverend. Honestly, I don't think they know at this time either. I am unaware if there is a plan or not."

Reverend Wallace was growing impatient. "Father Mathias, this demon says that Father Desmond and Mr. Aitken are returning to Virginia and that they are taking this key to Lucius Rofocale. Is that true?"

The Council chamber was abuzz as the members whispered to one another. Reverend Wallace slammed the gavel down and demanded silence. He once again asked Father Mathias, "IS IT TRUE?"

Father Mathias knew there was no hiding it. He lowered his head and said, "Yes. It is true."

Reverend Wallace turned to Imam Daws. "We need to alert the Grand Council immediately. We also need to contact Anna Grieve."

Father Mathias raised his head and, with a quizzical look, said, "Anna Grieve? That is impossible. She is dead. She was a casualty of the massacre."

Reverend Wallace stared Father Mathias down and said, "That is what we wanted you and Father Desmond's acolytes to believe. After somehow surviving the massacre, she agreed to assume a new name and identity to be JESU's boots on the ground in Virginia. She has been undercover for the past ten years, keeping an eye on that gate in Culpeper."

"Security!" Imam Daws yelled. "Take this *thing* to the warded cell in the basement."

"Escort Father Mathias back to Desmond's apartment for further questioning," Reverend Wallace directed. "There is a vast store of information in Desmond's library. Maybe we will find something there we can use to find out what Desmond is really up to."

***

Jack and Father Desmond arrived at the Abilene Municipal Airfield. They found Tracy Guidry's hangar and began packing the plane for their flight to Manassas. The last item Jack put on the airplane was the knapsack with the box inside of it. Father Desmond was on his phone, and when he finished, he returned to the aircraft.

"Are we all packed up?" he asked.

Jack replied, "Yes. I just put the knapsack on board."

Tracy Guidry approached the duo and said, "We should be able to leave on time. We are just finishing up the fueling now."

Father Desmond responded, "That is great, Tracy. Thank you."

Tracy left to finish fueling the plane, and Father Desmond turned to Jack. "I have been trying to reach Father Mathias, but he is not answering my calls or responding to my texts. I assume he is still involved with the Council meeting. I would have liked to have spoken with him before we left, but I am not surprised that I cannot get a hold of him. I am sure the Council is going through that report thoroughly and comparing it closely to Abraham's version of what happened yesterday."

"Father, I've been wondering, what happens if Lucius's people do not see me at the airport or train station?"

"It is possible, perhaps likely, that they will figure out you are not really on the plane or the train. However, last night before I went to bed, I purchased an airline and rail ticket in your name. If someone inquires about you, they will find your name on the manifest. Additionally, I contacted a colleague who I feel resembles you and suggested he take a last-minute trip at my expense. It is likely that anyone that Lucius may send to verify that you were on the plane or train probably has never seen you in person. Maybe we will get lucky…"

Jack chuckled. "Is there anything you haven't thought of?"

"I am certain there is, but I concede that I am making up most of what we are doing as we go along. We just need to stay focused and start planning how we are going to defeat Lucius and save your family."

The plane engines roared to life, and the propellers started to spin. Tracy Guidry said, "Time to go, Father."

The two men climbed into the plane, and as it taxied down the runway, they began to discuss the next steps in their plan.

Father Desmond could not help but feel a pang of déjà vu. He never thought he would be heading back to Virginia and the location of the most traumatic event of his life. He could not help but feel a sense of danger and foreboding beginning to build up inside him.

Chapter 20

October 31st
Air space over Kentucky
10:30 a.m.

Father Desmond was comfortable flying in a single-engine aircraft, but this was a first for Jack. He was surprised at how smooth the flight actually was, although the plane was small. Three people in the aircraft were a tight squeeze, and it was loud inside the cabin. They had to wear headphones to drown out the noise, and the two men had to yell at one another to conduct a conversation. The noise prevented Tracy from hearing them discuss their next moves.

"Jack, I have already arranged for someone to meet us at the airport. We will go directly to the Wat Lao Buddhavong temple in Catlett."

Located forty-five minutes outside of Washington, DC, the temple complex was the perfect meeting place. The Father had informed it was built in 1993 by monks who emigrated from Laos, and it was a quiet refuge for meditation and study. It was sixty acres of secluded land in rural Northern Virginia, ideal for detailed operational planning and the solemn ritual.

"What exactly is the Michaelmas, Father?" Jack yelled over the engine.

"Pope Leo XIII commissioned a formal prayer to the Arch Angel Saint Michael in the 1880s. It is the closing prayer of the Catholic Church's old Latin mass. This plea to Saint Michael evolved from protecting the church's sovereignty to hoping for its restoration after the 1917 communist revolution in Russia. It also was invoked during the rite of exorcism, which was published starting in 1890."

Jack rubbed his chin, listening intently as Father Desmond continued, "JESU developed its own ceremonial rites utilizing the text of the prayer as the centerpiece. It was not only a request for protection from evil but an appeal for offensive power to oppose, defeat, and destroy evil in any and all forms that it might assume in circumstances where Saint Michael could not intervene directly. The ritual was conducted only in the direst of circumstances and included a special blessing for the individual who would be the ultimate warrior for good."

"Ultimate warrior? Is that you, Father?"

"You are the warrior, Jack!" Father Desmond shouted.

"Me? It can't be? I have no military training. I have no fighting skills!"

Father Desmond replied, "The legend says that a compromised soul, to break the chains of perdition and atone for his sins, will fight on the side of God in Saint Michael's place. The mass will help channel Saint Michael's fighting spirit into that soul."

Father Desmond placed his hand on Jack's shoulder and looked him in the eye. "Remember, Jack; all things are possible with God's help. You must have faith."

"I understand," Jack said reluctantly. "Candidly, it is not my soul that concerns me. I am fighting for the lives of my family. That is all the incentive I need. I am not naïve. I realize that I am taking on a force that I have only begun to comprehend, but I also know the consequences of failing. It is more than just about me and my own. I am defending all that is good in the world. I know there is no margin for error. I am prepared to push myself to the limits of my own endurance and beyond. I do not want to die, but I will sacrifice myself if it will mean defeating Lucius."

"You won't be fighting alone, Jack. I have recruited several of my peers who have fought by my side before. If the element of surprise is on our side, we can choose where, when, and how we will fight and hopefully keep Lucius off balance."

Jack smiled. "And pray?"

Father Desmond nodded in agreement.

Just then, Tracy broke in over the radio, "Manassas tower, this is Abilene Flight 162, over."

The Manassas Airport Controller responded, "Flight 162, we hear you, over."

"Tower, we are about thirty minutes out on a southeast approach, over."

"Copy that, Flight 162. The air space is clear for your approach, over."

"Copy that, tower." Tracy yelled over the engine noise to Father Desmond, "Father, I'm making preparations to land. We'll be on the ground in about a half-hour. Right on time. Do you need me to wait around? Is this a quick trip, or will you be in the area for a while?"

"Things are up in the air at the moment," Father Desmond shouted.

"Okay, Father. I was planning to stay here for a few days. Once we land, I'll text you the information about where I will be staying. If you need a trip home, just let me know."

Jack and Father Desmond finalized their plans. First, they would hold a tactical planning session with other JESU members to discuss fighting Lucius and his demon minions and rescuing Amanda, David, and Louis. Immediately afterward, the Michaelmas would take place, and upon its completion, they would head to Culpeper.

Jack checked his messages. He hoped for some communication from Amanda, but there was none. There were, however, several voicemails from Detective Bishop. Due to the bulletin he found while in Kansas, he already knew she would be looking for him. Going home would be out of the question as it would almost certainly be under surveillance. He wanted to avoid a confrontation with her at all costs. Fortunately, Father Desmond had already requested one of his friends obtain clothes for the two of them, and they would be at the temple complex when they arrived.

At 1:05 p.m., the plane touched down on the Manassas Regional Airport runway and taxied to a nearby hangar. Jack stepped off the plane, stretched his muscles that had tightened in the cramped cockpit, and soaked in the bright sunshine. He looked around the airport and was impressed by the scope of the facilities.

He had lived just a few miles away from this location for more than two decades and never imagined it was as extensive as all this.

Monk Maha Bounmy greeted Father Desmond with the Laotian variation of the Thai greeting known as *the wai*. It consisted of a slight bow with the monk's hands clasped together as if he were in prayer. Father Desmond reciprocated, but the monk's hands were held high and his bow lower than Father Desmond's, a sign of great respect. Father Desmond introduced Jack, who responded to a similar greeting from the monk with a nod and a smile. He led them to a car to take them to the temple.

Jack was familiar with the route they were traveling. As they drove on Route 28 South, they passed by a sign for the turnoff to Linton Hall Road, which would have taken Jack back home. He glanced right as they entered the intersection and closed his eyes as they drove through it. He thought of his family and wondered if they would ever be together again in their beloved yet straightforward suburban home. He was not sure of the answer to that question, but as they turned onto a dirt road that would take them to the temple, he knew that after tonight, nothing would ever be the same.

"Yes, Chairman," Anne Bishop said. "I understand. I'm on my way there now."

Anne Bishop ended the call with the JESU Grand Chairman, turned to her driver, and said, "Step on it, Ross."

The driver immediately complied, and their vehicle sped South on Route 29 toward Charlottesville, Virginia. They already had passed Culpeper and would reach Charlottesville in roughly an hour. It should be just enough time to take up appropriate positions, which would enable them to take Desmond and Aitken into custody peacefully. At least that was what she hoped.

It had been ten years since she had last seen Mark Desmond. Her real name was Anna Grieve then. It was right before they had entered the forest around Culpeper, just before the massacre. As a matter of fact, unless he had managed to unravel the best-kept secret within JESU, he most likely believed that she was dead.

There were very few survivors that day, and though seriously wounded, she had managed to find, somehow, her way out of the woods and to Route 29, where she was picked up by a passing vehicle and driven to a hospital.

A few weeks later, when she'd sufficiently recovered, she contacted colleagues at JESU and was informed of the extent of the massacre. At the same time, Anna received orders to prepare for a long-term mission. She would be JESU's boots on the ground around the Hell Gate and covertly monitor the area. Her physical injuries healed much quicker than her emotional ones, but the mission had enabled her to move forward from the massacre and its aftermath eventually.

She assumed the name Anne Bishop and concocted a real-life identity for her new persona. This ruse was so effective she stopped thinking of herself as Anna Grieve altogether. It was almost as if Anna had never existed. For many years there was little if anything to report. This respite helped Anne come to terms with what had happened. She viewed her mission as an opportunity to redeem herself for participating in an operation she believed caused lasting damage to JESU.

Things had changed roughly a year ago when demon activity in the area spiked significantly. Anne later surmised that someone of importance had moved into the region and that the increased activity coincided with this event. Her cover as a police detective enabled her to keep tabs on crimes in the Culpeper area and covertly investigate those that had the potential to be tied to satanic ceremonies and rituals.

However, finding out the identity of this evil entity had proven to be difficult. Anne had to investigate cases carefully, as capturing and interrogating too many demons could bring unwanted attention to herself and blow her cover. She also was unable to re-establish relationships with JESU members so that her identity could remain hidden even from her former friends and colleagues. Sometimes, she lost herself so profoundly in her role as a detective that she could almost forget that she even was still a member of JESU. Today's call from the Chairman had instantly changed all of this, and hearing the name Mark Desmond stirred emotions within her that had long been dormant. Feelings that she had been unsure even still existed.

Anne had known Mark for many years before the massacre. He had been her mentor and eventually became her best friend. There was no denying that she loved him, and she believed that Father Desmond loved her too. She knew his fidelity to his religious vows would never allow him to act on such feelings, nor would he ever acknowledge them to her. Still, he would frequently discuss and debate religious doctrine, and from time to time, that included the topic of celibacy and if priests should be allowed to marry. Above all of this, she thought to herself; *a woman knows when a man has fallen for her.*

Even for a time after the massacre, her relationship with him would invade her daily thoughts, and when she slept, she would revisit it all in her dreams. She never blamed Mark for the massacre. She never thought him to be solely responsible for what had happened in the way that the JESU Grand Council had. She did concede he had a blind spot for family and friends. In retrospect, it was easy to see how he could have been taken in by those he felt were close to him. At the same time, he was a true warrior. He was selfless and willing to lay down his life for loved ones and his God. This willingness on his part to sacrifice everything for the greater good enabled her to see her role for JESU in Northern Virginia as an honorable one. If Mark could make such sacrifices, then so could she.

It pained her not to be able to reach out to him in what she was sure was his darkest hour. To bring him some comfort and help ease his pain. In one sense, they had both suffered the worst of losses: their friendship. The mission had to take precedence, so she trained herself to drive out all thoughts of reuniting with Mark. Initially, the days were long, and the nights were longer, but her JESU training and the right forged documents allowed her to obtain a job that she could throw herself entirely into, body and mind. Her soul, however, remained conflicted between her feelings for Mark and her duty to JESU.

Now, the mere mention of Mark's name caused every banished memory to come flooding back to her like a raging torrent. As they got closer to the train station in Charlottesville, she fought back the tears. Arresting Jack Aitken was one thing. For all, she knew he could indeed be responsible and need to be held accountable for the disappearance of his family. She was trying to understand what could bring Mark back to the location of his most profound agony? Accepting the truth of what JESU was telling her about the threat represented by this key, would she still be able to do her duty to recover it and arrest Mark too?

She was about to find out. They pulled into the parking lot and made their way to the platform. Anne checked her watch and saw that it was almost two o'clock. The train was just pulling into the station, and she started scanning the cars looking for a sign of Mark.

All the years of training made it easy to spot a suspicious-looking man and woman at the far end of the platform. She suspected they were here for the same reason as she. She continued to size the two individuals up as the doors opened and the passengers began to exit the train. When all of the passengers had left the train, there was no sign of Mark or Jack Aitken.

Anne and her driver started back to the car. Anne chuckled and, under her breath, said, "Vintage Mark Desmond!"

***

Jack's head was spinning. For several hours, he'd participated in the most intense planning session he had ever experienced. Father Desmond had assembled a team of JESU members that he personally selected as much for their military prowess as their friendship and loyalty to him. The discussions were candid and very detailed to avoid any mistakes or oversights that would lead to failure. What was at stake was far too significant to warrant nothing less than the most exhaustive preparations.

Jack could not be sure, but the room appeared to be constructed for one purpose only, secrecy. There were no windows. A heavy, wooden door with ornate iron hardware was the only way in and out of the room. It looked like something from a medieval fortress or castle. Out of curiosity, Jack had hit a wall with his fist. It felt like hitting concrete and barely made a sound. Whatever discussion took place in this room went unheard by anyone passing it in the hallway.

Rabbi Evan Strouse was the leader of a synagogue in Fairfax, Virginia. As a member of JESU, he had training in intelligence gathering with particular expertise in surveillance. His methods included both boots on the ground scouting and technology that included drones. He'd found the area heavily guarded by more than a dozen demons and two Hell Hounds. Jack shuddered at the mention of the Hell Hounds, having become all too intimately familiar with them during his previous visits to the gate. Rabbi Strouse then told Jack he knew where Amanda and the boys were currently.

"Amanda and your sons are imprisoned in a cell located in the basement of the Bradford house. They are under constant monitoring, including guards on duty around the clock."

Jack asked pleadingly, "How are they? Are they okay?"

"I do not know, Jack."

Father Desmond interjected, "Jack, while Lucius is bloodthirsty, I do not believe he would harm Amanda, David, and Louis. Without them, he loses significant leverage over you. No doubt, their stay has been highly stressful, but I anticipate they will be physically unharmed."

No amount of reassurance would be sufficient for Jack, but he knew coming unglued at this moment would not help his family, nor would it instill confidence in the team of his ability to fulfill his role in this mission. He nodded his understanding to the group members gathered around the table, and the meeting continued. Hindu Priest Sriman Raghavacharya reached into the bag on the table in front of them and pulled out bracelets he handed to each team member. As a JESU member, he had considerable knowledge of weaponry and protection from the influence of evil. Each bracelet contained hematite, obsidian, and a tiger's eye.

"These bracelets will provide defense against the evil that we will be facing. The stones work together to provide strength and protection. Hematite brings with it feelings of calm and heightened mental energy. It will help us to focus on our mission. Obsidian is a volcanic rock whose black color shields a person against negative energy. Finally, the tiger's eye represents good luck and increases one's willpower to resist evil."

The priest reached back into his bag and pulled out additional weapons, which he distributed to the team.

"Eraka Grass," he said. "It is an herb that will transform into an iron spear in the hands of a penitent and contrite soul. Once we complete Michaelmas, this weapon will automatically transform into a spear made of an iron that will kill demons."

Next, the priest handed out an object that looked like a flute.

"This is a specially made blowgun. The darts can travel up to 350 feet per second and are accurate from up to twenty-five yards away. I dip the tips of the darts in holy water infused with dill, lavender, oregano, and parsley."

The team members examined the weapons the priest had provided to them.

"I chose these weapons for their power, potency, and ability to kill a demon without making noise. They are light, and their small size makes them easy to carry without impairing the need to move swiftly and nimbly. Silence and the element of surprise will be great allies in a mission such as this. Silence and surprise will help disguise our numbers, which are clearly inferior to our enemy. We can close that numerical gap utilizing stealth and daring."

"Thank you, Sriman," Father Desmond said. "Weapons like these are just what we are going to need tonight."

Speaking directly to Jack, Father Desmond continued, "These weapons are far more sophisticated than they may appear. After this meeting, but before the Michaelmas, Sriman will be giving you a crash course in their use."

Jack nodded and acknowledged that he understood.

Father Desmond went on, "During the massacre ten years ago; the demons used guns. Sriman, do we have any idea of what their stockpile may include?"

"Each demon is likely to be armed with similar weapons as they used back then. A demon's primary weapon is to possess humans; deception and their ability to influence people to do evil. They have also effectively adopted the technology of mortal men for their own devices. Their physical strength is greater than the average human. There is no doubt that we will need to use the weapons we have and use them with great skill. The Michaelmas should help us prevent them from 'getting into our heads,' so to speak."

"Now, I want to talk about the ultimate goals of our mission," Father Desmond said. "How do we close this gate forever, and how will we liberate and rescue Jack's family? Let me introduce Imam Shamima Wadud, who will share her plan to secure the safe return of Jack's family. She has been a JESU member for fifteen years and an Imam in a mosque in Denver, Colorado, for even longer. Her expertise is hostage extraction and rescue. She has led multiple successful missions for JESU all over the world. Imam Wadud, the floor is yours."

"This is a complicated scenario," the Imam stated. "There is no guarantee that during the encounter with Lucius Rofocale that Mrs. Aitken and her children will remain in the Bradford home. They are far more likely to be moved in the next few hours to another location. However, if they are still in that prison cell in the basement, we might be able to rescue them. I am going to propose a two-pronged approach. Mark, can you provide some background on the Bradford home for us?"

"The Bradford home is at this location for a reason. Indeed, my research indicates that the Bradford's were suspicious of the burial mound in the area centuries before we became aware of its existence. They built the home to research the origins of the burial mound and monitor any activity in the area."

"What happened to the family?" Jack asked. "Their cemetery has numerous tombstones, and the home appears not to have had any occupants for many years."

Father Desmond responded, "We are not entirely sure. Virginia suffered several epidemics in the 1800s, including a cholera outbreak in 1848. It also could be that Lucius Rofocale became aware of their presence and decided to kill them to protect the secrecy surrounding the gate."

Imam Wadud interjected, "Mark, tell the team about the basement entrance you located."

"The Bradford's were involved in the mining industry. There is an entrance to their old mine at the current Bingham & Taylor Iron Plant in Culpeper. Look at this map."

Father Desmond placed a yellowed document on the table and unrolled it.

"This map indicates the mine entrance actually connects to an entrance in the Bradford basement. It is likely not far from where Amanda and the boys are at the moment. It may be a longshot, but I think it is worth considering a rescue attempt using this passageway."

"I agree with Mark," Imam Wadud said. "It is possible we can surprise the guards and help Jack's family escape. At the same time, we need to consider the alternative scenario: Amanda and the boys at another location. My experience tells me that Lucius would want them to be near him."

Rabbi Strouse joined in the conversation. "Based on the surveillance I did, wooded areas surround the mound. It would be easy, particularly in the dark, to hide Jack's family there."

Imam Wadud turned to Jack and said, "Jack, when you get to the area around the gate and confront Lucius, you should demand to see your family before you agree to give him anything."

"Okay, but Lucius has not been too receptive to my demands. The more I push him, the more pissed off he gets."

"You have to be firm, but do not insist that he do it," Father Desmond counseled. "What you are requesting is not out of the ordinary, and I would expect Lucius to comply with it just to show you that they are unharmed. It would be in his best interest to do this to ensure your compliance. If he refuses, you can tell him that you won't turn over the key without seeing them."

Imam Wadud continued, "Let us assume he brings them out and keeps them close to him. As the confrontation with Lucius unfolds, and particularly if it escalates, we need to do something to protect your family from reprisals by Lucius or his demons."

Imam Wadud handed each team member a plastic bag containing a gray powder and a lighter.

"This is fennel powder, used to ward off evil in Islamic mystic traditions. It is made from ground fennel seeds and infused with gunpowder to act as a propellant. It receives a blessing from a Sufi Islamic mystic. It can be spread in a circle around your family and ignited. The circle of flames would then protect your family from being physically harmed by Lucius or any of his demons."

As the tension in the room increased, Father Desmond tightly gripped the edges of the table. "Now, let us discuss deployment. Jack, you will take the trail to the gate that you have used previously. On the chance that we have managed to fool Lucius, we want you to appear as if you are alone. Imam Wadud and I will access the mine entrance west of the Bradford House. Our goal will be to extract Amanda and the boys if they are still there. If they are not, we will eliminate any of Lucius's demons that we can find and make our way to the gate. We will take a path that circles behind the mound and will allow us to approach the area in the opposite direction you will take."

Father Desmond pointed to an area on the map.

"Rabbi, you and Sriman will come in from a direction that is on Jack's right."

Rabbi Strouse added, "The data obtained by the drone indicates this is a heavily forested area with no formal trails. We will need some extra time to traverse this terrain and engage and remove any demons that we may come across. We will park and hide our vehicle along Route 29 rather than utilize the same parking lot that Jack does."

Father Desmond concurred. "You should leave immediately after the Michaelmas. Imam Wadud and I will depart at a time that hopefully will allow us to all be in position when Jack arrives at the gate. I hope that by all of us approaching simultaneously, even if one team loses the element of surprise, the others might remain undiscovered. If Lucius moves demons from one area to meet a known threat in another, it could lead to a weakness that we might be able to exploit."

Father Desmond paused, then stated firmly, "Now, I want to make sure I am clear on a few other things. We all know what is at stake here. When you use your weapons, you use them with the intent to kill. Protecting Jack's family is a priority, and if you can shepherd them to safety at any point, do it. I know we would all like to kill Lucius Rofocale, but he should not receive any disproportionate attention. Lucius is not an ordinary demon, and there is no guarantee that any of our weapons can affect him, let alone kill him. Finally, there is a very high likelihood that some or even all of us will not survive. Above all else, that gate must be closed forever."

The planning session came to an end, and the team dispersed to begin preparations for the Michaelmas. Father Desmond pulled Jack aside and asked, "Do you have any questions, concerns, or need clarification on anything we discussed?"

"No. I am sure I understand. I also appreciate you gathering such an impressive team. My confidence has increased significantly after listening to all of this. The depth of knowledge and expertise is impressive. They have had an extensive amount of training, and I am sure you had something to do with that. I just want to thank you for all of your support and for believing in me."

Father Desmond placed his hand on Jack's shoulder. "You have become entangled in a web of intrigue, a conspiracy that you were totally unaware of until it was too late to change the road you were on. You might have listened to Amanda and even your own instincts to change the direction you were taking, but once a person starts down the *'Highway to Hell,'* they often find there is no way off. From one man to another, I understand why you did what you did and continued with the project."

Jack forced a weak smile but shook his head. "Thanks. I cannot help but continue to ask myself, how did I get here? Why me?"

"I am a man of faith. Jack, we are all sinners. All sinners are required to atone for those sins. As imperfect as we are, there is always a chance at redemption. Second Corinthians chapter twelve, verse nine, states, 'My grace is sufficient for you, for my power is made perfect in weakness.' I believe that God's glory will be made manifest in your weakness."

Father Desmond continued, "Saint Paul went even further in the same chapter, but in verse ten, 'So I take pleasure in weaknesses, insults, hardships, persecutions and in difficulties, for the sake of Christ. For when I am weak, I am strong.' I believe that all the challenges you have been through in your life and the horrors of the last few days have tempered you into steel. God has chosen you for the role you are now about to play. Just have faith and believe that you are ready to serve his purpose."

Jack stood up straighter, suddenly feeling more in control of his destiny. He knew he was walking a tightrope, but Jack decided right then, he would no longer look down. His focus would be on saving his family and doing what was necessary to help Father Desmond close the gate for good.

However, he knew the only way to fulfill these aims was to do one thing. He would need to kill Lucius Rofocale.

Chapter 21

October 31st
Prison cell, Bradford House
5:30 p.m.

"I dreamed a dream in times gone by. When hope was high and life worth living," Amanda softly sang to David and Louis. Jack always told her she had the voice of an angel, and this song from *Les Misérables* usually settled the boys down.

"I had a dream my life would be so different than this hell I'm living."

Amanda could find no better way to describe the last week than to call it living in Hell. Her family had been kidnapped, then psychologically tortured. Meanwhile, her husband was racing against time to save their lives and souls. All of this masterminded by an arrogant, devious, and vicious entity that made her skin crawl and evoked dread in her heart every time she was in his presence.

She used the word entity only because she was not sure what to call the bastard that held them captive, and there was no way to refer to him as a human being. She had sensed something wrong with Lucius Rofocale from the moment she and Jack had first met him. When he had assumed the form of quite possibly, the most frightening figure she had ever laid eyes upon, it made him something else altogether. The word evil did not come close to describing him. He was beyond evil, and he evoked both fear and an intense hatred she never thought could possibly emanate from her.

David began to stir slightly, and Amanda rubbed his back to soothe him and help him sleep awhile longer. She was not sure exactly what time it was but based on the sun's rays shining into their prison cell; she surmised it was late afternoon. Amanda hoped the boys would sleep a little longer, as it was impossible to know what would happen later that night. She only knew it was going to occur around midnight. The timing was one of the few details that Lucius had chosen to share with her. She found herself yawning. None of them had been able to get any restful sleep for days, and to say they were suffering from sleep deprivation was an understatement. She just hoped that pure adrenaline would carry them all through.

She closed her eyes and wondered about Jack. Lucius had not allowed them to have any contact with one another for several days. All he had told her was that Jack had obtained "the key" and was on the way back to Northern Virginia.

At one point, Lucius had pontificated for more than an hour about his grand plan and how his brilliance had turned an old legend about a compromised soul into reality. The only thing bigger than this achievement had to be Lucius's ego, but Amanda understood enough of what he was saying to know that he believed Jack was this compromised soul and that the key would open a portal to Hell. Initially, it all sounded surreal, but after everything that had occurred this week, it was all too believable.

Louis opened his eyes and looked up at Amanda with a smile. She smiled back and stroked his hair. She encouraged him to go back to sleep and watched as he cozied up closer to her and David. The boys had become very clingy since the most recent incident between David and Lucius. Every time Lucius entered the room, Louis dashed to the corner of the cell that was furthest from him and shook with fear. It was difficult to watch the two of them go through this, but Amanda could not be prouder because, despite everything, they had held up tremendously well.

Just then, the door to the room swung open, and a man entered carrying a tray of food. Amanda knew it must be around 6:00 p.m., as this was typically when their meals arrived. Amanda always found mealtime to be somewhat amusing. Lucius and his minions quickly became aware of the power and control that autism could have over a group of people.

The first night after their kidnapping, they brought in hamburgers. Both boys refused to eat. Lucius himself came to the room and initially tried to intimidate David and Louis into eating. Still, even the "great and powerful" Lucius Rofocale could not get them to consume the food. It was the one test of wills where her family had been able to declare victory over Lucius. Amanda reasoned Lucius knew he had to keep them all alive and in good health to ensure Jack's compliance.

Exasperated, he finally asked Amanda about the boy's dietary requirements. She could not help but smile when she told Lucius that the only thing David would eat was Chick-Fil-A. She imagined one of Lucius's demon stooges having to drive through Chick-Fil-A, a faith-based Christian company, to buy food. Amanda took great pleasure reminding him he would need to buy two meals on Saturday as Chick-Fil-A would not be open on Sunday. While she was sensible enough not to verbalize it, "up yours" was the thought that came to Amanda at the time.

While David and Louis ate, Amanda could not help but replay the week's events in her mind. She was not the type to armchair Quarterback herself, but she did have one honest regret above all else; she had been far too trusting. When Lucius's henchman had come to the door and informed her Jack was involved in a car accident, Amanda should have asked questions. Instead, she had reacted out of profound fear and concern and never asked to check their identification. She quickly grabbed her things, including a cell phone, and ran to the car waiting for her.

As if anticipating her needs, the men offered to collect Louis and David before she could even mention the necessity of planning to pick David up at school and Louis from work. They drove first to Patriot High School, where she arranged to have David excused from the rest of his classes. They then went to AutoZone in Manassas and picked up Louis from work. She told the boys that their father was in an accident and they would go see him right away. She only became suspicious when the car began heading west, the opposite direction of Fairfax Hospital. That was when all three of them received a face full of chloroform, and the next thing she knew, they were in the prison cell where they had resided for the past week.

So many times during the week, she had wondered if the outcome would have been different if she had been less deferential at that time, but there would never be any way ever to know the answer to that question. She would have done anything to spare her children all of this. Lucius tried to tell her he had intended to leave the boys out of this "affair," as he referred to it, but he indicated Jack's rudeness and failure to follow directions put him in a position of having no real choice in the matter. Amanda called bullshit on that one. She knew Lucius derived far too much pleasure in tormenting the four of them to give up the chance to treat them like they were toys to be played with by the family cat. He was relishing all of this, every bit of it.

After finishing their meal, perhaps their last one, the three of them retreated to the cot at the rear of the cell. The boys hugged Amanda, and she comforted them as they began to whimper. It was as if they knew that something significant and terrible was about to happen. She had tried not to show them she was scared, but she feared they sensed her apprehension. The light in the cell was waning, sunset only a few minutes away. Once again, she heard the lock turn, and the door opened. The two guards quickly snapped to attention, which told her Lucius was entering the room. As he did, Louis hurried to the corner of the cell while David squeezed Amanda even more closely than before.

"Good evening, Amanda," Lucius said. "I trust your meal was satisfactory?"

Amanda responded abruptly, making it a point not to thank him for it. "It was fine."

Lucius nodded and said, "Well, good. How are the boys?"

While Lucius had not mentioned them by name, the boys sensed he had asked about them. This inquiry immediately caused them to get behind Amanda as if she could shield them from their tormentor.

"You can see them for yourself. Just how do you think they are doing?"

Lucius grinned broadly. "Actually, they seem to be behaving nicely. You and Jack should be thanking me, you know. They have both been far more compliant since I disciplined David." He paused. "A lesson you might take with you when this is all over, perhaps?"

Amanda ignored Lucius's obviously obnoxious and disingenuous insinuation about the possibility of there being a tomorrow at all. She retorted, "There is nothing that I need or want to learn from you. What do you want with us now?"

Lucius clasped his hands behind his back and paced back and forth in front of the prison cell. After a few moments, he said, "Mrs. Aitken, we have begun the final preparations for our gala spectacle that will commence in a few hours. It will become necessary to move you and the children outdoors to a site closer to our ceremony's main location. You will be escorted and looked after by my staff, but I am anticipating your full cooperation. Any resistance is futile, and retribution for non-compliance will be swift and, shall we say, painful. Am I getting my point across to you without alarming your children further?"

Amanda replied sternly, "I understand, but do us both a favor, stop pretending that you care about my children. You don't give a rat's ass about them. If you did, you would let them go. If I thought it would do any good, I'd beg for their release, but I am not going to do that."

"Yes, please do not do that, Mrs. Aitken. It would be very unbecoming of a woman of your resilience to start groveling now. You may not believe this, but I hold you in high regard. While foolhardy, your dedication to your children is somewhat admirable, I suppose."

Amanda snapped back, "The last thing I need or want is your appreciation for my mothering skills. You cannot possibly know anything about the bond between a mother and her child. The only things you really know about are playing games with people's lives like they are part of some sort of sporting event and your constant, over-inflated sense of narcissism."

Lucius's expression quickly turned, and the tone of his voice became far more ominous. "Be careful, Amanda. My compliment was in no way implying that I will tolerate any defiance from you.

Your life and that of your children depend entirely upon your submission to my demands. Anything less will result in the immediate termination of your life as well as that of David and Louis. There will be no second chances. No opportunities for redemption or forgiveness."

Amanda gritted her teeth and said, "I understand."

"Good. Now, I will briefly require your guards' assistance, so I will be leaving you alone in this room for an hour or two. Of course, you will remain in your cell, and mind you; there is no chance of escaping. No cavalry is coming to save you. Rest up if you can, as our event will not commence until much later in the evening."

One of the guards held the door open for Lucius as he exited the room. Before the door closed behind him, he paused, turned to face Amanda, and said mockingly, "Of course, you might consider praying to your God for help."

The door locked behind him and, Lucius stood in the hallway, laughing.

After Lucius left the room, both boys quickly huddled next to Amanda. She thought about what Lucius had said about God when he left the room and then began to hum and sing another song from *Les Misérables* to soothe the boys' concerns.

"God on high, hear my prayer. In my need, you have always been there."

Amanda looked down at Louis and stroked his hair. She continued to sing, *"He is young. He's afraid. Let him rest. Heaven blessed. Bring him home."* As both boys' breathing slowed, a tear slowly ran down Amanda's cheek. She placed her arm around David's shoulder and pulled him closer. Their eyes met, and David smiled as Amanda sang, *"Bring him peace. Bring him, Joy. He is young. He is only a boy. You can take. You can give. Let him be. Let him live."*

The tone of her voice grew softer, and her song became more and more like a prayer, *"If I die, let me die. Let him live. Bring him home."* As the room grew darker and became quiet, Amanda silently pleaded for God's intervention and mercy. She also begged Jack to hurry.

The doors swung open, and Lucius strode into the chamber. Instantaneously, all the demons assembled in the room stood stiffly at attention as he made his way to the podium. Lucius paused to glance around the room at his legions. All eyes were on him, and he grinned as he looked at their faces and basked in their adoration. His hour of triumph was drawing near. He almost shuddered at the thought of the power he would wield once he became the fourth member of Lucifer's inner consortium. The tales of his glorious achievement would live on forever, along with himself, of course. His immortality would be assured.

Lucius gathered his subordinates around a map of the burial mound and the surrounding area. Pointing to the area adjacent to the knoll, he indicated that the guards could transfer Mrs. Aitken and her children there after the meeting. One of the demons asked, "Master, should they be shackled together or restrained similarly?"

Lucius responded, "No. Those two boys are so scared they will not be going anywhere. Their mother is their protector, and she would never leave them behind. She has no physical power or any other power, for that matter, that can hurt any of us. I want them out in the open so that I can personally keep an eye on them. I want Mr. Aitken to see them when he arrives at the burial mound to reinforce to him his need to comply with my demands."

Lucius then pointed out where he wanted other groups of his demons to station themselves. He suspected Jack would be approaching the area utilizing the same route he had used previously. He pointedly stated, "You will signal to me when you spot him and apprise me of his progress every fifteen minutes after that. It should be obvious, but if you do not see him, report it to me immediately."

The demons all nodded in unison and confirmed the understanding of their orders. Lucius then showed several of the guards a secret passageway behind the wall in the basement. "Several of you will remain in the house in case someone attempts to make use of this secret passage. Everything I know right now indicates that Aitken will be arriving alone, but he has been meeting with Mark Desmond, and we need to prepare for all contingencies."

The demons around the table looked at one another. While none of them dared speak, they were all familiar with the stories surrounding Mark Desmond. Lucius sensed this information about Mark Desmond was raising some concerns amongst his legions.

He slammed his fist down on the table to get their attention and said, "You all know what happened here ten years ago. Mark Desmond is no match for me! There is nothing for you to fear. Follow my orders, and you will all be witnesses to history and the rise of a world dominated by our Lord and Master Lucifer. A new world we have been waiting for thousands of years to arrive is only hours away. Now go! Do your jobs!"

The demons around the table all spoke in unison, "YES, MASTER LUCIUS!" The chamber emptied as the legions set about fulfilling Lucius's orders.

Left alone in the chamber, he stared at the map in front of him. While he was confident in his plan, there were a few nagging details that were troubling him. His scouts had indicated they spotted a man looking like Jack Aitken get on a train at the Charlottesville station earlier in the day. However, a few hours later, when that train arrived in Manassas, Virginia, Jack was not on the station platform. Jack was not answering his cell phone either. However, he had someone go to Jack's house, and they found a charger on the counter. He suspected that Jack had left the charger at home in his haste, and since his phone likely had no charge, he was incapable of receiving any calls or messages.

Still, while the explanation was plausible, something told him this had Mark Desmond's fingerprints all over it. The last text he received from Nadia, however, indicated that Desmond was still in his apartment.

Lucius finally concluded that none of this really mattered. Even if Jack was in the wind, so to speak, he had to be returning with the key. He knew his family was doomed if he failed.

He reached for the sword of Saint Michael inside the sheath that hung from his waist. Even if Desmond had cooked up something, this weapon would trump everything, and there were always alternatives if something unanticipated were to occur. Lucius swept away any doubts he had and was confident that nothing could stop him now.

***

As she watched Louis and David sleep, Amanda closed her eyes and thought about Jack. She wished she could get a message to him somehow, but Lucius informed her he was blocking the signal on her cell phone. He reinforced his total lack of concern about her ability to communicate with the outside world by permitting her to keep her phone to allow her children to play games and keep themselves occupied during their imprisonment.

There were things she wanted to tell Jack, but she worried she might never get that chance. While she hoped Jack would find a way to defeat Lucius and save them, she had to admit the odds were not in their favor. She took out her phone and stared at the screen for a minute. The guards would be returning soon, and she decided to take the opportunity to write an e-mail to Jack with the hope that when this was all over, he would have a chance to read it.

My Dearest Jack,

David and Louis have finally fallen asleep. Although I am unsure for how long, I am writing this e-mail hoping that you might read it when this is all over. I cannot lie and tell you that I am optimistic. I know the reality of what is happening, but I have faith in you, my love. I have been allowed to hold on to this phone solely, as this bastard Lucius puts it, "to keep your damned children occupied." The son of a bitch tries to make it appear as if he is magnanimous, while at the same time, I know he delights in the psychological torture that he imposes on us.

He has blocked all communications, so even if I had information I could share with you about how we are doing and where we are now, it would not go through anyway. Perhaps, I am really writing to you as a way to deal with my own fears, which have frequently been put on the back burner while I try to help Louis and David navigate all of this. How I wish you were here to assist me with the two of them. They are so frightened. However, you would be as proud as I am at how they have held up under such intense stress and pressure.

The other day, David attempted to defend me against Lucius's taunting, which caused Lucius to assume his supernatural form. Yes, Jack, I have seen the face of our mutual tormenter. He nearly choked David into unconsciousness. As I am sure that you do, I want to kill Lucius in the worst way possible. However, I do not know of any means humanly possible to do so as he is not human. He is an abomination and eviler than anything I possibly could have imagined. Several days ago, I would have scoffed at any discussion that even alluded to the Devil, but having seen Lucius face to face, I know that real evil does exist. I find it even more frightening to realize that it was seemingly right here in our own backyard all along.

I am sure you have been asking yourself, "Why is this happening to us? How is all of this even possible?" Jack, I know you are blaming yourself. Thirty years of marriage and growing up with you, as my best friend tells me this. I know I implored and begged you to stop your research. After whatever happened to you back in September, you did what I asked you to do. Only in the aftermath have we seen that Lucious set in motion events far beyond anything we could control or comprehend.

Regardless of what may happen now, you must not blame yourself. I do not blame you. I understood why you needed this book project even while I was asking you to give it up. I do not hold you responsible for all of this. Lucius is who should be accountable for it all. I realize that my words alone will not deter you from taking on the responsibility for this horror show, but you must somehow see that he is the monster, not you.

Sleep has been difficult to come by these last several days, as I am sure it has been for you as well. My dreams, however, have not all turned to nightmares. They have been replays of the most beautiful times of our life together. Sometimes dreams fade in the minutes, hours, and days after they occur, but not my reveries. I have seen you as the handsome young man asking me out on our first date. Do you remember the name of the ice cream parlor? I could smell the Racquet Club aftershave on your face as I kissed your cheek in appreciation for such a wonderful time. We were two children, each of us nervous yet exhilarated at our new romance, and I still feel that way today, Jack, as I know that you do.

We have known one another for well over half of our lives. Our relationship has seen high school and college graduations. In my dreams, I once more had the chance to relive your marriage proposal at Jones Beach as the sun began to set. Saying 'yes' to you was the best decision I have ever made. My dream also gave me one more chance to gaze into your eyes as we exchanged our vows to one another. Then, it was onto our honeymoon in Bermuda with its pink sand beaches and that rum swizzle cruise. We have worked hard building a life together, which led to our most beautiful creations, David and Louis.

We have cried together and supported one another through so much when it comes to our children. Most of all, we have loved and appreciated them quite possibly more than we might have if they were not autistic. I know this has been incredibly difficult for you as a father. All of those things that fathers and sons do together, such as teaching them to play soccer or watching their little league games, were not yours to have, my love. I know the hurt you have buried for years, and I want to assure you that you never allowed your private pain to get in the way of our family's well-being or happiness. You are a wonderful father, Jack, and I am blessed to be your wife.

You have stood by me through my darkest days and nights and believed in me even if I did not always believe in myself. You never saw anything but the best in me. When something went wrong in my life, you fought to make it right, my knight in shining armor. When I was weak, you were resilient. When I lost faith, you found a way to restore it for me. I have leaned on you all of these years, which has prevented me from falling into despair. Your love made me believe that all things were possible and allowed me to find a voice that I never knew I had.

You have brought joy to my life far beyond anything that I could ever have imagined. The reality of marrying you has exceeded any fantasy that I may have had. You have shown me love and respect beyond anything that I might have imagined. Some men talk a good game about how they treat their spouses, but you backed up every word with your actions. What a man does is far more telling and meaningful than what he says.

I know that regardless of the outcome of all of this, our love will be more robust, and our children will thrive. Together, we will rise from the ashes of our darkest hour and fulfill the vows we made to one another. I know you remember them, my love, for better or for worse, for richer or for poorer, in sickness and in health, and if death does cause us to part tonight, I know the survivor will carry on for the sake of David and Louis. Though heartbroken, our spirit and love for one another will remain unbroken. The bond between us is indestructible. Neither Lucius nor Satan himself can break our covenant, which will remain intact forever.

I can see that the day has turned to night through this prison cell window, and my time is growing short. My love, I still believe that the strength of our relationship can get us through the trial to come, but I am not naive. The Bible states it is better to give than receive; let us pledge to do our part tonight. Let no setback discourage you, and I promise that I will not be afraid. We will make Lucius pay the highest price for our lives and our souls. We will not go quietly or without the fiercest fight that we can bring, and regardless of what our ultimate destiny might be, we will at least leave this world knowing that we were together at the end.

I love you more than you know, Jack.

Love always and forever,
Amanda
XOXO

Amanda hit the send button and saw the e-mail sitting in her outbox. She pushed the power button on the phone off and put it down on the floor next to her. Footsteps were coming down the hallway, and as the door opened, Amanda closed her eyes and said to herself, "I love you, Jack."

Chapter 22

October 31st
Wat Lao Buddhavong Temple, Catlett, Virginia
4:45 p.m.

Father Desmond led Jack to a room adjacent to the temple sanctuary. As they entered, Jack saw robes, priest vestments, and other religious attire hanging on hooks attached to the walls. There was a small altar where the monks would pray before entering the sanctuary, which they would access through a second door on the other side of the room. In the middle of the room was a small card table with several chairs around it. There was also a cabinet on the wall opposite the altar, which contained religious icons and ornaments.

Father Desmond motioned for Jack to have a seat at the table. He remained standing and said, "We are finalizing the preparations for the Michaelmas that we will conduct in the sanctuary. While you are waiting, I have a guest that I think you might like to speak with."

The door that Jack and Father Desmond had just gone through opened, and a monk led an older gentleman into the room then closed the door behind him. Jack got up from the table to introduce himself, and to his surprise, he recognized the man. He reached out to shake hands and exclaimed, "Reverend Miner! What are you doing here?"

"One of your friend's colleagues picked me up at your house, Jack," Reverend Miner said. "Your call the other day worried me, and I thought some additional spiritual guidance from an old friend might be helpful."

Father Desmond shook Reverend Miner's hand. "It is a pleasure to make your acquaintance Reverend. Jack has shared a great deal about you over the past few days. He was indeed fortunate to grow up in a church with someone in the pulpit who clearly had such a significant influence on his life. Will you both, please excuse me? I have to finalize the arrangements for our ceremony."

Father Desmond left the two men in the room. Reverend Miner took a seat at the table and said, "Jack, it is good to see you. I was sorry to hear about your parents' passing. After they retired, I kept in touch with them for many years, but as often happens, these communications suddenly stopped. It is usually an indicator that something significant has changed. They were both good and pious Christians. I am sure you miss them greatly."

Jack smiled at the mention of his parents. "I do. I think of them often. It's truly a blessing to see you, Reverend. I can't believe you came all this way," he said gratefully.

"How are Amanda and your boys?" Reverend Miner asked.

Jack's shoulders slumped, and his eyes glanced down toward the floor. "Your instincts were correct. I can use all the support and guidance I can get right now. Has anyone told you anything about what has happened?"

Reverend Miner shook his head. "When I spoke with Father Desmond's friend who found me at your house, he indicated you were suffering a crisis of faith. He suggested that it would be better for the specifics to come from you. What is going on, Jack?"

For the next half hour, Jack poured his soul out to Reverend Miner. He skipped no details and confessed it all to his friend and religious mentor. Jack held nothing back. He spoke with great trepidation about his loss of faith, all the time worrying what Reverend Miner must be thinking of him. *What a disappointment I must be to him,* Jack thought to himself. He could not think of a time that he felt greater shame. It was not unlike how Jack felt as a boy when he would confess to his parents about some wrongdoing or poor decision he had made. The decision, in this case, was worse, as Jack was now a grown man and not a naïve child.

After Jack had finally finished his confession, there was a moment of silence while he waited for Reverend Miner's reaction.

While Jack was speaking, Reverend Miner had sat and listened. He was both stunned and heartbroken by what he had heard. Revered Miner felt for Jack. His own grandson had been born deaf, and, on some level, he felt like he understood Jack's pain about his sons' autism and the sense of loss Jack had described. As a man of faith for more than fifty years, he had never personally experienced evil on the level that Jack had shared with him. Did he believe it was possible? The answer was an emphatic yes. Yet, he never imagined it could be this real. He found this aspect of Jack's story to be illuminating, and it only served to reinforce his own faith.

Reverend Miner turned his chair slightly so that he was facing Jack. He placed both hands on Jack's shoulders, looking him squarely in the eyes while saying, "I am so very sorry that you and your family have had to go through all of this."

"So, you believe me?"

"With every ounce of my being. Jack, we have known one another since you were a teenager. Above all else, you are not a liar. You will forgive me when I say that you have always been a bit too reflective and your desire for perfection is a double-edged sword. It has pushed you to succeed in everything you have tried to accomplish in life, but it also left you vulnerable to the influence of evil. Please do not take what I am saying as a critique or criticism. I have counseled many Christians who develop an obsession with their own high expectations. Failure or perceived failure usually leads to disappointment. If an individual endures too much disappointment, it can cause them to become discouraged. This discouragement can lead them down a dark path as they search for ways to soothe their pain or cut corners while striving to overcome it. It is in this state of despair that a person allows Lucius and his acolytes an entry point into their lives, usually at the cost of their soul."

"Thank you so much for your support, Reverend. You have no idea how much it means to me. I was so worried that you would think less of me as a person and as a Christian."

Reverend Miner smiled. "I do not believe that at all. These days, often by necessity, families, and friends are often required to leave one another. I only wish I could have been there for you, Jack. Perhaps, I could have helped you with the grieving process that you have gone through with your boys."

Jack wiped a tear from his eye. "You just did, Reverend. I will be able to take this conversation with me, and I am certain it will help me move forward."

Suddenly, there was a knock on the door. One of the monks from the temple poked his head into the room. "Mr. Aitken, preparations for the ceremony are almost complete. I will be back in five minutes."

"Thank you," Jack replied.

"If I may, Jack," the Reverend said. "There is one more observation that I would like to share with you. It is related to what I mentioned on the phone the other day."

"Please do," Jack said, curious about what Reverend Miner was going to say.

"I have been a religious man all of my life. I believe that most of the men and women I have worked with and the members of the congregations I worked for have been good people. You have shared some information with me about JESU. Honestly, I have never heard of the group before today. On the surface, it sounds like an organization whose purpose is noble. However, I want to caution you that just because this is a religious organization does not make it totally devout. What I am trying to say is that any organization run by human beings is always going to have flaws and imperfections."

Jack hesitantly replied, "I am not sure I understand."

"Let me put it this way. Religious organizations and institutions have leaders that are not dissimilar to government officials. Government representatives can fall into several categories. Some are truly well-intentioned; others are naïve about how things really work and fail to realize that some of their peers have agendas that are not always in the country's or their constituent's best interest. Some public servants are honest and intelligent, and some servants of God are liars and ignorant. Unfortunately, both religious and governmental institutions are susceptible to the influence of individuals who are evil and whose intent is to lead those they represent astray."

Jack pondered what Reverend Miner had just said. "I appreciate your insight Reverend. As I told Father Desmond previously, I understand the bigger picture of what is at stake tonight, but I am focused on one thing. I have got to find a way to save Amanda and the boys."

"I agree with you, Jack," Reverend Miner said. "What I am saying is that saving them is not necessarily the primary concern of JESU. While your goals are not mutually exclusive, they do not have to save you, Amanda, and the boys to achieve their aim. I hate to use the word expendable, but it does come to mind."

"I understand. Father Desmond has said some things that lead me to believe that he might have his own reservations about JESU. Fortunately, he has personally vetted our team."

"Jack, be careful. Life is always more complicated than it seems or than we wish it to be. It is not black and white, right or wrong, and you cannot just tie it into a neat bow. The reality is that dealing with evil can create a paradox; sometimes you can damn yourself while trying to save someone else."

"Will you pray with me, Reverend? For the safe return of my family."

Reverend Miner smiled. "Certainly."

The two men bowed their heads. Reverend Miner placed his hand on Jack's head. "Lord, I pray for your protection over Jack's family. Shield them from evil and be their refuge and strength. Make them strong in the face of danger and courageous when they feel any vulnerability. Assure them that you will help them overcome all injustice and make everything right that is wrong in their world. Give them emotional and physical shelter in the arms of Jesus. Finally, Lord, please grant Jack the perseverance to see this all through and the power to save Amanda, Louis, and David. In your name, we pray, Amen."

As they finished praying, Father Desmond entered and said, "Jack, we are ready."

"Okay, Father."

Jack turned to Reverend Miner and said, "Thank you for coming all this way. You have no idea what this has meant to me."

"Good luck and God speed, Jack."

Father Desmond opened the door and showed Jack into the sanctuary. He turned to Reverend Miner. "Reverend, I will have one of the monks take you to the airport."

"Thank you, Father. God bless you."

Reverend Miner sat down in the chair with his gaze fixed on the entrance to the sanctuary. He feared Jack might be in over his head. Were it not for his advanced years; Reverend Miner would help Jack himself. But his age prevented his participation. He was curious about what might be taking place in there.

While Reverend Miner was thinking about the ceremony, he did not hear the person entering the room. The figure slowly snuck up behind him and then skillfully placed the wire garrote around Reverend Miner's neck. The elderly clergyman could not put up much of a fight and soon slumped limply in the chair. The figure then picked up the body and exited the room without a sound.

***

Jack stepped through the doorway into the temple. He looked around the sanctuary and found it to be quite beautiful. The front of the shrine had mats on the floor where people could kneel to pray or meditate. Buddha's statue was behind the altar, sitting lotus style, wearing a bright orange robe with gold sandals on its feet. Covering the sanctuary's walls were murals depicting Buddha in various prayer positions in multiple natural settings. The central aisle of the temple, which led to the altar, was bisected by another corridor, and where the two walkways met, the center of the temple, was a hexagonal-shaped baptismal font made of marble. The baptismal was not a permanent fixture in the structure, and Jack surmised it had been placed there solely for the ceremony.

Father Desmond handed Jack a white, handwoven cap, commonly used by Muslims, along with a prayer shawl that looked like those that a Jewish Rabbi would use. He motioned to Jack to remove his shoes, standard etiquette in a Buddhist temple. When Jack had entered the temple, it was empty and quiet, but he soon noticed that two monks were placing an altar in the central aisle in front of the baptismal.

Jack whispered, "Father, is there anything I need to know about the ceremony?"

"I will lead the mass and guide you through it. There are contributions from all the major religions."

"Do you know the last time this ceremony was conducted?" he asked.

"Tonight is the first time that I am conducting these rites, and to the best of my knowledge, no one else has either."

"I guess that speaks to what is at stake tonight. It's more than a little intimidating. Saint Michael is obviously a critical figure to JESU."

"Saint Michael is the patron saint of JESU and important to many faiths. In Islam, believers know him as a Wali. In the Jewish tradition as Tzadik. Hindus refer to him as a Rishi and Buddhists as Arhat. Saint Michael is most often painted holding a shield and spear and is the leader of God's army. He is always on guard, ready for battle, and is the guardian and protector of all the religious faithful. He is the ultimate warrior against evil. We pray to Saint Michael to protect us in our spiritual battles and guard our organization, its members, and their families. Saint Michael will defend all who love God and defeat all who seek to spread the influence of evil."

Father Desmond paused, then said, "It appears that we are ready, Jack."

Jack watched the other team members begin a processional toward the middle of the sanctuary. Monk Mahabounmy carried a tray with a decanter and a loaf of bread on it. Rabbi Strouse, Imam Wadud, and Priest Raghavacharya followed silently, each placing an object on the altar. Jack and Father Desmond met the group by the baptismal, and the mass began.

Father Desmond said, "Brothers and sisters, more than a century ago warriors of JESU, desperate and on the verge of defeat, called upon Saint Michael to intervene on their behalf and defeat Satan and his demons. We know the limitations of our human existence prevent us from defeating evil on our own. Only through God's power and mercy are we able to emerge victorious over the Prince of Darkness and his agents of evil. Like our brothers and sisters before us, we now face our own apocalyptic threat from Satan's multitudes, and we once again call on Saint Michael, the patron saint of JESU, to stand with us in battle. "

Jack and the team spoke a profession of faith in unison. "I believe in God the Father almighty and his servant, the Archangel Saint Michael, who would deign to aid us in our battles against Satan and all of his unclean spirits who roam about the world pursuing the destruction of the human race and seeking the ruin of souls. Amen."

Father Desmond motioned Jack to step forward. Buddhist Monk Maha Bounmy held a candle, which Jack lit as a gesture of penance. Jack lit the candle that each participant had and then instinctively prostrated himself before the altar.

Jack was in shock. How had he known that at that very moment, he should kneel? Suddenly, he heard a voice in his head telling him to lead the others in prayer. Despite never speaking another language other than English, Jack offered a Buddhist prayer of repentance.

"The evil karmas I have done with my body, voice, and mind result from greed, anger, and delusion, which are without a beginning in time. Before Buddha, I now supplicate for my repentance. I repent of all sins, the cause of hindrances, and I reject all the roots of evil."

In awe of what was unfolding, Jack, wearing his yarmulke and a prayer shawl provided by Rabbi Strouse, began to speak again. This time, however, it was in Hebrew.

"After requesting penance and confessing our desire for forgiveness, we must atone for our sins before granting said forgiveness. The Kol Nidre is spoken on Yom Kippur to begin the process of atonement. All vows, prohibitions, oaths, and consecrations whether called Konam, Konas, or any synonymous term which we may vow or swear or consecrate or prohibit upon ourselves from the previous day of atonement until this day of atonement and from this day of atonement until the next day of atonement, we do repent."

Jack pulled the prayer shawl over his head, and the rest of the participants followed his example. They bowed their heads as Jack held up the bread to the Lord for his blessing.

"God, we offer these gifts of bread and wine as reparations for our sins. We consume them so that we may commune with you personally to ask forgiveness for our individual transgressions."

Jack broke the bread in two and turned to the other participants.

"My brothers and sisters, Bannock bread is made from barley, oats, and rye. Monks made it with no metal instruments. It is a simple bread made in honor of Saint Michael, who, according to the book of Daniel, is an advocate and defender of Israel. Eating the bread is considered good luck, and all of us must partake in it."

Jack began passing the bread around, and as each participant consumed it, he marveled at his transformation. He felt different. A swell of confidence was building, and Jack felt his faith growing along with it

He then picked up the decanter, poured wine into a chalice, and held it up to the Lord for his blessing.

"Blessed are you, Lord our God, King of the universe, who creates the fruit of the vine. Amen."

Jack placed the cup to his lips and sipped the wine. He then passed it to each participant, who drank from it.

"Brothers and Sisters, our reconciliation with God, is complete. Let us share a sign of peace with one another."

The participants kissed one another on each cheek as a sign of peace and reconciliation.

The rites continued for the next thirty minutes, with Jack leading the team in a series of prayers and incantations. Imam Wadud joined him on a prayer mat before the altar, and with their outstretched hands and in a prone position, they prayed together in Arabic.

"There is no God but Allah, and Muhammad is his messenger. Prayer is a pillar of Islam, and we seek strength and courage for the challenges we must face. O my Lord, expand my chest and ease my task for me and remove the impediment from my speech so they may understand what I say."

Jack took a small tub, filled it with water, and knelt before each participant, and washed their feet in an additional act of purification.

Once he had washed their feet, Jack returned to the prayer mat and beseeched God, "Give me friends to advise and help me that by working together, our efforts may bear abundant fruit. And, above all, let me constantly remember that my actions are mine unless guided by your hand."

Filled with strength and courage, Jack stood in front of the altar. Still being led by forces he could not understand, he instinctively struck a match and held it to an incense stick. Once the rod began to smolder, he inserted it into a brass holder on the altar.

Raising his hands, Jack said, "My friends, I light an incense stick to request protection for all of you from the influence of evil. Breathe deeply and take in the incense essence in order that it may ward off the powerful evil spirits and demons that will surround and oppose us this night."

The area surrounding the altar was full of the sweet smell of incense, and each member of the team closed their eyes and inhaled the smoke that hovered around them. The sanctuary was quiet as each member silently prayed.

After a few minutes, Jack broke the silence and said, "Now, I will chant the Rudra Gayatri Mantra, whose purpose is to ease tension and remove fear. It will help us realize the ultimate truth of life and keep our body, mind, and soul healthy."

"I pray the mightiest of the Gods, the ideal Purusha, Mahadev. Bless me with the intellect and enlighten me with knowledge."

Jack continued, "The Durga Gayatri Mantra is a plea for protection from our enemies. The Hindu Goddess of the universe,

Goddess Durga, loves all her children and nothing is possible in life without her blessing."

"Om, let me meditate on the Goddess, who is the daughter of Kathyayana. Oh, maiden Goddess, give me higher intellect and let Goddess Durga illuminate my mind."

Jack turned and knelt at the altar with his hands raised, and head bowed. "Finally, the Rudrayamala Tantra Mantra is a powerful prayer against black magic. It comes from the ancient Rudrayamala Tantra book and is spoken only in the direst of circumstances. It only protects those whose heart is pure.

"Thus, protect me from the evil one who wishes to dominate this world."

As Jack completed his chant, he glanced at Priest Raghavaharya, who closed his eyes and nodded his approval. Jack turned to Father Desmond and said, "Father, I believe it is time for the Call to Arms."

Jack stepped aside, and Father Desmond moved in front of the altar. He removed a small Bible from his pocket, opened it, and began to read.

"A reading from the book of Matthew, Chapter 14, verses 22–31.

"Immediately, Jesus made the disciples get into the boat and go ahead of him to the other side, while he dismissed the crowd. After he had dismissed them, he went up on a mountainside by himself to pray. Later that night, he was there alone, and the boat was already a considerable distance from the land, buffeted by the waves because the wind was against it.

"Shortly before dawn, Jesus went out to them, walking on the lake. When the disciples saw him walking on the lake, they were terrified. 'It is a ghost,' they said and cried out in fear. But Jesus immediately said to them, 'Take courage! It is I. Do not be afraid.' 'Lord, if it is you,' Peter replied, 'tell me to come to you on the water.' 'Come,' Jesus said.

"Then Peter got down out of the boat, walked on water, and came to Jesus. But when he saw the wind, he was afraid and, beginning to sink, cried out, 'Lord, save me!' Immediately Jesus reached out his hand and caught him. 'You of little faith,' he said, 'why did you doubt?'"

Father Desmond concluded his reading, placed the Bible back in his pocket, and said, "May God grant us knowledge, spiritual wisdom, and understanding through his holy words. Amen."

Father Desmond paused, took a deep breath, and began to speak. "What does it take to defeat evil? While this ceremony is about Saint Michael and his skill with a sword, the Book of Revelation in Chapter 12, Verse 7 says, '*And there was war in Heaven, Michael and his angels fought the dragon.*' You see, no man or angel is an army of one. Even Saint Michael needed help."

Father Desmond looked at Jack. "I may be showing my age and Jack's too, for that matter, but in the 1980s, a movie about naval aviation and warfare was very popular. That film was *Top Gun*."

Jack smiled at Father Desmond and knew the theme of the sermon instantly. It was the same one that Reverend Miner had delivered many years earlier.

Father Desmond continued, "The main character, a pilot who goes by the call sign 'Maverick,' attends the Naval Fighter Weapons School in San Diego, California. This school is commonly referred to in Navy vernacular as 'Top Gun.'

"As his call sign suggests, Maverick is a brash, cocky pilot who is always flying as if he has something to prove. With few exceptions, his recklessness manages to alienate his fellow pilots and instructors. During one training mission, Maverick commits the 'Cardinal sin' of naval aviation tactics: he leaves his wingman. A wingman is responsible for supporting his fellow pilot's blind spot. The failure to do so can be lethal to the pilot that the wingman is supposed to be helping.

"Maverick abandons his duties to test his dogfighting skills against the best of the best, the Top Gun director, whose call sign is 'Viper.' Maverick becomes so fixated on defeating Viper he fails to fulfill his responsibility to his wingman. His failure dooms the pilot he was supposed to be guarding as well as himself. After they return to base, the second in command of the school, call sign

'Jester,' tells Maverick, 'That was some of the best flying I have seen to date. Right up to the point where you got killed. You never ever leave your wingman.'

"In the scripture reading, during the storm, Jesus has caught up with the disciples in the boat; Peter tests Jesus by asking him to come out of the boat and walk on water to him. At first, Peter succeeds, but he allows distractions to take his focus away from Jesus, and he begins to have doubts, which results in his starting to sink into the water. Peter failed at being Jesus's wingman, just like Maverick had failed his fellow aviator who had taken the lead in the combat exercise. Both Peter and Maverick suffered negative consequences arising from their actions.

"During a combat situation, late in the film, Maverick faces a similar scenario. Remaining the wingman for his fellow aviator is his primary responsibility. However, fulfilling his duty as a wingman puts Maverick's own life in jeopardy. Maverick's co-pilot tells him they need to get out of there, but Maverick states, 'I can't leave Ice,' referring to his fellow aviator and main antagonist, Iceman. When his co-pilot reiterates the peril, Maverick responds forcefully, 'I'm not leaving my wingman!'

"In a few hours, we will all go face to face with the ultimate evil. While Jack will wield the sword of Saint Michael, he too, just as Saint Michael did, will need our assistance. Let each of us now resolve to stand by one another. Cast away any doubts you may have and repeat with me, 'I am not leaving my wingman. I am not leaving my wingman. I am not... leaving my wingman.' Amen."

***

Father Desmond remained at the altar and began to speak once again.

"While all the religions that we represent are deeply rooted in the tenants of peace, there is a recognition that from time to time, it becomes necessary to wage holy war on the agents of evil and protect our followers from the snares of Satan. We have arrived at one of those moments.

"More than 150 years ago, in Stull, Kansas, a sword wielded by Saint Michael himself defeated Satan's forces and sealed a gate to Hell. Unfortunately, we have discovered that there is more than one entrance to the abyss. That sword shattered while breaking the locking mechanism to the very door to Hell itself. This act permanently sealed that door but also destroyed our most potent weapon against evil. Tonight, we will replace that weapon with a sword even more powerful than its predecessor."

Father Desmond motioned for Jack to join him.

Imam Wadud stepped forward and picked up what appeared to be a simple block of wood from the altar. It was shaped like a square with two slots perfectly inset into the block, making it appear to be three equal pieces joined together. Both of the block's outer sides had three holes bored into them, where one would insert dowels or another similar nailing mechanism to secure whatever was in the slots.

Imam Wadud immersed the block in the blessed water from the baptismal and then removed it. Upon doing so, she said, "This block of sacred wood comes from a beam taken from Noah's Ark. A Muslim cleric obtained it from Mount Ararat more than two millennia ago."

Imam Wadud handed the block of wood to Jack.

Jack could scarcely believe what he was seeing. A piece of Noah's Ark? As a young boy, he had always wanted the story of Noah and the flood to be true. Now, here was proof of that truth right in front of him. He stared at the item, agape, and felt a current of power flowing from it into his hands.

Jack stood holding the block of wood while Rabbi Strouse approached the altar and picked up a second wooden object. It was carved in the shape of a handle and pitted to enable the warrior who wielded it to grip it firmly. The Rabbi took the handle and immersed it in the baptismal.

While still holding it in the water, he said, "This handle is from wood that Levites used to carry the Ark of the Covenant. The resting place of the Ark remains a mystery, but Moses, by the instruction of God, had this wood passed down from Aaron to his descendants for safekeeping."

Jack was astonished. Now, wood from the Ark of the Covenant? Were it not for the events of the past few days, he would have asked how this could be so, but he knew better than to ask that question. He felt a surge of adrenaline run through his body and knew what was in front of him was real.

Father Desmond glanced quickly at Jack with a solemn look on his face and then went to the altar himself. He carefully picked up a wooden object that looked surprisingly like a blade whose length reminded Jack of a katana. There were also three wooden dowels in Father Desmond's other hand. He placed the remaining objects in the holy water and said, "This blade and these dowels came to the early Christian church via the apostle Peter; after he too was crucified, but before he ascended to heaven. They are all carved from wood that was part of the cross on which Christ suffered his crucifixion."

Jack was mesmerized. He held the block while Father Desmond and Rabbi Strouse inserted the handle and blade into the slots, and Priest Raghavacharya and Monk Maha Bounmy then pushed the dowels into the three holes. There was no need for hammers or tools. It was a perfect fit, and the weapon was obviously the work of an exceptional craftsman. A carpenter...? Jack wondered if the hands could have indeed made it...

"Jesus Christ," Father Desmond said, anticipating the very thought in Jack's head. "The master carpenter built this weapon from materials representing God's Holy Trinity. The wood from Noah's Ark represents our Father, the creator of heaven and the earth. The Ark of the Covenant's handle represents God's Holy Spirit, which resides among men and women of faith. The blade made from the cross of Christ's crucifixion represents God in the form of his only son who lived among us and understood our trials, pain, and suffering."

Jack held the sword in his hands, and as the team members placed their hands on him, Father Desmond shouted, "Wield Saint

Michael's resurrected sword with the same strength, courage, and honor that he showed JESU's warriors more than 150 years ago!"

Energy he'd never felt before coursed through his veins. A golden, yellowish glow suddenly enveloped him. He looked at his limbs in awe, trying to understand the significance of the light that surrounded him from head to toe. Jack scanned the rest of the team's faces, and they all had looks of amazement on their faces too. Jack was unsure what the light wrapped around him meant, but all his doubts about God's love for him faded, and he was full of gratitude. Jack looked at his team while raising the sword above his head, then said, "Glory to God in the highest! Praise his name!"

Jack motioned for the team to kneel before the altar. They bowed their heads as Jack prayed in Latin.

"Saint Michael the Archangel, defend us in battle, be our protection against the malice and snares of the devil. May God rebuke him we humbly pray, and do thou, O Prince of the Heavenly host, by the power of God, thrust into hell Satan and all evil spirits who wander through the world for the ruin of souls. Amen.

"Come to the assistance of men whom God created in his own likeness and whom he has saved from Satan at a high cost. JESU honors you as its guardian and protector. God has entrusted the souls of the redeemed to be led into heaven by you. Offer prayers on our behalf to God that he may have mercy on us always.

"Join this day our battle against the army of darkness and the spirits of evil. Through your servant, Jack Aiken, and his brothers and sisters, cause our enemies to flee at the sight of our righteousness. Help us drive out demons, their legions, and all satanic power that we encounter. Through your grace and in the name of the Father, we pray, Amen."

***

With the ceremony concluded, the team set about their preparations for the final confrontation in Culpeper. The moment of truth was nearly here.

Father Desmond pulled Jack aside and whispered cautiously, "Just remember, this sword won't make you immortal or invincible. Victory is not guaranteed."

Jack tempered his enthusiasm just a bit and said, "I understand, Father, but clearly, the sword in Lucius's possession is a fake. That is what you were going to tell me back on the trail to Stull Cemetery."

"That's right, Jack."

"For the first time, Father, I feel like we have a fighting chance."

Chapter 23

Jack seemed to hit every light after he left the temple parking lot. He was sure not to speed, but he still felt like he was pulling into the parking lot earlier than he had anticipated. Jack glanced at the clock, which read 9:15, before slamming the door behind him and heading for the barricade. He'd now been here so many times that it was like he could find his way blindfolded. This time, however, felt quite different.

He could not find the words to describe what he was feeling. He was unsure if it was the joy of seeing Reverend Miner again or the humbling power of the Michaelmas, but it was as if his past and future were now one, and he had discovered a reservoir of strength. The golden light that had enveloped him during the mass was no longer visible, but upon entering the forest, he felt as if his years of wandering the wilderness of fear and despair were at an end. He was not dismissing Father Desmond's cautious warnings about what he was facing, but as Jack clutched the sword in his hands, he felt confident. He adjusted the special harness he was wearing under his sweatshirt to conceal the weapon and slid it into the sheath on his back. He thought back to Sunday school and remembered Romans 8:31. *"What, then, shall we say in response to these things? If God is for us, who can be against us?"*

He reasoned that although he was not Saint Michael, he had God's power at his fingertips. How could Lucius or even the Devil himself stand up to that?

As he passed the Bradford Cemetery and entered the forest, he felt a breeze across his face and saw what leaves remained on the trees rustling in the wind. The night air was growing colder, and

Jack's breath condensed in a cloud of water vapor as he exhaled. He realized he had failed to remember it was still Halloween. Jack could not help but recall his sons dressing up and trick or treating. Louis would always come up with the most challenging costumes. One year he wanted to be Luigi from the Mario video game, and another, he wanted to go as a shark. David, on the other hand, was more interested in the candy than in the costume. He smiled at the pleasant memories and the knowledge that he would soon see them and Amanda once more. It felt like he had not seen them in quite some time, but the reality was it had only been a few days.

Jack continued to move quickly through the woods. He guessed that having made several trips on the trail over the last month, he had trampled some of the underbrush, which freed up his movement. Regardless, Jack was not attempting to hide his presence. He wanted Lucius to know he was coming. Jack's thoughts again drifted back to his family and, specifically, to Amanda. How was she? He knew that taking care of Louis and David could be complicated, even in the best of times. These last few days must have been challenging beyond anything he could imagine.

He knew if anyone could get the boys through this, it was Amanda. Her patience seemed limitless, and her serenity while the storms of life surrounded her was something he always marveled at and admired greatly. Amanda was always there for him. How would he ever make this up to her? Jack realized that shepherding his family to safety would be a great start. He felt for the sword and silently prayed to Saint Michael for the strength to do just that.

***

The car's tires crunched on the gravel of the driveway of the Bingham & Taylor Iron Works. Father Desmond found a spot to park the car. He turned the lights off and shut down the motor. A cool breeze was blowing across the exposed storage yard of the plant. The moon was full and bright, allowing them to pull out the map from the planning session, which revealed the abandoned mine entrance.

Once they had oriented themselves, Imam Wadud pointed toward the far corner of the property, and the pair headed in that direction. While continuing to scan the yard for demon activity, Father Desmond said, "Shamima, I must admit that I am feeling a little apprehensive."

"What's bothering you, Father?"

Father Desmond turned up the collar of his jacket against the chilly wind. "I can't quite put my finger on it. It's just a feeling I have."

"You seemed a little on edge on the way over," the Imam replied. "But if you need reassurance, you don't seem as jumpy to me now."

Father Desmond noticed the Imam using the same breathing exercises he had taught as her instructor. Their friendship began many years ago, and despite what happened in Culpeper, she had remained steadfast in her support.

"I am grateful that you have stood by me all of these years. Shamima, it has meant a lot to me."

"Mark, although JESU has been accepting women and Muslims for nearly a millennium, there were still plenty of hurdles that a female Muslim Imam had to navigate within the organization. You were always my strongest advocate. That is why when you called and asked for my assistance, all I asked you was where and when."

Father Desmond smiled but then said solemnly, "It is no secret that I have fallen out of favor with many in JESU. You are taking a significant career risk by helping me."

Iman Wadud quickly said, "I believe loyalty and friendship are more important than any organization or group."

Over the years, they had worked so many operations together that even though none of them were recent, they still knew each other's movements and were clicking like a guard throwing a no-look pass to a teammate in a basketball game. They both wore black clothes to camouflage themselves right down to Imam Wadud's hijab. Father Desmond and the Imam moved around a scrap metal pile and came to a sheer cliff face with a boarded-up entrance. There was a sign warning of the dangers of the abandoned mine.

Checking the mine entrance, Imam Wadud said, "I think we're in the right place."

Father Desmond pulled a few loose boards away, which created just enough space so they could squeeze through and enter the mine.

"My research suggested that while old, the timbers should be safe enough."

Father Desmond helped the Imam through the hole and was hit by the smell of wet rock and damp soil. Adjusting to the darkness, he felt the cave walls which had sharp edges. He dislodged a piece and handed it to Imam Wadud.

"The recent assessment by Culpeper County, at the request of the fire department, confirms there are still veins of coal in here. According to the report, if coal remains intact, the mine should be safe."

As Father Desmond stared up at the ceiling, he thought to himself; *I sure hope that inspection report is correct.*

***

Detective Bishop left the interrogation room, thoroughly frustrated. She was exasperated and feeling the pressure from JESU headquarters to find Mark Desmond and Jack Aitken. Her instructions were to stop them before it was too late. Too late for what exactly? According to JESU investigators, who were questioning a demon they captured, Mark was assisting Mr. Aitken in delivering a key to Lucius Rofocale. Anne could not believe this was possible after what had happened a decade ago. It did not sound like something the Mark Desmond she knew would do. Perhaps she just did not want to believe that he had "gone rogue," as the JESU Council asserted.

Unfortunately, the demon either did not know the details of when this delivery was to occur, or she was able to withstand their interrogation techniques. Anne had already figured out for herself that the two men were heading to the burial mound, but where were they now? After discovering that neither man was on the train, it took a few hours of meditation and thinking as Mark would to figure out how they got back to Virginia. She had checked the manifests at Dulles, Reagan National, and Marshall Baltimore Washington International Airports and found no aliases that fit either man's description. This unsuccessful inquiry led her to check the smaller airports in the local area, and that was where she saw Tracy Guidry's name as the pilot of a flight that had arrived at Manassas Regional Airport.

Anne knew Mark had used Tracy on many missions in the past, and it did not take long to track her down at the hotel where she was staying in Manassas. Unfortunately, she had just finished speaking with Tracy, and she knew next to nothing about what Mark and Jack were doing. Anne guessed that part of Ms. Guidry's value to Mark was that she did not ask many questions and knew how to keep her mouth shut.

"Where are you, Mark?" Anne muttered to herself. She frowned at her inability to figure out her best friend and mentor's intentions.

Suddenly, something came to her. The legend of the impaired soul! Mark had mentioned it several times over the years. She struggled to recall the details. "What did Mark say?" Anne mumbled to herself. "The date!" she yelled. How could she have forgotten? She grabbed her coat and headed to her car. As she fumbled for her keys, she glanced at her watch, then said under her breath, "I only hope I can get there in time."

***

Lucius stood near the ceremonial bonfire burning near the burial mound. The earth around the knoll heaved and quaked in anticipation of the ceremony, which was to commence shortly. The Aitken family, who was to his left roughly twenty-five feet away, huddled together, trembling in the cool autumn night. Lucius was not sure if their trembling was a response to the outside temperature or intense fear. As he complimented his Hell Hounds, Barghest and

Gwyllgi, for their obedience and stroked their fur, he hoped it was the latter. The very thought made Lucius grin.

As part of his plan, he divided the area surrounding the mound into four sectors, with each zone patrolled by a legion of his demons. So far, all reports had indicated no activity, but suddenly he felt in his head that one of the patrols was seeking to contact him.

"Yes, Eblis," Lucius said. "What is it?"

"Sector A reporting, Master. Our sentry just saw Jack Aitken, and he is making his way through the woods in a Northwest direction, straight to your position. Just as you had indicated... he is alone. He has a knapsack slung over his shoulder."

"The key would be in the knapsack Eblis. I want reports every fifteen minutes moving forward. Is that understood?"

"Yes, my Master."

Lucius turned to the Aitken family and said sarcastically, "Good news for you, Amanda. Your *savior* is on his way." Lucius laughed with great enthusiasm, and it echoed through the woods.

Amanda gathered David and Louis closer and said reassuringly, "Boys, Dad is coming. He will be here soon." For the first time in days, both boys smiled.

Lucius then turned back toward the bonfire and telepathically demanded, "Sectors B, C, and D, what have you to report?" In sequence, he heard the following.

"Sector B, Kasadya reporting. Eastern approaches are being patrolled with no activity to report, my Master."

"Sector C, Preta reporting. Master Lucius. The Bradford House remains quiet."

"Sector D, Vapula reporting. My Master, the Northern and Western approaches report no activity thus far."

Lucius responded, "Very good. As of now, Sectors B, C, and D will report to me every fifteen minutes. I sense another presence. Someone other than Jack Aitken. Are we clear?"

Kasadya, Preta, and Vapula replied in unison, "Yes, Master Lucius!"

Lucius muttered to himself, "What are you up to, Desmond?"

Lucius reached into his pocket and tossed a treat of raw meat to Barghest and Gwyllgi, who ravenously devoured their reward. He estimated it was around 10:30 p.m. Running his hand through his slick, jet-black hair, he said out loud, "Jack should be here in an hour."

Turning toward Amanda with his fiery red eyes, Lucius's angular eyebrows drew downward in a menacing stare. "That is when the fun will really begin, Amanda."

Amanda looked warily at Lucius but did not respond. She refused to let him see her lose her composure or show him that she was afraid. However, there was no way to deny that deep down in her soul; she was genuinely terrified for her family and herself.

Due to the illumination from the full moon overhead, Priest Raghavacharya and Rabbi Strouse continued their steady progress through the dark forest. Rabbi Strouse was familiar with the terrain due to his drone surveillance, so he'd been leading the two men through the woods for the past forty-five minutes. The Rabbi put his hand up to signal the Priest, who quickly slowed down and remained stationary. Rabbi Strouse was sure he had heard something coming toward them, and he crouched down to avoid detection. Priest Raghavacharya moved forward and stood next to the Rabbi. The two men scanned the darkness for the source of the noise.

It didn't take long for a patrol of demons to come into view. There were four of them in the group, and they were talking amongst themselves. The only visible weapons were holstered handguns on their hips. Each of them had a flashlight, which they were using to scan the forest that surrounded them. They were laughing, and their demeanor indicated they were unaware of the presence of the priest or the rabbi, no indication they were expecting any action in their sector.

Rabbi Strouse signaled the priest that they would need to take offensive action against the patrol to fulfill their mission. Through years of practice, the priest loaded a dart into his blowgun while maintaining total silence and no discernable motion. Priest

Raghavacharya handed the weapon to the Rabbi, who then passed a second blowgun to the priest to load. While each blowgun was loaded, neither man took their eyes from the patrol.

The two men then took out the Eraka grass, which magically transformed into an iron spear. They leaned the spears against their bodies in such a way that they could quickly pick them up to use them. They carefully managed their breathing while bringing the blowguns to their lips. At the priest's signal, they targeted two patrol members and simultaneously blew darts at the demons.

Their aim was perfect, and the darts found their targets. The two security patrol members dropped dead immediately. The remaining members, bewildered, frantically searched the forest with their flashlights, looking for the source of what had killed their colleagues. Before they could get a fix on the rabbi or the priest, each was struck with an iron spear in the chest, dead before they hit the ground.

The priest and rabbi slowly moved forward to confirm the demons were dead and searched the area for other patrols. The dense undergrowth in the forest provided an ideal place to dispose of the remains. Once they had finished covering the demons with the brush, the two men resumed their mission and continued in the direction of the burial mound.

Father Desmond knelt at the wall at the end of the mine shaft. He listened intently for any sounds emanating from the room on the other side of the wall. The hope was that it would be Amanda Aitken and her children, but based on his knowledge of Lucius Rofocale, Father Desmond had little hope that they would be there. He and Imam Wadud had found the shaft flooded in several areas, so their progress was slower than he had anticipated. The mine was dark, but while their cell phones had no reception, the light from the devices helped them navigate the mine.

Hearing no activity at all, he began to feel around the wall for a mechanism to open the secret passage into the basement of the Bradford House. Imam Wadud joined in the search, and she eventually came across a loose brick in the wall. With Father

Desmond's assistance, the Imam pulled out the brick and felt a handle like a sink faucet. She turned the handle to the right, and it released a latch, and the wall slid to the left, the basement room now accessible.

Imam Wadud stepped carefully into the room and glanced toward the corners to ensure the space was indeed empty. She saw a vacant prison cell. They were too late! Amanda and the children were not there. She signaled to Father Desmond that the room was clear, and he stepped into the empty chamber behind her. He moved toward the door as if he were familiar with the layout of the room. He leaned against the door, listening for any noises in the hallway. He heard nothing and slowly opened the door.

The light in the hallway outside of the prison room was dim. Father Desmond peered down the hall one way and saw no one, then looked in the opposite direction and confirmed the hall was empty. He stepped into the hallway and waved for Imam Wadud to join him. Father Desmond turned to the left and headed for a stairwell that led to the main floor. He crept up the stairs carefully to maintain their silent presence. Imam Wadud followed him upstairs, but suddenly Father Desmond signaled her with his hand to stop.

Voices floated down from upstairs. Father Desmond could not make out what they were saying, but he guessed it was probably a contingent of demons stationed in the home by Lucius. He suspected Lucius was undoubtedly aware of the secret passage and wanted to ensure no one could use it without being detected. Father Desmond motioned for Imam Wadud to retreat down the stairs, and they slowly made their way back into the basement.

Father Desmond turned to the Imam and whispered, "I am sure I heard at least three different voices. These are demons left here by Lucius."

Imam Wadud nodded her understanding as Father Desmond continued, "King Solomon would trick demons by using bright, shiny objects to lure them into a trap. I will flip the light switch on and off several times when I believe someone upstairs may be watching. Perhaps, we can get them to come down to investigate."

Imam Wadud positioned herself in a dark corner at the bottom of the stairwell. She loaded her blowgun and signaled to Father Desmond that she was ready. She heard voices coming from upstairs. It sounded as if someone had exited the hallway, and there was only one set of footsteps. Father Desmond started to flip the light switch on and off.

It did not take long for the target to begin to investigate. The demon got halfway down the stairs and paused to look around. The guard saw the light in the ceiling in the middle of the hallway, blinking, and continued downstairs. As soon as the demon stepped onto the floor, Imam Wadud blew a poison dart into its neck, and it immediately dropped to the floor. Father Desmond waited to ensure no one else was in the upstairs hallway and checked the body, finding no signs of life. He then quietly dragged the corpse into the prison cell.

A few minutes later, another demon entered the hallway upstairs and asked, "Akuma, where are you?"

Father Desmond waited to see how the demon upstairs would react. The guard searched from room to room on the main floor and, upon finding no one, returned to the hallway. Father Desmond jumped into action and, once more, began flipping the light switch on and off.

The voice from upstairs said, "Akuma, are you down there?"

The demon slowly came down the stairs and asked once more with a tone of desperation and frustration, "Akuma, where are you?"

As soon as the demon stepped onto the floor, Imam Wadud nailed the target in the neck and watched it collapse to the floor. Father Desmond again waited, and there was nothing but silence coming from upstairs. He and the Imam dragged the body into the prison cell and tossed it on top of the other dead demon. A third demon came looking for the other two and soon joined them as another corpse in the prison cell. Father Desmond and Imam Wadud went up the stairs and searched the house for any remaining demons.

They found the rest of the house empty, and upon exiting the building, began walking through the woods. They hoped the route they were taking would allow them to approach the area around the burial mound from a direction that would take Lucius and his legions by surprise.

The recent cold snap had quieted the sounds of the creatures of the night, but Jack had barely noticed. His confident gait allowed him to maintain a steady pace, and he found himself in the clearing where one of the more frightening encounters of his original journey through the Culpeper woods had taken place. Jack was back at the haunted well.

While the memories of the experience with the ghost were fresh in Jack's mind, he was surprised to find himself unafraid. Jack intended to keep moving, but he tripped and fell to the ground before he could get too far. Brushing the dirt from his knees, Jack rose to his feet.

"Damn it! I could have hurt myself."

Searching for the source of his fall, Jack found the culprit in the high grass just off the trail. A rusty chain hidden by the foliage was almost impossible to see. Jack knelt to examine it more closely. The links were roughly the size of his fist, and they loudly creaked when he picked them up from the ground.

"Man, this is heavy."

Jack followed the chain through the grass until he ended up at the well. At the base of the wall surrounding the well was a large rock where the chain was attached.

"I don't remember this being here the last time."

Jack looked around the clearing, then peered down the well. Unlike the last visit, no apparitions or voices were calling out to him. Just silence. Jack stood scratching his chin.

"I wonder what poor soul Lucius chained here?"

As he made his way back toward the trail, Jack shifted the harness containing the sword on his back. Since leaving the temple, he'd periodically checked for the sword, and it was reassuring knowing it was there. Jack paused, and reaching behind him, pulled the sword from its sheath.

He marveled at the craftsmanship, and despite its simple appearance, Jack could feel its power. He carefully felt the sharp edge of the blade and then took the handle in both hands, held the sword overhead, and plunged it down into the chain. A flash of orange and yellow sparks flew, and Jack looked down to see a shattered chain.

"Why did I do that? It was like something else was controlling me!"

Briefly startled, Jack quickly put the sword back in the harness and hurried back to the trail.

"Here I come, Lucius," Jack said euphorically. "Ready or not!"

Once he was out of sight, the spirit of Alsoomse appeared. Now free from her chains, she drifted toward the heavens.

For the tenth time in the last half hour, Louis Aitken asked, "Mom, where is Dad, and when is he going to get here?"

She told him once more that Dad was on his way, but this did nothing to make Louis feel better. He continued to stick closely to his mother and David and sat as far away from the bad man as he could. This man scared him, mainly when turning into that monster. He tried not to look at him and his dogs. Louis had always been interested in dogs and could recognize almost any breed on sight, but he had no idea what type of dogs the bad man had. He just knew they were as scary as he was.

The wind blew leaves off the trees, and Louis began to shiver. He was cold and hoped they would be going to the car soon to go home. Louis missed Dad and did not want to go back to the house with the prison cell. He smiled a little as he remembered telling Mom he thought the mansion looked like something he had seen in a Scooby-Doo cartoon. Louis thought about Shaggy telling Scooby to do something about his chattering teeth and started saying the line repeatedly. It made him feel better to do this, and he sat and rocked back and forth while he did it.

David positioned himself between his mother and "the bastard" who had hurt him. He heard his mother call him that, and he repeated it over and over, but in a low voice so no one else could hear him saying it. David tried saying it like he thought his dad might do. When Dad got here, David hoped they would all get to hit "the bastard" in the head. David did not like him hurting his mother or scaring his brother and wanted to hit him so he would stop doing it. When they had dropped Dad off back in September, he remembered that the number 666 kept coming into his head, and he started to hear it again.

"Six-six-six," David said.

Amanda immediately turned and asked him, "David, honey, what did you say?"

"Six-six-six.''

Amanda dropped to her knees and hugged him. "It's okay, David. Dad will be here soon."

David smiled and began to make guttural noises, which were something he did when he was excited. He looked down the trail back toward the house and saw someone come out of the bushes.

"DAD!" he shouted.

Louis and Amanda quickly looked in the same direction. Amanda said, "JACK! Thank God!"

Jack was uncertain if it was his familiarity with the trail or his intense desire to see his family, but he felt like the last hour had flown by quickly. As he had passed through one gate after another, revisiting places such as the well and the cabin, Jack felt his determination growing. He made up his mind that nothing was going to stop him now, and it was only a matter of time before Lucius would feel his wrath. What had started as a slight swell in his heart and soul during the Michaelmas was now a tidal wave, and he planned to drown Lucius Rofocale in his tsunami.

The church pews with their skeleton congregation still seated as if they were waiting for a satanic service to begin came into view. As Jack silently prayed for the poor souls sacrificed on its unholy altar, the burial mound loomed ahead. Jack stepped carefully around the bones that still littered the ground in reverence to the sacrifice they made ten years ago. As he made his way into the clearing in front of the burial mound, Jack heard a familiar voice shout, 'Dad!'

"LOUIS! I'm here!" Jack yelled. "DAVID! Are you okay, buddy?"

Finally, Jack saw Amanda. He waved and shouted, "AMANDA! I LOVE YOU!"

David and Louis tried to run to Jack, but two of Lucius's demons physically restrained them. The two Hell Hounds left Lucius's side. Snarling and growling, they moved toward the boys. Amanda instantly inserted herself between the dogs and her children. The boys immediately reached for their mother, who backed slowly away from the Hell Hounds without taking her eye from the two animals. The demon guards released the boys, who hugged their mother.

Before Jack could react, Lucius said, "Barghest and Gwyllgi. Where are your manners?"

The two Hell Hounds immediately obeyed and returned to Lucius's side. He then continued in a sarcastic tone of voice, "Jack. How nice it is to see you again. Are we not all just one big, happy family? You see that I have held up my side of our bargain. Your family is unharmed, at least for now."

Jack replied forcefully, "Let my family go, Lucius." He held up the knapsack. "I have the key here. Let them go. Your business is with me. You do not need them anymore."

Lucius's voice was cold. "It does not work that way, Jack. They are as much a part of this now as you. I like them exactly where they are."

Just then, more of Lucius's demon legions appeared. They surrounded both Jack and his family. The smell of Sulphur became more intense, and the ground around the burial mound shook. Jack saw the metal door embedded into the knoll. The only thing standing between an unsuspecting world and the forces of Hell. It glowed fiery red as an intense source of heat was impacting it.

The Hell Hounds began to growl, and Lucius leaned over and asked, "Barghest and Gwyllgi, what is it?"

Several of Lucius's demons emerged from behind the burial mound with two hooded figures in front of them. Then, to Jack's right, more demons arrived with two other hooded figures in their custody.

Sector B leader Kasadya pushed the two captives forward and said, "Master Lucius, we caught these two intruders, just where you said they would be."

Sector D leader Vadula stepped forward and stated, "Master Lucius. We caught these two trespassers trying to sneak around behind the burial mound. I think you might find one of them to be of particular interest."

Vadula removed the hood of one of the figures. Lucius gleefully said, "Father Mark Desmond. Well, this is indeed a surprise."

Then, the guards took the hoods from the other three figures. Imam Wadud, Priest Raghavacharya, and Rabbi Strouse looked around as dozens of demons surrounded them. A great look of concern was apparent on each of their faces.

Lucius turned to the trio and said mockingly, "Friends of Father Desmond, I presume. Well, welcome to all of you. Is this not a nice surprise? Now that all the actors have arrived, we can bring up the curtain and begin our show. Do you all agree?"

Jack was stunned. *What do I do now?*

Chapter 24

"So much for the element of surprise," Jack mumbled. "I sure hope there's a Plan B."

Jack shot Father Desmond a glance and slowly reached for the sword on his back, but something in Father Desmond's face told him to stop. Jack could feel the power of the weapon permeating into every cell of his body and wanted nothing more than to release the pent-up fury inside him that was intensifying each second that he stood within reach of Lucius, but he hesitated.

Perhaps, it was the sheer number of demons surrounding them or concerns about his family and the team, but Jack wondered what was going through Mark's mind. Why were they not attacking anyway? Jack wondered. But Father Desmond had gotten him this far, and Jack was not going to leave his wingman! Jack brought his hands back down to his sides and waited for the signal to strike.

Lucius knew he had the upper hand, and he intended to make the most of this moment. His crowning achievement was within his grasp, and he intended to take a victory lap or possibly two before he revealed the full magnitude of his triumph. He planned to inflict upon Jack Aitken the most incredible suffering he could imagine. Before he would be allowed to die, Jack would watch the pain and agony of each member of his family as they were tortured and slaughtered as part of a satanic ritual. A ritual like the one Jack had witnessed during his initial visit to the burial mound and a ceremony most appropriate for the evening's proceedings.

However, before Jack Aitken's final farewell, there was his old adversary, Father Mark Desmond, to address. Lucius enjoyed

331

toying with his victims and, turning toward Father Desmond, said tauntingly, "Mark. May I call you Mark?"

Father Desmond stared icily at Lucius, and not taking the bait, responded firmly, "Call me what you wish, Lucius,

Lucius was slightly disappointed Father Desmond would not play along but continued, "Come with me, Mark. I have something I would like to show you."

Reluctantly, Father Desmond followed Lucius to the fence that surrounded the burial mound.

Lucius pointed at a tombstone. "Here, Mark. Read this. I am sure you will find it interesting."

Father Desmond read the inscription: *'In Memory of Joseph Rogers. At Least He Is Warm Now... in Hell!'* He stood staring at the tombstone.

"Mark, I thought you might like to know what happened to Joseph. After all, you helped me put him here."

Ignoring Lucius's mocking barbs, he maintained his silence as he was led back to Imam Wadud's side. One of Lucius's demons then stepped forward, holding an arsenal.

"Master, when we captured these intruders, they were all equipped with these."

Lucius studied the equipment, then looked warily at Imam Wadud, Rabbi Strouse, and finally, Priest Raghavacharya. All three had their hands zip-tied in front of them.

"Interesting, which one of you is responsible for choosing such an eclectic array of weapons?"

The three JESU members glanced over at Father Desmond and maintained their silence.

"Speak up," Lucius demanded.

Unsure of what Lucius might do if he did not cooperate, Priest Raghavacharya stepped forward. "I did."

Lucius admonished his demon army, "This is why I have always counseled you to take Father Desmond so seriously." Nearly praising Father Desmond, Lucius said, "I am impressed with your choice of a weapons expert. Clearly, this priest selected them very carefully."

Lucius turned back to Priest Raghavacharya. "My compliments. I understand that you used both very effectively against my demons." Now scowling, he continued, "We found the bodies in the brush."

Priest Raghavacharya stood stoically silent in front of Lucius.

"So, why not give us a demonstration of your prowess with one of these weapons? I myself am already familiar with Eraka Grass."

Lucius picked up the Eraka Grass, which turned into an iron spear as soon as he touched it. As he grabbed it, steam began to emanate from his hand. He took the spear and jammed it into the ground next to him.

"A little hot to the touch." Lucius scoffed. "I am sure you are aware that while this would kill one of my demons, it would not do too much to me. So, that leaves the blowgun and dart. Now, what will we use for a target? We already know this will kill a demon, but what about a human?"

Jack watched what was unfolding with an increasingly uneasy feeling. He wondered if he should intervene before something terrible happened. He, too, was looking at Father Desmond for some sign that he should reach for the sword, but Mark seemed spellbound by Lucius's antics. Jack wondered if memories of the massacre were affecting Mark in some way. He appeared distracted.

Jack looked over at Amanda, whose eyes were wide. Her hands were shaking, and her lips quivered in a combination of fear and horror. She looked at Jack pleadingly, and he tried unobtrusively to move closer, but Barghest and Gwyllgi began to growl and positioned themselves between Jack and his wife.

Lucius watched his pets flank Jack and tossed them each a treat for their obedience. Then, with a flip of his finger, one of his demons roughly pushed Rabbi Strouse to the burial mound fence and tied him to the railing. Lucius turned to the Priest and commanded, "Pick up the blowgun and load it."

Sensing some hesitation, Lucius reached back for the iron spear and held it in front of Iman Wadud's face.

"Do it now, or I will shove this spear through the Imam's eye socket."

Priest Raghavacharya tentatively picked up the blowgun and placed the dart inside the chamber.

"Now, shoot the rabbi," Lucius instructed bluntly. "Do it, or the Imam will die."

Lucius motioned to one of his demons, who stepped forward and placed a gun to the back of Priest Raghavacharya's head.

"I see that look in your eye," Lucius said menacingly. "Even if you shoot me, this will not harm me in any way. It will be like a bee sting might be to you, and trust me, I am not allergic to whatever toxin you may have infused into the dart."

Despite the brisk night air, Priest Raghavacharya felt a bead of sweat roll down his back. He had a choice to make, and he needed to make it quickly.

"Times up, priest!" Lucius yelled.

The demon cocked the gun behind his head. Priest Raghavacharya looked over at Rabbi Strouse. Priest Raghavacharya knew they were of one mind as he silently prayed and shot the dart at the rabbi. The priest watched the rabbi's body go limp and then felt the iron spear pierce his own heart. As he fell to the ground, he prayed with what life still coursed through his body for forgiveness and that their deaths would not be in vain.

Jack could no longer stand by and reached for the handle of the sword. Before he could make a move, however, the two beasts were on him. Jack struggled to keep the vicious predators at bay. As Barghest and Gwyllgi scratched, clawed, and bit Jack, Amanda and the boys screamed.

"Dad!"

"Stop it! You're killing him!"

Lucius laughed at their concern. "That's the general idea, Mrs. Aitken. Good boys," he urged the beasts on. "Enjoy yourselves and make sure to give him an especially nasty bite for me."

Jack continued to try to reach the sword strapped to his back, but the two creatures were overpowering him. He was surprised that despite the savage attack he was experiencing, he did not feel any pain.

Lucius continued to laugh and said, "You know, Jack, I have special plans for you and your family, but there is no reason not to have a little fun before we get down to business."

As his demons dragged the bodies of the Priest and Rabbi to the mound for burial and his hell hounds continued to attack Jack unmercifully, Lucius looked at his watch, smiled, and said sarcastically, "Mark, your Good Book talks about an eye for an eye. Their deaths make us even."

Lucius leered at the Imam.

"But where are your manners? You have not introduced me to your other associate. Who is this lovely creature standing next to you?" Smirking at Father Desmond, he said, "I thought Catholic priests were not allowed to date women."

Lucius laughed aloud and delighted in the look of rage that appeared on Father Desmond's face as he disrespected the Imam.

"I am Shamima Wadud."

"Based on your clothing, a Muslim cleric, I presume?"

Imam Wadud nodded yes.

Lucius circled the Imam.

"Why would you want to align yourself with a group like JESU, my dear? I am told that they do not treat women especially well." Lucius smirked. "Of course, if you worked for me, I would treat you with the utmost respect."

"If that is a recruiting proposal, you can save it. I would never join the likes of you."

Lucius frowned. "Do not be so quick to dismiss me or my proposition, my dear Imam. Many of my demons have engaged in combat with you over the years. Their grudging respect tells me that your abilities are quite impressive. I am proposing a role for you in my organization that JESU would never offer. The leader of my armies. The head of each of my legions would report directly to you. You would report to me. JESU has never offered a similar position to a woman. Isn't that true, Mark?"

"That is correct, Lucius, but you are wasting your—"

"Let the Imam speak for herself!"

"I will never forsake Allah and join you. I would rather perish a devout and loving Muslim than live as a corrupt and evil soul like you!"

Lucius looked Imam Wadud in the eye and coldly said, "Very brave, Imam, but foolish. Your wish is my command."

Lucius grabbed Imam Wadud by the throat with his right hand and raised her into the air. He gazed into her eyes as she struggled to breathe. He slowly dug his fingers into her throat and began to crush her windpipe.

Lucius's attention shifted to his beloved Hell Hounds and their brawl with Jack Aitken. He dropped the Imam at Father Desmond's feet, who knelt to check on her condition. Father Desmond knew she was dead and prayed for his fallen comrade but never stopped monitoring what Lucius was doing. He had been carefully loosening the zip ties on his wrists and had finally managed to slip out of them.

"That is enough, boys," Lucius said sternly.

Barghest and Gwyllgi immediately ceased their attack and returned to Lucius's side.

Jack slowly got to his feet and caught his breath. He waved to Amanda and the boys to assure them he was okay. He then looked back at Lucius, who now had a puzzled look on his face.

"Why are you not hurt?" Lucius asked. He appeared baffled. "There is not a scratch on you. No cuts, wounds, or blood."

Lucius eyed Jack skeptically. "You look different. What are you wearing? That was not there before."

Jack looked at his arms. The golden light that had surrounded him during the Michaelmas was visible once more. Jack was amazed as he looked at his torso and then down at his legs. Some type of body armor protected his entire body!

"Jack, it has to be a gift from Saint Michael," Father Desmond called out loudly. "I have seen this type of armor depicted in tapestries and read about it in medieval books and scrolls. It looks like iron armor that the Knights Templar used to conquer the Holy Land during the Crusades. Muslim warriors had no weapons that could pierce it."

Father Desmond taunted Lucius, "And, evidently, neither can Lucius's mutts."

Lucius shot a look in Father Desmond's direction at the mention of Saint Michael. Except for Jesus Christ and God himself, Saint Michael was the most despised figure in demon lore. No one dared mention his name in Lucifer's presence without the risk of being instantly disintegrated. While initially shaken at this development, Lucius felt for the sword inside his cloak. He felt reassured that there was nothing to fear from some protective gear while the ultimate weapon remained in his possession.

"Master Lucius," one of the demon guards said, alarmed. "He said, Saint Michael."

Murmurs could be heard through the demon ranks.

Lucius snapped his finger, instantly disintegrating the jittery guard.

"Move Desmond next to Mr. Aitken."

A guard roughly shoved Father Desmond to a spot next to Jack. Father Desmond was sure to keep his hands held together in front of him with the hope that no one would notice he had slipped out of the zip ties.

"Mark, I am sorry about your friends. I wasn't sure if I should intervene or not."

"I know, Jack. You did what you thought was right. Your family looks okay."

"Yes," he replied. "At least for the moment."

Suddenly, the ground around them began to shake, and the door embedded into the burial mound began to swell as if someone were trying to push it open from the other side. It was a reminder that midnight was fast approaching, and something exceedingly evil was anticipating its release.

"Enough with the theatrics. Time to get down to business," Lucius said, ignoring Jack's glowing armor. "Jack, you have proven to be a far more formidable adversary than I believed you were capable of being. I hope for your family's sake that your ingenuity and resourcefulness have extended to your ability to recover the key. I see your knapsack on the ground. Is it safe to say that the key is in your bag?"

Jack picked up the knapsack from the ground. It had become dislodged during his tussle with Lucius's Hell Hounds. He held up the bag.

"Lucius, if you want your precious key, free my family now and allow them to leave safely."

Lucius was infuriated. "Jack, your insolence tries my patience. You know the situation you are in leaves you in no position to make demands, yet you choose to provoke me. You leave me no choice. Bring Mrs. Aitken to me," he demanded. "Her blood will be on your hands, Jack."

The guard ruthlessly pushed Amanda toward Lucius, and Louis and David struggled to free themselves from their captors.

Jack reached over his shoulders with both hands and drew the Sword of Saint Michael from its sheath and shouted, "Get your hands off my wife, you demon bastard."

The guard paused, and Jack pointed the sword in Lucius's direction, declaring, "Now, we are going to make a new pact. You are going to let my family go, or I am going to shove this sword down your miserable throat, you demonic son of a bitch."

Lucius's grotesque laugh echoed through the trees.

"Jack, Jack, Jack, look at your sword! You know that it is a wooden weapon, don't you? Have you taken leave of your senses?" Lucius mocked. "Did you at least dip it in holy water or something else to make it sting a little when you 'shove it down my miserable throat'?"

Jack, brimming with confidence, said sarcastically, "Come here, *Master Lucius,* and let us find out."

Lucius reached his hand inside his cloak and pulled out the sword he first showed Jack just a week ago.

"Is this not familiar to you, Jack? Look at it closely. Now, let us end this ridiculous standoff before it goes any further."

Jack gripped his sword tighter in anticipation of an attack that he was sure was coming.

Amanda yelled, "Jack, behind you! Turn around!"

But before Jack could react, he heard a click as something pressed against the back of his head.

Chapter 25

Jack closed his eyes, instantly knowing he was in trouble.

"Jack, drop the knapsack."

He complied but knew the voice immediately. He opened his eyes, turned slightly to the left, and saw Father Desmond holding a gun to his head. Jack was stunned. He could not believe what he was seeing. *How? Why?*

"Mark, what is going on? What are you doing?"

Father Desmond picked up the knapsack without taking his eyes from Jack. "Harmony and balance, Jack. Peace and order."

Jack looked at Father Desmond, bewildered. "What are you talking about?"

Father Desmond ignored Jack's question entirely and said firmly, "Give Lucius the key, Jack."

Jack shot a look at Amanda, who huddled with their children, still heavily guarded by Lucius's demons.

Jack whispered, "Mark, I cannot do that. If he gets the key, he is going to open that gate. *All Hell will break loose.*"

"Jack, we have gotten this far together," Father Desmond said pleadingly. "You are going to have to trust me."

Jack shook his head in disbelief.

"I know who we are dealing with and what he is capable of doing. Remember what *The Art of War* says, 'If you know your enemy and you know yourself, you need not fear the result of a hundred battles.'"

"Give me the key, now," Lucius demanded.

Father Desmond nodded to reassure Jack as he tossed the knapsack at Lucius's feet. Lucius picked up the bag and removed the ornate box from it. He held the box and gazed at it from all sides with a look of cautious optimism on his face.

"None of the other keys had such an elaborate box. Why is this key treated differently than the others?"

"It is demon folklore that references the creation of the keys," Father Desmond replied. "While I am well versed in your legends, I am not a demon, so I cannot tell you any details about the keys beyond what is in your books on demon lore." Rolling his eyes, he continued, "You are on your own with this one. Why not open the box and see what it looks like?"

Lucius opened the box and picked up the key to examine it. It certainly looked like the other keys he had in his possession. There was only one way to be sure, though. As everyone else anxiously looked on, Lucius made his way over to the door embedded in the burial mound. The ground around the burial mound continued to heave and shake as the entities inside the grave struggled to free themselves.

Wasting no time, Lucius carefully inserted the key into the locking mechanism. He tried it several times, but the key was not a match for the lock. Lucius realized it was a fake. He stormed back to the ceremonial area and confronted Father Desmond.

"It is a fake! Where is the real key, Desmond?"

Father Desmond smiled cunningly. "I assure you it is somewhere quite close."

Lucius clutched the sword in his hands as his fury grew. He wanted nothing more than to plunge the blade through the heart of his greatest enemy. It took nearly the complete application of his demon power to contain his rage. He reasoned that if he wanted the key, however, he needed to restrain himself.

Father Desmond pointed to the Sword of Saint Michael that Jack held and said, "Lucius, I think this would be an appropriate time to break this news to you as well. The sword you have is worthless. The first Saint Michael sword shattered during the battle at Stull Cemetery in 1857."

Lucius looked down at his sword and studied it more closely. He then looked up at Father Desmond with suspicion. Thus far, Father Desmond had managed to be one step ahead of him. Why would he now disclose that the sword he had was a fake? He decided he would call his bluff.

"Prove it," Lucius said, throwing his sword in Father Desmond's direction. "The two of you can fight it out, and we will see which sword is the real one."

Lucius's demand caught Jack off guard. He was still processing what was happening. Now he was supposed to fight Mark? None of this was making any sense. Mark holding a gun to his head? What the hell was he thinking? Jack also observed that the clock was also literally ticking down for Lucius to complete his plan to release Lucifer. Still, he didn't seem to be in any particular hurry to execute it. Why?

Then, Jack heard Father Desmond. "Jack, raise your sword."

"Mark, I cannot fight you. The thought of the two of us engaged in mortal combat is beyond insane. Why don't we take the weapons we have and kill Lucius?"

"Even if we get to Lucius, Amanda and your boys will be dead before we lay a hand on him. There is also no way to spread and light the powder that Imam Wadud gave us. There are too many of Lucius's demons around them."

"So, what do we do next?"

"I will attempt to stab and cut you with the sword. Do not worry; the armor you are wearing will protect you."

Jack reluctantly did as Father Desmond instructed him. He assumed a fighting stance but allowed Father Desmond to wield Lucius's sword against him. First, Father Desmond took his sword and struck Jack in the arm, attempting to slice through his armor. Then, he lunged toward Jack and tried to run Jack through the abdomen. Lucius's sword glanced off Jack's armor in both instances, leaving him uninjured and the armor intact and undamaged.

Jack grinned back at Father Desmond and then glanced at Lucius, who stood scratching his chin with a perplexed look on his face.

"Jack, now take your sword and strike Lucius's sword with it."

Jack raised his sword and then swung and hit Lucius's sword that Father Desmond held upright with both hands. Lucius's sword shattered into several pieces, with Father Desmond holding the broken sword's handle in his hands.

Jack smiled, breathing a sigh of relief. Were it not for the cautionary words that Father Desmond had given him just a few minutes ago, he would have swiftly pivoted and lunged at Lucius. Jack was still struggling to understand what Father Desmond was doing. Based on the look of surprise and concern he now detected on Lucius's face, perhaps the goal was just to get Lucius to back down. The failed attempt to get Jack and Father Desmond to fight one another and the knowledge that Jack and Father Desmond possessed both the Sword of Saint Michael and the key to the gate left Lucius with few options, did it not?

Father Desmond heartily laughed as he threw the map that Jack and he had used to find the key at Lucius's feet. Father Desmond acted as if everything occurring was mere entertainment.

"I guess you figured out that this is a forgery, just like the key that we supposedly found with it."

"You can keep it to display in that museum where you have been working," Father Desmond scoffed.

Lucius glared at Father Desmond. If looks could kill, then Father Desmond would have been lying on the ground, but nothing Lucius was doing seemed to bother Father Desmond in the slightest.

"We had an arrangement," Lucius said to Father Desmond indignantly.

"We still do, Lucius. I just like these new terms better."

Jack looked at Lucius and then back to Father Desmond and said disbelievingly, "Arrangement? What arrangement? Mark, what the hell is he talking about?"

Father Desmond moved closer to Jack, put his hand on his shoulder, and said, "Jack, you need to open your eyes. It does not matter if it is Lucius, Lucifer, or JESU. They are all the same, and each wants to control the other. You and me, they consider to be disposable. We are pawns in a game of chess. They move us around the board, and when we are no longer of any use, well, you know what happens. They all want to rule the world, Jack. I am just trying to even the playing field for our side."

"Have you gone insane, Mark?" Jack asked in amazement. "You are a man of God. I do not have to caution you about deals with the Devil, do I?"

Jack pointed a shaking finger at Lucius. "He is as close to the Devil right now as you are going to get! Why, Mark? Why are you doing this, and what does it all have to do with my family and me?"

"I am not insane, Jack," Father Desmond countered. "Far from it. You have asked me several times this week about what I believed about good and evil. I would submit to you that one cannot exist without the other. Wasn't Lucifer once an angel? In a way, JESU and Lucius's demon legions share a link because of the relationship between good and evil. It is therefore highly logical that we might be able to come to an agreement of some kind that acknowledges this connection."

"Mark, I thought the mission of JESU was to destroy evil," Jack said incredulously. "You are suggesting a repudiation of everything you swore you believed in when you joined the organization. Lucius has terrorized you for most of your life. How can you possibly believe a thing that he tells you?"

Father Desmond responded with some frustration, "Jack, one of the key tenants of the *Art of War* is something you probably have heard many times. 'The enemy of my enemy is my friend.'"

Jack interrupted Father Desmond, "Are you saying that JESU is your enemy?"

"Not the organization, but many within the society fail to grasp things have changed, and the organization needs to evolve. JESU is decaying from within Jack. As I told you, our numbers are dwindling, and replacements are becoming hard to find. The balance between good and evil, the status quo, if you will, is threatened by this. This imbalance is as potentially destructive to the world as having one side be victorious over the other."

Jack rolled his eyes. "Mark, how could you possibly believe that if JESU were to defeat Lucius that the world would be just as bad off as if Lucius were in control?"

"Jack, you are naïve," Father Desmond said dismissively. "There is no utopia of the good. The balance needs to be maintained somehow, and that currently unknown evil that would arise could be worse than the proverbial devil we know. Are you familiar with the Cold War doctrine of Mutually Assured Destruction?"

"Jack!" Amanda suddenly shouted, pointing toward the gate to Hell. "Look at the door!"

The door, which had previously been a fiery red, was now an eerie blue-violet color.

"Mark, we don't have time for this," Jack said impatiently. "You know that door needs to be closed, permanently. NOW! That color is hotter than orange, yellow, or red!"

"Jack, you haven't answered my question. Do you know what MAD stands for?"

"Jesus, Mark!" Jack shouted indignantly. "Are you blind?"

Ignoring Jack's tirade, Father Desmond answered his own question. "It is a theory of deterrence. Each side has no incentive to start a war of annihilation as they both have the means to destroy one another if one were to initiate a pre-emptive attack against the other."

Father Demond grabbed Jack's arms and shook him. "Can't you see? That is what an agreement with Lucius will bring. By ensuring a reconfigured JESU and Lucius's legions are on a level playing field, it will ultimately decrease violence between the two organizations, which would be beneficial to the world."

Jack looked at Father Desmond in disbelief, "Now who is being naïve, Mark? As I said before, how are you going to trust Lucius?"

Lucius, who had been silently listening to the exchange between the two men, interrupted them. "Jack, look at what time it is. Have I opened the gate? That is not an accident. I know that Mark has the key and sword, but did it ever occur to you that perhaps I decided I did not really want to open the gate?"

Jack looked at Lucius skeptically. "And now are you by some miracle transforming into a benevolent and generous entity? A change of heart? I was pretty certain you did not have one."

Lucius replied coldly, "I do not, Jack. However, I have grown to enjoy the power I wield, and I am not quite ready to relinquish it to anyone, including Lucifer. My agreement with Father Desmond will allow me to add to my demon legions' size as he rebuilds JESU. Once we have achieved parity, then our agreement will be at an end."

Lucius's piercing red eyes stared at Father Desmond. "This pact is, of course, contingent upon him giving me the key."

Jack shook his head. "I will correct my earlier assertion—you are both insane! Mark, which one of you cooked up this scheme?"

Jack then looked Father Desmond in the eye and said dejectedly, "You've been using my family and me, haven't you? Mark, I trusted you."

"I am not insane, Jack. However, I am pragmatic, and sometimes the ends justify the means."

Jack grew furious and grabbed the lapels of Father Desmond's jacket.

"Jack, you have to know that this is not a plan that I just came up with out of the blue. I have thought this through thoroughly and have worked on it for several years. If I do not change the dynamic, JESU will fail, and as we have talked about, a veil of darkness will descend upon humanity."

Jack interrupted and said coolly, "I see. You will ride to JESU's rescue, of course. Reclaiming all of the influence that you lost as a result of the massacre ten years ago and enhancing your personal power has nothing to do with any of this, right?"

Cocking his fist, he clenched his teeth and reared back to strike Father Desmond.

Jack heard Lucius's voice. "Jack, turn around."

Glancing over his shoulder, he saw Amanda and the boys on their knees with guns pointed at their heads. Jack backed away from Father Desmond.

"Jack, you may find this hard to believe at the moment, but I still believe that good will always ultimately triumph over evil."

Lucius stared at Father Desmond coldly and said sarcastically, "We will see about that…Father."

Father Desmond turned to face Lucius.

"Remember that change to our agreement I referenced? Well, ownership of the key is another one of those adjustments."

Father Desmond reached into his jacket and held up an object. He waved the real key in Lucius's direction. "I will be holding onto this for safekeeping."

Lucius's eyebrows narrowed and deep furrows formed in his forehead. Visibly angry, he said, "That was not the agreement, priest. You and your friend Jack pontificate about your inability to trust me. The real question should be, how am I to trust you?"

"Calm down, Lucius," Father Desmond counseled. "Once we achieve equality in the level of our forces, then I will give you the key. You will have the ability to open the gate, but I will retain the sword and the ability to close it for all eternity."

Lucius turned to Jack and said, "You know, Jack, Father Desmond is correct about one thing. Not everything JESU does is good. You may wish to speak with the good Father about a few things. Perhaps, he would like to explain to you how he appears to have used his old friend Joseph Rogers to deliver a fake sword to me. What *man of the cloth* would do that?"

Father Desmond looked at Lucius angrily but maintained his silence.

"You might also want to ask him why he would allow me to terrorize you and your family as part of this ruse."

Father Desmond interrupted, "You bastard! Jack, do not listen to him. You know Lucius isn't to be trusted. He is a liar."

"Bastard? Liar? That is no way to refer to someone who is your partner."

Jack glared at Father Desmond. "Mark, you told me I was a compromised but not yet a corrupted soul. Were you really talking about me, or were you trying to convince yourself that you had not crossed over from one to the other? You have obviously become very educated about military history. You referred to Sun Tzu's *The Art of War* several times in the past week. I do not doubt that you have studied Roman military history as well. Do you recall the story of Julius Caesar crossing the Rubicon? It seems to me that you have done just that. There is no turning back from all of this, and while Caesar became dictator, you know what happened to him."

Father Desmond frowned. "Are you comparing me to a dictator?"

"If the shoe fits…"

Father Desmond slapped Jack across the face. "Jack, you have got your weaknesses too. Your tendency toward introspection and self-flagellation regarding how things impact your family made you an easy target. You set this entire affair into motion. You were a convenient tool, and you are far too trusting."

Jack looked at Father Desmond with fury in his eyes. "You killed him, didn't you! Reverend Miner is dead, isn't he? All this talk about introspection. You were listening!"

Father Desmond nodded. "Collateral damage. Of course, I knew what he was telling you. Don't you think I have spies of my own? He stuck his nose somewhere where it did not belong."

Lucius smirked and folded his arms across his chest. He was not above gloating and said with delight, "Ah…now we are getting somewhere. It appears that none of us can avoid the betrayal that is now the defining theme of this evening's event."

While Lucius was speaking, Father Desmond whispered to Jack, "Jack, I'm sorry that I slapped you. That was for Lucius's benefit. We must not let Lucius divide us. There has never been a member of JESU who does not have a degree in religious studies. You have demonstrated that you have what it takes. I can offer you a special role within the reconfigured organization. Together, we can eventually defeat Lucius."

Jack stared at Father Desmond with a puzzled look on his face. "Mark, you just talked about mutually assured destruction and maintaining the status quo. You said there is no such thing as utopia. Now, you are telling me we can destroy Lucius. Which vision will you try to sell me on next?"

"Jack, all of that was for Lucius's consumption," Father Desmond said, trying to convince Jack of his sincerity." You remember, don't you? We talked about it on the plane. Sun Tzu said, 'All warfare is based on deception.' I need Lucius to believe that I am his partner. Another lesson from the *Art of War* that we did not discuss was always to leave an enemy a chance to escape. This way, they do not fight as hard as they would if their backs were against the wall. It makes it easier to appease them. We can lull Lucius into a false state of security, and when he least expects it, we will strike."

"You just lost three of your best warriors! They all admired you and valued the friendship they had with you. What did you offer the three of them? How will their loss win you favor with the remaining members of JESU?"

"They knew what they were getting into, Jack. I must demonstrate that I learned from the mistakes of the past. *'Making no mistakes is what establishes the certainty of victory.'* We are fighting a war, Jack! I need to show JESU's remaining membership that I understand that relying on friendship blinded me in the past. Think about it. When you approached me a week ago, I had to make sure that you were not part of another attempt by Lucius to set me up. I only knew you were for real when you specifically mentioned Lucius by name. None of the friends who betrayed me previously did that. Subtle adjustments such as this are what will restore my position and reputation within JESU."

Jack shook his head angrily. "You allowed your three friends to risk their reputation and their lives. You may as well have killed them yourself. Their blood is on your hands! All so you can show an organization that treated you like Judas over the past ten years that you have learned your lesson?" Jack looked over at Amanda and the boys. "Count me out! I see quite clearly now what friendship means to you."

"Jack, you are far more perceptive than I thought," Lucius said, attempting to exploit the rift between Jack and Father Desmond. "I suspect that you observed that Father Desmond took no action to prevent me from, shall we say, removing his pawns from the chessboard? You realize that was no accident, don't you?"

Father Desmond shouted furiously, "You demon bastard!"

Jack stared at Father Desmond, his mouth agape.

Lucius persisted, "You set the precedent that our agreement was open to renegotiation. Had you given me the key as agreed, I would have kept my word. All bets seem to be off now, don't they?"

Lucius turned to Jack and said, "Desmond allowed me to kill his friends as part of his agreement with me. Let us call it a 'test of trustworthiness.'"

"Let me guess the other part of this trustworthiness test," Jack said in disgust. "Mark will keep the key until his death, at which time it will pass to Lucius. Of course, Lucius will get to torture and kill us all and take our souls."

As Jack finished his sentence, he heard a click and felt the barrel of a pistol pushed against his temple. He looked over at Amanda, and the boys, who were on their knees with guns, pointed at the back of their heads. Amanda looked at Jack with fear in her eyes. The boys were struggling to sit still. He knew without looking that Father Desmond was holding the gun to his head once more.

"I regret this, Jack. I truly do. I meant it when I said there was a place in JESU for you. Remember, I did warn you. There were no guarantees your family was going to get out of this, and they won't."

Lucius had been pacing back and forth. He interjected, "Jack, remember, *you* dragged your family into this. Anyway, I need to show Lucifer that I got something from this deal. Oh, he will be on a rampage about my failure to open the gate, but there really is not much he can do while he is still locked in Hell. Ultimately, he will come around and be satisfied by the increase in our demon force levels and the corresponding surge in the number of damned souls. My Master will be particularly pleased knowing that the soul of the human at the center of the legend will be his to torment for all eternity. Your family, well, that will be a bonus that will delight my—"

Lucius's monologue was interrupted by the sound of beating drums echoing through the forest. Everyone in the proximity of the burial mound looked around for the source of the drumming, which grew louder and seemed to surround the entire area.

Lucius looked at Father Desmond and demanded, "Is this another one of your schemes?"

Father Desmond looked around warily. "Your guess is as good as mine."

Deep in the woods behind the burial mound, a glowing white ball appeared. It seemed to hang in the air for a moment and suddenly began to move up and down. The ball started to move toward the burial mound, and as it went forward, it continued to move up and down in lockstep with the drumbeat.

Lucius's demons started to whisper to one another about what they were seeing. "What is it?" one of the guards asked. "It is moving toward us," said another. There was anxiety in their voices.

Jack's attention alternated between the glowing ball and his family. He made eye contact with Amanda and removed the bag of fennel powder from his pocket. While the demons were distracted, he tossed the bag in Amanda's direction. He made a circular motion with his finger in the air, hoping she would understand his instructions on what to do with the powder.

The glowing ball had nearly reached the burial mound when it began to change shape. It almost instantaneously morphed into a horse galloping to the drums' beat, whose rider appeared to be a Native American wearing an elaborate headdress. Jack stared at the figure, and from his research on the Manahoac tribe, he recognized the apparition was wearing a war bonnet, worn only by individuals who earned great respect within the tribe, on and off the battlefield.

As the rider reached the burial mound, he pulled on the reins, and the horse stopped and reared up on its hind legs.

"Eluwilussit," Lucius whispered to himself.

Lucius looked at Father Desmond, sure that he was responsible for the entity before them. Father Desmond looked back at Lucius and shook his head to assure him that he was not responsible for who or what they were seeing.

The guards had stepped back from Amanda and the boys. David and Louis stared at the entity while Amanda stealthily picked up the bag that Jack had thrown toward her.

The horse confidently cantered back and forth with its ears pricked forward. Its blowing and snorting created a mist exhaled through its nose. Yet the animal was translucent, as was its rider, who suddenly began to speak.

"Ni Lawa Maneto We Leme Wa. Ay Sasakiwa Maneto Hke Wa. Mya Sihta Wa Wi Ci Mi Nexpetoni Ni Mata. No Nsye Swa Kexkinawa Te Lemena Mya La Ci Melwe Lemewa Akw Wi Oani. Ma Maw Melwihtwa Wme Ya Wi Weokici Ki Watawe Wa Ki Hki Hkime Wa Akw Manahoac Akosiwema."

Lucius and Father Desmond locked eyes. Both were bewildered, and neither of them understood what the entity was saying. Jack, however, heard every word: *"I am Eluwilussit. A Manitou. The Great Spirit. Fight with me my brother. You are not impure like these evil double tongues. Together, we will right the wrongs inflicted against the Manahoac people!"*

Jack clutched his sword tightly, looked at the figure on horseback, and nodded his agreement. The ghost warrior waved the spear he held in his hand, and a single ball of fire materialized in the forest behind him. The second ball of fire appeared next to the first, and one by one, similar balls of fire emerged until the area around the burial mound was encircled and illuminated in a circle of fire.

Lucius, his demon legions, and Father Desmond looked all around with astonished looks on their faces. While trying to understand what they were witnessing, fear began to build up inside of them. They all searched for a path that would enable them to escape, but they were surrounded, out in the open, with nowhere to run and nowhere to hide.

The drumbeat became louder, and the tempo grew faster and faster. Lucius's Hell Hounds, snarling and drooling, looked straight at Jack. Shadow figures became visible in the forest, and the fireballs, suspended in the air, grew brighter. Jack saw that Amanda had figured out what to do with the contents of the bag despite the chaos. She managed to encircle herself and the boys with the blessed fennel powder. Amanda looked at him, lighter in hand. She lit the powder, and the resulting flame caused the demon guards to reel backward.

"Get them!" Lucius demanded.

The guards tried to recapture Amanda and the boys, but the result of every attempt to do so was a burn more painful than their demon hands could endure.

Lucius frowned and said, "Barghest, Gwyllgi, slaughter Mr. Aitken." The beasts, no longer restrained by their Master, leaped in Jack's direction.

Jack raised his sword, blunting the attack from Lucius's Hell Hounds. He then heard a scream and realized that his sword had inadvertently pierced Father Desmond's upper body. Father Desmond fell to the ground. At the same time, Jack overheard the ghostly presence say, "Now, my brothers, let vengeance reign!"

The shadow figures complied with the command, and the sky was teeming with flaming projectiles emanating from the forest. The previously dark night was now afire. The fiery missiles reached the apex of their trajectory and began their downward flight back to earth. As Jack battled the Hell Hounds, some of Lucius's demons began to lose their nerve and attempted to reach the cover of the forest. Those that stood their ground found themselves skewered by flaming spears that left them as a pile of ash. The few that made it to the tree line came face to face with the shadow figures who impaled the demons, sending them to the same fate as their colleagues.

Jack held Barghest at bay with his arm and ran his sword through Gwyllgi's chest. As Jack removed the blade, the beast writhed on the ground in agony. Jack saw demons dropping all around him. Clouds of ash, the residue of their once physical form, littered the ground. The putrid smell of Sulphur hung in the air. Jack pushed Barghest away to create some space between himself and the Hell Hound and, with a sweeping and slashing motion, severed Barghest's head. Jack watched as the remains of the Hell Hound smoldered and turned to dust. He turned and saw Gwyllgi motionless on the ground. Jack moved quickly to the carcass and cut off its head to ensure it was dead. It flared up and then fell to dust.

Lucius looked on in horror as he saw his precious pets disintegrate before his eyes. He watched his demon legions turned to ashes, and their death screams echoed through his head. Father Desmond lay on the ground. He was still and appeared to be dead. Lucius watched Jack cut off Gwyllgi's head, and it was more than he could stand.

While his demons could not stand the pain of the flaming fennel power, Lucius gritted his teeth and reached through the blaze. He grabbed Amanda by the neck, but before he could drag her through the fire, David picked up the remaining fennel powder and threw it into Lucius's face. Lucius dropped Amanda and fell back in agony. Lucius's anger now turned to blind rage.

His eyes turned blood red, and rough, black, reptilian-like skin emerged as the clothing tore away from his body. His fingers lengthened, and claw-like fingernails grew from the tips. His lower jaw protruded as two enormous canine teeth emerged. Pointed, dog-like ears rose from the sides of his hairless head. His torso broadened, and the shoulders retracted, revealing a chiseled, muscular chest. Lucius was now fully transformed into his hideous true self. An eight-foot-tall behemoth who turned and looked for Jack.

Jack saw him approach and braced himself for Lucius's onslaught. Lucius took the iron spear that he had jammed into the ground earlier and, with all his strength, thrust it into Jack's chest. Jack was driven to the ground by the attack, but the armor he was wearing saved him from what should have been a lethal blow. Jack quickly got on his feet and sliced Lucius's arm with the sword. Lucius let out a roar of excruciating pain. Lucius, his attention totally focused on Jack, did not see the figure coming up behind him.

The Manitou said, "Your Red-Eyed Warriors are dead. Now he who has an evil heart, it is your turn!"

Lucius roared in a deep, menacing voice, "Aitken, the time for you to meet your true fate has come!"

Jack watched the Manitou raise its spear and ram it through the back of Lucius's neck, down through his chest, and out the front of his body, impaled and pinned to the ground. His tortured scream reverberated through the woods. The body let loose one last lengthy gasp before it twitched and went limp.

The scream left Jack shaken, and he slowly made his way toward Lucius's lifeless corpse. He stepped over Mark's body and paused just for a moment, and prayed that he would find peace somewhere and somehow. Jack was going to make sure Lucius was truly dead and that he would never be a threat to his family again. He checked for signs of life. There were none that Jack could detect. He spent several minutes waiting to see if anything would change. Once Jack was confident there were no signs of life, he raised the Saint Michael sword, which ignited into a flame. Wielding it with righteous indignation, he separated Lucius's head from his body.

The area fell eerily quiet. A gentle breeze rustled the leaves in the trees. The forest was now dark but somehow no longer felt as foreboding as it once did. Jack looked up, and the Manitou atop his horse nodded and said, *"Blessings to you, my brother. Peace to you, my brother."*

The horse and its rider turned and trotted back toward the woods from which they had appeared. Once past the burial mound, they began to fade away. Jack watched them disappear. He then turned to see his family waving to him. Amanda was smiling, and the boys were holding on to her. Jack smiled back, returned the sword to its sheath, and started walking in their direction. He took a deep breath and thought to himself; *It is over. Thank God!*

"Well done, Jack," a familiar voice said. "I could not have done it better myself. "

Jack instantly knew it was Father Desmond. Wounded but not dead, the man he thought was his friend once again held a gun to his head.

"Mark, there is no need for this. Lucius is dead. It is all over."

"Jack, I am afraid not. Do not get me wrong. You have done the world a great service today. After the British forces' victory over the Nazis at El Alamein, Winston Churchill told the British people, *'Now this is not the end. It is not even the beginning of the end. But it is, perhaps, the end of the beginning.'* That was one of World War II's turning points, so today is the same for us in our war against evil. JESU now needs to consolidate its power. That won't happen without me. To assume control of JESU, I need to tie up loose ends, which means I need you and your family out of the way. I promise that I will make this quick and painless. I will give you all a Christian burial."

Jack shifted his weight to reach the sword. Father Desmond sensed what Jack was trying to do. He turned the gun on Amanda

"Jack, please do not try it. She will be dead before you get your hand on the sword. Now, get down on your knees with your fingers laced together. Hold them behind your head."

Jack knelt as Father Desmond commanded. He continued to point the gun at Amanda.

"Mark," Jack pleaded. "Please do not do this."

Father Desmond began to press the trigger and quoted Sun Tzu one last time, *"Thus it is that in war, the victorious strategist only seeks battle after the victory is won.* Sorry, Jack. You came close, but not quite close enough."

A shot rang out. Jack flinched, striking Father Desmond's arm. He heard a thud next to him and wondered for a moment if he was dead. He slowly turned and saw Father Desmond on the ground next to him. The key, the real key to the Hell Gate, had fallen from Mark's jacket and lay next to his body. Jack quickly pushed the key under Father Desmond's body to hide it and looked in the direction from where he thought the shot had come.

Detective Anne Bishop emerged from the woods.

She carefully made her way over to Jack and checked Father Desmond's neck. Her facial expression told Jack there was no pulse. She then went over to Lucius's body and shot six bullets into it. She looked at Jack, waved her gun, and said, "Garlic infused silver bullets. Just in case. Go ahead, Jack. Take your family and get out of here. I will take care of this."

Stunned, Jack said, "Thank you." He got to his feet and turned to reunite with his family. There was no sign of Amanda, but he saw the boys kneeling on the ground. He realized they were shaking Amanda and saying, 'Mom! Mom! Wake up, Mom!"

Jack raced over and saw Amanda's unresponsive body lying motionless on the ground. The trampled grass surrounding her was crimson from the blood rushing out of her body.

Jack stroked her hair. "Amanda. Honey, please. Amanda. Say something. Oh, God! Someone help! please!"

Holding Father Desmond's gun, Detective Bishop called out, "There is one bullet missing."

With a wave of nausea, he realized that when he had flinched at the sound of Detective Bishop's gunshot, he had struck Father Desmond's arm, redirecting the bullet.

Jack screamed, "NO!"

Detective Bishop rushed to their side. She pulled her cell phone out and said, "This is Detective Anne Bishop. 10-33 emergency. 10-52, I need a medivac helicopter to the GPS coordinates that I am sending to you now."

It felt like an eternity before the helicopter arrived. Miraculously, Amanda had a pulse. There was no room for Jack and the boys in the helicopter. They were going to have to walk through the woods to get back to the car. Jack watched the helicopter lift off and saw paramedics through the windows feverishly working on Amanda. The helicopter quickly disappeared.

A gentle, cleansing rain began to fall. Jack thought back to the nightmare he had a few days ago. The one with him kneeling with his face in his hands next to Amanda's body. A nightmare that now was his reality.

He prepared to lead the boys through the woods to begin the journey back to the car. Then Jack remembered the key hidden under Father Desmond's body and realized he must retrieve it for safekeeping. As he fought back the tears, Jack thought to himself, *Now, I really understand the toll that one must pay to travel the Highway to Hell, and it is a price that is more than I can bear.*

Epilogue

February 28th
Inova Schar Institute Fairfax, Virginia
4:00 p.m.

Jack was jolted awake by the door opening. At long last, the nurse had returned, and she maneuvered the bed into the room. David was still asleep, and with the procedure now complete, Jack could breathe a sigh of relief.

It had started before dawn, with Jack waking to the sound of pouring rain hitting the windows in his bedroom. By the time David would shake off the effects of the anesthesia from the lumbar puncture he had just received, it would be dark. They would be traveling at the height of rush hour, which meant it would be a long drive home.

While Jack was tired, he knew that David was the one bearing the heavier burden. Shortly after the incident at the burial mound in Culpeper, David began to complain of headaches. Jack took him back to the pediatrician several times, but the doctor insisted he had the flu. In mid-December, they were back in the emergency room so David could receive fluids for dehydration. The attending physician in the emergency room ordered a CAT scan as a precaution. Fifteen minutes later, David was in an ambulance rushing to Fairfax Hospital. He had suffered a stroke, and there were blood clots in his brain.

Jack still had a hard time convincing himself that this was possible. *Seventeen-year-olds do not have strokes;* he kept telling himself. Still, unfortunately, the MRI said otherwise. David's illness was a significant blow to all of them, occurring so soon after Amanda's injuries during the events on Halloween. Jack had no way of knowing that things were about to get far worse.

David appeared to recover quickly after the stroke, but he was not feeling well again by early January. During David's hospital stay in December, the blood drawn showed no irregularities, but the same tests in January revealed that David had Acute Lymphocytic Leukemia. He started chemotherapy immediately in a phase of treatment known as induction. Several weeks into treatment, David suffered a seizure at home, which led to another hospital stay. Another medication was added to his already heavy daily regimen of pills to address this new complication.

Despite the seizure, the induction phase of David's treatment seemed to go well. Hopes were high that his bloodwork on February 1st would show that his body had little to no Leukemia cells left. Jack was devastated to hear that not only had the treatment not worked, but it was so unsuccessful that David's odds of recovery had plummeted. What had been a fight to drive Leukemia cells from David's body now became a fight to save his life.

Days later, Jack received a call from David's teacher about obtaining updated documentation for the school about David's illness. When Jack picked up the paperwork from the doctor's office, David's pediatrician told Jack that he personally never had a patient suffer such a sequence of life-threatening illnesses. He went even further, telling Jack that everything that happened to David was so rare that each year fewer than five people in the world are afflicted with anything resembling it. Jack could not help but question if David's condition might have been a consequence of his kidnapping and captivity. He wondered if being in Lucius's evil presence, even for that brief period, could cause such terrible things to happen.

Starting in early February, David began receiving powerful medications daily, and every Friday, a spinal tap introduced additional drugs into his spinal fluid. These drugs took a toll on his immune system, which resulted in the need for blood transfusions. Today was to have been a shorter day, but the need for a blood transfusion had turned it into an all-day affair. Jack tried to support

David as much as possible but being autistic only added to David's challenges. The need for the transfusion had thrown off the entire schedule for the day and resulted in David needing a sedative to calm down.

It was breaking Jack's heart to see David's suffering. The physical changes, such as David's pale complexion and the dark circles under his eyes, were bad enough, but to see him regressing socially, including rarely speaking and withdrawing from his preferred activities, was almost more than Jack could take. At the same time, Jack had deep admiration and respect for David's bravery. He never complained nor tried to avoid any of the treatments he was subject to, no matter how uncomfortable or debilitating they might be.

After more than an hour in the car, they finally arrived home. Louis greeted Jack and David at the door and started asking Jack questions in a rapid-fire interrogation.

"Why are you so late? Is David okay? Is David going to eat dinner now?"

Jack attempted to settle Louis down while helping David get changed for bed. Once he was able to restore order, Jack went back downstairs to the kitchen. His mother and father-in-law were there, as they had picked Louis up from work. Jack filled them in on the status of David's treatment, and they agreed to pick up Louis in the morning. While Louis had returned to his job, he was still filled with anxiety and continually asked if his brother would die and what happened to his mom.

Amanda's family had difficulty understanding and accepting what had happened to her. He felt terrible, particularly for her parents, for all that they had been through over the past several months. Each time he saw the sorrow in their eyes, he sensed that they both blamed him. It was just one more burden that Jack had to bear.

The phone rang, and Jack excused himself to answer it. He waved goodbye to Amanda's parents and said, "Jack Aitken speaking."

"Good evening, Jack. How did David's treatment go today?"

Jack recognized the voice as belonging to Anne Bishop. She was one of the few people Jack interacted with these days. Jack knew he was forever in her debt. Not only had she stopped Mark Desmond from murdering his family, but she had tied up the loose ends of the investigation surrounding Amanda's disappearance. She convinced the authorities that the entire matter had been a kidnapping and that she had to shoot Father Desmond in self-defense. The inquiry had been brief, and the case was closed with little fanfare. She found Reverend Miner just as Jack had told her she would. She confirmed he died from strangulation. It was difficult for Jack to hear, but something good did come out of it. Anne resigned from JESU.

In the aftermath of the investigation, Anne had told Jack about her relationship with Father Desmond. She spoke with Jack of the feelings she once had for Mark and that she could not stop asking herself, *Was it the darkness that Mark lived in after the massacre that changed him or did that darkness already dwell in his soul and does that mean it lives inside of each of us?*

Regardless, she knew that Mark had indeed transformed into a variation of the very thing he himself would have once destroyed. She admitted, however, that having to shoot her best friend was something that she would never get over.

Jack, in turn, had shared with Anne Reverend Miner's concerns and his own about JESU. These observations, along with her own personal grief over Mark's death, convinced her that JESU was no longer the organization that she had thought it once was, so she left. Jack wondered whether it was indeed possible to leave an organization whose clandestine activities relied so heavily on its members' loyalty and silence. Would she be allowed to just walk away with no hard feelings and no strings attached? He hoped for her sake that a clean break was possible.

Jack thanked Anne for her kindness in asking about David's condition and hung up the phone. He headed upstairs and found that both boys had gone to sleep. He watched them from the doorway of their room and wondered how long it would last. Both boys had nightmares about everything that they had experienced during their week of captivity. Lucius was dead, but he lived on in their subconscious. Jack had tried to engage both boys in conversation about their fears and what had happened to them, but they refused to discuss it. Jack closed the door and headed back downstairs.

He reached the landing and walked across the hallway to the study. As he entered the room, the only noises he heard were those of the medical monitoring equipment. Jack checked the monitors and tubes, then looked down at his beloved Amanda lying still on the bed. He brushed her hair, then sat in the chair next to the hospital bed to read the daily report on her recovery. The update was always the same, with no movement or responses to stimuli. Amanda remained in a coma with only the rhythm of the life support systems to keep her alive.

Jack put the daily log down on a table next to the chair. He went to the kitchen and got a beer. Returning to the room, Jack reached down to his hip and pulled his cell phone from its protective case. As Jack sat down, he turned the phone on and re-read Amanda's last e-mail to him, as was his nightly ritual. She had composed it on Halloween, but Jack was unaware that she had sent it until days later when she was still in the hospital. Jack broke down the first time he read it, and every time since.

During the final moments of the confrontation in Culpeper, a bullet, likely from Father Desmond's gun, had struck Amanda in the neck, perforating her carotid artery. It was, in truth, a miracle she survived the airlift to the hospital or the marathon operation that saved her life. After Amanda's condition stabilized, she remained unresponsive and was on life support. When the hospital told Jack there was nothing more they could do for Amanda, he investigated the option of moving her to a rehab hospital. The nearest facility that could meet her needs was several hours away. Jack knew he needed to have her closer to him, so he arranged to have her come home instead.

During the day, he paid for full-time nursing care. He took the night shift, sleeping in a chair next to her bedside each night when he slept at all. Fortunately, their financial advisor had included a rider in Amanda's life insurance policy that allowed for early withdrawals for long-term care. Jack's employer had been either unable or unwilling to support the balancing act required to manage Jack's personal affairs and work-related responsibilities. Jack found himself unemployed, and it took a great deal of negotiation to finally convince the insurer to allow him to use the policy to help pay for her care.

Jack finished rereading Amanda's e-mail and wiped a tear from his eye. He took a deep breath and began to speak to her. Jack described how David's treatment had gone that day and told her that Louis had a good day at work.

He paused, lowered his eyes, and said in a heartbroken voice, "How am I supposed to go on without you, Amanda? I am trying to hold things together. I know that is what you would do, but I never was as strong as you."

He looked upward and asked out loud two all too familiar questions, "God, where are you? Why have you abandoned us?" Jack shook his head. The why it always came back to the why. Never any answers, just more questions.

Jack sat back in the chair, rubbing his eyes. His body was weary, and his mood somber. He could not help but wonder if it were his destiny to watch those he loved to slip away until he would be the only one to remain. He was afraid of what would occur next, and he felt powerless to stop what was happening. Jack turned on the radio that he played to pass the time on some of the longer nights. His instincts told him that this was going to be one of those. 'King of Pain' by The Police was playing. *How appropriate*, Jack thought, feeling immensely sorry for himself as he turned the radio off.

Jack's thoughts drifted back to another subject that was never far from his mind. *'How could Mark have turned on me as he did? Could I truly have been so blind not to see that even he was capable of such treachery?'* Jack recalled that Mark Twain once wrote, *'Everyone is a moon and has a dark side which he never shows anybody.'* Jack tried to find reassurance in the quote, but he just could not shake the question from his psyche. He had trusted Mark with his life and the lives of his family members, and Mark betrayed him. Jack found that he was having problems trusting people in general and organized religion particularly.

Weeks after the incident at the burial mound, JESU made overtures to Jack, like what Mark Desmond had offered him.

When Jack turned them down, their approach became confrontational. They demanded Jack return the key and sword to them immediately. Jack rejected their demand and hid them in the house. The key was now snugly buried in the insulation in his attic. Jack had taken the precaution of nailing plywood boards on top of the rafters over the insulation under the auspices of creating additional storage space in the attic.

The sword was also never far from Jack, buried in the basement under the sump pump tank. Jack looked at both artifacts as an insurance policy of sorts. If they were in his possession, neither JESU nor the remnants of Lucius's demon legions had control over him, and they each had to worry about the other obtaining the artifacts. While his life felt like it was falling apart, he did maintain a steely resolve not to yield to JESU or anyone else when it came to possession of the weapons. He was becoming a sentry of sorts. His goal was to protect the arms and, in doing so, maintain the status quo and the balance between good and evil.

Jack still had one particularly worrisome, nagging feeling. The specter of Lucius Rofocale never seemed to go away. Sometimes, Jack thought he could still feel his presence. While Father Desmond had taught Jack how to keep Lucius out of his dreams, there seemed to be no way to heal the damage that Lucius had already inflicted on Jack's consciousness.

Only yesterday, while Jack was meditating, he had a vision of standing by Amanda's bedside, asking her to open her eyes. Suddenly, her eyes opened in response to his request, but they were blood red. A voice that was not Amanda's asked, *"Jack, do you not recognize me?"*

Jack shuddered at the very thought of it, and while he had personally beheaded Lucius, he worried that he was still, somehow, out there.

While Amanda was still in the hospital, Jack had reread his journal repeatedly. For some reason that he could not quite explain, it led him back to the burial mound. Jack explored the possibility of purchasing the acreage around the knoll from what remained of the Bradford family. He wanted to ensure that someone would not inadvertently do something to open the gate or resurrect the evil that Jack had only recently been able to exorcise from the land.

Out of respect for the JESU members who had been massacred there ten years earlier and to pay homage to the Manitou of the Manahoac for saving him, Jack spent days burying the remains that Lucius had previously seen fit to defile. He prayed that God would provide an object, possibly made from the same wooden materials as the sword, that would allow him to seal the gate forever if that were even possible.

The truth, however, was that Jack wanted to be sure Lucius was dead. What bothered him was that even after all the measures he was taking to cleanse the area, there were still no bird sounds, nothing but dead silence. He found it troubling and unsettling, and while he was okay being there in the daytime, he knew deep down in his soul, he never wanted to be in these woods after dark ever again.

The events of October 31st replayed in his mind repeatedly. He was still struggling to come to grips with them. He wanted to forget, but that was impossible. However, there was one part of it all that was intriguing, The Manitou. After everything he had been through, Jack thought he would never ask the question again, "*How was this possible?*" but he wanted to know more about the Manitou. He needed to learn more.

Jack researched it further and what he found out was truly mind-blowing. He discovered that while evil comes in and takes on many forms, so does good. The concept of the Manitou was rooted in Iroquois culture. It was the fundamental, spiritual life force that resides everywhere. There were *Otshee Monetoo* (Bad Spirit) and *Aashaa Monetoo* (Good Spirit). The Manitou could manifest as just about anything. It could be a plant, an animal, or as in Jack's case, a warrior on horseback.

During his research, Jack also found out that according to Native American beliefs, a distinct type of energy, metaphysical or supernatural in form, could be associated with specific locations or 'sacred sites' where people would gather for worship and prayer. Many such holy sites dotted the Northern Virginia landscape. The locations included areas where council meetings took place or quarries, not unlike the mine that the Bradford family dug. These sites could unite through spiritual lines that allowed energy to flow between locations or merge at a precise location, such as a burial mound. It all sounded so unreal.

Jack's thoughts wandered back to the present. He held Amanda's hand and watched the drops in her IV fall one by one. Jack began to weep and kissed the back of Amanda's hand. *I am so afraid that I am going to lose you. What do I do if you do not wake up?*

Suddenly, Jack felt something brush across his fingers. He looked down and saw nothing. He looked at Amanda's face, and her eyes were still closed, the expression on her face unchanged.

"Wishful thinking," Jack whispered.

Several minutes passed, and Jack found his eyes drooping. He leaned his forehead against the rail of the hospital bed and started to doze. Jack was almost asleep when something brushed across his hand once more. He looked down, and this time he was sure that Amanda's finger was not in the same position it had been in before. He watched intently for another minute, and this time, he was sure. Amanda's finger had moved!

Jack sat up immediately and looked at Amanda's face. Her eyes were open, and she was looking around. She saw Jack and smiled weakly. Jack smiled back and kissed the hand that he had been holding.

"Amanda! You are back! I knew you would come back."

Amanda replied in a raspy voice, "Jack, you look so tired. You have lost weight too."

"I am okay, Amanda. Can I get you some water?

Amanda nodded yes, and Jack gave her a sip of water. She was able to speak more forcefully. "Jack, listen to me."

"Amanda, I just need to call the doctor."

She quickly replied, "No, Jack. Wait."

Jack was trying to contain himself. It was a miracle! It was as if the storm clouds surrounding them had parted, and the sunlight finally had returned. Jack thought to himself; *perhaps God was listening after all.*

"What is it? What do you need?"

Amanda looked lovingly into Jack's eyes and said, "I fought back from wherever I was for a reason. I just had to get a message to you. You have to let me go, Jack."

"What... what do you mean let you go? What are you talking about?"

"Jack, I cannot feel or move my arms and legs."

He was stunned. A moment ago, he had the first sign of hope in months, and just like that, it seemed to disappear. It was as if the clouds now had swallowed the sun in its entirety, and the bitch that was the storm itself would not let them go.

He said pleadingly, "But...but your finger moved."

"I do not know how that happened, Jack. I cannot flex it now, no matter how hard my brain tells it to move. Jack, I know that David is sick. I heard you telling me about it."

Jack lowered his head. "I do not understand why these things keep happening to us, Amanda."

"Jack, I know," Amanda replied. "But we have discussed this before. The boys are your priority. You cannot take care of me and do what you need to do for them. I am never going to get better. I do not want David and Louis to remember me this way."

"Amanda, please do not ask me to do this," Jack begged. "I cannot do it."

"Jack, you know I am right. I know you are afraid of what tomorrow might bring, but you must face the reality of what is happening today. David needs you, Jack. I have had a chance at life and was blessed to have the three of you in it. David's life has only begun, and he must have a chance to live it to the fullest. Louis needs you too. Please, Jack, do it for them."

Jack thought about what Amanda had just said. He understood what she was trying to tell him. He always referred to it as the Godzilla Paradox. In the original *Godzilla* film, the only weapon capable of destroying Godzilla was an oxygen destroyer. A scientist accidentally came across a formula to remove oxygen from water, rendering everything in it a lifeless corpse. The scientist considered its potential use to be so terrifying that he wished to destroy the formula. He faced the possibility that his discovery could fall into the wrong hands, who would use it for nefarious purposes. This what-if scenario contrasted with the reality that was Godzilla, a monster who would destroy Japan and kill millions if the scientist refused to allow the use of the oxygen destroyer. He and he alone had to wrestle with the decision.

Jack knew Amanda was concerned that he would allow the hopelessness of her recovery and his own fears about tomorrow to get in the way of the reality of David's own life and death struggle and Louis's future needs. A decision was required, and Jack would have to decide between taking vital resources, financial and otherwise, from his children and, by doing so, compromising, impairing, and possibly killing their future. The alternative was to prolong Amanda's life to find a cure for her condition, an improbable outcome.

The choice that Jack feared above all else and never wanted to make now stared him in the face.

He glanced down at his watch only to see that it was nearly 3:00 a.m. He was sure only a few minutes had passed since Amanda had regained consciousness, but it was, indeed, several hours ago. Since that time, Amanda had drifted back into an unconscious state and demonstrated no additional signs of life. Jack knew her wakefulness was not his imagination, and it was far too fleeting. He spent the time since Amanda's awakening lost in his thoughts and at war with himself over the decision he now faced. It was a decision he now felt compelled to make.

Jack brushed Amanda's hair. He smiled and kissed her lips. "Amanda, you are the love of my life. You have always been my heart, my soul, and my world. I promise you that I will do whatever is necessary for you and the boys."

He reached up, and one by one, shut down each machine that was keeping Amanda alive. He felt her hand slowly slip out of his grip. Her breathing slowed, and while she let out her final breath, he tenderly whispered to her, "Amanda, I will love you, always and forever."

Jack stood and watched over Amanda. He thought about her inner beauty and the sacrifices she had made for him and their boys.

He muttered to himself, "We helped save the world, but at what price? At what cost? It was a pyrrhic victory that brought no consolation." He bowed his head and chokingly said, "I will miss your strength, Amanda. How do I do this without you?"

He reached for the phone to call the paramedics.

As he dialed the number, he heard a roll of thunder and looked out the window. It was snowing. *Thundersnow?* Jack thought to himself. *Very unusual for us here in Northern Virginia.*

Jack never noticed the figure that had been standing in a dark corner of the room or its red eyes that opened as Jack dialed the phone. He did, however, recognize the voice that emanated from the darkness when the entity said, "Jack, I can see that your grief is profound. Please accept my condolences."

Jack put the phone down without turning around and closed his eyes. "Lucius."

"That is right, Jack. You know she is not going to answer you, but she could if you want her to. We need to talk. I have a proposition for you, Mr. Aitken."

"There are horrors beyond life's edge that we do not suspect, and once in a while, man's evil prying calls them just within our range." H.P. Lovecraft

Made in the USA
Middletown, DE
30 November 2022

16530879R00215